THE WRENCH IN THE MACHINE

A NOVEL OF LOVEHOLMESIAN MYSTERY AND STEAMPUNK HORROR

BY BONSART BOKEL

Dedicated to Luci Forbes (1976-2021)

Special thanks to Stephan Ballance

The Wrench in the Machine

Revised Edition

ISBN: 9789083199405

Cover art by Staranger

Interior Art:
Associate 212 vs. C-33 by Alex Castro
S-36 by Octofox
Cityscape by Rebecca Harrie
C33 by Luci Forbes
Aqrabua by Yohan Alexander
Associate 321 by Yohan Alexander
Mr Brass by Yohan Alexander
S-36 by Yohan Alexander
S-06 by Bonsart Bokel
Dr. Jenever and S-36 by Peter Kuhn
Macarthur by 47ness

Table of Contents

Chapter One	5
Chapter Two	16
Chapter Three	31
Chapter Four	51
Chapter Five	84
Chapter Six	112
Chapter Seven	133
Chapter Eight	164
Chapter Nine	177
Chapter Ten	199
Chapter Eleven	238
Chapter Twelve	259
Chapter Thirteen	284
Chapter Fourteen	299
Chapter Fifteen	311
Chapter Sixteen	319
Chapter Seventeen	339
Chapter Eighteen	360
Chapter Nineteen	383
Chapter Twenty	403

CHAPTER ONE

"Good morning Dover. I am Frank Dimbleby of Dover Public Broadcast. This news bulletin was provided by the Kent News Network on the 7th of May, 1875. It's one minute past eight.
Here are some of today's highlights. The discussion on the expansion of Kent's Rescue Services. The controversy around the proposed Home Army Bill that is about to enter parliament. And, finally, a debate on the question, is our entertainment being weaponized? This discussion was sparked after a reviewer of the London Journal accused a playwright's latest stage play of being Signalite propaganda.
But first! More protests at Utter-Krapp's main office after the company announced the expansion of its space program. The protesters claim the weaponization of rockets is inevitable. They displayed drawings of Napoleon the First throwing R2 rockets at England, with the phrase 'Never forget'... More demonstrations have been announced, including one near the Pendleton Park War Memorial in Dover.
Excuse me... Our Producer just came in with a special bulletin…
This is just in. The Dover Borough Police announces Dover Priory Railway Station has been locked down. This is due to a crime committed at the premises last night... They advise the public to use other means of transportation for the remainder of the day. They apologize for the inconvenience."
"On with the program..."

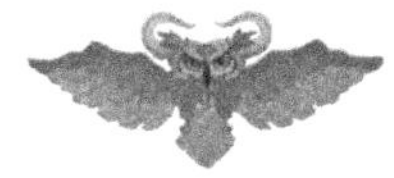

The rhythm of galloping hooves slowed down as the coach pulled in front of the Dover Priory Railway Station. The moment the carriage came to a standstill, the door swung open. Inspector David Ol'Barrow stuck his head out of the tobacco-smelling coupe and coughed. As he got out, he breathed the spring air in through his nose and sighed. On this breezy morning, the scent of wet fauna drifted in the air. But the moment Ol'Barrow began to move, he felt clammy, and the sunlight revealed the unkempt state of his brown tweed waistcoat.

Inspector Bigsby followed him outside, ready to produce another cigarette, despite finishing the last one just moments ago. Ol'Barrow didn't mind his younger colleague's smoking habit that much. It was the stale smell of smoke that bothered him.

As Ol'Barrow brushed off the fluff from his vest, a young - well, to the inspector's standards - constable dressed in a knee-length coat in police approached him in a huff. Ol'Barrow greeted him first, as was his custom.

"Morning, Derby. What do you have for us today?"

The young officer saluted and gave his report. "Mornin', sirs. It's a weird one. Two saps dead. Both night watchmen. They're cut up bad by the maniac. But that is not the weird thing," he added ominously.

"Double homicide is not good enough?" asked Bigsby.

"You better see it for yourselves, sirs," Derby said, nodding, and walked away like a young boy with something to show off. The inspectors found this behavior odd, but shrugged their shoulders and followed the constable.

The young officer wasn't kidding about the railwaymen. Their lifeless bodies were found beside a train that had been scheduled to be unloaded that very morning. Both victims were elderly guards, merely present as a deterrent against petty criminals at night. Now, they lay there in the same positions as when they were slain. Quite efficiently, or so Ol'Barrow thought.

Derby explained the situation to him. "Barry Wilts and Jonathan Slober, aged 57 and 68. Worked for LCDR for several years now. Started working the night shift a few years back."

Meanwhile, Ol'Barrow looked at all the signs. The men were killed where they stood. Wilts had been stabbed in the throat with such force his back was pressed against the sides of the railway carriage and left a trail of blood on the rough boards as he collapsed.

Mr. Slober had dropped to the ground in fright.

Ol'Barrow imagined the poor man looking up at his murderer as he tried to shield himself with his arm, which consequently got severed at the elbow. The limb was slashed with such force that it lay six feet away from the body on the terminal floor. Slober was then stabbed several times in the throat and chest, as if he was a pincushion.

Ol'Barrow bent to his knees and inspected the severed arm on the terminal floor, clutching the handle of an electric lantern. The cut seemed clean… surgical even. No axe could have done this without rending the flesh. Too much force had been applied for a knife. A saber, perhaps? The inspector still found it unlikely.

Squatting, Bigsby carefully observed the corpse of Mr. Wilts. "One straight horizontal stab through the artery and went straight out the back of the neck, right into the panel behind him," Bigsby remarked as he rose to his feet. He then pointed out the deep cut mark in the sideboards near the top of the blood trail. "The murderer severed the spine, looks like."

"That rules out an axe," groaned Ol'Barrow as he raised himself. "Bigsby, look at the distance between these bodies."

His colleague took position between the corpses and spread his arms wide. "Both in arms reach. Seems a bit neat for some ordinary criminal," he concluded. "I suppose the victims found the trespasser. Approached him, and once in reach, they were attacked."

"Indeed," said Ol'Barrow, looking at the severed arm. "They were too close together to be stabbed by a saber like that. And the murderer couldn't have looked that threatening if they approached him voluntarily."

"He carried a concealed weapon, then?" Bigsby thought out loud. "How about a butcher's knife?"

Ol'Barrow considered it but shook his head. "The puncture wounds look too narrow. Maybe the coroner can come up with something." Ol'Barrow turned to the young officer. "Constable Derby! Anything taken? Like their wallets or badges?"

"No, sir. Nothing is missing," the lad answered. "Not even from the cargo inside the wagon, we think."

Ol'Barrow looked at the open carriage door beside the body leaning against the carriage. "Is that what you wanted to show us?"

The constable nodded, gesturing for them to follow him. What they discovered inside the cargo hold was indeed something to behold.

Cold fumes arose from within the crate as the inspector stared at the body curled up inside. Above it, scratched crudely inside the interior of the lid, was a number: 54.

Bigsby stroked his fingers through his hair. "This is something you don't see every day."

"Indeed," murmured Ol'Barrow, distracted by the number scratched into the broken lid. The fact that it was just a number was ominous enough. But for some reason, it had a stripe struck through it, like a notch on a gun handle. The many scratches that comprised the numbers had been carved vindictively into the resin, which was in stark contrast to the executions outside. "What do you think it means?" Ol'Barrow asked, scratching a burn scar on his right jaw.

"Calling card?" guessed Bigsby.

"Like a villain from one of those wave serials?" remarked Ol'Barrow. "I swear, those things are a bad influence." He looked inside the crate. "And what about this fine gentleman?"

Defrosting ice was dripping down the body's eyebrows as they observed the middle-aged man lying in a shallow bath of icy water. Ol'Barrow concluded that the man was probably a working-class stiff – no pun intended. The inspector based his assumption on the victim's worn and old-fashioned clothes, which were not that dissimilar to his own. A broad purplish line around his throat betrayed that he'd been hanged before being stuffed into his container. The inspector lay his hand on the smooth sides of the crate's yellowish interior and scanned the surface with his fingers. The lid, which lay discarded on the ground, had a similar inlay. It felt similar to amber resin, but more flexible and without discoloration. "What are the sides made of?"

"A plastic, I suspect," responded Bigsby. "Utter-Krapp claims plastic will replace amber resin and most metal alloys in the next twenty years." Bigsby was always on top of new developments. Maybe it was just his generation, hooked on wavecasters and eager to hear what the future has in store for them. Ol'Barrow knocked on the plastic with the knuckle of his index finger, producing a hollow sound.

"It's probably a vacuum in there." Bigsby continued. "That is how the contents remained frozen until the murderer broke the lid."

Meanwhile, Ol'Barrow was looking at two other crates of similar sizes that had been broken open. These contained boxes and random trinkets. But no apparent damage from a crowbar, or other implements, was to be seen. Whatever the case, the murderer had been looking for something.

Ol'Barrow turned to Bigsby. "How long do you think the body has been in here?"

"Based on the French labels on the box, I'd say less than two weeks. I can hardly tell if rigor mortis had time to set in due to the ice."

Ol'Barrow moved the victim's trouser leg up and laid bare the purplish-blue skin. "Does this look broken to you?"

"Trauma to the lower leg. Mostly heavy bruising and abrasions due to being tied up. There are similar injuries on his wrists. The ankle seems to have contracted oddly. Might be due to trauma."

"So, he was either in a fight or tortured. Then he was hung by his neck." Ol'Barrow put his hand to his sides. "Why bother breaking into the carriage after murdering two men just to open this crate?"

"Maybe they wanted us to find the body?" Bigsby suggested. "You know, get us on the trail of those who put him in there?"

The other inspector finished his thought. "And then we take care of their competition?"

"Other than that," Bigsby pondered out loud." If the body itself was so valuable, why leave it?"

"Maybe he was expecting something else?" suggested Ol'Barrow.

The constable stepped forward with hesitation in his step. "According to the station master, this crate was supposed to be picked up from the depot this morning," he said softly.

"By whom?"

"Howard and Chambers Logistics," announced Constable Derby.

To the young man's delight, the old inspector nodded approvingly. "Good work, constable."

"I never heard of them," mumbled Bigsby.

"Neither have I. That will be our first stop then. Constable, take care of the Frenchman."

Bigsby stepped closer. "If he is indeed foreign, this needs to be reported to Scotland Yard."

"Indeed. And I don't want to be bothered with the paperwork. That is why we'll find out where this Howard and Chambers lot hangs out."

Derby wanted to protest. "But sir, if you don't-"

"Look at it as valuable work experience, constable," Ol'Barrow rebutted. "Also, you get to show your face at the Chief Inspector's office when he needs to sign the final forms."

"I suppose."

"Good man! Give me the address, and we are good to go. Come, Bigsby."

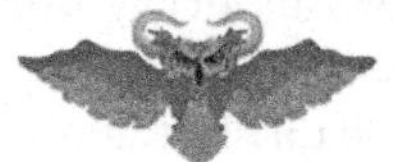

Under way to the old industrial district, the inspectors' carriage drove past the working-class apartments of Dover. Ol'Barrow was in luck; this was a non-smoking cabin. The interior didn't even have that stale tobacco smell like most carriages. Bigsby, however, was already fidgeting with his feet. "Are you sure you wouldn't rather sign forms?" he asked. "This might be a foreign affairs thing."

Ol'Barrow pouted his lips. "Probably. But if we have smugglers in our town, they are our responsibility."

"True enough...," Bigsby paused. "Funny, last night there was an episode of The Shade on the caster called Cold Case."

"I am sure there was," responded Ol'Barrow, half-heartedly. While Bigsby was summarizing the plot, the old inspector was staring out the window. He got distracted by a blimp passing over the city parading Utter-Krapp's tagline: Bringing you Tomorrow's Future, today!

"Do you even have a wavecaster, David?" asked Bigsby.

"Hmm? No..." responded an absentminded Ol'Barrow. "I was born before that time, and I always managed to keep myself occupied."

"With dolls, sir?"

"Hell no. I was an animal man!" Ol'Barrow announced proudly. "I preferred the wilds and the sensation of the wind in my face as I rode around on my hobby horse, with a pan on my head like the knights of old." All of a sudden, he felt an unexpected sense of melancholy. "But one day, I realized I had no idea where I left that hobby horse. My father made it for me, and I just forgot about it. When I recalled the horse, I just..." The inspector changed the subject. “Do parents still make toys for their kids, Tom?”

“My grandfather did,” Bigsby answered. “After his retirement. I mean, these days, we can't make stuff as cheaply as the companies can. Things are changing.”

Ol'Barrow looked at the blimp again. “You don’t say.”

“That cool box,” Bigsby began pedantically. “Imagine that cool box. If we can save bodies that way, we can preserve food.”

“Did you just use the words ‘food’ and ‘body’ in one sentence, Bigsby?”

“W-Well,” he muttered, caught off guard. “You know what I mean.”

The coach slowed down, and the driver announced, “This is as close as I can get, gentlemen. This place is a mess. Abandoned crates and junk everywhere from here on out.”

“How come?” Bigsby asked as they got out.

“Lots of abandoned warehouses and closed down companies. They just left their wares on the street.”

“Another score for progress, I assume,” Ol'Barrow mumbled. “Know anything about Howard and Chambers by any chance?”

The driver seemed surprised by the question. “Just know the name. But I never have seen them around, if you catch my drift.”

Ol'Barrow nodded. The statement confirmed his suspicion that H&C was probably just a front. Because Dover was the gate to England, there was no shortage of such companies. The government, on the grounds of Liberal principles, didn't allow the police to perform invasive investigations of private property. Not until somebody complained anyway, and thus these fronts could flourish.

As the inspectors entered the district, they realized the driver wasn't kidding either. The alleys, originally intended for freight transport, were cluttered with abandoned wares and rusting devices. Some warehouses were converted to workshops by craftsmen who obviously didn't require all that space. But the building owners would take on any tenants at this point.

Finally they found it. An unremarkable warehouse, with a large sign in front displaying "Howard and Chambers Logistics.” It had an entrance gate for a single wagon and a normal door beside it. The paint was flaking off the weathered brickwork, but the building didn't seem in too bad a condition otherwise.

Ol'Barrow knocked politely on the plain door and waited.

No response.

The Inspector knocked again.

“This is working hours,” Bigsby complained. “They should be in.”

This time, Ol'Barrow slammed his fist on the door. "Anyone there? This is the police! We have questions for you."

"Allow me," Bigsby said when no reply came. With a loud thump, the inspector knocked down the door and broke it off its hinges. "Ah, bloody hell!" he cried, keeling forward.

"Be careful, inspector!" Ol'Barrow grinned at his colleagues' expense. "I am not the only one growing older." Ol'Barrow's smile disappeared when he heard a child's giggle in the distance.

"Just help me up, will you? I hurt my knee," cringed Bigsby.

"Oh, right," Ol'Barrow responded, distracted while aiding his colleague. "You heard that?"

"Heard what?" Bigsby groaned.

He listened for a moment. "Never mind," said Ol'Barrow, looking around the interior. Everything seemed to be in order. Stables, a shaft, and a pulley system for loading and unloading. A staircase to the attic. It didn't appear in disuse, but there was no obvious cargo either.

"Looks empty to me," Bigsby stated while brushing himself off.

"I can see that. It's probably a front," Ol'Barrow mumbled.

"Just to move a body? Seems a tad extreme."

A loud thump shocked the inspectors' nerves, and they immediately fixated on the ceiling. It had sounded like a box hitting the floorboards

Chins raised, the inspectors stared upward.

Bigsby pulled out his service pistol, with his eyes focused on the attic. "Who's there?"

"Put it away, man!" warned Ol'Barrow. HIntensely he intensely observed the plans overhead. Then, from the corner of his eye, he saw a shadow move between the cracks. He glanced at Bigsby, who nodded to confirm he saw it too, and they moved slowly to the staircase.

"Come on. We know you are there," said Ol'Barrow sternly. "Show yourself. We are with the police." Making no sudden movements, the inspectors walked up the steps. Carefully, they raised their heads above the floorboards and scanned the attic for any movement behind the sacks, crates, and barrels.

"We just want you to answer a few questions," Ol'Barrow repeated, but there was no response.

The layout of the floor was simple. At the front end, there was an enclosed office area. On the other, nothing but a broken ceiling window just above some stacked barrels. Too small for adults, but just big enough for a child.

Ol'Barrow gestured to his colleague to head for the office, and he moved in the opposite direction. "This is your last chance. If you keep resisting, we'll have no choice but to…" he raised his voice dramatically, "...BRING YOU IN!"

Another loud bang made the inspector jump off his feet as the weight of the fallen object reverberated through the floorboards. Startled, Ol'Barrow turned around to see Bigsby staring at the fallen crate in front of him. "Bigsby?"

He looked at him in denial. "I swear I did- Sir! Behind you!"

The inspector turned around to spot the shape of a child climbing the pile of barrels toward the broken window. "Stop!" he cried, giving chase. But the youngster had already made its way to the roof.

"Stop, you!" Ol'Barrow yelled again as he climbed the bottom barrel. "I just want to- ah!" He lowered his leg as his thigh cramped up. And there it was again: that childish laughter. He looked at the window where a small girl was giggling at his expense, her hair reflecting bright orange sunlight. "You little-" he stopped as he noticed a weird reflection of light in her left eye, like that of a cat. Then she dashed away.

"Are you alright?" asked Bigsby as he came over.

"I'm fine!" he shouted, holding his thigh. "Go after-"

"I can't fit through that hole, man!"

The dismayed officers fell silent as they looked around idly.

"What the hell happened?" complained Ol'Barrow.

"I swear that crate moved by itself!" Bigsby responded defensively.

Ol'Barrow looked away in disbelief.

"I wasn't even close!" he reiterated and relaxed with a sigh. "How's your leg?"

"I'm fine," the old inspector grumbled as he staggered toward the office. The door of the room was unlocked, and the officers moved in to inspect the place. It was obvious somebody was staying here. There was a makeshift bed, and on a desk lay drawings of young people with freakishly large eyes. Candy wrappers smelling of raspberry toffee lay scattered on the ground. Beside the pillow on the bed, there was an odd rag doll. It looked a bit impish, with a large oblong head, X-shaped eyes, and a wide, stitched smile. Its fantastical robe, shell-shaped hat, and red mop of hair made him suspect it was supposed to be a witch. Whatever it was supposed to be, he had never seen any toy like it.

"Now what?" Bigsby asked.

Ol'Barrow spotted a note on the desk and picked it up. The moment he glanced at its contents, he squinted his eyes in dismay. The writing seemed to be an odd mixture of Arabic and Gothic letter styles. Any attempt to mumble out the phrases ended up in nothing but nonsensical gibberish.

But there was a sentence he did make out in forced English handwriting. "Castlehill Road 44," Ol'Barrow whispered to himself. He knew it wasn't that far from Priory Station.
"Found anything, David?" yelled Bigsby from the other room.
"Nothing," he answered. "We tell them we found an empty warehouse."
Bigsby walked in, dusting off his bowler hat. "And the child?"
"You want to go look for an urchin in Dover? Be my guest," he answered in jest. "I have enough to do."

CHAPTER TWO

8TH OF MAY, 1875, 10.04 AM. CASTLE HILL ROAD, DOVER.
The high-pitched ringing of the store bell broke the silence as the door closed behind the Inspector. Aghast, he looked at his surroundings as the smell of sweet perfume and dust overwhelmed him. Wherever Ol'Barrow looked, toy monkeys looked menacingly at him. Bears with unkempt fur in dress uniforms yawned. And, of course, porcelain ladies in pretty dresses looking disinterested from atop their shelves. The store was far too small for the number of toys it contained. But maybe a child could feel at home - here - in Hendrick's Doll Haven.

Cautiously, the inspector made his way past the tables, careful not to knock over any toys. In the far corner at the back, a tranquil woman in a lavender dress sat behind a sewing machine, undeterred by the ringing of the doorbell. Dark flowing hair covered her cheeks as she mended a plush lion with a needle and thread.

Ol'Barrow took off his hat. "Uhm, excuse me."

Startled, she looked up from her craft. "I'm sorry," she spoke with a hoarse gentle voice. She got up, brushing the fluff of her skirt. "Can I help you?"

Gently moving aside a baby carriage, Ol'Barrow asked. "This is number 44?"

She nodded, while swiping an untidy braid from her cheeks. "Yes, that is right."

"Oh, good. I am Inspector Ol'Barrow, and I'm looking for a child."

She seemed a bit puzzled by the question. "Well... children come here," she responded with uncertainty in her voice.

Ol'Barrow noticed a bear in a Napoleonic uniform behind her, staring bloodthirsty into the distance with its jaws wide open. "You don't say... Do you have a child living with you?"

She shook her head politely. "No. I am not even married."

"I see." He was looking around until a hobby horse caught his attention. "Excuse me, where do you get these toys from? I used to have a horse identical to that one."

"Yes, these used to be made by a local carpenter a long time ago. Sometimes I find one. They are quite rare these days. People prefer to buy new toys."

A shiver went down his spine. "Made by a carpenter, you say?" He always believed his father had made it with his own two hands, just for him.

She nodded awkwardly. "Anyway, children often bring them to me. They find them in the trash or places like that. I give them candy for their effort."

He noticed the way she kept her hands folded in front of her lap and the suede gloves she wore that covered the hands down to the tips of her fingers.

"I see. Did an urchin with ginger red hair come around by any chance?"

He noticed her eyebrows move. "No," she said abruptly. "Can't say I have seen him. I don't really notice what happens in front of the store," she answered, smiling gently.

He smiled along with her. "I noticed. So, is there much demand for refurbished dolls?"

"I mostly make my money with repairs, to be honest."

He glanced at the bear in the Napoleonic uniform again, knowing he had seen it somewhere before. But he let the thought slide and prepared to leave. But then he turned around. "One more thing. Did you ever do business with a company named Howard and Chambers, Miss Hendricks?"

Her face seemed frozen for a moment. "Oh, no." she responded aloof. "My brother's name was Hendrick. Hendrick Boerhave."

The inspector squinted his eyes. "I am sorry, Miss..?"

"Henrietta Boerhave."

He raised an eyebrow. "Is your family Dutch, Miss Boerhave?"

"Our parents were refugees from the French Empire. Orange Royalists, you see."

"And this place is your brother's?"

She answered, shaking her head. "It used to be." There was a certain sadness about her movements.

Ol'Barrow nodded sympathetically. "Well, I will not bother you any longer, Miss," he said, and left for real this time. The bell rang again when he closed the door behind him. As he walked down the street, he wondered if she dodged the question about Howard and Chambers intentionally. Regardless, he was convinced she knew about the girl. Another fact. But was it worth pursuing?

Back at the station of the Dover Borough Police, the old inspector sat behind his desk, reflecting on the day.

The ground floor of the old building, on the corner of Park and Ladywell, was bustling with activity. The desks were surrounded by the balustrades of the the second and third floors, giving Ol'Barrow the sense he was sitting at the center of a cathedral. The only way up was by a black oak double staircase that came together on the first floor, with a half landing in between. The stairs to the second floor were more straightforward, as if the Tudor designers had given up at that point. The whole interior of the place felt like style over substance. But it was a blessing it survived the bombardments by Napoleon, as it was an ever-rarer link to the past. The building used to be a convent. After the reformation, it was rebuilt to serve as the weighing house. Then a manor - that fell into disuse. That is when it was decided it would serve as the headquarters for the new borough police.

Ol'Barrow's father had been one of the first men to join the constabulary of Dover, after its founding about 30 years ago. That man walked the beat till the end of his days. Seven hours a day, seven days a week. Of course, Ol'Barrow did not appreciate his father's commitment then, as he did now.

Ol'Barrow turned to the picture of his father hanging on the wall, next to two other officers who died in the line of duty in the department's three decades long history. The portraits of the other two peelers still wore the uniforms that resembled the civil fashion of the day, including top hats. How things had changed.

The once spacious office was filled with three rows of desks now. The plastered walls were covered in paintings and photos related to the department's history, including newspaper articles on past successes. One even included Ol'Barrow's name, but he preferred not to think about it. The first-page article was regarding a house fire that happened ten years ago. It used to hang in a more prominent place too, near his desk. But after a year or so, his colleagues got the hint, and silently relocated it. He wouldn't have minded if they removed the frame all together.

The Peelers were meant to chase drunkards, thieves, and other petty criminals for 14 shillings a week. Then constables became firefighters as well. It wasn't a terrible idea. But, as the events ten years prior had proven, Dover would be better off with a professional fire brigade. Ol'Barrow was asked to be one of its founding members, but he hadn't even bothered with a reply.

Relieved of their firefighting responsibilities, the police were allowed to raid the bordellos and other places of ill repute. Anything to prevent crimes from occurring in the first place. Some new measures allowed them to fulfill their tasks more dutifully. Others, well... In Ol'Barrow's experience, inventing new crimes just created more criminals.

Regardless, the borough police proved its worth in an ever-changing world. It was Ol'Barrow himself who managed to convince his superiors that he, and his peers, should wear civilian clothes during investigations as it made the citizens more cooperative. This was during a time when a Bobbie without a uniform was a big taboo. Yes, he was a hot-blooded man back then.

Ol'Barrow lay a hand on his belly. He had become a bit of a mister plump lately. with a sigh, he crossed his arms and leaned back in his chair. As he stared at the dark wooden beams that supported the high ceiling, his mind dwelled on the day's events. There was no motive, no witnesses. Just an empty warehouse and a mysterious number left on the lid. "Fifty-four," he mumbled.

"I wouldn't put too much thought on that number," said Bigsby, as he walked past. With a thud Bigsby placed a lunch bag on his desk and dropped himself into a chair. "So. Where have you been today?"

"Oh, please Tom, we are not married," jested Ol'Barrow. "You didn't tell anyone about the child, did you?"

"Not yet. Why?" he asked, before taking a bite from his sandwich.

"Just a hunch," Ol'Barrow mumbled. "Tom, have you seen the constable who took care of the crime scene?"

"Yeah, Derby took care of the paperwork and left."

"That was quick," the inspector responded, impressed. "Efficient lad, isn't he?"

"I'm sure he reminds you of yourself, senior inspector," jested Bigsby.

"I wouldn't give him that much credit," Ol'Barrow sneered, deadpanned. "Did you find out who owns that Howard and Chambers warehouse?"

Bigsby sighed. "I requested the information from the Chamber of Commerce, but they said it's going to be a while."

Ol'Barrow looked at his colleague. "They are having problems with their Archival Engines again, I'm sure... The only thing those machines are good for is producing excuses."

His junior offered him a sandwich. "Well, be prepared," Bigsby began. "The Revenue Service is going to start the mechanization process next year."

Ol'Barrow took a bite and let the taste of roast chicken with walnut fill his mouth. "Well, in that case," he said, mauling his jaws, "We might never have to pay taxes ever again."

"I wish," Bigsby responded cynically. "Everything is going downhill in this town, except my property value... You know who was on time?" he asked pedantically.

"The folks who pay our salaries?"

"The Metropolitan police who picked up the Frenchman."

Ol'Barrow blinked sheepishly. "That's fast," he responded, surprised. "That reminds me. Found anything about the box the victim was in?"

Bigsby shoved his fingers together. "That's a dead-end I am afraid. Crates with PVC-inlay are already quite common in the Kingdom of the Netherlands. They use them in the fishing industry. About a half a year ago they started using these to transport sea-fish by train into the German Kingdoms, and beyond. Anyone can get one on the continent." Ol'Barrow slanted his shoulders and shook his head. "Everything is changing so fast, it is getting ridiculous."

"Somebody told me the other day," Bigsby began philosophically. "If you want to change your line of work, learn to solder. Ever tried getting an electrician to fix your wiring?"

Ol'Barrow ignored it. The Dover he knew was gone. The world beyond seemed to become more alien as well.

Then a clear voice pierced the humdrum of the office from the other side of the room. "David!" Ol'Barrow looked over his shoulder to the chief inspector who stood on the half landing of the stairs, just to the side of his office. "Can you come over for a moment?"

The sweet scent of pipe tobacco triggered a mild dizziness as Ol'Barrow sat unwillingly in front of the chief inspector's desk. Opposite him, Mayfair blew out another smoke plume before continuing one of his typical rants.

"David, you really should consider offering yourself up for promotion... Sure, you might sit behind a desk. But why not?" he exclaimed enthusiastically. "You are not getting any younger..."

The inspector had sat there, pretending to listen till he finally responded.

"Oh, stop it. You sound like my housekeeper."

"Don't you mean your wife?" Arthur responded in jest.

"Not funny. She is a widow, for Pete's sake."

"Didn't her husband die years ago?"

"How does that matter?"

Mayfair blew out a final plume of smoke and started to clean out the bowl of his pipe above a trash bin.

"You know what your problem is? You are a brave man but are scared of long-term commitment."

"Hm," David groaned.

"Life is passing you by, you know," Arthur said with some dramatic flair.

"Uhum."

"I mean, you committed yourself to this. Surely, you can commit yourself to something... different."

"Uhmm...." Ol'Barrow heard similar speeches so many times before, he learned to shut it out. He was where he wanted to be. Doing what he enjoyed and was good at. Surely, that was enough? But deep down, he knew the chief was right. Still, it didn't feel right.

"I dunno Arthur. I couldn't do what you do," Ol'Barrow responded, self-deprecating. "I mean, now you need to deal with that door we broke down this morning."

Mayfair smiled dismissively. "If only we could find the owner."

That raised an eyebrow. "Didn't get the impression that the warehouse was in disuse."

The chief shrugged his shoulders. "So, maybe some smugglers are using it. I doubt they'll be back. Regardless. Some suits at Scotland Yard can go through the process to find out who this Frenchman could be."

Tilting his head, Ol'Barrow asked. "What about the dead railway men?"

The chief put down his pipe. "All we know is that the murderer stabbed them with two identical daggers."

"Two what?" Ol'Barrow responded with a mixture of surprise and dismay. "This guy now sounds like a villain from these audio dramas everyone is listening to."

The chief nodded in agreement. "By the way, did you know the last show was called? The Cold Case-"

"Yeah, yeah," Ol'Barrow groaned. "The episode of the Shade. Tom already told me all about it. Villains using exotic weapons and leaving calling cards. If this keeps up, criminals like these will become the rule rather than the exception."

"Are you referring to the mysterious number 54 the perp left behind?" the chief asked.

The inspector nodded when their conversation was interrupted by a knock on the office door.

"Come in," said the chief.

A man in a long coat and neatly ironed pantaloons, holding a bowler hat to his chest, appeared in the entrance. "Sorry about disturbing you," the man began apologetically with a neat academic accent. "I am inspector

Sterling from the Home Office. Apologies for being late. The wheel of our car broke the moment we wanted to leave. But now we are here to collect the body."

"Really?" responded the chief, surprised. "Another one?"

The other man shook his head in confusion. "Excuse me?"

"Yes," the chief began. "Some of your colleagues were here this morning to collect a Frenchman, we... found," He slowed down as the eyes of Mr. Sterling grew wider and asked concerned. "Say, don't tell me you are here for the Frenchman?"

A few moments later...

The cry of a man in anguish reverberated through the ancient halls. "They what?" The chief leaned over his desk when he heard the news that a corpse had been stolen from the morgue.

"Yes," Bigsby admitted. Both inspectors stood in front of the chief's desk, while Mayfair sunk away in his chair growing paler every passing second. "It appears the ones who collected the body this morning were imposters masquerading as metropolitan police," Bigsby continued. "They even had an enclosed cart in police trappings. We sent word to the patrols."

Mayfair groaned as he buried his face in his hands. "This is disgraceful. How am I going to explain this to the commissioner?" The panic in his voice was palpable.

Ol'Barrow cleared his throat. "Who assisted these imposters?"

"Constable Derby, sir," responded Bigsby reluctantly.

A chill ran down his spine. "Derby?" repeated Ol'Barrow. "I only told him to do the paperwork." He now regretted his laziness, although he could forgive himself because of the sheer ridiculousness of the situation. "Where is he?"

"We assumed, on patrol," Bigsby said, "But now we are not quite sure. Anyway, witnesses claim they saw an enclosed police carriage heading west. They could be heading for London Town."

The Chief Inspector straightened himself. "I need you to find out what happened," he insisted. "If the metropolitan police find the thieves first, we'll never hear the end of it."

Ol'Barrow tried to remain positive. "Don't worry Arthur, I have a hunch. But it's a long shot."

The chief slammed his fist on the desk. "I don't care! Find them."

The two inspectors looked at each other. "Will do, sir... Come, Bigsby. There is somebody I want to keep an eye on."

"Where to?"

"I'll explain later," Ol'Barrow answered while putting on his bowler hat. "We are running out of time."

Nearly an hour had passed, and the flow of people in the street grew thinner while the sun descended behind the townhouses. The officers waited on the corner of Castlehill Road. They got there fast, thanks to a new addition to the police force. Bicycles. It just bothered Ol'Barrow that the Utter-Krapp logo was printed into the metal of the frame. Barely visible under the dark blue paint. But it was there, nonetheless.

Meanwhile, Bigsby was sitting down on a bench, pretending to read that day's newspaper while keeping an eye on Hendrick's Doll Haven. The top article was, of course, "The Priory Station Stabbing".

Bigsby read the finely printed words critically. "Listen to this," he began. "Dover's first serial killer! Ha, they seem to have forgotten all those arsons from back when."

"A good headline can make people forget about a lot of things," grumbled Ol'Barrow cynically. "Crooked politician being investigated? Announce a long-awaited book. Economic recession? Talk about how one of the queen's dogs died. The folks care more about their tea than the empire collapsing."

Bigsby raised his eyebrows after listening to his rant. "Guess it's a nice diversion from the recession. Oh, look. There is no mention of the Frenchman in this piece."

Ol'Barrow sighed as he stood with his back against the wall. "Probably for the best. Considering how the relations with the continent are at the moment."

"We always need to think about that big picture, I suppose."

"It's enough to drive a man mad," Ol'Barrow complained. "So, most chose to ignore it."

"So, who is this woman then?" Bigsby asked, peering past the newspaper at the store.

"That is what I want to find out," responded Ol'Barrow. "It's unlikely she can support herself by repainting toys in this economy, that's for sure. And we find her address in a smuggler's den."

"Alleged den- wait." Bigsby folded up the newspaper. Miss Boerhave just left the store and walked up to a passenger coach. The moment she got onto the carriage, the officers put on their cycling goggles and stepped on their bicycles.

And so, the chase began.

Tailing the carriage from a safe distance, the inspectors followed the cab to the west of the city and beyond its boundaries.

Puffing and groaning, Ol'Barrow felt his thigh acting up and he developed saddle pains. "How is your - knee, Bigs-by?" he asked with exaggerated bluster despite his heavy breathing.

"Speak for - yourself - old man," Bigsby retorted.

The scent of the sea grew stronger as the officers paddled on, and so did the wind. They had to rise from their seats and put their full weight on the paddles to keep up.

Finally, the coach reached its destination - the perimeter of the abandoned harbor. The officers stopped and observed Miss Boerhave when she got off in front of the gate to the old piers. The brick boundary around the area was covered in soot and bird droppings, and one-half of the gate was forced open by vandals. The few people that still worked here cared little for public property these days, and the sound of industry has been replaced by the cries of seagulls.

It was not so long ago this place was rife with activity, but the old docks of Dover could not handle the increasing ship sizes and payloads. Meanwhile, London's harbors expanded, and companies had taken their business westward. All that remained was a collection of dilapidated buildings at the dead-end of the rail tracks, being eaten away by the salty sea wind.

Quietly, the officers followed Boerhave from a distance as she paced up to the yard. Here the workers used to maintain the cranes and other machines that moved up and down the rails by the piers.

Careful not to take any risks, the inspectors took their time approaching the complex. The large building consisted of riveted cast-iron beams that supported the sloping roof.

Beside the wall, in the shadow of the depot, the peelers spotted activity. From behind a fence, the officers observed how two men were hastily painting the exterior of an enclosed coach black over police blue while the horses were patiently waiting in place. They quickly concluded it was the vehicle that carried away the Frenchman's body. Ol'Barrow inspected the coach in more detail. It seemed like a typical cart used for moving cargo, but it seemed remarkably close to the ground.

Reaching for his service revolver, Bigsby remarked: "I think we found them."

"There could be more," warned Ol'Barrow. "Let's avoid them for now."

Moving from rust-brown container to container, they entered the roofed area. Overhead, between the rafters, remained some of the chains, cranes, and platforms that were used in machine maintenance. On the tracks stood a small steam locomotive, still attached to some carts it used to haul around the area. It made Ol'Barrow wonder if Dover was doing so poorly it couldn't even find work for such an engine.

Beneath the depot's roof, there were other structures like storage rooms and small terminals. One of these was a single-story building that might have belonged to the management staff. Here, behind a window on the ground floor, burned a faint light that attracted their attention.

"Are we just going to barge in? "Bigsby whispered as they moved closer to the structure.

"No, I want to see for myself what they are up to," Ol'Barrow said and glanced around the corner of the entrance.

A grainy tune played in the background as they peered into what appeared to be a locker room. At the back, there were two doorways. One led to a cafeteria of sorts with two large tables and a bench covered in grime. The other seemed to be a small office space with its furniture trashed. Quietly, they went inside. Despite the static-laden music, reverberating voices were audible from a room beyond the cafeteria. Some men and a woman.

"Oh, look," Bigsby pointed at the wireless device on the cafeteria table. "A genuine Utter-Krapp Mark II," he remarked pedantically. "That thing could be as old as I am."

"Thank you for that," Ol'Barrow responded apathetically as he observed the interior.

From this angle, he could see light coming from another room but not the doorway itself. Just the shadows that moved across the floor.

As Ol'Barrow looked over his shoulder, some light spots were projected on the surface of a locker door. He checked the small office space. It turned out there were several holes in the wall there, left by looters presumably. Ol'Barrow went in and pressed his face against the moldy boards. His open eye struggled to adjust to the bright lamp light as he peeked inside the chamber at the other side of the barrier. The space was arranged like a makeshift operating room. Beside the table was a standing lamp, its light focused on the shaven head of the missing Frenchman, that was mostly covered up by a blanket.

Ol'Barrow reached for his notebook and penned down his observations.

He heard Boerhave speak from beyond the line of sight of his pinhole. "You are taking too great a risk," she said. The woman did not sound as gentle as back at the store, but it was most definitely her.

A man responded with a loud laborer's voice that was accustomed to talking inside a factory. "The longer you are going to complain, the longer it's gonna take. Just take it out."

"An inspector came by today," she said.

He seemed shocked. "And?"

Miss Boerhave stepped into view with several implements in her gloved hands. "And nothing," she answered while laying out her tools on the table and inspecting a small rotary saw.

"What? Just a casual visit?"

"They were just looking for a pickpocket."

Ol'Barrow frowned at that statement as he watched her plug the cord into another device. The circular saw made a nasty zooming sound as the blade started to spin, and the inspector cringed as the electric saw did its work on the scalp of the body.

Ol'Barrow noticed Bigsby's concerned look. He was anxious to do something. Anything. But Ol'Barrow kept observing. This was about more than just a body in a box. He'd encountered some red herring in his career before, but nothing this baffling.

Finally, the electric device was turned off.

The inspectors could not get a detailed view of the proceedings, but they could hear the squishy sounds of her poking and prodding with the tweezers. "I found it," she said pulling something out from within the cranium.

The man stepped into their sight. His rolled-up sleeves revealed the thick arms of a laborer with an arrow-shaped tattoo. Arrows were of course no uncommon motif, but this one was so straightforward it seemed to belong on a street sign.

"So, is this it?" he asked. "Did the man really hear the frequency through this device?"

Boerhave opened a container. "We'll learn more back at the lab. Let me get this ready for transport."

Ol'Barrow stuffed away his notebook and turned away. Silently, they moved out of the office back into the locker room and carefully made their way to the exit, when suddenly, the Wavecaster in the cafeteria appeared to change channels. As the frequencies changed, between the inaudible chatter of skimped broadcasts and the white noise, the device started to play ominous-sounding music. This melody was arranged with electronic tunes that the peelers couldn't associate with any known instrument. Even though the strains themselves seemed cheerful, the individual tones droned deep and dark, accompanied by a background chorus of white noise.

"I know that tune," Bigsby whispered. "But I can't place it." He hadn't finished his thought when an eerie woman's voice started to speak. It sounded like lifeless, with the same buzzing at the end of every word. "8, 54, 68, 122, 321."

Ol'Barrow froze as he heard the number 54 and turned to the Wavecaster.

"8, 54, 68, 122, 321."

The tattooed man from earlier walked up on the Wavecaster. He was dressed like a typical working-class chap, with brown pants hanging from suspenders. "What the hell is this about?" he asked.

The Officers quickly took cover behind the locker doors and peered through the three venting slits. Ol'Barrow opened his notebook again and listened closely as he noted down the seemingly random numbers being repeated on the Wavecaster.

Another more stylishly dressed man joined his friend in front of the device. He seemed to be a well-off man dressed in black pantaloons.

"You know what this is?" asked the other, clearly concerned.

"8, 54, 68, 122, 321."

"Could it be?" the second man whispered in reverence.

"Could be what?" The other snarled, but then his expression changed, and he responded in disbelief. "No-oh!"

The gentleman hovered his hand over the Wavecaster with venerative gestures.

Ol'Barrow squinted his eyes. He could not see clearly, but it seemed the man was missing two fingers on his right hand.

In the meantime, they went on. "Maybe it responded to the receiver we just pulled out of his head," said the gentleman.

His friend seemed amazed at the suggestion. "But wasn't that bloke a terrorist? Why would-" He turned around. "Sister! Did you hear this? Miss?"

There was no response.

The two men looked around, confused. "Where did she go?"

Meanwhile, Ol'Barrow stepped back. Maybe it was the dark droning of the numbers being recited, but a sense of dread fell over him. "Something's off," he whispered.

"No kidding," Bigsby replied anxiously.

Without further comment, they slipped out of the room into the yard itself and scanned their surroundings. The descending sun had tinted the environment orange, and long black shadows shrouded the depot's interior.

Ol'Barrow froze when he heard unfamiliar sounds reverberate among the rafters above. As he looked up, one of the heavy chains swayed from side to side while the other ones remained motionless as if frozen in place. There was no way that could have been the wind.

"Let's get out of here," Ol'Barrow whispered to Bigsby.

They barely stepped outside when a scream cut through the silence. They turned around and looked around the corner of the door opening. There, on the cafeteria floor, they saw the legs of the man in black pantaloons lying motionless on the floor.

Bigsby's voice quivered. "What the hell?"

Ol'Barrow grabbed him by the shoulder. "Let's get on with it!"

Scared out of their wits, they hurried across the depot grounds, jumping over the tracks as they did. While on the run, they heard the rumbling noise of a horse and wagon approaching at an alarming speed. To their astonishment, the coach from earlier sheared past at a reckless velocity, leaving the scent of fresh paint in their wake. Yet, the driver cracked the whip to make the horses go even faster. Ol'Barrow's heart skipped a beat when the rampaging cart's wheels collided with the sides of the rail track, bending the steel axle.

"What on Earth is happening?" Bigsby lisped.

Ol'Barrow, not even bothering to respond, ran toward the red light of the setting sun. They just passed the locomotive when suddenly, a shadow moved just beneath the roof.

Startled and out of breath, they looked up at the rafters.

"Did you see that?" asked Ol'Barrow.

Producing his sidearm, Bigsby nodded as his eyes scanned the ceiling.

The inspectors both faced the same direction when a sudden banging of colliding metal pierced their ears.

Cast iron links rattled overhead as a shadow descended from a chain.

With the grace of a trapeze artist, a tall female figure dropped down in front of them. Her knees folded up at the moment of landing, and the sides of a tailored coat elegantly draped themselves around her female form. Then she rose up effortlessly as if the impact meant nothing to her slender frame.

As Ol'Barrow was blinded by the light from the red sun behind her, it was hard to distinguish her face, apart from the outline of her thin features and silvery hair that hung down her shoulders.

The inspector got distracted by the numbers tattooed in her neck. It wasn't a single series of numbers either, but many running down her chest and shoulders, some of which seemed crossed out.

"Who are you?" was Ol'Barrow's involuntary response.

There was a strange clicking noise as she tilted her head. Her squinted eyes had a blank expression, not unlike the dolls at the store. But behind those eyes, that was a faint spark of curiosity.

Bigsby stepped forward. "We are with the police! You are interfering with an investigation."

The corners of her mouth curled upward with joy as two flashes of steel appeared from atop her wrists with such speed Ol'Barrow could barely register what just happened.

"Don't move, or I'll shoot!" screamed Bigsby, but she came at them regardless.

Ol'Barrow stepped between them but was ruthlessly pushed aside, toppling him. As he hit the ground, two deafening shots reverberated through the depot. Ol'Barrow shifted his eyes as his ears were ringing, but it was already too late. The woman leaned against Bigsby who had his back against the locomotive. She looked the man in the eyes whilst the blades pierced his chest and blood ran down his waistcoat.

In a flurry of panic, the inspector produced his weapon and pointed it at the assassin. But as he was about to pull the trigger, she stepped sideways with such speed her form became a blur. His trembling hand tried to follow her, but she already lunged at him.

A cold, shearing pain went through his fingers. They were gone!

Blood ran down his arm as he stared at his maimed hand with a mixture of disbelief and dread. How could this be happening!?

Struck with a sudden flash of reality as he lay there, Ol'Barrow looked up into the woman's reflective eyes. He couldn't help but stare into her eyes that gazed at him with delight in his suffering. Why?

She moved her arm slightly, but it was enough to make Ol'Barrow recoil and raise his arm in an attempt to shield himself.

Two ear-bursting blasts launched rubble dust between the two of them, knocking the assassin over on her side.

A man stepped into the red sunlight, wearing a peculiar beaked-shaped mask over his mouth and thick oval-shaped glasses that were so reflective it blinded the inspector. The masked man stepped forward, aiming his large revolver as he hissed: "Got you now, you skank!" and fired another two shots.

She leaped away, her arm hanging limply by her side as she gave him the slip and vanished inside the maze of rusting hardware.

Then silence. All the inspector could hear was the heavy breathing of the masked man, possibly pondering if he should give chase.

“Don't do it,” Ol'Barrow wanted to say. But his life was flowing out of him.

The man then turned toward him. He was dressed strangely. Baggy trousers bound at the shins with spats, a tight-fitted leather jacket, and that mask that seemed to belong to a character from a penny dreadful cover.

Ol'Barrow tried to scramble up while he peered into the man's oval glasses. Even in the twilight, he could make out his own reflection in the silvery shades. “Who are you? What was she?” Ol'Barrow mumbled.

“Associate 212.” As the masked man kneeled down, his glasses reflected Ol'Barrow's paling face “Worry about yourself,” he said with a muffled voice.

“Bigsby!” Ol'Barrow looked sideways.

Bigsby sat with his back against the locomotive, a trail of his blood staining the boiler behind him. The old Inspector lost all feeling in his arm as darkness encroached on him.

“Not, like, this...” he stammered as the sun turned into a black disk.

I have things to do.

I need to live!

"What are you up to now?" asked a heavy familiar voice. "Why are you laying there?"

"Why do you care?"

"You've been skipping school again, haven't yea."

"So, what?"

CHAPTER THREE

"Listen, you little shit! If I get one more complaint from Jenna, I swear."

"She's not my real mum!"

PAF!

"Oh, you're gonna cry now! Get out of my sight! I will deal with you when I get back... I'm not gonna lose my job over this shit."

"I hate you!"

The man's eyes widened. That phrase reverberated through the mind of a man who never had the opportunity to take it back. As he awoke, the man was unable to move his body. There was no way to distract himself from the scare that had marked his consciousness since the day his father died.

Back in the present, a woman in a white dress walked by his bed. She didn't pay any attention to him. As his right arm felt inflamed, and his legs were swelling, he parted his lips and attempted to move them up and down, but no sound came out.

"Ah-Auw."

The nurse turned towards him when he managed to squeeze the words out. "Mr. Ol'Barrow?" she asked almost to the point of condescension. "Are you awake?"

He managed to nod.

"I'll get the doctor right away," she replied, and off she went.

Laying there, the inspector tried to organize his thoughts. He didn't recall how he got there. Just the beak-masked fellow and Bigsby sitting lifeless against the locomotive. His wrist was nothing but a stump now, wrapped in bandages. The hand might be gone, but the memory was still there, likely forever.

A surgeon had told him. "I am sorry, Mr. Ol'Barrow. We could not save your hand. The risk of inflammation was deemed too great."

That same morning, Chief Mayfair visited to inform him of what he already knew. Bigsby was dead. Killed by the Priory Station Slasher. And Ol'Barrow was the only witness.

"No," Ol'Barrow responded with a hoarse voice. "The woman of the Doll Haven was there. And another masked man who shot at her."

"Her?" Mayfair asked. "The woman of the Doll Haven?"

"No. The Stabber!"

"The Slasher is a woman?" the chief responded, surprised.

"Yes, she has blades on her arms. She is not human. But this masked man attacked her and drove her off."

The chief closed his eyes as he grimaced. "Why did she attack you?"

"I dunno," he lisped. "Must have something to do with the- the thing inside the Frenchman's head. The Doll Doctor took it out of his brain."

Mayfair nodded incredulously. "Well, we did find his body at the crime scene. Unfortunately, his head is missing."

"Slasher must have done so... Or the Doll Doctor."

The chief nodded with pursed lips. "Hmm, we'll have a proper debrief once you are better. I'll talk with our department physician about what we can do about the hand. Meanwhile, we have specialists in these types of cases. They'll find who did this to you."

"I wanna be fair," he mumbled as the dose of morphine started to kick in.

"You what?"

"I wan to-," he spat out the words. "Bwe in the investi-gation!"

The chief put his hands inside his pockets. "Focus on getting better... I'll be back after work. You're in the minds of everyone at the department."

15TH OF MAY, 1875. BOROUGH POLICE STATION, DOVER.
A week after the incident, Ol'Barrow was welcomed back at the precinct as was to be expected. However, the usual banter Ol'Barrow was accustomed to appeared awkwardly absent. Bobbies getting injured was not uncommon. But when one of the lads broke an arm or nose, they were greeted with the knowledge their wounds would heal. A Bobby could respond with phrases like, "You should see the other guy", or similar bravado. However, in this case, there was no glory. Nothing to brag about other than he had faced an illustrious killer and lived to tell out about it.

Ol'Barrow sighed when he saw Bigsby's neatly arranged desk lacking any papers. In front of the chair there was a lone picture of him with some flowers.

Without saying a word, Ol'Barrow sat down at his own desk. He too was missing files. But it didn't matter. He still saw the woman looming over him as he closed his eyes. The curling of her lips into a wicked smile.

Those squinting eyes that gleamed with a fiery determination and-something else. Something malicious he couldn't identify.

He rubbed his face as if to wipe away the memory from his imagination when a familiar voice called out his name. "David?"

Ol'Barrow looked up at Mayfair who was standing beside him. Despite this, his voice seemed far away from where his mind was.

"Mind joining me in my office?"

While Ol'Barrow was trying to find out how he could hold his maimed arm comfortably sitting down, Mayfair lit up his pipe. Smoke passed his lips as he nervously shook the match till the flame was extinguished. "Did you enjoy the service?" he asked.

Ol'Barrow shifted in his chair. Even after a few days, he felt like he didn't belong anymore. "Yes... It was nice. I do feel the commissioner's speech was a bit, how do you say..."

The chief blew out a long plume of smoke. "It wasn't his first eulogy. He probably recites it in his dreams by now."

Ol'Barrow nodded in contemplation. "How about you, Arthur? How do you prepare your eulogy?"

"I'd rather not," admitted Mayfair, with a sigh. "So, I force myself down and start writing. I recollect the words of my grandfather. How we deal with death is as important as how we act in life. However," he sighed," it is hard to be honest when you don't want to speak ill of the dead."

Ol'Barrow inhaled deeply as he stared at the stump where his hand used to be.

"Did you try it yet?" the chief asked, responding to Ol'Barrow's posture.

He put his wrist inside his pocket. "Last time I tried the wound was still sensitive. But speaking of life," he began to change the subject. "Any trace of Constable Derby?"

"Not yet. You still believe he is the one who reported what happened at the yard?"

Ol'Barrow shook his head. "If not he, then who? The masked man?"

"We have no evidence the constable was there."

"What if Derby followed the thieves?" Ol'Barrow suggested.

"Why not say so?" the chief rebutted. "We may have to face the fact that he has deserted us."

The inspector nodded admittingly. "What about the investigation into Bigsby's murderer?"

The chief put down the pipe. "Like I told you. We have a specialist on it."

"Who?" Ol'Barrow insisted. "Is he from a different department?"

The answer was as evasive as it was apologetic. "The matter is outsourced," the chief replied.

"Outsourced?" Ol'Barrow responded indignantly. "Are we hiring private detectives now? Like in the United States?"

"It's more complicated than that. The woman you described is considered to be of special interest, as they call it."

Ol'Barrow raised an eyebrow. "They?"

"Please, David. It is beyond my position to talk about these things."

Straightening himself, the inspector raised his chin. "In that case. I volunteer to be a witness."

"David-"

"No! I am the only one who was there! How can I not be part of this investigation?"

Mayfair crossed his arms. "It's out of my hands."

"It's what? Well, if this private eye isn't interested to hear what I have to say, maybe the tabloids will."

The chief's eyes grew wider. "David, that's outrageous!"

"This is outrageous!" Ol'Barrow bellowed, red-faced. "Three, no, five people are dead because of her!"

The chief looked past him with a concerned look on his face. When Ol'Barrow turned around he saw a dozen or so stunned faces looking up at them through the office window. Enraged, the inspector opened the door and walked up the balustrade. "What this?" He snapped from atop the stairs. "You're looking at a Punch and Judy show? Get back to work!" The glass trembled as he slammed the door behind him and turned to the chief. "Write me down as a witness, Arthur!"

The chief stared at him with his hand in his pockets. "You understand I will have to make note of your behavior."

"You do what you have to do," Ol'Barrow said as he put on his hat. "I'll do mine."

There was an unexpected knock on the window. It was Buckton who came in with a rather boyish grin on his face.

"What's going on, constable?" asked the chief.

Buckton pointed with his thumb over his shoulder with a wide smile. "There is a lady downstairs to see you, sir." He leaned in closer and whispered: "It's Miss Carla Lantry, sir."

It rang a bell in Ol'Barrow's mind, but he could not place the name. "Wait, are you talking about the actress?"

"Surely not," Mayfair responded.

"Surely is! Sir," he said with a wink. "Legs and all. You can't fake those."

Ol'Barrow frowned an eyebrow. "Her, legs?"

"Yes, sir. Those are peg legs," he said gleefully. "But it's impossible to tell."

The officers looked at each other. "Why would an actress come all the way to Dover?"

The constable's face reacted. "You're making it sound like there is something wrong with Dover. Sir."

"That is not-"

They got distracted by disruption on the first floor. A lady, dressed in clothes far more flamboyant than is typical of Dover, barged in. The thick braids laced with glittering netting at the back of her head seemed heavy enough to break her neck. Yet she forced her way past the officers elegantly and unencumbered. His colleagues seemed frustrated with the stranger at first. However, they forgot the indiscretion the moment they recognized her. It was hard to believe, but renowned stage and voice actress Clara Lantry walked the station floor as, or so Ol'Barrow imagined it, only an actress could. The men's faces lit up when the lady asked them something and directed her to Mayfair's desk. With an elegant but determined strut, she marched up the stairs toward the office. Without knocking, she flung the door open with a theatrical swing of her arms and tilted her head as she asked with a deliberate and sensuous voice, "I am looking for Chief Inspector Mayfair." Her voice was so sultry, sibilant, and clear, it seemed unreal, just like on the speaky.

Mayfair stood straight up and straightened his vest. "T-That would be me," he said, flustered like a schoolboy.

She walked up to him, closer than was decent, and offered him her hand to kiss it. "I am Clara Lantry. Pleased to make your acquaintance, chief inspector."

Mayfair politely held her hand but refrained from kissing it, probably dissuaded by Ol'Barrow's disapproving glare.

Without asking, she sat herself down in a chair. "I am here on behalf of the Followers of the Signal."

"Ah," Mayfair responded, grinning like he had a toothache.

"Yes, when do you intend to release the bodies of our brothers?"

"Your. Brothers. Well..."

"The Commissioner promised to return them today! They must be conveyed before the day's end. Please, don't tell me these were taken, too?"

Ol'Barrow couldn't take it anymore and interrupted them. "Excuse me. Conveyed?"

"Yes! Ensure their minds are still intact for future ascension."

Mayfair stammered: "Well..."

Ol'Barrow again butted in. "We need those for the investigation."

She turned to him, smiling. "Excuse me, but who are you?"

"Inspector Ol'Barrow. I was the last man to see 'your brothers' alive." He held his bandaged wrist just where she could see it.

It seemed to put her on the defensive. "Did you? I heard rumors about a survivor. That was you, I take it?"

"That is correct. Unfortunately, the force lost a good man that day."

Her cheeks creased uncomfortably while she maintained her smile. "So, did we?"

Mayfair raised a finger. "To get back to the point. As my colleague explained, we can't just release their bodies without their family's consent at this time."

"If their own testaments don't suffice, officer. We can return the bodies afterward."

"Afterwards?" Ol'Barrow wondered out loud. "You are not going to bury them?"

The actress sighed. "We just need their minds," she said impatiently.

He raised an eyebrow. "You mean, you want to save their brains?" He had heard some rumors about the Signalites. He just thought they were exaggerated.

She averted her eyes, aghast. "It will suffice," she conceded. "I assure you, our surgeons are very careful during the proceedings."

"I'll have a word with the Commissioner," the chief said.

"And with that, you mean, consider it done. Don't you, Mr. Mayfair?"

"Well, I-"

She clutched her hands together as if ecstatic. "Oh, thank you so much, Chief Inspector!"

"I-"

"I am a busy woman, Mr. Mayfair. Please, if I need to sign the paperwork, could you arrange it as quickly as possible?"

Ol'Barrow, having enough of this charade, reached for his hat, to which the chief responded. "Just a moment, Miss... David, where are you going?"

"Don't worry," he replied while opening the door. "Just going to the bakery."

Frustrated, Ol'Barrow walked down the stairs. He noticed his colleagues, the males in particular, keeping a close eye on the chief's door, hoping to catch another glimpse of the actress.

Outside, as the inspector walked off the station's steps, he noticed a pristine white electric car whose dashing appearance was in steep contrast to the drab appearance of the Dover street. An art piece on wheels, whose white glossy paint reflected the sun in a mirror image. *The lady sure knows how to attract attention*, Ol'Barrow thought disapprovingly while inspecting the abstract symbols on the side that reminded him of some technical schematic. That is when he noticed an arrow pointing upward. The inspector frowned. "Ascension."

Meanwhile, the driver, dressed in a well-fitted light gray uniform, leaned against the back of the vehicle whilst smoking a cigarette. Curiously, his legs were braced down from the ankles up to, and including the knees, by a silvery carapace similar to the leg protector of ancient Greek armor. The inspector had seen such contraptions before, but these were by no means ordinary medical braces. These were too sleek, made from materials he couldn't directly identify... Bigsby undoubtedly might have known.

The driver noticed Ol'Barrow eying him. And when their eyes met, the inspector recognized him immediately. The driver's mouth fell open, and after a brief pause, he disdainfully threw his cigarette into the gutter. The brace's joints moved fluidly as the man approached the inspector. Now Ol'Barrow knew for sure it was him. His hair was shaved now, but he still had that disdainful glare around his eyes. "Well, look at that," the driver began as he approached. "Constable David Ol'Barrow," he says mockingly. "Fancy meeting you here."

"So, they let you out, MacArthur. I expected you to be in the dock for at least- What? Another decade?"

"Well, my case got reviewed, and my sentence was suspended due to," he tapped his leg braces with the side of his shining boots. "The circumstances surrounding my arrest."

Ol'Barrow inhaled deeply through his nose, refraining from taking the bait. "Is that so? And now you just happen to work for a celebrity? Does she know?"

"Actually, Miss Lantry is quite a champion for the victims of the system."

He rolled his eyes. "Did you still dare to call yourself a victim?"

"How do you see yourself... Where is your uniform, constable? Or did shattering my kneecaps get you a nice promotion."

His heart was pounding as the blood rushed through his head. "Listen you-"

"Is there a problem?" asked a sultry woman's voice.

As they turned to Miss Lantry, McArthur's demeanor changed immediately. "Oh, no problem at all, miss. Just speaking to an old friend," he said, smiling, and rushed for the car door. The disdainful glare had disappeared entirely leaving a loyal yet friendly gaze that could fool anyone.

Her eyes lit up. "Ohhh, Mr. Ol'Barrow, was it?"

"Inspector Ol'Barrow," he said, smirking.

"I see. Well, for what it is worth, I hope you find the assassin," and added sardonically: "Inspector."

With that said, McArthur opened the carriage door and let the actress in.

Ol'Barrow peeked at her feet, but all he could see was her glossy ankle-high stilettos. If she had leg prostheses, it was indeed impossible to tell.

"Oh, come now, inspector," McArthur remarked loudly enough for other people to hear. "One knows better than to look at a lady's ankles."

Ol'Barrow peered at him from underneath his thick eyebrows as he noticed the curious stares of onlookers.

With that smarmy smile of his, Macarthur turned around and entered the car.

Ol'Barrow had turned his back to them as they drove off and pondered: if Miss Lantry had a man like McArthur working for her, what does that say about the actress? Was it a coincidence that, of all the men he arrested during his career, she brought him? Or maybe he was just overthinking it?

As he made his way inside the vehicle depot of the police station, the drained inspector looked for an available bicycle. But once he did and grabbed one of the handles, he stopped. How to get on this thing without his second hand? He tried swinging his leg over the frame, but he was too stiff, and he couldn't hold the bike straight up. To make matters worse, two constables were watching his dilemma.

"Need help, inspector?" one of them asked carefully.

He sighed. "No, I- I have an aid."

Ten minutes later, Ol'Barrow was finally cycling through Dover's streets, though he still struggled with finding a proper angle on how to control the stir with the hook on his wrist. The prosthesis was strapped to his lower arm and shoulder. It irritated the scar tissue, but it was manageable. Just a painful reminder that the simplest thing seemed a struggle now. This morning, he grabbed a pot of chutney from the kitchen shelf, realizing he had no way to unscrew the lid. Or properly prepare his breakfast. Or tie his shoes. Or button his cufflinks, and so on. Dressed like a slob, he appeared at Bigsby's funeral service and tried to stay out of sight.

All this was his fault. If only he had filed the bloody forms himself, or maybe it had been more aggressive when he first met Boerhave. Or...

Ol'Barrow tried to make the self-flagellating thoughts slip and squeezed the brakes. One last stop at the bakery, he thought, inspecting the store displays with fresh bread, scones, and delicious buns. He nodded approvingly. "That should do it."

The afternoon was getting warmer. A powerful breeze swept up the dust from the cobblestone road as the inspector drove between the buildings of the old industrial area. In front of the Howard and Chambers building, he stopped. Groaning, he struggled to keep his balance as he got out of the vehicle. At this point, he developed a love-hate relationship with the bike, but at least he got the hang of driving it with his disability.

As he straightened his jacket, out of a nearby alley, a lone dog emerged. An old mutt with some terrier in him and rough fur comparable to a floor mat. It held one of its hind legs up while it limped up to him, growling at the bag that hung from his side.

Ol'Barrow pressed the bag demonstratively against his chest. "It's not for you. Now, shoo."

The mutt tilted its head, yammering pathetically.

Ignoring the animal, he approached the door that was boarded up by the police, but Ol'Barrow came prepared with a crowbar and used it to remove some of the boards as gently as possible. Meanwhile, the dog was watching him critically. "You're not getting anything. Get lost," the inspector warned while dislodging another board. Finally, he made enough room for himself to squeeze his body through. If only he was younger. Dusting himself off, he rose to his feet and looked around. The dog followed him inside and sat belligerently beside him as to say, "You sure you are not missing anything?"

"Nothing seems to be different," he mumbled. Then he walked up to the middle of the space and raised his voice. "I know you are here!" he cried and reached inside the paper bag. "I brought some sweet almond buns. They are all yours. All you need to do is answer some questions."

When he held up the bag to open it, he realized he had no hand to do so. Instead, he used his hook as a coat hanger from which he suspended the bag and took out a pastry. He then took a big bite. "Hmm, I haven't eaten these in years. Good bakers are hard to find these days."

The dog growled and squeaked greedily as he tap-danced from left to right.

Ol'Barrow gave the mongrel a disappointed look, "Well, I guess if she is not here. I suppose they are all yours. I can't finish so many," he admitted as the dog impatiently held his nose up.

"Fine!' he heard a girl callout. The two turned their gaze upward as a ginger-haired girl stuck her freckled head out from behind some crates that were covered in burlap. Ol'Barrow looked in amazement, intrigued by her differently colored eyes. A natural emerald on the right and a not-so-normal crystal blue on the other with a slightly translucent look to it. She approached him with slanted shoulders and a rather apathetic expression on her face. Not surprising for a teenager, but she wore a pastel green robe as if she belonged to some neo-druidic order of some kind, complete with a collapsible hood that covered her shoulders. It wasn't some historical reproduction. Instead, all the layers had triangular shapes that overlapped over each other like scales. Whatever she was, she was no ordinary urchin.

With a rebellious glare in her eyes, she looked up at him. "What do you want to know?" she asked with a peculiar francophone accent.

He smiled. "Why don't you sit down and eat something first," he said while offering her a cinnamon bun.

After taking the pastry, she sat on the barrel opposite to him and greedily bit into the bun, mauling excessively.

"You like it?"

She nodded, be it reluctantly. Meanwhile, the dog looked at her with his hungry eyes. She tore off a piece of the pastry and threw it halfway across the room. The dog gave chase as his meal flew overhead and nearly tumbled over as he ran past its goal. But within moments, he gleefully devoured it, dust and all.

"You are just encouraging him, you know," Ol'Barrow remarked as the dog returned to its starting position.

"You are doing the same with me," she remarked, shrugging her shoulders and taking another bite.

He ignored her observation and asked: "What's your name?"

"None of yurbuznez," she answered with her mouth full.

"Alright, miss None-of-your-Business. Do you know who owns this place?"

"It says so on the front," she responded as if it should be obvious.

What a brat, he thought. "Alright. Who are Howard and Chambers?" he asked, but she didn't respond. The inspector sighed, reached into his bag, and took out some candy. "You like Raspberry Taffy?"

"You want to bribe me with candy?" she responded, insulted. "I am not a child, you know."

He raised an eyebrow in disbelief.

"I am sixteen!" she said, raising her voice.

He looked her up and down. She was no taller than a fourteen-year-old.

Arms crossed, she added: "I am small for my age, okay?"

The inspector held up the bag of candy with a questioning look on his face.

In return, she glared. "Alright, fine," she said as she reached out her arm.

He handed her the paper bag and asked: "So, who are H&C?"

She shrugged her shoulders. "I dunno. I just sleep here."

"Fine then. Miss Boerhave, the lady at Hendrick's Doll Havens, is involved in a case that got a fellow inspector killed this week," he said sternly. "Now, I am about to go to her and arrest her if you don't give me a proper reason not to."

She scowled when hearing the remark. "Doctor Jenever doesn't kill people!"

"Doctor?" he repeated. "So, you do know each other."

She looked down at her bun and then threw it away, to the dog's delight, who ran after it. "Sometimes, she takes care of me. But you can't tell her I am here!" She insisted.

"Are you hiding from her?"

"It's not like that," she protested and bowed her head. "I just wanted to be left alone. I'll return home next week."

Not wanting to get involved with the girl's personal life, he considered the situation. But Ol'Barrow didn't like the idea of leaving her with a person who cuts up corpses. “My friend,” Ol'Barrow began. “His name was Tom Bigsby. He was murdered by a monstrous woman who appeared to be half machine. Before she attacked, there were numbers recited on a nearby wireless. Does that mean anything to you?”

She hesitated for a moment, but the description didn't seem to surprise her. “She sounds like she could be an Outsider. As for the numbers...”

“Did you say, Outsider?” Ol'Barrow interrupted her.

“Sure. You know of them, right? Creatures and people that come through the Rifts.”

“Well...” He thought about it for a moment. He heard of these anomalies called Rifts. These appeared all over the world, and there were many rumors about them. But the average person cared as much about Rifts as they would worry about dormant volcanoes. They knew the risks and dangers, but these also made good tourist attractions. A couple of years back, Ol'Barrow read about a major incident in the Kingdom of Lothringen. An accident that occurred during the Franco-Prussian War caused a rift to rupture if he recalled correctly. This made "Creatures from another World" run rampant. But the threat was contained by the Imperial army. But then some actor died. What was his name again? Roger Houwer or something? And people just forgot about it.

“Alright,” Ol'Barrow pondered out loud. “What is an Outsider doing here?”

Shrugging, the girl answered: “I know there is a Rift near the harbor. Her eyes started to light up. “I can show you!”

His eyebrows rose. “You can?” It was about more than the investigation now. He had never seen a Rift before.

“Tonight,” she said. “But. I want a week’s worth of food in return.”

Ol'Barrow tilted his head. That was it? He crossed his arm. “Well... Hmm, very well. It had better be worth it,” he said, playing up his skepticism.

“Fine.” She slid off the crate. “Meet me at the large park, near the glasshouse, ai.”

“Pendleton Park?”

“If that's what it's called,” she replied aloof.

He nodded. “Fine then. I'll see you tonight.”

National Republican.

OL. I. WASHINGTON, D. C., MONDAY, MARCH 4, 1821. No. 81.

Mankind's first launch into space ends in a Ball of Flames

Oh, the Humanity!" I heard a reporter scream into his microphone as an astounded audience looked at the ning ruble that was supposed to be, not only the awnser to humanities oldest ambitions, but it greatest achive-nt. Onlookers counted down expecting a momement of triumph, but when they cried: "Zero", The Comet exploded ing all souls onboard.

he day the people of all ons were anticipating ended agedy. From all around the ised world there are stories eople who woke up behind r radio sets (they bought just e a witness of this event) vinced they woke up from a tmare. Many friends itted to me they cheered as heard the roaring voilence, ming it were the engines iting, but alas. The ylon personnel barely aged to contain the fires and y visitors jumped of f the orm in a panic into the r below. I and other okers had to volunteer to these poor people from the n as the staff was to busy ng the fire under control. unatlely 'we'were successful ing everyone, but the crew dedicated their lifes to this ion.

Comet did not leave the lon Launch Platform. rocket was supposed to ch 8 am local time, enter 's gravitational field and the Elysium-Object three s to take photo's up close eturn. The crew of six was osed to land in a capsule ing from a parachute as the avy would pick them up eturn the cosmonauts the al Babylon Platform in the le of the Pacific Ocean. All this planning was naught. Now everyone is asking how this could have happend? As of yet, there are no answers. The head of the project Ghulam Ali is under fire, as the designer of the Comet, who is not known to take critism well. And his opponents have also taken this time to, once again, remind the public he developed AR-1 explosive rocket that terrorised the coast of Britain during the reign of Napoleon.

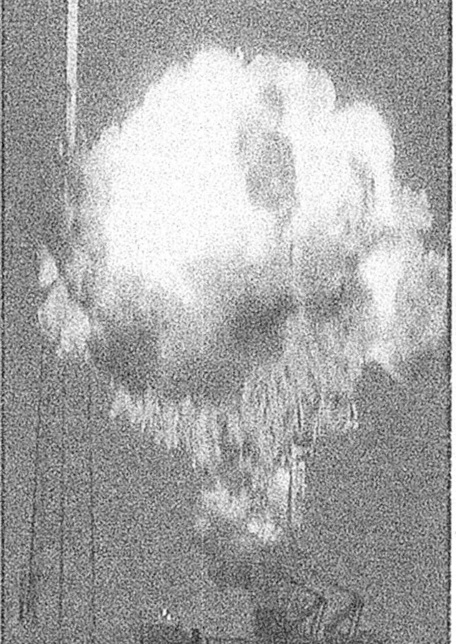

Is this the end of the Babylon Project?

Ali Says: "No!"

Prof. Ali proclaimed the Babylon Project can prepare. the next launch within a couple of years, while they get to the bottom of the incident. World leaders have offered they condolences to the families who lost loved ones and have proposed to establish a independent committe to investigate the cause of the accident. "It's a thinly veiled attempt to spy on our efforts", Ali claimed. Meanwhile senator Walker stated in congress yesterday."There has been a severe lack of oversight on the taxpayers expense and these brave cosmonauts paid the price." No goverents or sponsors have come forward on their decision to continue supporting the project.

The crew of The Comet who gave their lives for this mission from top left to bottom right.
Thomas Daily (Cpt.), Maria Estaphan (Computor), Lerom Jurkins (Pilot), Georgy Remek (Pilot), Jule Cameron (Photographer), Jan Yurchikhin (Physicist)

FREE  **PRESS.**

No. 8. HALIFAX, N. C. FRIDAY, MAY 14, 1824. VOL

UTTER-KRAPP IS SHOOTING FOR THE STARS

"We'll have men on the moon by *1830*" Utter-Krapp spokesperson Miss Spelling declared. In the wake of the failed second attempt to launch a manned vehicle to Elysium it looks like the Babylon Project is about to collapse. Several investors have already announced retracting their funding and there are rumors of Ghulum Ali being sued for matters of deception, negligence and fraud.

What happened to The Comet II and who is responsible is still a matter of discussion. But the competition doesn't waste any time taking on Ali's former employees who are leaving the launch platform where they constructed the Comet rockets. "The conditions were getting unacceptable, but we kept working. We wanted to keep supporting each other," Jan-Kees the Bruin explained. "We wanted to redeem ourselves for what happened the first time. But now, we had to say, enough is enough." Mister de Bruin is one the many Members that found new employment after the Comet II incident. "It feels like a second chance. The goal is the same, just the target is different... Now we have a new team and a fresh set of eyes. It might have been the thing we needed in the first place." We found the same sentiment along other former staff members. "We want to apply the knowledge gained in more fields than space travel," miss Spelling proclaimed. "We are talking rocket proppeled blimps, coaches and to replace the pony express while we are at it." Regardless of their other ambitions, Utter-Krapp has announced their space program includes landing cosmonauts on the moon and developing means to create a permanent presence there.

on May 3rd, After the much anticipated launch, The Comet II disappeared from sight just when it left earth orbit as it approached Elysium. "As far as we can tell it just vanished." Mister Burke, a member of the astronomical society says. "We tracked the rocket's flight very closely with our telescopes and suddenly it was gone and it's smoke trail just ended... No explosion of falling debris." After weeks of investigation, there is still no answer The conspiracy savy have suggested it might actually have been "smoke and mirrors" and some parties have created models on how the Babylon Project used actual magician tricks the create the illusion of a rocket launch. Ridiculous? Experts responded to these reports with: "It is as good an explanation as any other."

This photo was taken right after the Comet II disappeared from sight.

Babylon will not prevail

As credibility diminishes funding is being pulled from the project. "The whole thing has been a waste of money." MP Watts-Russell stated in an interview. It was an investment in one man's dream that wouldn't have payed even if it succeeded." Parlement decided to suspend further funding.

"Monsiour Ali has a lot to explai The MP continued. "He should so be held to account for his actic during the war and his crmies against the British people."

It seems accusers and angry inv tors are closing in on the entrep eur, who hasn't made any publi appearances since the 1st of Ma Meanwhile, companies like Ut Krapp are picking up the pieces former staff members are looki for new employment. What els can we conclude other than Babylon will not prevail.

Twilight had come to Pendleton Park. One of Dover's cultural highlights was designed and paid for by the man to whom the park owed its namesake. It had one of the biggest greenhouses outside of London at its center. The complex consisted of four wonderful glass domes arranged in a clover pattern, with a cupola on top of the main dome. The beams were curved in elegant angles and overgrown with ivy and other evergreens. The top of the central tower looked similar to that of a lighthouse, which contained a small observatory. Truly a wonderful public work. But in these austere times, maintenance wasn't what it had been, and algae was growing on the glass.

Ol'Barrow walked slowly across the slate pavement. The bag dangled by his hook at his side. The pastries inside were cold at this point, but the scent had reinvigorated his appetite. As a faint distraction, he looked up at the darkening sky as the waning moon revealed itself, the bell-shaped Elysium in its shadow.

Elysium. The legend goes that Sir Pendleton had an odd obsession with that mysterious object that followed the orbit of the moon since the 1790's. The heavenly body looked like a blue shining beacon. Was it a relic? A crashed alien ship or a city? It was an ancient riddle that was for sure. Despite its disappearance millennia ago, and knowledge of the object was obscured in myth, it inspired religions, philosophy, and even space travel. All attempts to reach it, however, ended in catastrophic failure. A curse on its creator, who used the same rocket technology to bombard the English coast during the time of emperor Napoleon Bonaparte the First.

Ol'Barrow stood at the edge of the crater left by one of the so-called Vengeance Rockets. Pendleton left the hole intentionally. It was said a chapel once stood here in which people sought shelter when a wave of three of such monstrosities came at Dover. Ol'Barrow wasn't yet born then, but his father told him of the horrible wailing sound its engines made as they crossed the channel. It was also the task of the Dover police to fight the fires. Seven rockets in total would hit the city during those years. The people in the chapel were lucky in that regard. Afterward, many joked that even in the house of the Lord, nobody was safe from man's ingenuity. Yet, others proclaimed it a miracle that the rocket had not exploded.

Now, the remains of that very missile rose from the crater as a macabre reminder of what had happened all those years ago.

Ol'Barrow looked over his shoulder. Two haggard men passed by, clearly intoxicated. An increasingly common sight. It was no place for a child at this hour. The park was losing its splendor. If it wasn't for local volunteers, it might have degraded to nothing except for trees surrounded by undergrowth.

Enthusiastic barking in the distance broke the silence. When Ol'Barrow walked toward the source of the noise, he found the strange girl sitting on a swing, accompanied by the mutt. She had her hood pulled over her head this time. The swing's chains creaked as she played fetch with the dog, who returned with a bigger stick every time.

"Hello miss, None-of-your-business," he began. "I see you made a loyal friend."

She shrugged her shoulders.

Proudly, Ol'Barrow held up the sack. "I got your reward," he teased. When she reached out, he kept the bag just out of her reach. "Point me to the rift first, missy."

She pouted and stuck out her left hand.

Ol'Barrow squinted his eyes for a moment. Did he see that right? The girl appeared to have a device in the palm of her hand: a tattoo of some kind. The ink in her skin lit up as she directed the two opposite triangles right at him. Suddenly, Ol'Barrow felt a tug at the bag, and before he could comprehend what was happening, it was pulled from his grasp. It was as if a ghost dragged the sack through the air and delivered it straight into the girl's hand. Even the dog looked surprised as she held up the bag of pastries with an impish smile on her face.

Frozen stiff, he looked at her. "You did that?" Ol'Barrow asked, perplexed. "How did you do that?"

She pulled out a loaf from the sack and put it straight in her mouth. "Iet a sek-let."

Now, it was his turn to frown. "Fine then. Where are we going?"

She slid off the swing. "Follow me," she said and walked off.

As they strolled in the direction of the greenhouse, in the warm light of the lanterns, Ol'Barrow spotted a cluster of bumps on her head. "What's with the bruises?" he asked.

Embarrassed, the girl pulled her hood down. "I bumped my head."

Multiple times? he wondered. But he decided not to comment.

They stopped next to a separate wing of the glasshouse. A side building in the same style, but the panes were made of frosted glass. A sign near the door read, "No entry. Property of Utter-Krapp". Because of course, it was.

Ol'Barrow asked. "It's a storage area of sorts?"

"You'll see," the girl said as she reached underneath her hood and pulled out a hairpin. To the inspector's dismay, she then stuck it inside the lock of the door and started to pick it.

"What are you doing?"

She remained undeterred. "You wanted to see the rift, right?" she replied as she unlocked the door with relative ease.

Staring at the open door with his mouth agape, he asked. "Is this something you do often?"

"I can do a lot of things," she said proudly and wiped away the sweat on her forehead.

"Are you alright?" he asked.

"Sure. It's just humid. Let's go inside."

They entered the restricted area. Ol'Barrow looked around, but there was nothing here except for a large black-and-white checkered block, about twenty feet in all directions.

"Is this supposed to be art?" he asked.

"More like a puzzle, but I can imagine people not knowing the difference."

"Bit cynical at your age, aren't you, young lady?" Now that he thought about it, he still didn't know her name.

"Maybe I am just smarter than most people my age," she bragged while holding the tattoo in her palm to the checkered panels.

"What are you doing?"

That was an audible turning of gears coming from behind the plates. Then, one of the checked squares was lodged free. Ol'Barrow nervously stroked his fingers through his hair as the panel floated out of its slot. It revealed a safe lock secured by a numerical dial.

"How did you do that?" he asked.

Smug, she knelt in front of the dial and lay her hand on the panel.

Apart from not contributing anything, the inspector grew concerned he was dealing with an actual witch. "What are you doing now?"

"I can see the mechanism inside it," she explained. "Because it's so smooth, I can easily move the gears behind the panel that way. Guess they didn't count on a wizard, ai?"

"Oh, dear," Ol'Barrow mumbled, stroking his clammy head and feeling very uncomfortable because he had teased her before.

Meanwhile, she stared intently at the panel until there was a clicking noise coming from behind the cast steel, and she turned the handle. There was a slight thump, and a large hatch raised itself up.

"Amazing," he thought aloud. "You're a wizard, you say? Are you actually using magic?"

Her smile disappeared suddenly. "Of course not!" she cried, insulted.

"Well, sorry. This is all new to me," Ol'Barrow mumbled, shocked by her overreaction. Then again, he did feel a tad silly for raising the question.

"Right... Never mind, let me open the hatch," she said and unlocked the mechanism.

Dust drifted across the floor as one of the cube's sides tilted upward.

Curiously, Ol'Barrow bent over so he could peek inside the large vault. He could not believe Utter-Krapp had gone through all this trouble. There was nothing apart from a strange dark powder on the floor that scattered like fine ash as he trod inside. Behind him, the dog moaned nervously and paced back and forth as if he were walking beside a river.

The girl sighed, disappointed. "Fine then," she said to the dog. "You wait here."

The dog lay down, with its snout between his paws, and observed them anxiously.

Ol'Barrow swiped his finger over the floor and inspected the dust. "What is this gray stuff?"

She knelt and grabbed a handful of the powder. "Nothing can stay away from their plane of origin for long," she explained and let the powder pour down from her hand. "So, floating leaves, animals, and non-living matter. Whatever comes through a Rift turns to powder in a month or so. Unless it returns, that is."

"Humans, too?" he asked.

"Humans are animals," she reiterated.

"Right... Where is the Rift then?"

"Look closer," was all she said, staring at the wall.

He scanned the cube. It felt like a tomb that had been uncovered in the desert - a black desert. Then he noticed a faint ripple in the air like a vertical mirage hovering just above the ground like smoke rising from the end of a cigar. The longer he observed it, the larger it seemed to become. Moving closer still, the mirage seemed to widen, and colors around it started to fade to a grayish haze.

"Don't come near just yet," she warned, standing behind him. "Rifts don't respond the same to everyone."

Awestruck, he stared at the hazy ripples. "So, it's all true then?" he said. "Inside that... There is another world?"

"Want to see it?"

He looked at her. She had a childish twinkle in her eyes.

"Don't worry. It's safe," she reassured him. "I've been there before."

He turned back to the Rift. In his imagination, he could hear the train whistle blowing. Was it time to get off? Or...?

"Let's get on..." he answered.

"Hm?"

He straightened his jacket. "Let's get on with it, I said! How does this work?"

"Just walk through it," she answered plainly.

"Alright, let's go!" He sniffed. "Ladies first."

She grinned and stepped forward, shaking her head. Without hesitation, she walked into the mirage and faded away like a ghost inside the darkness. Just like that, she was gone. leaving nothing but an odd ripple in the fabric of reality itself.

He swallowed while his feet felt stuck to the ground. But, not to be outdone, he cleared his throat and loosened his shoulders. The dog's concerned yammering broke his flow, however. "Don't stop me!" he warned and looked at the challenge in front of him. "All aboard!" he cried and strolled straight at the rift. He could feel it now. A strange chill enveloped him, and then....

Nothing?

CHAPTER FOUR

15TH OF MAY, 1875... NOWHERE

What is nothing? Is it the same as non-existence? The traveler wasn't sure, but this felt close to something like that. Oblivion. A sense that nothing but its consciousness existed and nothing beyond that. It wasn't even sure why it was doing what it was doing. It just was. It had no attachments nor desire. It feared nothing. It wanted nothing. It was content if that word held any meaning.

Then, a light appeared. It grew larger in size as a violent torrent spiraled around the precipice. Suddenly, he felt like something was going horribly wrong as he was sucked toward light like a leaf getting washed down a drain. Ol'Barrow was stunned by the many impulses that flooded his senses. It felt like a torrent of water rushed through his head while he seemed caught inside a cocoon that was wrapped around his body.

Or were those just his clothes?

Reality washed over him like a surge of cold water.

Shaking on his feet, Ol'Barrow rubbed his face before opening his eyes. In the twilight, he saw the girl standing waist-deep in a sea of tall grass, observing him as he paced around in confusion.

Behind him sounded the rushing of waves crashing against the white cliffs. Was this Dover? His question was partly answered when he saw a herd of creatures in the field beyond. They looked like rhinos with two horns - one in front of the other - and draped in a thick brown fur.

He looked around in awe. His mind was overwhelmed by new sights, smells, and the sounds reverberating in his skull. "Where? What is this place? Did we go back in time?"

"I told you. It's a different world," the girl answered impatiently. "A different England. Well, it doesn't have a name here, but you know what I mean."

It surely didn't smell like England. He scanned the environment that consisted of untamed plains with the outline of thick forests on the horizon. But even in this alien landscape, in the shadow of a tor, he noticed an anomaly. Something that seemed to resemble a man-made hovel surrounded by a makeshift barrier. "What is that?" he asked as he moved in for a closer look. "There are humans here?"

"Oh, that." She didn't seem surprised. "We can go there if you want. But it's kinda creepy."

"Why is that?"

She started walking. "You'll see."

Weeds had overgrown the barrier surrounding the yurt at the center of the primitive camp. The yurt itself, covered in washed-out hides, looked like an isle in a sea of grass. The scent of burned wood and moldy leather grew stronger as they approached the tent, and like she said, there was something ominous about the site. Maybe it was the moonlight coming down a hole in the top. Perhaps it was the primitive drawings on the inside of the tent. Despite its archaic appearance, the yurt's interior looked impressive. Based on what she told him, its builders needed to hunt and gather supplies right here. It must have taken them many days, if not weeks.

Looking around in awe, he asked. "You know who built this place?"

"Nobody knows for sure. They are travelers like us, but we never spoke with them. They build these yurts on other planes near rifts as well... for some reason."

He peered at her past the corners of his eyes. "Who do you mean by 'we'?"

She looked startled. "Uhm... I mean, people who traverse the rifts."

"Hm, sure you do," he answered skeptically. "Can you at least tell me what I can call you?"

She turned her eyes away for a moment. "Igraine."

He reached out his hand. "Well, nice to meet you, Igraine."

She suddenly looked smaller, and she retracted her lips. She hesitated as if intimidated by his gesture but then responded in kind. As her cold fingers grabbed his hand gently, Ol'Barrow could feel her tattoo tingle inside his palm. As she let go of him, she acted awkwardly, as if she was embarrassed.

Ol'Barrow, pretending not to notice, turned his attention back to the faded drawings on the sides of the interior. It reminded him of cave paintings whose meaning was lost to time. One depiction in particular interested him. A white one-eyed giant with a long conical head, or hat, who appeared in various scenes. It was fighting monsters and taking on various poses that appeared to have some significance. "Do they make all these drawings in their other tents as well?"

Igraine shrugged her shoulders. "I assume so. I haven't seen the others."

"Hm." Hand inside his pocket, he walked back out. From on top of the barrier, he observed the herd of rhinoceros grazing peacefully in the twilight, surrounded by the brushing of tall grass swaying in the wind while the roaring of the sea caressed his ears. It was so tranquil here, unlike the world he knew. Was this what Pendleton tried to protect? The reason why he built a park so pretty nobody considered looking past the glass panes?

Igraine stood awkwardly beside him. Ol'Barrow didn't really know what to do with her. They had nothing to say to each other, nor did he intend for her to get involved. And yet... She could help him find Bigsby's murderer.

"Listen," he began diplomatically. "I am looking for a dangerous killer. Can't you give me something? A nudge in the right direction? A place where I can find more clues on her whereabouts?"

Igraine gave him a sheepish look. "All I can tell you, the lady sounds like an Outsider like them." She pointed at the herd. "If those would enter our world, they would be considered Outsiders. Kinda like what we are now in this world."

"So, we are Outsiders now?" he repeated philosophically. Then he turned toward her. "Wait, does that mean there is another rift near Dover?"

He stopped as the girl walked back in the direction of the rift without any notification.

"Wait, where are you going?" he cried after her.

"To where my bed is," she said with a weak voice. She swayed uncomfortably with every step.

"What's going on with you?" Ol'Barrow asked, following her.

Suddenly, she sat down on a slab that was part of the barrier and stared strangely into the distance like her consciousness was a million miles away. Before he could ask what she was doing, her eyes went cross-eyed, and she toppled sideways.

Ol'Barrrow called out to her, "He, what's hap-"

Her body started to convulse as she lay there on her side. She bounced her head against the stone surface until she rolled off. He was just in time to catch her and pressed her against his chest as she shook erectly like somebody getting electrocuted. The eyes turned inside their sockets, and saliva ran down the corners of her mouth. Her expression was both terrified and terrifying, like an unearthly force just took possession of her. He immediately thought of the white giants. Could it be?

"No! Don't be foolish, man!" he thought. "The Rift then? Cut it out! This isn't helping!"

"What do I do?" he cried as her body attempted to break his hold as if intent on hurting itself. And it just went on and on, and no way to turn it off. He wrapped his arms around her. But it only led to her head butting his jaw. Then Ol'Barrow put her into a headlock but abandoned that idea as he feared she would snap her own neck. What kind of horrid affliction could make a person convulse as if possessed? Finally, the spasms ceased. Her eyes were finding their bearings, and her muscles relaxed. But she was still limp, and her speech was little more than gibberish.

He rubbed his hand through his hair as he looked at the stricken girl. "Now what?"

"Cu-coo..! Cu-coo..! Cu-coo!"

16TH OF MAY, 1875, 10.00 AM. OL'BARROW HOUSEHOLD, DOVER

The squeaking of the mechanical bird hurt the inspector's ears as the grandfather clock announced the new hour. Groaning, Ol'Barrow lifted his head from the kitchen table. Daylight already shone through the windows, and the treading of dog feet approached him at great speed. Popping sounds from his back reverberated through his body when he straightened himself. Meanwhile, the mongrel jumped up against his shins, as well as it could with one hind leg.

"Yea, yea," Ol'Barrow growled, petting the animal on the head. He could barely recall how he made his way home. With some effort, he got up, stretched his back, and shuffled his way to the bedroom. There, the girl lay in his bed, facing away from him. The strange doll he found in her bag glanced at him over her shoulder, with its cross-shaped eyes and reassuring smile. He knew she was awake. But he was too tired to deal with this right now, so he chose an easy option. "Be free to stay here for now," he told her. "There are still some cinnamon buns. We'll talk when I'm back. You know, if you are still here."

Ol'Barrow should have been rushing to work, but instead, he sat down again, resting his chin on the palm of his hand as he leaned on the table. "Just a cup of tea," he mumbled.

Idly, his gaze swept the room. Many would envy the size of this old home. It was the legacy of his parents, a fact he was rather proud of. Not once had he considered moving. There was nothing wrong with it. He even bothered with installing electric wiring to keep up with the times.

Ol'Barrow glanced at the Utter-Krapp Wavecaster model II, with its diamond-shaped console, for a moment. The device was as old as Bigsby. Its reception here was bad, even on clear days. But now... His tired mind started to drift.

At that moment, somebody pushing a wheelbarrow passed by his door. The scrapping of its wheel was reminiscent of wave-static. It was hypnotizing him in his tired state. Suddenly, he was alarmed by a woman's voice cutting through the static, reaching out to him across the waves. He shook as he broke out in a cold sweat. It was her. "Mr. Ol'Barrow!" she cried.

The dog's barking gave Ol'Barrow such a fright he nearly fell off his chair.

"Mr. Ol'Barrow?" cried a woman from outside while the dog ran at the door barking.

"Come here!" Ol'Barrow said to the mutt, who surprisingly listened. "I am coming!" He quickly tidied his hair a bit and answered the door. Slowly, he opened up and peeked outside. There she was, a middle-aged woman in a modest dress with a wide, cheerful smile on her face. It was Diane Appletree, his housekeeper and old-time acquaintance, holding a plate covered by a blanket.

"Mrs. Appletree?" he stammered.

"Oh, hello, sir, "she said in her shrill but friendly voice. "I saw you were in, so I thought I could go back to work."

"Actually, I overslept," he said. "I should be on duty."

"Oh, no, sir. You look exhausted," she said indignantly. "I heard what happened. You should be resting."

"That - is very kind of you. But-"

She forced him aside as she came in. "It's the least I can do. Here, I baked you a cake. Just something to sweeten your day."

"Oh, I can't-"

"Please," she insisted, putting the cake on the table. "What kind of world are we livin' in if neighbors are not even allowed to take care of each oth-" She froze at the sight of the red headed girl laying sideways on his bed, still dressed in her robes.

"What do we have here?" Mrs. Appletree asked out loud.

Unawares, Igraine rubbed one of her eyes as she awoke. "Wut?"

Ol'Barrow stepped in. "She... This is Igraine..." he said, trying to maintain some composure. "She's my niece..."

Mrs. Appletree looked from Ol'Barrow back at Igraine. "You don't say."

"We are related by marriage," he added. "A niece of my brother Edward."

"Oh?" she responded open-eyed. "And what brings you here, young lady?"

"Uhm," was all the confused girl could produce.

Mrs. Appletree took a closer look at her. "You have two eye colors?"

Igraine looked at Ol'Barrow in a panic.

Ol'Barrow stepped forward. "Actually, she is here to recover."

"From what?"

"Well..."

"Oh, look at me. I am prying," Mrs. Appletree apologized. "You want some cake, dear?"

Although she stayed quiet, she failed to hide her gluttony.

Ol'Barrow gave up. "Well, I-Uhm. I'll make some tea then?"

"I would love some."

As he stood in front of the counter while holding the kettle beneath the faucet, he realized he was lacking a hand, at which moment Diane gently forced him aside with her small but robust frame. "Oh, let me help you."

He shrugged his shoulders in self-loathing.

"Oh, I'm sorry, mister Ol'Barrow. I didn't mean to walk over you like that."

"No. It's fine," he said, throwing his hand up in surrender. "I need to learn, and-" He sighed. "Accept this is my body now."

She lay his hand on his shoulder. "Oh, don't worry, Mr. Ol'Barrow. You cope with it in time. I've seen it with plenty of men. You be do-in' everything like nothing changed."

"Thank you," he said, smiling. But in reality, Ol'Barrow wished he shared Mrs. Appletree's optimism. In no position to argue, he sat down at the table. Opposite of him, Igraine leaned on the palms of her hands, smirking like a little imp.

"What are you smiling at?"

She looked past him at Mrs. Appletree.

"Don't stare," he warned. "It is impolite."

"Is she your mistress?" she whispered.

"No," he snapped with a hushed voice. "She is a childhood friend."

She tilted her head in disbelief or to provoke him. He wasn't entirely sure which.

"What to do with that girl?" he mused. Witnessing last night's seizure probably took a year of his life. Judging by the fading bruises on her head, it wasn't the first one either.

He looked at his neighbor. "Mrs. Appletree? Could you do something for me?"

"Of course," she said while preparing the stove

"Mind keeping an eye on my niece today?"

Igraine's eyes woke up suddenly. "What?"

"Oh, sure. I'll be busy here anyway."

"I can take care of myself," Igraine protested.

"Just for today," he said, a bit on the smarmy side, and grabbed his coat. "I need to go to work. Will be back when I can."

Igraine puckered her lips at him as Ol'Barrow closed the door but was quickly distracted by the scent of fried eggs.

Back at the station, Ol'Barrow absentmindedly greeted his colleagues and sank into the chair behind his desk. He wasn't even sure what he was going to do today. He barely had any time to think. And after last night... David rubbed his face. He had set foot on another world, in a different reality. How was that possible? Going to London was a journey for him. People bragged for months when they traversed the Atlantic. But last night, he'd left the planet.

A voice called out to him from across the room. "Inspector!" It was Mayfair, standing at the door opening to his office with his hands in his pockets. He then beckoned Ol'Barrow. "Come with me, please."

Ol'Barrow looked at the ceiling. This is about yesterday, isn't it? Reluctantly, Ol'Barrow approached his superior. "What can I do for you, chief?" he asked as they walked up the flight of stairs and took a left at the half-landing in the direction of the commissioner's office.

"Well, David," Mayfair began. "I forwarded your request."

Ol'Barrow braced himself. He expected his previous outburst didn't sit well with the commissioner.

But then the chief continued: "The specialist has been waiting on you for an hour."

Ol'Barrow raised an eyebrow. "He, what?"

"The 'Private Eye' you wanted to see," Mayfair reiterated.

Perplexed that they agreed with his request, Ol'Barrow's concerns turned to curiosity. In a moment, he would figure out what was so special about this "Specialist".

They stopped in front of Interrogation Room 4, and the chief knocked on the door.

A deep but lively voice answered. "Please, come in."

Eagerly, he went inside where, behind the table, a black man rose. He was tall and broad-shouldered like a sailor, stretching the fabric of his rococo shirt. From his sunken eyes alone, the inspector could tell this was a man who had seen many hardships yet weathered them all. But despite his strong build, the black man needed to support himself with an oddly massive cap stick. "Hello, inspector," he said with a slight American accent. "Let me say I am sorry for your loss," he said and reached out his right hand in greeting.

Baffled, Ol'Barrow hesitated. "I'm sorry," he said as he returned the gesture. However, he had forgotten he had no right hand to offer.

About to shake hands, they both froze and stared astonished at the prosthetic.

"Allow me," said the man, embarrassed as he quickly switched hands. The inspector did the same, and they finished the ritual.

Mayfair cleared his throat. "Inspector Ol'Barrow. This is Associate 321. He is an adviser with the Association of Ishtar."

321? The number triggered memories of the transmission he heard over the wireless before the Slasher struck. "Ah," responded Ol'Barrow, trying to retain his composure. As for the Association of Ishtar. He had heard of the name, but it just invoked a group of eccentrics who fancied the esoteric. "Welcome, I am inspector Ol'Barrow. Your name is...?"

The Associate just gave him a friendly nod. "Please, have a seat, Inspector."

A bit baffled, Ol'Barrow pulled up a chair and sat down. "The Association of Ishtar?" he began. "Aren't you something like the Freemasons or something?"

"I'll explain..." the Associate responded and spread his arms theatrically. "We, Inspector, are international agents and experts on Rift Related Activity. We seek out and explore the Planes and assess the potential threats and opportunities."

Ol'Barrow tilted his head. "Threats? Are you referring to the assassin?" he asked. "The Priory Station Slasher?"

The Associate turned to Mayfair, who was still in the room. "Chief Inspector, would you excuse us?"

With a nod, the chief left.

The moment the door was shut, the Associate shoved his fingers together and rested his hands on the table. "Before I tell you my suspicions, how about you tell me if you saw or heard anything of value during the incident." Ol'Barrow took a deep breath and tried to recall the events. "It started with the Wirecaster. It changed the channel by itself and then these numbers were recited. I wrote them down. 8, 54, 68, 122, and finally, 321," he emphasized.

"That is very interesting," commented 321 unfazed. "Anything else?"

Disappointed he didn't get a rise out of him, Ol'Barrow continued. "One of the suspects seemed to believe it came from a receiver they pulled from the Frenchman's head. Then he addressed the doctor as, 'sister,' for some reason."

"Was that all you heard?"

"No. The other man referred to the Frenchman being a terrorist. And there was this melody before the numbers were recited ... I know it, but not sure what it is."

"Roses in the Rain?" the Associate remarked with a mysterious smile.

"Excu-" Then Ol'Barrow recalled the song. He had heard on the Wavecaster long ago. The first song ever broadcasted by UK-BN.

"Woke up one morning half asleep," the Associate began to sing. "With all my blankets in a heap."

"...And yellow roses scattered all around," Ol'Barrow continued. "Yes. Yes, that was it. A corrupted version, but that was it," he whispered. "And after that, it recited numbers... Including the number 54. A number the Slasher left at Priory Station." Ol'Barrow looked at the Associate in the eyes. "Associate's numbers."

Ignoring his statement, 321 reached into his office bag and produced a folder. "It's not in our habit to share such documents with third parties, but this is a special occasion."

Ol'Barrow inspected the envelope labeled "S-36".

"Yes, Subject 36," 321 explained. Our organization has a vast archive of its discoveries and reported incidents. We use these to counsel our clients on Rift Related Activities. State agencies, local governments, armies, and, of course, police departments."

Ol'Barrow opened the file in front of him and scanned the pages.

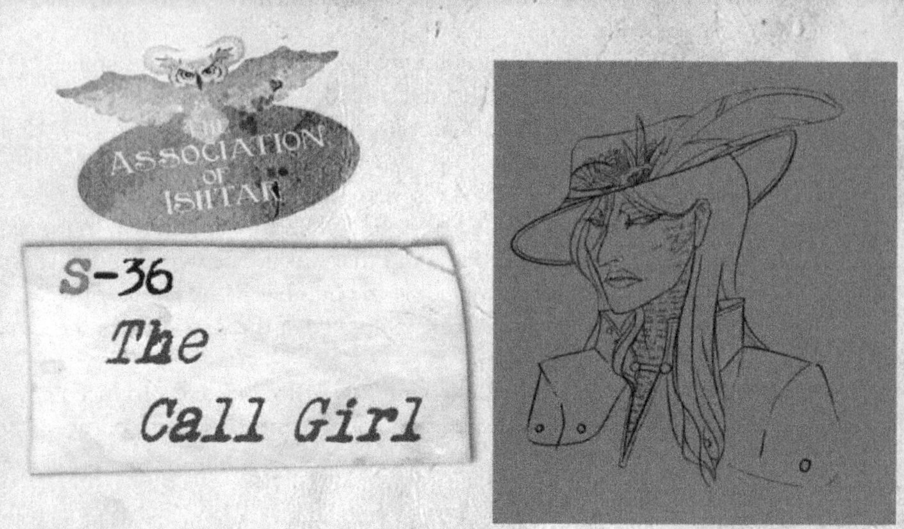

"When receiving messages from Subject-36, either on paper or audio, Associates are to call for reinforcements. If these options are not available, avoid being alone and especially in small spaces. S-36 prefers to ambush its victims."
- Dr Bourbon

Description

S-36 appears to be a female version of ███, based upon its prosthesis, above-normal reflexes and strength. Overall appearance is that of a young woman wearing clothes according to the latest trends in fashion within the local culture.
Most notable features of S-36 are her collapsible birdlike prosthetic legs and multiple tattoos of number-symbols that have been crossed out, covering her face, neck, and shoulders. We suspect these numbers might represent Associates who have gone missing on previous expeditions. This matter is still under investigation.

ENCOUNTERS:

Subject-36 contacts her targets in advance before attacking. Either she leaves written messages, making her intentions clear, or contacts them directly through Short Waveband (FM) radio devices or wireless telegraphs. These transmissions start off with a musical tune, played in punch tape tunes, followed by a string of numbers announced by a woman.

What follows is a recorded message, received on February 2nd, 1871. The recorded message starts after a punch tape tune starts playing that has similarities to the song 'Roses in the Rain' by The Blokes from Burningham.

...8, 14, 68, 54, 121, 251...

8, 14, 68, 54, 121, 251 ...

8, 14, 68, 54, 121, 251...

These numbers corresponded with the designations of the Associates present at the time, and is usually followed with an attack by S-36 within several minutes to an hour.

How S-36 acquired this information, or the Associates' frequency is unknown. Based on encounters on Planes 007, 067, 155 and 169 it is assumed S-36 is able to move through Rifts, making her exceptionally dangerous. Also, for unknown reasons, S-36 seems to have it out for members of the Association specifically.

S-36 prefers to ambush her targets and engage them in close quarters, for which she seems especially designed.

Associates described the Subject as agile and sadistic. During engagements, rather than defending, she acts evasively, using her ability to leap to great heights to disappear behind cover and strike from concealed positions. S-36 prefers to immobilize her targets before killing them. However, her agility comes at the expense of protection and most handguns can harm or damage her. See Log S-36 for an eyewitness account.

Transcript debriefing, Associate-8 on 1st of October 1870 by Dr. Jenever. The interviewed, Associate-8, returned alone from Plane-007 after he was ambushed by S-36.

Dr. Jenever: “Welcome back, Associate.”

Associate 8: “Ahh. Didn't think you cared, Doctor.”

Dr. Jenever: “Could you please take this seriously, for once?”

8: (The Associate slams fist on the table) “Let me tell you how serious I am, Doctor! Another two dead Associates at the hands of that, that thing. What the hell was that?”

Dr. Jenever: “... Well, that's why we invited you here. To find out-”

8: “You know exactly what it is... It knows who we are, our numbers even. And whose numbers were those tattooed on her face?”

Dr. Jenever: “We are investigating the matter.”

8: “That is not an answer, Doc!”

Dr. Jenever: “Could you please just answer the questions?”

8: (sigh) “Sure.”

Dr. Jenever: “Please, describe what attacked you?”

8: “Freaky looking lass with roughly built prosthetics limbs. Legs looked like those of a chicken.”

Dr. Jenever: “A chicken. Like, bird legs?”

8: “Yeah, she was quick on her feet as well. Could jump, run and everything. Never fought anything like that before. Arms and hands looked more normal though. Used straight bladed knives to off ██████ and ██████.”

Dr. Jenever: “What about her intelligence?”

8: “Human, I'd think. Too sadistic to be just a machine. Could see her smile as she cut into poor ██████”

Dr. Jenever: “Please refrain from using real names… Please.”

8: “Oh, sod off. Is that all we are now? Numbers to be crossed off a ledger, Doc?”

Dr. Jenever: “You know why... Associate?”

8: “Why don't you just call me ██████, ey? Makes it a little more personal, partner. Equals, as we used to call it back when I joined the Association. Oh, but how times have changed.”

Dr. Jenever:	"I will not discuss this matter with you. What else can you tell me about-"
8:	"She covered their faces with numbers. That creepy doll face has our numbers on it. Most are crossed out, but not all of them... She has your number too, Doctor..."
	[END OF TRANSCRIPT]

His mouth apage, Ol'Barrow lay down the file. "This is her," he mumbled. "An assassin who travels from one world to the next. And then there was the mention of Dr. Jenever. Boerhave was Dr. Jenever. But did 321 know?" Ol'Barrow looked at the Associate. "What is S-36 doing in Dover?"

321 leaned over the table. "That is what we need to find out."

"But according to this, she is after your organization specifically," Ol'Barrow observed. "If that assumption is correct, then why did she appear at the docks?"

A broad smile appeared on the Associate's face. "Truth be told I was quite pleased with your request to speak to me."

"Is that so?"

"First of all, secrecy is not our goal, inspector," 321 said reassuringly. "Secrecy is but a means to an end. Did you see the autopsy report on the dock killings?"

Ol'Barrow shook his head. "No, I was recovering in the hospital."

The Associate looked thoughtfully at the hook on Ol'Barrow's wrist. "Yes," he whispered and reached into the bag again. "Here it is." On the table he laid out some photos.

Ol'Barrow bent over slightly. These were pictures of the crime scene at the docks. Including one of Bigsby's body. Without saying a word, he picked up the image of his dead colleague, who sat with his back against the locomotive.

Associate 321 sat nonchalantly on the edge of the table and cleared his throat. "I am sorry you had to see this again. But I want you to remember what happened. In your statement, you mentioned a man who saved you."

"Yes..." answered Ol'Barrow suspiciously. Something about that question baffled the inspector. Didn't he know about the Associate at the scene of the murders?

321 leaned toward him. "Did you talk with him?"

Ol'Barrow snapped out of his thoughts. "Um, no... I lost consciousness. I just recall the mask and his peculiar weapon, like I mentioned in my statement."

The Associate nodded. Then he reached down and shoved one of the photos in front of Ol'Barrow. "I want you to look at the photo of this victim. Mr. Liggit. Especially what he has on his arm."

Ol'Barrow studied the image. It was the well-dressed gentleman he observed that evening. In the photo the victim had a very elaborate hand prosthesis with three grabbing fingers which made the inspector kind of jealous. He had seen similar designs in the past, but this seemed more elaborate. Thin cables and springs running underneath the exterior.

"They're functional, in case you are wondering," said the Associate as Ol'Barrow attempted to slide aside one of the photos with his hook.

The inspector leaned back. "Where did this prosthetic come from?"

The Associate groaned softly as he got off the desk and walked stiffly back to his chair. "There is only one group we know of who has the knowledge to make such a prosthesis. An esoteric organization is known as the Followers of the Signal. Mr. Liggit happened to be a member. Are you familiar with them?" he asked, curiously.

Ol'Barrow crossed his arms. "Well, yes... They are trans-humanists, aren't they?" asked Ol'Barrow, even though he didn't really know what that meant. "The Signalites have a lot of famous actors and scientists. Isn't that playwright that moved over the Atlantic...uhm, Boucicault, a member?"

"Indeed," 321 groaned. "We have a few of them in the Association as well. Miss Boerhave is among them."

"The Doll Doctor is?" Stunned by this revelation, Ol'Barrow looked back at the photo of the prosthesis. It wasn't a stretch to think that the Signalites could create something like those wrist blades. "It would make sense," Ol'Barrow thought aloud. "What do you think is the relationship between her and the Frenchman?"

"His number used to be 45," Associate 321 revealed.

Ol'Barrow processed it briefly." The man inside that locker?"

"That's right. He was what we call a Lost Number," Associate 321 explained. "An Associate who betrayed his vow years ago. He was put on ice a few weeks back."

"In France?" said Ol'Barrow perplexed. "You knew he had something inside his head, didn't you?"

"Hm, we suspected something, yes," 321 admitted as he sat down. "It is why we went to the trouble of transporting his body to one of our... Special facilities," he continued evasively. "And that's why we must recover Boerhave and this item as quickly as possible. We have no idea of its significance at this point. Or why Boerhave has not returned it to us."

Ol'Barrow crossed his arms. "Are you implying she is a 'Lost Number'?"

"I am implying we can't rule out the possibility."

Mechanically, Ol'Barrow straightened himself in the chair thinking if this woman Boerhave, or Dr. Jenever, was a traitor, then was the Associate who saved Ol'Barrow from S-36 was an accomplice? He cleared his throat. "What's S-36's part in all this?"

"She hunts associates," 321 answered bluntly. "She knew we would go after that item."

The inspector blinked. "You mean, it's bait? That simple?"

"Some people just need a simple purpose," 321 responded.

Something about that statement made Ol'Barrow's blood pressure rise. "That is why she murdered two men at the station? Just for that?" he asked indignantly. "And Bigsby? Why? What have you done that she hates you so much?"

The question made the Associate pause. Once again, he reached for his bag, took out another folder, and like a clerk browsed its contents with an air of indifference. "I read your file, inspector," he began coldly, speaking as if it was a performance review. "Despite your rather notorious early career, you have been commended, and you even turned down promotions." 321 peered from beneath his eyebrows at Ol'Barrow. "Now seems to be a very good time to take that offer," the Associate said pedantically. "Have you considered it?"

"No," Ol'Barrow said distrustfully. He felt that he was being baited.

"Why have you not taken that promotion?" 321 asked, puzzled. "You are fully committed, so responsibility isn't the issue. You have no family. You do have the skills and personality. There are no practical reasons why you shouldn't. What is holding you back?"

Ol'Barrow sniffed his nose. "I just don't think it's for me."

With a loud bang 321 slammed the folder shut. "That's a coward's reply, Mr. Ol'Barrow!"

Ol'Barrow sprang up from his chair. "How dare you judge me?"

The Associate raised his voice. "On the contrary," he responded indignantly. "I want to know how committed you are. Let me tell you how I got here," he began. "I joined the West Africa squadron of her majesty because I wanted retribution. But before I got to shoot my slave trader, I got a bullet in my leg, and it has been lodged in there ever since! But I kept serving in the West Africa squadron despite my injury, until I found a new calling and took my vow as an Associate."

Not understanding the point of this tale, Ol'Barrow simply responded with, "West Africa squadron… That's commendable."

321 got up and leaning forward, looked Ol'Barrow in the eyes. "I am not seeking your approval, inspector. The point is I learned something about myself." After a brief pause, he continued. "The truth is, I didn't give a damn about the cause. I cared about the killin'. Revenge is a very powerful motivator, Mr. Ol'Barrow. Makes it quite easy to assume you can do no wrong, as long you target the right people."

That made Ol'Barrow pause. "Well, if your question is if I have been there. Yes..." He nodded admittingly. "Yes, I have."

"You have?" 321 repeated. "But what drives you now, David? How motivated are you now, inspector, to apprehend those responsible for the deaths?"

Ol'Barrow contemplated the question for a moment as he stared back in the man's brown eyes. There was something about them that disturbed him greatly, like the bottom of a pit that was shrouded in darkness. Ol'Barrow blinked. "It's the only thing that helps me get up in the morning right now," he said. "It should have been me she killed..."

There was a moment of silence. It pained him to say it out loud.

Ol'Barrow finished his thought. "I think she didn't even consider me a threat."

321 straightened himself. "Your record would disagree with that, inspector."

Ol'Barrow nodded with a dark frown on his face. "Yes. Maybe old age has made me soft."

The corners of the Associate's mouth curled up again. "Good," he said with a wide pearly smile. "I want you to join me at the victim's, Mr. Liggit's, home. I want to see how you work."

Surprised by the request, Ol'Barrow nodded modestly. "Very well, then."

The Associate slapped his hands together. "Good!" he said with a smile. "Good. I expect you there at ten in the morning."

The gentle splashing of the raindrops on the cobblestone street was a pleasant distraction as Ol'Barrow made his way back home. But it did not keep him from getting lost in thought as he contemplated what this Associate had told him. Was Boerhave, this Dr. Jenever, a traitor in cahoots with S-36? He went over the events that transpired at the docks.

Boerhave just extracted the Receiver from the body. The Wavecaster had announced S-36's presence. Then Boerhave fled, and her carriage left the scene in a hurry, nearly colliding with the rails. Her flight might have been for show. But intended for whom, exactly?

His mind conjured up another scenario. Boerhave was preparing to leave when she heard the melody of "Roses in the Rain". Fled to the carriage and told the driver to make haste, causing them to nearly crash as they fled. But then, why did S-36 attack? "The numbers on the Wavecaster," he pondered. Did one of those numbers happen to be Jenever's? Then Ol'Barrow recalled the statement by Associate 8, inside the file. "She has your number too, Doctor."

The inspector's eyes widened. "Boerhave has a number!" he thought out loud.

Back home, Ol'Barrow stormed through the front door, hoping Igraine would still be there. The moment he entered the sound of dog paws approached. The mutt came running in that strange way of his and inspected Ol'Barrow from a distance before heading back inside the living room.

There the girl sat at the table, bent over a drawing she was working on, while the dog lay behind her enthusiastically gnawing at a thick branch that barely fit between his jaws.

"You are still here?" Ol'Barrow said, relieved.

"It's raining outside," she responded with a puzzled expression on her face. "And Mrs. Appletree made dinner."

"Well, I'm glad," he said while hastily pulling up a chair, and sat down. "We need to talk about Dr. Jenever. Or whatever her name is. I spoke to a certain Associate 321 today."

She continued drawing. "Good for you."

"He claims the Doctor is a traitor."

The dog looked up from his branch as Igraine slammed her hands flat on the table. "She would never betray the Association!"

"I believe you," he reassured her. "A matter of fact, I think she is in grave danger. Does Dr. Jenever have a number like the other Associates?"

Igraine slowly turned her head like the thought never occurred to her. "No... I don't think so. Why?"

"Maybe it's not important. What's she been up to the last few weeks?"

"I don't know. All she said was she would be away for a while... That was half a year ago," She added softly. Her disappointment was palpable.

"You missed her, didn't you?"

She ignored his statement. "She is with this group now."

"What group?"

"I think for those Followers of the Signal. I know it from some Wave celebrity who's a member."

"Yes. That is right!" he exclaimed, knowing he was onto something now.

"That doesn't make her a traitor!" Igraine protested.

Ol'Barrow curbed his enthusiasm. "Alright... Let's forget about that for now. What was Jenever doing?"

"She visited a manor. It's in South London, where it is really busy. So, I couldn't get near the place without being seen. And they have some creepy patients."

"Creepy, how?"

"You know. Like they just got out of prison. And many are maimed. I think they are getting prostheses there."

"That is very generous of them... Did she meet some people on a regular basis?"

Igraine crossed her arms and stared at the table. "Yes..."

Ol'Barrow leaned toward her. "Well? Who then?"

"Some of those cult members, I think. But they always met inside the toy store."

"Did one of them have a hand prosthesis?"

She nodded. "Yeah."

"Describe it to me."

"Didn't look that special. It was a three-fingered design. But..."

He raised an eyebrow. "But what?"

"Sometimes I saw them come out of the toy store. But I never saw them enter," she said ominously.

"How do you mean?"

"There is no back door," Igraine emphasized. "The only way in is through the front."

"Hmm. So, are you saying, there is a secret passage?"

"Unless you have a better idea."

Ol'Barrow looked out the small window above the kitchen till. Night approached. He got up and put his bowler hat back on. "I'll go and have a look in the store."

The mutt jumped to its feet, as Igraine stood up. "I'll go with you!"

"No," he said resolutely.

"If there is a secret space, you'll need me to get in."

The Inspector blinked while considering it. Then he picked up another frock coat from the rack on the wall. “Fine then,” he said as he threw the coat her way.

Igraine frowned. “What should I do with this?”

“You put it on! Dress how you like when you are on your own. But when you work with me, at least attempt to look inconspicuous.”

HALF AN HOUR LATER...

The twilight turned the streets of Dover to a purplish hue as they walked to Hendrick's Doll Haven. Ol'Barrow hoped the mutt didn't tear apart his house while they were out. Meanwhile, Igraine walked beside him, looking rather uncomfortable in the tweak frock coat that reached all the way to her ankles. Still, he couldn't help but feel she looked adorable with the matching flat cap on her freckled head.

Together they walked awkwardly down the street without saying a word to each other. The Inspector didn't really know how to deal with children. Let alone one that wasn't even from this world.

“So-um, when will you go home again?” he asked.

She hesitated. “Couple of days.”

“What is your home like?”

She looked down. “It's complicated. I guess it's kinda like an orphanage, or...” She didn't finish the sentence. “It's a special place,” she finally said.

“What happened to your parents?”

“Nothing,” was all she said. “What about yours?”

Caught off guard he mumbled: 'Well... I never knew my mother. My father raised me alone. Although I spend most of my time at a boarding school. After that, I learned to become a copper, like him.”

“Where is he now?”

The inspector contemplated his answer. “He is dead... Killed while on patrol.”

“Oh...” She seemed a bit embarrassed now. “Did you find the killer?”

He sighed. "I looked. But no," he confessed. "I kept investigating for many years."

"You stopped?"

"Yes," he began. "I was angry for many years. I suppose I still am. But I let it dominate my life in such a way, I..." He paused for a moment. "I had to forgive him, in order to move on."

"You forgave your father's murderer?" she sounded aghast.

"I did," he confessed. "I needed to do it in order to move on, lest I become like his murderer.'

"Wait. What about the Stabber?" she asked.

"Huh?"

"Will you forgive the Stabber for what she has done?"

"Well, um..." The memory of how S-36 smiled when she killed Bigsby sprang to mind. "I can only forgive her for what she did to me," Ol'Barrow answered as he showed her his hook.

"But will you?" she insisted.

Ol'Barrow didn't know how to respond. "She has a lot to answer for," he mumbled. "Why do you think she does it?" he asked. "Why does she hate the Associates so much?"

Igraine remained awkwardly silent. So, awkward in fact, they didn't arrive a moment too soon at the Doll Haven.

Inside, they looked for a way past all the furniture with a single beam of light from his electric lantern. Meanwhile, the white of the stuffed animals' grins stood out from the shadows while beady eyes reflected the orange street lamps. How could Boerhave stand all those lifeless eyes? he wondered and looked the other way. Suddenly, he noticed a bright eye staring at him in the dark. He jumped back, knocking over a table and as he tumbled to the ground he was covered by various plush animals.

"Huh?" Igraine looked at him as if paralyzed. "What's wrong?" Her left eye shone like a bright blue diamond in the darkness, reflecting what little light there was.

"Nothing," he lied, brushing the toys away. "I tripped, that's all."

At the back they investigated the interior of the storage for any concealed features, but all he could see were baskets filled with all manner of cloth, beads, doll parts. Meanwhile, cracked and dirt-covered faces observed them from the shelves. How were they supposed to find anything?

"There it is," Igraine said while pointing at a small wall cabinet. "I recognize that shape." She opened its door and revealed a console behind it. It looked similar to the dial on a safe. But there were several hinges.

"You've seen this before?"

"Something like it."

Ol'Barrow looked on, feeling a bit useless. "You think you can open it?"

She smirked. "I open locks like these all the time. Most of the time they don't even notice." After a couple of minutes there was a click and the floor hatch popped up slightly. The inspector lifted the panel and revealed a shallow staircase with another door at the end.

"Huhm. Well, you can always go to work as a locksmith," he said, impressed.

Her smile disappeared. "Sure," Igraine responded curtly and went down the stairs.

Ol'Barrow shook his head. There was no way to encourage her, was there?

The scent of mildew greeted them when they pushed open the door and peered inside the darkness. Ol'Barrow aimed his lantern and illuminated the chamber. It was a fully furnished room, which included some worn out baroque seats, and curtains to conceal the wall. Despite the classy, be it dilapidated, furnishing, it still smelled and felt like a basement and in one place mushrooms grew out of the wall. It was humid and cold, and the old baroque couch felt clammy when he touched the sunken-in seating.

"How did they fit this thing through that door?" he wondered out loud.

Igraine walked to the back of the room where a faded red curtain obscured the wall. She looked behind the red cloth and moved it aside to reveal another door that was being eaten away by mold climbing up from the bottom.

"That solves that mystery," he said. "But what were they doing here?"

He randomly shone his lantern around till he spotted a light fixture above a desk and with the flip of a switch, the orange light revealed the interior of the hideout.

On a table lay a pile of folders and office supplies. But what stood out was a rectangular shape in the layer of dust covering the desk, like the print of a cabinet or box that used to stand in that place. Whatever it contained, it must have been more important than the folders lying about. Then he noticed an electrical plug stuck between the wall and the cabinets beside the desk. He used his hook to reach behind the furniture to get a hold of the cable and once he managed to hold the cable between his fingers, he inspected the odd plug at the end.

"It's a radio plug," Igraine said.

"Oh, is that so? Why would they take the Wavecaster? Don't they need the power cable?"

Igraine corrected him. "That is not the power cable. It's a coaxial cable, to receive telegraphic signals. It's probably connected inside the wall somewhere."

"Still, why did they take the Wavecaster with them?"

"Maybe they really like those Shade reruns," she answered, aloof.

"Right," the inspector mumbled as he browsed the files. These contained newspaper clippings, maps of London's neighborhoods, unnamed schedules, and timetables. But without context, these were useless. He stopped browsing when one of the files grabbed his attention. It was the same type of cover as the Association folder he held this morning, labeled C-33. He showed it to Igraine. "Do you know what this is?"

Igraine's eyes became larger. "It's an Association file! C, stands for Construct," she said. "It's probably about a device, or something."

Ol'Barrow opened it and went over the text.

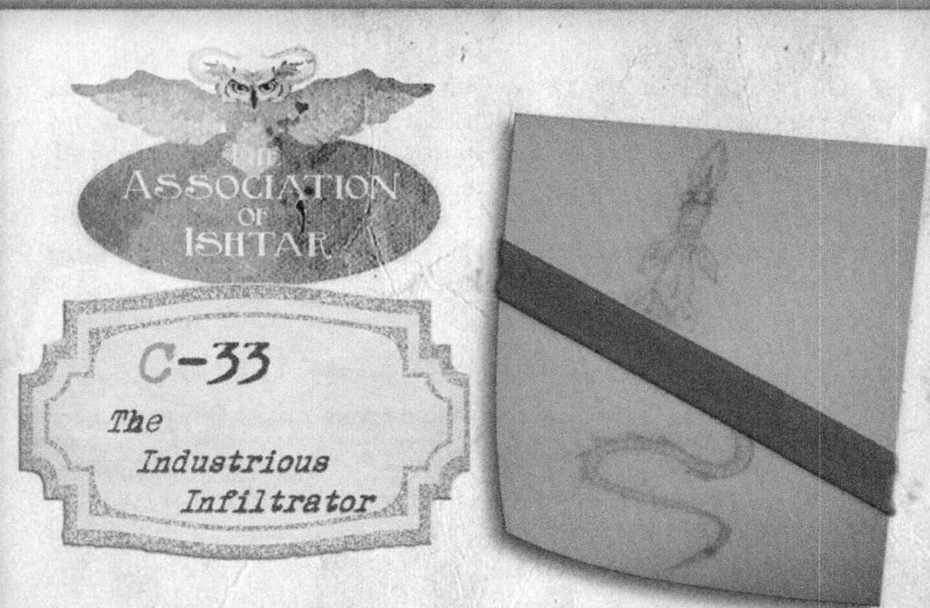

The capture of a live specimen of C-33 or C-33-A is currently a top priority for Associates. The Chair has assigned a special committee, The Resurrection Men, to identify possible C-33 activity and retrieve its victims to withhold knowledge of C-33-A from the public. If an Associate suspects they have come in contact with C-33-A, he must inform the committee at once and await further instructions.

Description:

C-33 looks like a brass-colored snake, about seven centimeters in length with a drill for a head. Who manufactured C-33 and the material composition of which the carapace was made is currently unknown. Its 'head' is a relatively powerful detachable surgical drill with which it borrows its way into its victim. Initially, it will attempt to drill its way into the base of the skull while its victim is sleeping to create an instance of C-33-A. C-33-A then disposes of the tail and any other evidence of the infection taking place.

C-33 only infects adult humans, male, and female. Various instances of C-33-A are currently known to exist. No reliable method of identifying C-33-A has been developed yet.

Known examples of C-33-A all involved members of the Industrial Elite. After the supposed infection occurred, the people closest to C-33-A started to notice a change in character. At first, C-33-A appears focused on a single goal. However, C-33-A also acts less rational than before the infection, turning from jovial to angry as soon as somebody refuses to follow certain orders. In some cases, C-33-A even became violent when their requests were not acted upon. These outbursts of anger and violence, usually work-related, become worse as time progresses. See Addendum B and C.

ENCOUNTERS: It is impossible to know how many C-33 have entered Atlas, or how many C-33-A instances are active. Areas infested by C-33 are extremely dangerous to unarmored personnel as C-33 waits in ambush, only striking when detected, or when an isolated victim has lowered its guard. When entering an area that is suspected to contain C-33, the use of fully enclosed reinforced suits is strongly advised.

Its brass interlocking carapace makes it very hard to smash or crush with blunt objects. Its flexible body makes it hard to contain, as the construct has an uncanny ability to find crevices and tears to hide in. It also displays tactical insight, and despite its slithering movements, it can move quickly to find a place to hide when it is caught in the act. During attempts to corner examples of C-33 by cutting off its escape route, C-33 immediately changed its path and found another way to escape the scene. If C-33 can't find an escape route, it will use its drill to force its way through material like wood, cement, flesh, and even material as strong as human bone.

REPORT C-33-1, SUMMARY: In 1868, a specimen of C-33 got captured by a shepherd near the village of ██████ When he caught an example of C-33 in his cabin, he threw an unshaven sheepskin on it. As a result, C-33 intertwined its drill in the fur and was unable to dislodge itself. The shepherd then handed the entire sheepskin over, with the C-33 trapped inside, to the local authorities. Unfortunately, C-33's internals were destroyed. Whether this was intentional, or due to the drill overheating, is unknown. The remains within the carapace contained metals, like copper and iron, and molten resin designated P-████. Regardless, this was the most complete specimen of C-33 the Association has managed to obtain.

Further investigation by Dr. Bourbon indicates that the carapace and internal parts have disintegrated, indicating Travelers Disease. This proves the origins are not of this world.

REPORT C-33-2, SUMMARY: This is a case that might involve a specimen of C-33-A. In 1863, a workshop owner, Mr. Jeffery Stalton, referred to as C-33-2, from the town of ███ threatened to push his brother-in-law, Mr. ███ who worked for his company for many years, into a furnace after he refused to fulfill an assignment that he considered detrimental to the company. The order in question was the fabrication of seven hundred miniaturized cogs with peculiar shapes. Although not impossible, it required a substantial investment in a product the brother-in-law deemed not profitable. Employees remarked that both men had always been on good terms and the owner's actions were 'out of character'.

It was when authorities confronted C-33-2 about the assault, the subject ran towards the nearest steam-hammer and laid his upper body underneath it. He resisted when those present tried to pull him away. C-33-2 was crushed from the waist up. One of our Associates was informed that, during autopsy, metal objects were recovered within the remains of the skull and are now in our possession.

REPORT C-33-3: In 1869 the Association caught wind of a possible incident involving C-33-3, name of the infected ███. She was the daughter of ███, an influential industrialist who made his fortune manufacturing standardized parts for machines such as Spinning Jennies. Associates managed to interview some members of the household.

Associate: "How would you describe your daughter?"

Interviewee: "Social. She enjoyed social events. Everybody liked her and she was very outgoing. Opinionated. Unfortunately, she didn't have the same passion for her responsibilities. I think she even joined those suffragettes, but I am not sure. She enjoyed living on the wild side, so to speak... I always feared she would give her mother a heart attack... Well, she nearly did me in.... It was just..."

Associate: "When did her behavior change?"

Interviewee: "Must have been a Tuesday... Oh, I don't know. I had stopped paying attention to her by that point. We considered her something of a lost cause, I must admit. I kind of got used to her asking for things I suppose. We gave her everything. Gave her every opportunity. It wasn't until she gave one of our servants a mouthful when he informed her the Sunday dinner was ready... Despite everything, she never missed the Sunday dinner. Even if we wouldn't say a word to each other. Well, that changed."

Associate: "Changed how?"

Interviewee: "All of a sudden she cared about my work. Even mentioned how I should run the company. At first, I thought she was taunting me... But then she started to make sense. Spoke like a prodigy even. I tried to raise my son to follow me in my footsteps for many years. God knows he tries. I am proud of my son, but even now I don't know if I can entrust the company to him... And then she sat there across the table, telling me to pay close attention to the colonial situation, as the African climate is very hostile to western men."

Associate: "Did she get involved in the company?"

Interviewee: "She wanted to... At first, I thought she was just boasting. Repeating what one of her many friends had said. But she kept insisting. And then she came home with a new, let's call him a 'friend.' A young army captain involved in a special committee for health and safety. He and I started talking business and before I knew it, I was up to my ears in a secret government program. All according to her plan I suspect."

Associate: "Plan to achieve what?"

Interviewee: "Who knows? Build a non-sentient army to conquer Africa... I just knew there was something wrong, but... Anyway, I kept her in the dark the best I could. We barely managed. She even broke into my office at the factory. When she was caught, I placed her under house arrest. Another underestimation on my part."

Associate: "Are you aware of a company called Warwick & March?"

Interviewee: "Yes, they have several weapon factories on the isle and the continent."

Associate: "We suspect she intended to sell the plans to them. The crown intercepted a letter from her to them and she bought a boarding pass to London."

Interviewee: [Interviewee is silent for a moment] "I guess I can't be surprised. They are ordinary arms traders... They tend to be morally flexible."

Associate: "Well, I guess that brings us to the night of ... Your daughter's death. Could you- are there any details that stood out apart from its conclusion?"

Interviewee: "Hmpf... The conclusion. Very well. I gave her house arrest after we ound her prowling around in my office. What else could I have done? Turn her in to the police? I guess I should have."

Associate: "I'm sure many would have done the same."

Interviewee: "Yes, well, she escaped. Forced the lock. One of many latent talents, I suppose. Then again, I barely paid her any attention... But she knew she could find me in my office. I couldn't sleep and I couldn't be idle. So, there she was. My own daughter about to knife me with a letter opener, demanding I divulge the code to my safe that contained the information regarding the project. Regardless of our relationship I had always given her what she desired. Not sure why, but not this time. Not for a moment did I believe she was ██████. Not a doubt in my mind. When I heard her spitting that godless language from between her lips, I knew she had been possessed."

Associate: "Are you well?"

Interviewee: "Obviously, I am not! Something turned my daughter into a monster. No... Something took her. Wore her body like a…a skin suit. Like an automaton."

Associate: "Sir, we can-"

Interviewee: "A servant came in, bless his heart. I managed to take advantage of the situation and threw her off me. We struggled. Managed to disarm her. But I let her go again. That was my fault."

Associate: "Why? What happened?"

Interviewee: "She ran off. Straight for the lounge. Locked herself in. Then came the shot. It disposed of her body with my father's hunting rifle. That is how my father used to make a living for his family. Of all the guns. It did it to spite us, I'm sure."

[End of transcript]

According to the servant involved in the struggle, it was not the father, but himself who allowed her to escape from the office because he had reservations about hurting a woman. We have no explanation for this contradiction.

After the struggle, while C-33-3 had locked herself up, the father ordered an evacuation of the manor. Before any action could be taken, a single gunshot emanating from the room.

With aid from the local authorities, they forced the entrance to the room where C-33-3 was last seen. C-33-3 had taken her own life with an 8-gauge hunting rifle. In this case, just like in case C-33-2, metallic objects were recovered from the remains of the skull.

An acquaintance of the aforementioned army captain informed one of our Associates of the event. Unfortunately, the whereabouts and status of the metallic objects are unknown. The constables claim this happened due to a clerical error.

REPORT C33-5:PRELUDE TO THE ENGAGEMENT: An instance of Construct-33 happened in a manor near the city of Amstan Junction. A maid was removing cobwebs from the ceiling while the master of the house was away combining a business trip with a family vacation.

When she removed another cobweb, a C-33 appeared from underneath the web and crawled across the wall. Terrified, she called other staff members for help, who gave chase to the construct. They cornered it in the kitchen where C-33 attempted to drill its way out through a cupboard panel. After stomping it, the staff managed to trap the C-33 underneath a wooden tub. One of the servants sat on the bottom of the tub to prevent it from being lifted. Unfortunately for the servant, C-33 decided to drill its way through the bottom of the tub.

When C-33's drill protruded from his body, all those present fled the manor immediately and authorities were informed. Local constables accompanied by members of the local militia entered the manor. They were unsuccessful, however, suffering heavy casualties; leaving one military member dead, three wounded and one of the constables died of organ failure in the hospital. See the interview section for more information.

This is when a local acquaintance informed the Association, and three Associates volunteered.

CAPTURE: After our Society was informed, three associates were dispatched to deal with the Construct. Staff and militia members present had been interrogated. See Interviews A and B.

Associates brought with them sheepskins, as this was a tried method, and large quantities of steel wool. The kind that is used for pest control. Associate 15 speculated that its brittle nature might slow down C-33's drill enough without overheating. C-33's container needed to be wrapped in sheepskin regardless.

INTERVIEW A, MILITIAMAN: In the aftermath of the capture of C-33, witnesses of the first attempt to neutralize C-33 were interviewed to learn more about its behavior. Corporal ████████ was there to lead his platoon.

15: “Please, have a seat. Thank you for your time. Could you state your name and function for the record?”

Corporal: “My name is ███████, Corporal. I have been with the ██████ militia for about five years.

15: “I'm sorry about what happened to your men, corporal. Could you tell me about your encounter with C-33?”

Corporal: “C-33 is too kind of a name for that ... thing, sir. I have fought strange animals before, but nothing like that ... We entered the manor and headed for the kitchen. The body of Mr. Ullie was still there. We followed the trail of blood it [C-33] left behind. That thing had crawled up against the counter into one of the cupboards. There we discovered it had drilled its way into the next room. It's a sneaky bastard like that. [...]
We finally cornered it. We had a metal bucket, with a lid, with us to contain it. We tried shooting it. We tried smashing it with a hammer. It was the most frustrating thing I have ever seen. Whatever that thing is made of it is so slippery that bullets and hammer strikes just seem to push it aside. “Then private ███████ tried to grab it while wearing welding gloves. He was new so I guess he wanted to prove himself... That turned out to be a mistake. Ever seen a man cutting himself? I heard stories of drug fiends cutting themselves because they hallucinate insects crawling under their skin, but this. We could see it crawl underneath his skin, destroying whatever was underneath. It soun... It ...

[The corporal recovers himself]

“Have you ever heard one of those automated meat grinders at work? It sounded just like that. Others tried to help him, and I just stood there. It got them too, just drilled its way through their limbs and escaped. Constable █████ nearly stopped him with the bucket but failed... The thing made its way straight through his abdomen and out through the back… That is when I aborted the operation. We carried away the bodies and evacuated the site.” [...]

[END OF INTERVIEW]

"My god," was all the inspector could say. The contents of the file sent shivers down his spine. "Is this what all this is about? Is this what they found in the head of..." He looked at the girl who was fidgeting on the couch.

"You don't have to hide anything from me," she said. "I know more about this stuff than you do."

Ol'Barrow considered it, but he couldn't involve her in something like this. *Should I tell 321*? he thought. *No, not yet. He'll ask how I got this. Then who*? He turned to Igraine. "Does Doctor Jenever have another hiding place?"

She shrugged.

"Fine then," he said as he laid down the dossier. He walked up at the curtain and swept it aside to clear the door. "Let's see what is on the other side."

The high-pitched creaking of the hinge reverberated through the cellar as he forced open the door. A humid draft greeted them as Ol'Barrow entered the tunnel on the other end, while the splashing sound of water was amplified by the low curved ceiling. It looked like they were beneath an old bridge completely integrated into the foundation of Dover. Their side was blocked off by dirt and other debris, but at the other end light came through the reeds that hid the tunnel's entrance from the outside world. "So, they are using the channel."

"Now what?" Igraine asked.

The Inspector looked down on her. "We go home," he replied. "It's past your bedtime."

CHAPTER FIVE

There was a rumbling of carriage wheels rolling over the tracks as a deep high-pitched whistle sounded in the distance. In a daze, Ol'Barrow passed through a blanket of white steam so thick it even obscured the marble tiles he walked on. The arrival hall around him was dreamlike, lavishly ornate, with polished stone walls, elaborate lamp fixtures and exquisitely crafted street furniture. Fifteen feet up in the air, suspended from various steel rafters beneath the leadlight roof, hung an enormous crystal chandelier that reflected a thousand lights.

Confused and unaware of how he got to this station, Ol'Barrow slowly strolled by a pristine train wagon, displaying "Howard and Chamber Express" on the side, with the line "an Utter-Krapp Company" underneath. The beige lines, painted over a pure emerald, looked so crisp they jumped out of the background. Even the train wheels looked unused, clean.

The locomotive hissed aggressively as it spewed out more vapor obscuring Ol'Barrow's surroundings yet again. As the steam lifted an older man at the other end of the carriage emerged for the smoke. Ol'Barrow froze when he recognized him. It was Mr. Slober, the dismembered man they found on the train station over a week ago. But now he was alive and in a conductor's uniform. Slober gave him a friendly nod and held his hand beside his mouth. "You need to hurry if you want to get on, sir. "

Scared out of his wits, Ol'Barrow obeyed the man without question and grabbed one of the handlebars beside the passenger entrance. He then attempted to pull himself up through the doorway, but his foot slipped. Fortunately, he managed to keep himself vertical, only hurting his pride.

"I wish I could give you a hand, sir," Slober said with a smile on his face, and lifted his maimed arm. "But you know how it is."

Uncomfortable with this whole situation Ol'Barrow just nodded, while grinning like he had a toothache, and climbed on board. Once inside, he found little amiss with the train. On the contrary. It was idyllic, in cleanliness as in decor. Electric lighting in the shape of a vintage oil lamps. Embroidered blinds in front of the windows on his left side. Comfortable passenger cabins on his right. Feeling compelled to go on, he walked quietly past the coupes, one step at the time. Ol'Barrow noticed number plates on top of the door frame. 42... 43... 44... His mind stopped for a moment. "Could it be?" he wondered when he reached Cabin 45. Ol'Barrow wasn't sure why, but he felt this was significant. He grabbed the handle and shoved the door aside.

When the path was open, the blood froze in his veins. He recognized the man on one of two opposing benches. It was the Frenchman, but very much alive. He looked up from the book he was reading, clearly annoyed by this unannounced visit. As the Frenchman raised his chin, he unwittingly revealed the grazes of a noose around his neck.

"Forty-Five?" Ol'Barrow exclaimed involuntarily.

The man frowned. "No, this is fifty-four," he corrected him, aggravated. "You are in the wrong cabin."

Ol'Barrow looked at the number plate again. 54? Baffled, he looked back at the man. "Terribly sorry. Must have misread." Ol'Barrow then excused himself and shut the door behind him.

Both embarrassed and feeling lost, Ol'Barrow continued down the hallway. Inside the cabins he saw vaguely familiar faces. But they didn't appear to know him and kept indulging in their own leisure as he passed by. He was fine with that, but the sight of one passenger made him pause. There was an older gentry woman sitting by the window wearing a modest bonnet. Her sullen face looked outside with indifference, until she became mindful of him. When she turned to face him, Ol'Barrow's already pronounced brow turned into a disapproving glare of contempt. The moment those brown eyes stared at him, he already had enough and walked on as if he hadn't recognized her, assuming the feeling was mutual.

Looking around to distract his mind, Ol'Barrow walked on. There did not seem to be an end to this carriage. Before, the end didn't appear further than twenty feet away. But it remained so, no matter how fast he walked. But he kept going, hoping he should reach the door at some point. From walking he turned to running, but the harder he ran the further his destination move away as if the hallway stretched itself like a piece of gum. The dissociating effect gave Ol'Barrow such vertigo it made him that Nauseous, he was forced to stop.

Catching his breath, he looked around again. Things seemed to have turned to normal, but he hadn't moved an inch, despite his efforts. Then, through an open cabin door, he saw another familiar face. He stopped to have a good look and exclaimed. "Derby!"

Constable Derby was just sitting there, in civilian clothes, smoking a pipe. Surprised, he took the pipe from between his lips. "Inspector?" he exclaimed. There was something about his inflection that made it appear he wasn't pleased to see him. "I didn't expect you to be on this train."

Awkwardly Ol'Barrow set a foot inside the cabin. "To be honest I am not sure what I am doing here either, ha, ha."

"Well, if you are not sure," he stated bluntly to the point of being insulting, "maybe you should get off before we leave."

"A-Ah," was all he could respond with. "I see..." Feeling rejected, he went back into the hallway. But maybe Derby was right, and he should get off now while he still could.

But before he could finish that thought, the deep train whistle blew, followed by the hissing of the engines. A sharp static sting coming from the speakers made his hairs stand on end. A melody started playing. It was that of Roses in the Rain. Then the train whistle blew, announcing their departure.

Ol'Barrow grabbed the seat beside him as the floor beneath his feet started to shake. Careful not to damage anything with his hook, he entered the cabin and sat himself down on the bench.

"Now what?" he asked himself. He never enjoyed traveling, and used the train only a few times before. Even then, he didn't like riding trains because he always had this nagging suspicion that he wasn't heading the right direction.

Meanwhile, the outside landscape was blurry. But not a blur in a speed sense. It was literally a smudge of shapes and colors. Even the murmur around him appeared to be an imitation of human speech, and so did the rhythm of the train itself.

Outside of the window, the colors started to fade. The world was turning dark, and the train sounds died away until these ceased to exist. All Ol'Barrow saw was blackness apart from infrequent streaks of light that sheared past like falling stars.

The silence persisted, apart from the beating of his own heart, and the impulses inside his brain sparked by his own insecurities. He tried to focus on the passing lights in an attempt to suppress the urge to count the strokes inside his chest. But all he managed to do is make his heart speed up the pace.

"Tickets please."

His heart paused for a moment when he heard the ominous phrase from down the hall. Like a curious rodent, Ol'Barrow peeked his head outside to see what was happening.

A few rooms away, two conductors were standing in a door opening addressing the passengers. "Good day. Tickets please."

He ducked back inside. Now what? Maybe he could go to the toilet? No, he didn't see one. Pretend to sleep? No-oh. But wait! Maybe he did have a ticket. Quickly Ol'Barrow explored his various pockets.

"Ticket, please!"

Ol'Barrow nearly jumped off the bench and turned involuntarily to face the conductor and said, "just a mom-"

He pressed himself against the back of the bench in fright. It wasn't because he didn't have a ticket. It wasn't even because of the conductor's pale corpse-like face, or his bloodshot eyes. It was because he knew him by name.

"Christopher?"

The conductor frowned his lips. "Have we met?"

"You're James Christopher," Ol'Barrow reiterated.

"Yes, sir," he answered plainly. "Now, can I please see your ticket?"

Flabbergasted, Ol'Barrow started to mumble. "Uhm, my ticket. Yes..." Rummaging through his pockets, he hoped that by some miracle there was a lost piece of paper somewhere. Meanwhile, Christopher observed him with a watchful, yet brotherly gaze as he failed to produce any evidence.

Then, a second conductor appeared in the doorway. "Well, well, look at that," he said with a familiar and very unwelcome voice. Ol'Barrow's body shuddered as he looked up. It was Macarthur, dressed as another conductor, sneering at him. "You are at it again, are you? He doesn't belong here."

"B-But I have a ticket," he said as he continued his desperate search.

The two men seemed to grow in size as they looked down on him.

"Sir, if you don't have a ticket," Christopher insisted. "I have to ask you to get up and come with us."

"Of course he doesn't have a ticket, you moppet," smirked Macarthur. "This one always tried to get a free ride. That's what happens when you let them get off the hook, James."

Christopher swallowed. "Please, sir. Your ticket."

Ol'Barrow's heart pounded against his ribs while sweat was forming on his forehead.

"I have one!" he mumbled as he reached inside his coat. Then his fingers located a carton box. "I have it right here," he exclaimed. But as he reached out his hand to present the item, he realized it wasn't a ticket to get out of this situation. It was a packet of- candy?

A third even taller man appeared behind the two conductors, wearing a top hat and an antiquated police coat. "What did you do this time?" he bellowed.

Ol'Barrow felt himself shrink even further as the policeman loomed over him. "I-I didn't steal this!" he cried with a boyish voice, while staring into his father's incensed eyes. "Someone else put them in my pocket. I swear!"

His father grabbed him by the wrist and grasped the candy away. "I've had enough of this, you lying little thief!" he bellowed and pulled him to his feet. Ol'Barrow was tiny compared to his father, who dragged him by the hand through the train carriages.

Even the passengers towered over him as he was dragged past their seats. Some, he believed, carried vague resemblance to people he had met. Others, he recognized from days gone. Days he tried to forget.

"There we have it again."

"Can you believe he's a copper's son?"

"Better keep your eyes on him."

"That one belongs in a workhouse, he does."

"You good for nothin'."

"You're a disgrace to your uniform!"

"No, please. This is a mistake!" He cried as he tried to pull free from his father's grasp.

"Don't talk to me about mistakes," his father sneered without looking back.

They reached the next carriage. There was a loud bang when his father swung the door open. Then he took his son inside the dark carriage, filled with boxes and other containers, and dragged him to a lone crate. As pulled off the lid, cold fumes rose from within.

"No," he cried as his father bent him over the edge. Ol'Barrow was horrified to discover the bottom of the crate was covered in lumps of ice. "No, please dad. Don't put me in! Don't put me in!"

"This is what you get boy!" he said as he lifted him by the back of his pants and tumbled him inside the crate.

"No, don't do this. I've done nothing wrong!"

"You had one job, you ungrateful shit. Get a ticket!" And with that, he raised the lid, which had the number 54 scratched into the bottom. The ice was already burning his shins as he tried to hold the lid back, but it was of no use. Within moments, he was locked up in the dark, while the freezing cold got a hold of him.

16TH OF MAY, 1875, THE OL'BARROW HOUSEHOLD, DOVER

There was a thunderclap when Ol'Barrow woke up. His body was so sweaty, it nearly fooled him into thinking he had been sleeping in the rain.

Igraine loomed over him looking stupefied and concerned at the same time, as she was standing beside his makeshift mattress with the mutt beside her.

Ol'Barrow blinked, feeling disoriented and not quite sure where he was. Gradually, it dawned on him he was back home. Home where he belonged. The splashing of rain on the windows, combined with the ticking of the clock, produced a soothing sound that gave him a homely feeling. Much better than the disturbing silence he experienced in his dream.

"What time is it?" he mumbled.

Igraine rolled her eyes toward the grandfather clock. "About nine."

"Nine!" He scrambled up. "I need to get to work."

Igraine didn't seem comfortable with this. But it was also for her sake. Or so he rationalized it. "I need to inform them of our find last night," he said as he put on his waist coat. "Assuming this C-33 thing is real, my superiors need to be informed. I mean..." He considered Constable Derby and his sudden disappearance. Could it be? He dismissed the idea, for now, and finished his thought. "You know what I mean."

"Where will we look next?" she asked.

Ol'Barrow froze. "We? Listen, there-"

There was a sudden knocking on the door. He wasn't expecting anyone, but now it seemed like a blessing. But who could be out with this weather?

It was Miss Appletree, wearing a mantle to protect herself against the rain. "I noticed you were in," she began bluntly. "I wanted to give you this. It was delivered while I was watching your niece."

"My niece? Oh, yes. Of course. Please."

She seemed hesitant to hand him the letter.

"What's wrong?"

"I'm sorry, Mr. Ol'Barrow. But I recognized the name."

He took the letter and read the sender. "Oltoak?"

"I'm sorry," she said again.

"Did you read it?"

Mrs. Appletree responded with another question. "Have you had breakfast yet? You should eat something first."

He gave her an annoyed glare, unfolded the envelope and scanned its contents.

"Dear sir, I regret to inform you that your father's widow, Miss Elisa Oltoak, has fallen ill and is not exc-"

Ol'Barrow stopped reading. So, she was dying. He didn't know how to feel about that.

"I'm sorry," Mrs. Appletree said. "I know you weren't close. But still..." She didn't finish the sentence.

Ol'Barrow folded back the paper. "So be it," he mumbled.

"Please, Mr. Ol'Barrow. Don't say that."

He grabbed his coat. "I need to leave now."

"But you look like you haven't slept at all. And neither does she. What have you two been up to?"

"I got sick last night!" said Igraine abruptly.

"Oh, poor dear."

"Yes, that's right," Ol'Barrow played along. "As matter a fact, would you mind watching her?"

"But I'm better!" Igraine protested.

"That's what they all say," Ol'Barrow said as he walked through the front door.

Mrs. Appletree walked after him. "Somebody should be watching you as well," she cried, judgmentally.

"I'll be home early. I promise," Ol'Barrow answered, hurrying down the street to discourage her from following. He neither had the time nor the energy to deal with this right now.

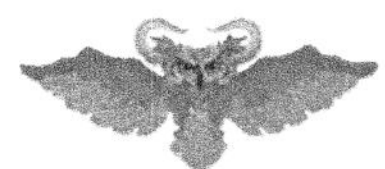

Moments later, beneath the gray sky, people in the street were running through the rain when Ol'Barrow's coach pulled up in front of the police station. The moment the vehicle stopped, he jumped out and was about to enter the station when someone called out to him.

"Sir!" the driver yelled with urgency.

Ol'Barrow looked up in fright at the man who sat about three feet above, looking down at him. "You still need to pay your fair, sir."

A mixture of shame and relief came over him. “Oh, terribly sorry about that,” Ol'Barrow said regretfully, and reached for his purse.

As soon as that was done, the inspector stormed up the station's steps. Despite a lack of sleep, he felt a weird type of energy soaring through his body, as if somebody rearranged his wiring, although that could just be sleep depravity. He ignored the usual humdrum of arrested drunkards and prostitutes in the reception area and marched on to the first floor, up to Interrogation Room 4 where "Special Consultant" Associate 321 had set up his office.

When Ol'Barrow swung open the door, the Associate looked up from the city map on the desk he was leaning over, clearly not appreciating the interruption. Peeking his head from behind the door, Ol'Barrow greeted the startled man. “Good morning, Associate. Mind if I interrupt?”

The Associate raised an eyebrow for a moment. “Of course not. How can I help you, inspector?”

Jaunty, the inspector stepped inside and turned around as he closed the door behind him. “I made some discoveries last night,” Ol'Barrow said as he reached inside his office bag.

“Did you now?”

“Yes.” He dropped the recovered C-33 file on the desk.

The Associate froze for a moment and inspected the cover like he was studying some illegible manuscript. After flipping it open, he glanced at the contents with a puzzled expression. “Where did you find this?” he asked, indignant.

Ol'Barrow couldn't help but gloat. “You think I couldn't find an Association hideout?”

Impatiently the Associate folded the file shut. “I am a busy man. What do you want?”

“C-33's. Are there any in Kent?”

A reluctant grin escaped his lips. “If I could tell you, there wouldn't be a problem.”

“What about this Lantry?” he continued unabashedly. “The celebrity Carla Lantry, she was here at the station the other day.”

“Is that so?” responded the Associate, plainly.

"Yes, she wanted to take away the two dead cult members we had in the morgue." Ol'Barrow elaborated.

"You better not call them a cult around her," the Associate corrected him.

"Oh, bugger that!" he snapped. "She didn't ask anything about those suspects who fled the crime scene. You know, her people."

"And?"

"And... And I don't like it!" Ol'Barrow responded, dismayed. "She is more concerned about dead members than live ones?"

"Why, you think that is?" asked 321.

"Why? Well, she said she wanted to take out their brains- Oh, I'm sorry, minds, for ascension," said Ol'Barrow mockingly, and raised his hook to shake it pedantically. "But what if she is hiding evidence? One of those *things*?" he reiterated by pointing at the file. "C-33-s?"

"I read nothing about any head wounds in the coroner's report," the Associate said.

Ol'Barrow turned away. "Right, darn it!" But then a thought occurred to him, and he raised a finger to his lips. "But what if the coroner is in on it?"

The Associate cringed at the statement. "Oh, please think before you speak!" the Associate replied indignantly. "Inspector..." After a deep breath 321 shoved his fingers together and tilted his head. "Inspector I can understand you are upset. But what is this intrusion really about?"

"I know these Followers are involved in this! Your lot must know something about them. Where do they get their technology from for example? They must use those rifts."

The Associate raised his eyebrows. "If only that were so simple. These are hard people to prosecute."

Ol'Barrow slammed his palm against the wall in frustration, took a breather and said "I must speak to that Lantry. She acted as if she knew those men."

"You think the victims were working for her?"

"Oh, I don't know," Ol'Barrow admitted. But the truth was he hadn't considered that possibility to begin with. "But she has convicted criminals working for her. Dangerous, dangerous criminals! And she dared to bring one right up to our doorstep."

The Associate's gaze grew more and more concerned. "Do you and she have history?" 321 wondered aloud.

"No. But her servant and I do. Macarthur. A pyromaniac I- We arrested a decade ago when he prepared to light up Dover Castle."

"Where the Norman fort is?" 321 asked bewildered.

"Yes!"

"And now you think she wants to do something with this MacArthur fellow?"

"Why else did she bother with getting him released?" said Ol'Barrow as if it would be obvious. At least it was to him. Of all the dirtbags Ol'Barrow had confronted, Macarthur had been the worst. Not even his accomplices wanted to work with him. They even turned him in, telling the police of his plans and where he made his incendiaries.

As the Associate looked at him, the inspector could see the assumptions forming behind his eyes.

"I admire your zeal, inspector," said 321, with a lowered voice. "But all of this seems very circumstantial... Did you sleep last night?"

At that moment, Ol'Barrow heard the bones in his neck pop. Blankets don't make the best of mattresses. He intended to clean out one of the bedsteads that he had been using as a closet but hadn't gotten around to it yet. Maybe he should make Igraine do it herself? It seemed only fair.

"I take your silence as a no, inspector," 321 responded, knowingly. "So, let me put your mind at ease. We located one of the victims' family."

Ol'Barrow's gloomy demeanor changed immediately. "You did?"

"Yes. Somebody at his post office recognized him. He appears to live like a recluse, but he still wrote to his sister in the North."

"Right."

"Inspector, you may have been out for a couple of days, but the world still goes on without you," 321 said, pedantically.

"What do you mean by that?"

"That you need to take a rest. You are not the only man at the department that wants you colleague to-"

"Bigsby!" Ol'Barrow corrected him.

"Yes, Mr. Bigsby will be avenged."

Ol'Barrow looked at him for a moment. "And?"

321 slammed his hand on the desk. "Go home and have some rest! We'll search Mr. Liggit's apartment and inform you of the finds."

Ol'Barrow shook his head dismissively. "No, no-no-no. I need to be there. I'm ready. We can go right now."

The Associate stroked his goatee. "If we go now, will you take the rest of the day off?"

"Sure, sure," he responded, nodding excessively. But no matter how much the inspector insisted, the Associate didn't buy it for a moment.

Igraine was tired. Tired of laying down and staring idly at the ceiling with yellow moisture stains.

Mrs. Appletree entered the bedroom. "Miss. Igraine. I need to get some groceries and run some errands. I'll be back before dinner."

"Alright."

When Mrs. Appletree had left, the bed cracked as she pushed away the blankets, and held up her doll. "I'm bored, Anwin," she said in her native tongue. She tilted her doll as if she were responding to her. "There must be something we can do?" she imagined Anwin saying.

"Like what?"

"Like... fixing the bed. There must be tools somewhere."

As an experiment, Igraine shifted from left to right. The bed moved along with her. "Fixing it might probably be a good idea."

She forced herself out of bed. To figure out what the problem was, she turned on the bulb of a wall sconce beside Mr. OlOl'Barrow's shaving mirror. It buzzed as if a fly was trapped inside and flickered slightly. Unfortunately, the sound did not just come from the lamp. Igraine realized something was wrong with the wiring. She pulled up a chair and climbed on top.

As she stood on her toes, the dog entered the bedroom. Curiously, he looked on as she was standing on the wobbly chair, checking the power lines.

"Oh. Hi, boy... Oh, no." She was horrified to find the cause of the problem. The wiring was covered by brittle cloth and stapled to the wall. In one place the staple cut into the cloth, exposing the wiring. It was a miracle the house hadn't caught fire.

Meanwhile, the mutt spotted Anwin laying on the edge of the bed and started to sniff at her. As he pushed his snout against the doll, Anwinfell down on the floor. Enthused by what he found he clenched the doll's dress between his teeth and dragged her away.

Past the corner of her eye Igraine noticed the dog making off with her friend. "No! Let that go!" she cried. The chair shifted because of her sudden movements. Unbalanced, Igraine tried to jump off, but the rickety chair toppled. Barely managing to break her fall she landed on the floor.

While recovering her pride, the dog observed her with guilty eyes while Anwin still lay in front of him on the floorboards.

Afraid he would run off with her, Igraine lunged at the doll, and glared at him, clenching Anwin to her chest. "Bad dog!"

He lay down with its head between its paws, in shame.

Now she felt sorry for him. She knocked on the ground beside her. "Come here."

Tail wagging, he got up and limped over to playfully rub his flank against her.

Her arms wrapped around her friends, Igraine looked at the chaos she just created. The chair was broken too. "I guess I'll fix those things as well, huh."

16TH OF MAY, 10.07 AM. DOVER.

Finally, the rain had gone. Instead, the inspector's nostrils were tormented by the scent of warm, humid garbage as he and Associate 321 walked beneath the clothing lines spun across Pelgrims Road.

These two-story buildings at either side of the street were home to the uneducated working class of the city. The impoverished state of the living conditions here was emphasized by the soot covering the walls which, ironically, hid the many cracks in the brickwork. Behind flaking window frames, improvised curtains were pulled shut to protect those who worked the night shift from the intrusive sunlight.

Ol'Barrow was well accustomed to the sight, for he had walked the beat in this neighborhood for years. Even then, these parts were not much to speak of. But at least these apartments would be occupied by a single family at the time. And one did not have to worry as much about pickpockets and robbers. He dealt with hawkers, drunkards, and the delinquent youngsters. And he could do it all on his own. Now, constables only dared to venture here in pairs, on ever lengthening patrols.

As the inspector reminisced on the past, Associate 321 walked beside him. He had his own issues as his foreign appearance attracted many curious eyes. Few black people arrived in Dover. Even fewer walked its streets. Despite the stares, the Associate walked on with his chin held high. "Don't mind it, inspector," 321 said reassuringly. "I'm used to it. I endured worse in the American South."

Ol'Barrow couldn't help but feel embarrassed by his countrymen. "In these parts I prefer to pay attention regardless of who I associate with. No pun intended." The inspector stopped walking and addressed the Associate for a moment. "What should I call you in public?"

"Mr. Wilkins," he responded right away without slowing down. "James Wilkins."

With a spring in his step, Ol'Barrow caught up with him. "Fine then. So, what are we looking for, Mr. Wilkins?"

"Evidence, clues. An indication of what Liggit and Miss Boerhave were working on."

The inspector grumbled. "You make it sound so mundane."

"And you seem a bit distracted, inspector," he rebutted. "Are you sure you are up to it?"

"It's just that I used to police these streets. It has become increasingly harder to patrol these parts. I used to unclog the drains, like this one over here. Now they are dragging bodies out of there."

The Associate raised an eyebrow. "Unclog the drain?"

"Yes. We used to do that type of thing. Clearing drains, clearing the street. Take care of the homeless. But even with thrice as many people, we can't do those things anymore. The population exploded. So much so, not even all these houses can hold them."

The inspector gradually came to a standstill in front of a general store. The fading sign on the facade read, "Houston's General Goods". Ol'Barrow recognized the proprietor who stood in front of the doorway. It was old Mr. Houston himself. A workhorse, and a cornerstone to the community who knew everybody by name. His business never was prosperous, and he had been the target of many robbers. But he continued regardless, for the sake of the neighborhood more than anything else. It was just the type of man he was. A rare breed, even then. Due to his apron, he looked like a picturesque example of a grocer. But his age was showing as he shuffled his feet over the sidewalk, hunched forward as he swiped the cobble stones. Every brush of the broom had a forced mechanical motion to it, like his arm joints where his serious need of greasing. But like a worn-out steam engine he persisted, until the inevitable point that the transmission would snap.

The corners of the old man's mouth curled up as he recognized the inspector's face. "Mr. Ol'Barrow?" he remarked with a hoarse, fragile voice.

"Yes, it is me, Mr. Houston."

"I haven't-" he paused to breathe." Seen you in years, constable."

"It's inspector now, Mr. Houston."

"Oh." He nodded, seemingly concerned he had forgotten. "Are you off duty?"

"No, inspectors don't wear uniforms anymore."

"Oh," he groaned once again, nodding sheepishly.

"Don't you have help, Mr. Houston?"

He shook his head like he shuddered at the thought. "I had help," he grumbled resentfully. "A constable arrested him after catching him stealing my oranges."

"Hm, who is walking the beat here these days?"

"Uhm. Hubs, Derby, and-"

"Derby?"

"Hm, yes," he grumbled. "Haven't seen him in a while. They come by fewer, and fewer."

Ol'Barrow noticed the Associate's impatient stare as he stood by him, hands in pockets.

"Did you know a certain Mr. Liggit?" Ol'Barrow asked. "Tall, chestnut hair, dressed above his station."

The shopkeep squeezed his lips together as he shook his head. "Nah."

"He had a unique artificial arm," he added.

"Oh, him!" Houston answered right away. "Yeah. Didn't like him. He wasn't one of us."

"How do you mean?" 321 asked. Apparently, he wasn't aware of the snobbery of the English working class.

"He was obviously a toff," the old man said. "You know the type. The cranks who like to pretend to be like us. But only so long they get to enjoy the wealth of their family, and forget about us the moment they get married, or a better job. I've seen their type all my life -" Houston stopped himself as a young woman approached. She would have looked pretty, if she had spent a moment to maintain any standard of hygiene. She held a reed basket so worn out it was held together with a dirty string. Meanwhile, dried dilapidated threads of cabbage hung from between the rush. An apt metaphor for the state of her clothes which has the elegance of a used burlap sack. Maybe that was all her parents were willing to afford, as alcohol tends to be the priority in such households. Prejudiced, perhaps. But Ol'Barrow had seen it too often before.

"Is the gin in yet? Mr. Houston, sir," she asked with a pitiful voice.

Oh, how he hated to be right. Ol'Barrow felt for the old man who knew too well that this girl, who was clearly underfed, was sent here just for the drink. Based on her avoiding his gaze, he figured she probably just earned that money too. Legal, or otherwise. But the alternative to not satisfying her family's addiction might be a beating, or other punishment. Regardless of her compliance, the end result would be the same. They would find their fix. The inspector had no qualms admitting the lower classes were underpaid, underfed, and neglected. But as a man who walked the beat for years, he learned the human tendency was to lose themselves and walk down a spiral self-destructive path.

Mr. Houston's hands trembled slightly as he put the jugs in the reed basket. Mr. Houston, pillar of the community, was supplying the abusive drunkards who prostituted their own children for longer than Ol'Barrow was alive. Of course, a shop owner could say, no. But did so at the risk of starving himself. And the result would be the same in the end. The drunkards would get their fix and blame society for their lot in a drunken stupor.

As the girl rummaged through her pockets for some pennies, the old man said. "I need to get back to work now, officers."

Ol'Barrow nodded. "It was good speaking to you, Mr. Houston," he said with a bitter taste in his mouth.

"What was that about?" asked 321 as they moved on.

"Derby was the one who disappeared around the time Boerhave's people stole the bodies from the morgue," Ol'Barrow whispered.

"And you think he is implicated?"

Ol'Barrow pretended not to hear the question and changed the topic. "Speaking of Boerhave. Am I right to assume Boerhave is also an Associate with a number?"

Wilkins shook his head. "No, Associates are all volunteers. The Doctors are unlike the Associates on retainer by the Chair. That's all I can tell you about them."

"But in the transcript of S-36, this Associate 8 refers to her number," Ol'Barrow reiterated. "Why did he?"

Mr. Wilkins turned his gaze away. "Even if I knew, inspector, I am not allowed to tell you."

They arrived at their destination. A tenement building that looked as grimy and overcrowded as the rest. All the windows were covered up, and paint flaked off the handrails as the men walked up the moss-covered steps. By the door hung a sign that read: "No vacancies". As Ol'Barrow knocked on the door with the back of his hook, he figured that sign wouldn't be around for much longer.

After a moment, a scruffy looking woman opened up and stuck her nose outside. Squeezing her eyes together, she inspected them, looking Mr. Wilkins up and down with suspicion. "W-who might you be?" she asked with a mouse-like lady's voice. Her wrinkled emaciated face still had an air of middle-class dignity about it. Undoubtedly a widow who invested her money in the building so she could at least cover her living expenses through its tenants. But not such critical things like maintenance.

Ol'Barrow nodded as he showed her his badge. "Dover police, madame. We are here to investigate Mr. Liggit's room."

With a hand on her chest, she opened the door wide. "Oh, finally! Will you take his stuff away as well?" she asked hopefully.

The men looked at each other. Ol'Barrow responded with: "Only potential evidence I am afraid. Have you contacted his family?"

"If only I knew how!" she complained. "He paid for a whole room by himself. Now that floor is littered with his stuff."

"What kind of stuff?"

"I think he studied medicine and made wooden legs and such. Each time he would leave his room with a new arm," she explained. "Now I need to get rid of all this junk before the new tenants can move in. There is enough room for five of them in there."

Ol'Barrow nodded reassuringly all the while. "We'll see what we can do, madame."

"Oh, good," she said, relieved. "I'll show you his room." She continued her statements as she walked in front of them through the cramped hall. It smelled of old tobacco and the floor was covered with many pairs of worn shoes. From inside some of the rooms, snoring could be heard. "I try to keep a tidy house," she said, "but some of these sods come back so early in the morning they can't see where they are going. Mr. Liggit was an okay tenant at first. But for the past month he has been coming in and out deep in the night." The steps squeaked loudly beneath their feet as they walked up the stairs. "He insisted he had important work to do... At least he didn't bring the strumpets home with him. I swear, if he didn't pay as consistently as he did, I would have thrown him out weeks ago!"

They stopped in front of a door. "This is his room. Fortunately, it is paid for till the end of the month."

She unlocked the door while Ol'Barrow asked: "How did he make a living? Apart from his family?"

"I think he mentioned working for a clinic. Don't ask me where." The lock made a rather satisfying click.

Mr. Wilkins asked. "Is that lock new?"

"Oh, yes," she groaned. "He even put in metal bars in front of the windows too. He paid for it, so I didn't complain. Somebody was after his research he said. Don't ask me why."

"Actually, that was very helpful."

"Well, there you go then. Don't walk around too much. You might wake the tenants downstairs." Then she left them to their devices.

The two men slowly walked inside, absorbing the interior of Liggit's room that was lit entirely by just two windows, protected by bars on the inside. Liggit wasn't a tidy man. His unmade bed was littered with magazines, notes, and anatomical drawings. Even an opium pipe lay beside the bed on the floorboards, right in the open. Displays of skeletal animal legs and human arms were scattered around the place. Some models rested on hastily arranged shelves while others stood on piles of books. Underneath one of the windows stood a workbench, surrounded by metallic parts, wires, and sheets of leather required in the construction of prosthesis.

Ol'Barrow picked up one of the intricate prosthetic arms. It had a skeletal metal hand with adjustable fingers, and a magnet inside its palm to stick useful items like utensils on. The arm found on Liggit's body must have been quite the improvement if he left a priceless piece like this at home.

Wilkins walked thoughtfully past the shelves. "Looks like the young man keeps himself busy."

Ol'Barrow rubbed his finger on the workbench and inspected the thick layer of dust on the top. "If he was, he wasn't doing much at home," he concluded and then pondered aloud. "What were he and Boerhave up to?" He turned to the Associate. "What do you know about his family?"

"Typical aristocratic family in the country. Old money. He seems to be the only member connected to the Signalites. He only wrote with his sister, but she claimed he never mentioned the group once."

The inspector tapped the hook against his chin. "Odd. I heard celebrities on the Wavecaster who wouldn't shut up about it."

"Not everyone enjoys praying in public, inspector," said Wilkins.

Ol'Barrow raised himself. "Or maybe his parents are proper Anglicans."

Wilkins nodded, admittingly. "Good point."

Not knowing where to start, Ol'Barrow browsed the magazines by the bed. "Typical really. Some young man, raised in the church. Come to the city and let go of every virtue he was ever taught. I used to meet them daily when I still walked the beat." As he idly flipped through the pages a photo dropped from one of the leaflets. When Ol'Barrow picked it up, it turned out to be an image of an erotic nature. "Just too many damned temptations," he whispered. "Before you know it, they are looking for new causes to believe in."

The Associate stared through the bars in front of the window and asked. "Are you a religious man, inspector?"

He put down the photo. "My stepmother dragged me to church until the day my father died." Ol'Barrow sighed. "I don't know what to believe any more. Just a few days ago I believed this was the only world there was... Now it turns out, we are just one world out of... How many?" he asked, somewhat disheartened by the thought.

"Regardless of what it means," responded the Associate. "You only get one shot at life. I, for one, wished I paid more attention to what is really important."

"You sound like an old man."

"I am getting old," Wilkins answered in a matter of course. "And so are you. And all this talking about meaning is distracting us from the very reason why we are here."

Ol'Barrow looked at the chaos around him. "You're right. Let's get to work."

Walking around, Ol'Barrow's gaze scanned the surface of piles of discarded crafting material. Beside a battered roll of leather and a coal bucket filled with metal parts, there was a rubbish bin. With his hook, he managed to dislodge the bin from its dusty and urine-smelling hiding place. Inside he noticed a bound manuscript that was clearly pulled out of its cover. He looked at the first page "Frankenstein: The Modern Prometheus by Mary Shelley."

"Wilkins?" Ol'Barrow said while flipping through the pages. "Have you seen the cover of a book titled Frankenstein somewhere?"

The Associate walked back, looking critically at the labels on the shelf. "Yes! Here it is."

'What's in it?" Ol'Barrow asked.

Wilkins opened it while Ol'Barrow watched on hopefully. "Well, this is odd," said Wilkins.

"It's not some story on the resurrection of a dead man, is it?" guessed Ol'Barrow.

"Well, it contains the blueprints for its limbs," Wilkins answered, dryly. He then laid out its contents on the workbench. Technical drawings of prosthesis. Schematics and a leather-bound notebook.

Curious, Ol'Barrow opened it and flipped the pages. "It's a journal!" he said, scanning the dates at the top of the pages. "Let me see... two months ago the lady said." He glanced at one folio after another. "There we go. He didn't write much. Ah, February 26th..."

"...I followed the instructions on the leaflet to this manor in Canterbury. I was quite amazed to find the manor was almost entirely re-purposed as a private clinic. Although, I suppose a convent would be a better word for it.

"From the start they made it quite clear they wanted me to join their little club. I emphasized I was here to learn more about prostheses. And they obliged. Inside what I can only call a showroom, they presented some of their creations. Automotion-prosthesis that moved with a mere thought. Their movements were slow, crude, but very promising. More promising than what they were talking about at Harvard. The academics left artificial limbs to artisans, deeming it unworthy of their attention. I would like to see their response when I manage to recreate my own automotion-arm.

"Unfortunately, there seemed to be a misunderstanding. They told me they could replace my current arm, but I am not allowed to share the knowledge of their precious Signal. Now, the concepts they showed me seem impressive, however I cannot help but wonder why their designs seem unfinished. I can't put my finger on it, but some elements seem rudimentary. Unless other parts are missing."

March 13th,

"I have been inducted as a novice in their order. All I needed to do was pay the admission fee. Unfortunately, money only takes me so far. They expect me to sacrifice my time in performing menial tasks. It did give me the opportunity to observe some of the patients coming in. Lots of commoners who, I doubt, could afford their treatments. I asked Janice about it, and she told me I should see them as volunteers for the study of implants and other modifications. In other words, they are lab rats.

"I wonder where they conduct these experiments. Despite my medical knowledge, I am not allowed to partake in them. I even offered to be experimented upon, but no. I lacked conviction.

"Conviction? I've seen who they let in. I would not trust them to hold my glass.

"But they have made me listen to the Signal. A recording played from a phonograph. It sounded like nothing but random bleeps to me like a form of accelerated Morse Code. Must be my lack of conviction. And this is what the so-called Recorders listen to all day? No wonder Janice seems so sheltered.

"They claim that the transmissions have not fully been translated yet and more information is still being received. I asked Janice if I could see these translations, but apparently one needs the advanced level of Translator to have access. I emphasized I am probably more qualified to look into them, but to no avail. However, Janice might sway for my arguments."

March 17th,

“I finally received my first electro-implants, or control sites, as they call them. These are attached to the ends of my redundant arm muscle and transmit signals to the pincher of my new hand. It is fascinating. The biggest issue is the weight of the damned thing. The inclusion of the alkaline battery doesn't help in that regard. And this one too has rudimentary parts, holes, and indentations. I cannot help but think they are copying an original model without understanding how it works.

“I tried to find one of the lab rats in the waiting room but didn't find one I recognized. I could ask for their whereabouts but... I think I am afraid to.”

March 23rd,

“After much insisting, I finally managed to get Janice to grant me a glance at some of the memos. It's quite intriguing, be it hard to translate for a layman like myself. They refer to things like Neuro-fibers, articulation sub-processors and bio-electric circuits. I need to make an analysis of these documents to figure out what these terms could mean.

“Janice claims that is the job of the Translators, who have access to all the transcripts inside the Main Temple. However, they have debates on the available wisdom at Lantry's place. A true believer, Janice called her. She told me Lantry had her second leg amputated just to be more like the Perfect. I admire dedication, but if it's true, these people are more insane then I previously assumed.”

March 29th,

“I analyzed the documents for three days, and after all that rigorous analysis, text comparisons, and consulting encyclopedias, I finally concluded that these people are frauds. Either they have no clue, or

they are making stuff up as they 'translated' these messages. These people are theorizing about non-existent technology and are imagining what it might be capable of! Hearing these people debate is like listening to those audio plays where two scientists discuss Interdimensional travel by means of a Transwarp Core and mushroom powered engines.

"I thought it was funny when yesterday a saner person interrupted their little stage- performance, asking about an abbreviation in the Signal. That didn't end well. I was afraid one of them would tear her apart with his new hands. But to my amazement, she didn't flinch. It was all rather cringeworthy. Like watching children argue which penny dreadful monster was stronger than the other."

April 2nd,

"I realize now that I am at an impasse. These people don't understand their own damned technology. There is nothing for me to learn. But I am afraid they are not going to let me go. I considered returning the arm and saying goodbye. However, they are not going to let me walk out of here. The best-case scenario is they sue me for everything I own. More likely they'll make me disappear like the other volunteers."

April 3rd,

"It's worse than I thought. I'm being watched. Janice doesn't want to talk to me. I assumed I was just imagining things, and I haven't been myself. But now I know they are moving against me. I saw a thing on the roof on the other side of the street when I was about to make an adjustment on my arm.

Its eyes. They looked like light reflections in the glass at first. But then I realized something was staring at me from the shadows. Right there, in between the windows. Its overall shape appeared human, but

its limbs were all wrong. And it resembles no animal anatomy with which I was familiar. No posture I have seen in humans. I don't know how long we stared at each other, as I was frozen stiff. But then it turned around, crawled up the roof like a lizard, and disappeared from sight.

I couldn't help but wonder, was that thing a lab rat?"

Ol'Barrow faced away from the pages and looked outside through the bars of the very window. Across the street, he saw two weathered hip roof dormers set in the pitched roof.

"What's wrong?" asked Wilkins.

The Inspector's eyes were focused on the soot covered tiles but spotted no evidence of anything ever climbing the roof. "Nothing," he whispered. "I'm nearly finished."

April 5th,

"I haven't slept in two days now. I show up at the clinic to keep up appearances, but sleep deprivation is making me paranoid. Or maybe not, and I am being threatened. But they cannot get rid of me. Nobody cares about disappearing pauper amputees. But they cannot disappear 'a Liggit' like that. Not without making it look like an accident.

"I talked to the raven- haired woman today. Her movements are intriguing. I can't help but imagine her to be like some sort of marionette. I assumed she might be involved with the experiments. But she became rather nervous when I brought it up and denied it. I insisted regardless. Or rather, I rambled. Might have made some promises I can't keep. Anyway, she invited me to her shop. She makes dolls."

April 12th,

"I stayed in a hideout these past days. Missus Hendrick revealed it to me. The Subliminal Signal. We worked tirelessly on isolating it. My head still hurts from listening to the noise so often. But now we found it, it's abhorrent. The second signal broadcasts on a slightly wider band than the main one. It took hours of dial-turning, but we finally found it on this Ultra-Low band. It sounds like an endless flow of beeps on the melody of a person groaning in pain.

"I couldn't help myself and asked what it could mean. Then she handed me this file. It included an autopsy report. She claims that this is something "They" are working on. But without some form of decoder it is just. That. Wailing.

"When I asked who 'They' are, all she said was "I am still working on that." But it is obvious she believes Lantry is involved."

That was all he wrote. Ol'Barrow closed the journal and stuffed it away in his coat pocket. He then summarized his finds to the Associate.

Wilkins rubbed his goatee. "Lantry, lab rats, and subliminal transmissions? But what's the meaning of all of this?"

"Maybe S-36 was stalking him all along," Ol'Barrow suggested.

"If you are referring to the creature on the roof," responded Wilkins, "he was an opium smoker. He could have imagined it."

Ol'Barrow nodded reluctantly. "Right... Well, this place in Canterbury shouldn't be hard to find.

"And then what? You intend to go in and ask if they are abducting the outcasts of Kent?"

"Please! The Association must be able to do something."

"You are about to walk into a hornet's nest," Wilkins said. We can smoke them out. But if you rattle their hive too much, their sting might paralyze you, setting back our progress something fierce."

Ol'Barrow slowly shook his head in disdain. "Why is everybody so afraid of them?" he asked, embittered.

"Know thy enemy, better than one knows thyself," Wilkins said pedantically. "If there is a connection between the Signalites and S-36, you know as much as I. You get what I mean?"

Ol'Barrow nodded, although he wasn't entirely certain. But one thing was for sure. They had no idea what the Signalites were capable of.

CHAPTER SIX

16TH OF MAY, 1875, 11.24 AM. PELGRIMS ROAD, DOVER

With Mr. Liggett's blueprints safely secured in his bag, Associate 321 gently closed the door behind him.

Down the hallway Ol'Barrow was already walking toward the staircase. His shoulders swayed slightly from left to right, suggesting the inspector was either intoxicated, or sleep deprived. To the Associate's annoyance, the wood beneath the officer's feet cracked loudly as he clumsily walked down the stairs.

"Please, Mr. Ol'Barrow," the Associate said with a stern, but subdued, voice. "People are sleeping."

The officer stared at him with glassy eyes for a moment. His unkempt hair and shabby sideburns gave him a nonchalant appearance unfitting to his rank and station. He shook his head as if he awoke from a dream and mumbled, "Oh, yes. Sorry about that."

The Associate sighed. It was clear to him now why he never accepted a promotion. Ol'Barrow was an embarrassment, even to himself. But there must be something about him if he was offered one in the first place. Then the Associate recalled what he read in Ol'Barrow's prior record, from before he became an inspector. That man, who slowly walked down the stairs one feeble step at the time, was potentially dangerous.

Outside, the Associate stopped himself from breathing in Dover's miasma through his nose. He'd seen poverty worse than this around the world. But at least he was spared the smell of cesspools mixed with burned charcoal and humid leather.

The inspector, on the other hand, irradiated an aura of nostalgia as he stood there, hiding his hands in his pockets. Then, Ol'Barrow looked over his shoulder at 321, and said, "Someone must have been after him. If not a Signalite on the roof, who then?"

The Associate took a deep breath. T hat what he was thinking about? Such a one-track mind. "If there was anything at all," 321 reiterated. The Associate was getting tired of the inspector's conspiracies. "I suggest you head home, Mr. Ol'Barrow. Get some rest, and let this affair sink in."

He nodded, admittingly, probably because he was too tired to argue. "Fine then. What will you be doing?"

"Continuing my own investigation," he answered, intentionally obtuse.

"Ok... Where will you be going?"

"Mr. Ol'Barrow, please! Go home."

"Alright, Alright, I'll be off then," he said as he turned away, and nonchalantly waved the Associate goodbye.

321 observed the inspector walking down Pelgrims Road with the aloofness of some vagabond and turned his attention to more pressing matters.

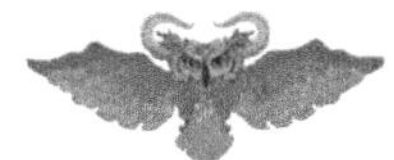

At the edge of the district, the Associate grabbed a cab and told the driver to take him to Lighthouse Road. It was quite a long ride through the center of the city and past the old harbor. But it gave him the oppurtunity to consider his next move. As 321 sat there, he looked outside at Dover Castle that rose above the city. A mostly medieval bulwark, so resilient it appeared to be immune to the passing of time. That old, it had symbolized various regimes and weathered just as many conflicts. It was a mountain crowned by a massive medieval wall, with another ring of walls beyond that, and a tall citadel at its center.

A dark melancholy fell over the Associate. It wasn't because of Ol'Barrow's suspicions about this Lantry woman, but because 321 felt envious of that ancient relic. That castle, just by existing, gave meaning to these people. The British people. But not to him. A former slave from the Americas. What did he have to call his past? And for that matter, how could his kin create a legacy? He sought to make one for himself in Africa, like in Liberia, but was greatly disappointed. Not only were these places not the utopia he was promised, but because these were quite the opposite.

As for Great Britain itself, he had imagined the whole island would be one enormous castle. And that there would be a huge gate that separated the river Thames from the sea. But there was no such splendor. Just another city, but older. Dover Castle on the other hand, was unlike anything he has ever seen before. From a distance, the Key to England didn't seem all that impressive. But when he was standing at the foot of Castlehill, then he understood. A man-made mountain the island inhabitants had erected ever higher over the course of possibly millennia. What would it be like over the next two-thousand years?

He recalled Ol'Barrow mentioning a former convict had attempted to blow it up. Maybe the culprit wanted to be the next Guy Fawkes? After all, it was used by the military to this day. 321 discovered this when he visited the museum inside the walls. Some parts were off limits, while the central citadel was apparently undergoing repairs.

The fort should be obsolete. But even after his brief stay, the Associate could not imagine this city without it. Be it for better, or for worse, it was a part of the city's identity. That fact made the Associate wonder why anyone would bother to destroy it. To him, this anachronism wasn't just a connection to the city's past, but also its future. By destroying it, one would sever ties to both. Therefore, he figured, arguing for its destruction for the sake of the future wouldn't just be a fallacy. It would be arguing for desecration.

England, he thought. The island of white folk who created an empire on which the sun never set. Sure, it had its marvels. But it wasn't at all how he expected it to be. The British officers he served under spoke of their Island as if it was the center of the world. Nothing like those rebels in the United States who, back then, still had to cease their enslaving ways. Humans are strange creatures that way. Even on their own Plane they couldn't agree on what reality they were living in. And he worked for an organization that operated in multiple realities. Not to speak of all the nuances of why they believed what they believed.

Before he joined the West Africa squadron, the former slave had assumed the Anglos would be all alike. Especially the landowners, be they from the west of the Atlantic, or the east. But now, despite not blaming anyone for making such an assessment, he noticed some nuances.

The Southern landlords would say, "I do what I want, and you do as I tell you." But the British officers would say, "You do as I tell you, and I do as I ought to."

Even though the distinction was easy to miss, it was there. While Americans resent authority, the Brits seem more accepting of it, as long the hierarchy is based on tradition and not government policy. More ironic is that the Americans call the British outdated for their monarchy and their colonies. Meanwhile, the Brits looked down on the 'colonials' for the barbaric practice of slavery. And even after the Civil War, they still do.

Humans are strange creatures indeed.

Not to mention his own people. Or so he was expected to call them by merit of their skin color. He traveled to Monrovia, Liberia, to get away from his stigma, like so many others. But once he got there, he discovered they continued their slaving ways by subjugating the local populace instead. Never did he imagine seeing a black man subjugating another. But once he did, it broke something inside of him. Something he had been trying to fix ever since. That's why he was eager to visit England. To see if the white folks treated each other any better. Although he did not see a whipping yet, he didn't notice much change when it came to the heart of things. Just a difference.

Humans are strange creatures indeed.

Take this Ol'Barrow-man. Sure, he wasn't the first self-destructive element he had encountered. But most of those involved drinking or other forms of substance abuse. The inspector on the other hand was suffering from a different kind of intoxication. Not of the moralistic or religious kind either. Nor did he seem driven by revenge. Something else was consuming him. Survivor's guilt perhaps? 321 had seen it plenty before. He was probably an example himself.

Associate 321 snapped out of his contemplations when the carriage came to a standstill in front of a Tudor-style tavern. The howling of the wind that pulled at the carriage made his hairs stand on end - as did the cold gray sea in the distance. Getting out, the Associate held on to the brim of his top hat, lest a loud gust of wind would carry it away. In front of him stood the Watch Tower Tavern, with the sea stretched out to the horizon behind it.

The age-old establishment was on Lighthouse Road, just off the Upper Road between Dover and Saint Margaret to the north. As the name implied, the road connected the various lighthouses dotting the White Cliffs. These were by no means as tall as the mountains he grew up around. But these white rocks had borne the brunt of the cold waves for millions of years - A thought that was just as uplifting, as it was terrifying.

Clasping his collar, the Associate made his way inside the sixteenth century tavern - the spitting image of what the buildings in England were like in the minds of foreigners. Past the oak door, he entered an entirely different atmosphere. Dry air, warmth, and the howling of the wind was subdued by the crackling of the fire inside the central hearth. Surrounding it were tables neatly arranged by the walls and windows, but barely any patrons. Those present were probably tourists.

Behind the bar stood a balding man cleaning glasses who, despite being middle age, looked like he came with the interior. He glanced at the Associate sideway, and immediately pretended not to know him.

321 took off his hat and asked the bartender. "I would like a room without a view."

The innkeep looked at him, still rubbing the glass. "That is an odd request." he mumbled hoarsely.

"The sea frightens me," the Associate responded. "You never know if there is a monster beneath the surface."

The innkeeper stopped what he was doing and turned to a small cabinet on the wall behind him, from which he produced an item. "Here you go, sir," he said, handing over a key. There was a short chain attached to the key handle that held a coin at the end. The silver plaque displayed the antiquated depiction of a woman, wearing a crown with bullhorns.

"Much obliged," answered the Associate. "I'll head straight for my room then, and don't want to be disturbed."

The man nodded as he went on with his business.

The Associate made his way down a shallow hallway on the end of the guest area, passed the staircase and stopped in front of the door to his chamber. A spacious guest room, and the only one with a hearth. Of course, this room wasn't intended for just any visitors. On the front of the ledge, just above the fireplace, was a small bronze hand from which hung a poker. Its palm was open, like it was waiting to receive something. The Associate pressed the coin, attached to the key, into the palm and the fireplace started to move. Silently the hearth turned around its own axis, swiveling open so smoothly it seemed to drift on air.

Mindful not to get his frog coat dirty, he squeezed himself past the shallow opening and walked down the steps on the other end. It was like a basement staircase that descended into the cliff itself.

Downstairs, 321 entered the lodge where indistinct music played in the background. Some Associates enjoyed playing music from different Planes, just to get away from the monotony of today's. 321 however, thought it was unnerving. He preferred the familiar tunes that could be heard on Wavecasters all around the world. Popular music was the constant in his life. Be it in America, Africa, or Europe, music made him feel at ease wherever he went. As for the room itself, a well decorated basement with the comforts of a decent smoking lounge, and some modest sleeping accommodations. There were several doorways into other parts of the White Cliffs. But those were closed, even to him.

Inside a tufted ear chair, beside a mahogany table, sat a man contemplating the contents of a file. Associate 122 wasn't a particularly imposing man, due to his shallow jaws and protruding cheeks, but something about his eyes made him fierce. Traces of a prior, more adventurous lifestyle perhaps.

He responded to 321's presence rather sluggishly, but finally got up from his chair and spoke with a hushed voice as if he was afraid somebody could be listening in. "It is good to see you again, 321. How have you been?"

"Still searching," 321 answered. He had no desire for small talk.

"Still no clues to the identity of 175's murderer?"

"Not one. Still, I feel I am on the right track."

"The Signalites, you mean?"

"My best guess, yes," confirmed 321. "You found anything on 175's movements?"

The corners of his lips curled up in glee as he adjusted his spectacles. "Apparently, he was in Spain, just after that terrorist attack in Saint Augustine"

"Yes, I know. I was tracking a known royalist from South America at the time."

"Would this suggest a connection between the terrorists and his murder?"

"I say we can't rule out the possibility... What are you reading there?" 321 asked.

"A file on a missing Subject S-06, who is suspected to be in the Dover area. Are you familiar with her?"

"I can't say I am."

He shoved the file toward him. "Might as well keep an eye out. She has been missing for nearly three weeks and needs to be returned."

He looked at the picture of an unhappy-looking girl dressed in a long white robe and hood-like hat that made her look like she escaped from a picture book. "This is an Outsider?"

"Yes. She has been in Association's custody for a couple of years."

"Years?" he repeated, astonished. "An Outsider? How is that possible?"

"Need to know," 122 responded abruptly. "Apparently, she has run off before, but usually returned within ten days."

"You believe she's escaped?"

"She is highly intelligent, has knowledge of tier 5 technology, and a knack for breaking our security measures."

The last statement made him raise an eyebrow. "Is that so?"

"I regret to say," was all he answered. "But what did you want to talk about?"

321 shoved his fingers together. "I just found out some interesting details about a shared acquaintance of ours."

His eyebrows rose. "You figured out what Jenever is up to?"

"No. But I can confirm she has interacted with Carla Lantry."

"Interacted?"

"Yes, she met a man named, Liggit. Apparently at one of the Signalite's clinicians."

"That doesn't help us much. We can't investigate those places. Not without upsetting either the Chair or the Signalites."

"I know. But the constabulary can."

122 nodded thoughtfully, but his skepticism was palpable. "What do you think of this inspector you've been talking to?"

"Ol'Barrow?" 321 sighed. "He is willing, but his superiors seem to be as hesitant as ours. Also, the inspector seems to be a restless workaholic. I think we can trust him. It is his reliability I am concerned about."

"Sounds like a typical Associate to me," responded 122 jokingly.

321 frowned his lips. "No," he mumbled, shaking his head slightly. "No. He knows where he belongs."

"Hmm?" 122 tilted his head. "Are you implying we are some kind of lost souls?"

"I prefer to think of us as wanderers," said 321, somewhat whimsically. "Wanderers who are searching for answers that cannot be found in this realm of existence."

122 pursed his lips, seemingly intrigued. "Hmm. I am not sure we are all looking to answer the same question."

321 grinned.

"Speaking of answers," 122 continued. "What do you have there?"

"Ah, yes." 321 reached inside his bag and took out the blueprints they recovered. "I found these drawings inside Liggit's apartments. They seem to be Tier 4 or more advanced prostheses."

122 put on his glasses and glanced at each of them, lifting the folios, one after another. "This is strange," he remarked absentmindedly.

321 leaned closer. "What is?"

He kept browsing the pages. "There are obvious screw holes and fittings in the images, but no parts assigned to them."

"Liggit mentioned something about that. But do you think these are functional?"

He nodded. "Yes, yes... But these are obviously not complete."

"So, who designed them? Could they have gotten these from a Rift?"

"Well, obviously. I mean, maybe Utter-Krapp could have reverse engineered something like this. But this is not like any of those I have ever seen."

"You think it is enough to convince the Chair?"

"Not without proving the origin of these designs. You said these belonged to a cult member?"

"A reluctant one," 321 added, and raised a finger. "I might have a lead... C-33."

122 looked up for a moment. "That's a bit of a stretch."

"Ol'Barrow managed to break into Jenever's hideout beneath a toy store."

"What?" said 122, baffled. "How did he get in?"

"That is not important right now," said 321, who didn't want to get derailed. "This would explain why she took a body from the police morgue and prodded in its brain. Furthermore," he continued, "back in the fifties, Mozellian, the founder of the Signalites, one day changed from being an eccentric hermit into a guru for London's esoteric set. Then, a month later." 321 snapped his fingers. "He died. His followers cremated his body before even his family could even pay their respects."

122 hesitated. "I suppose, it's possible," he admitted, cautiously. "But it is circumstantial evidence at best."

"How about this?" retorted 321. "You can still go to the Association's library and, if you can, find any records related to whatever previous instances of C-33 infestations Associate 175 had been investigating. I'll bet manufacturers of artificial limbs were among them."

122 shifted his gaze down at the drawings for a moment. "Of course I can, but... what if they find out? If they are related, they might become suspicious that we are onto them."

"Then be discreet."

"You mean? Without permission?"

"If that is what it takes," 321 insisted. "It could be the proof we need."

After a moment 122 nodded, be it reluctantly. "I need a couple of days."

"So do I," said 321 assuringly.

"What is your next step then?"

"I might do some background checks on suspects. What do you know about Clara Lantry?"

"The actress?" he asked, puzzled. She is an actress in various Speakies. Was she in that musical one? I don't recall enjoying her work that much."

"When the Songbirds Leave for Winter," 321 said, quite proud of his knowledge on trivia.

"Yes. And soap commercials."

"Soap?"

"Don't you recall the whole, 'Get off your soapbox' thing? You know. The one in which they preach about the importance of hygiene."

He already cringed at the recollection. "Oh, god. That one."

"People have been washing their hands more since then,"122 said, somewhat dismayed. "It made her career."

"Oh, great," 321 sighed. "A benefactor. No wonder people don't dare to touch her... No pun intended."

"That, and her celebrity status. She is part of a new generation of saints. Be careful what weapon you bring to this fight."

"What do you suggest? A stake?"

"In the past they would have used holy water, or a bible to expose a demon. Not sure what they used against false shepherds, though. Beside thumbscrews and a pyre."

Subject-06
She can't go Home Again

S-06 a day after being detained

S-06 currently resides in Sanctuary under Association custody where she will remain until a more suitable solution been found.
Arrangements have been made for private tutoring and she is allowed to go to social events and festivities under supervision for no more of then one day each week. During such events, any claims S-06 makes relating to engineering, technology, and the foundations of her worldview are to be left undisputed for the time being. Priority lies with S-06's wellbeing until accommodations have been negotiated for her return.

-Note
S-06 receives monthly medical and mental evaluation. When visiting, do bring crafting supplies as a present.

ADDENDUM:
Due to changes in relation to her Plane of Origin, our priorities should be proper assimilation in view of S-06's future on Atlas. The Chair regrets this, but there are no suitable alternatives at this moment.
- IV

ENCOUNTERS:
In 1868 S-06 was recovered in the French province of Brittany, after reports of a strange girl dressed in outlandish robes were received by the Association.
According to local authorities, S-06 was wandering the marketplace of ██████ alone and distressed, addressing pedestrians in a language foreign to the region. The people ignored her due to the language barrier and her appearance until the market closed. Then a fishmonger finally grabbed her by the hand and brought her to the local gendarmerie.
Not equipped for this type of situation, the officer on call decided to house her in one of the cells for the night. This distressed S-06, who then pushed the officer away with incredible force that lifted him off his feet and sent him flying through the hallway. The officer on call claimed she didn't even touch him. Then she fled the scene and disappeared into the night.
The Association was called in to investigate the matter. They found her trail when a store owner in the nearby town of ████ reported the door of his store was torn from its hinges, but only food was stolen.
After a day, S-06 was found in a shed of a shepherd who came to the gendarmerie, claiming a witch was doing something to his sheep.
S-06, too afraid and tired at this point to resist, was taken into custody and brought to the local lodge for interrogation.

What follows are the first impressions by Associate-143 after detaining S-06:

"What can I say? She is a child who lost her way and wandered into a Rift, somehow. She explained this by drawing this into a notebook she had in her bag. She looks like a student of sorts who has no business being here.
She claimed the Rift was in the forest near the Carnac monument. We looked but there was no sign of any Rift. Still, she insists it should be around... It was heartbreaking to see her run around looking for

something that clearly wasn't there.
The poor girl wants to go home, and she has been here for a couple of days. Fortunately, there is no sign of Traveler's Decay. When we returned, I managed to give her a good wash and gave her something from my daughter to wear. Her robes still reeked of barnyard animals, but she is protective of them. I will try to give them a wash while she is sleeping. She should be down for a while."

DESCRIPTION:
S-06 is a girl about 12 years of age with "Tier V" enhancement implants in her arm, granting her the ability to lift and hover objects many times her own weight, as well as slight cognitive enhancements. The nature of these enhancements is unknown, but apparently these surgeries are typical for children born into her social class on her Plane of Origin. Her height is typical for girls her age, has chestnut-colored hair, and her eyes are two different colors due to augmentation, her augmented eye being clear blue, and the natural one greenish brown.
An "Astral Manipulator" is located in the palm of her left hand and resembles a tattoo in the shape of two triangles, each pointing in the opposite directions. This device is connected to her nervous system, or may have even replaced it, and is controlled by thought and finger gestures that are based on "Magical Runes." It's an ability she is fond of using, but also exhausts her. She claims this becomes less tasking with experience and age.

DISCOVERY:
Our linguists determined she speaks a mixture of Gaelic and Saxon. S-06 claims she is from the Dominion of Gaul, which is governed by a Council of Seers, who are the most powerful Wizards in her country. She explained that she was born a Wizard, just like her parents. Those who are not Wizards, work 'outside'. What type of work these outside people did, she does not know because she is too young to go 'outside'. She may only leave the city when she is old enough, but her father told her, "The people out there are too dumb to understand anything," and S-06 thinks her father argues with them often.
How S-06 traveled to this world is unclear. In the fragment below Associate 105 interviews S-06 on this matter.

[AUDIO FRAGMENTS STARTS]

105: Hello, S-06." [There is no response.] I heard you got your own room today... Do you like it?
S-06: I don't want it.
105: Well, you can't go home for the time being... You understand why we need you to stay inside, right? [...] Good. Now, let's talk about how you got here. Do you remember what happened?"
S-06: Non.
105: You don't remember, or you won't tell me? S-06, if you want
us-
S-06: I'm not a number! My name is ▒▒▒▒.
105: Listen, if you won't tell us anything, we can't help you. You want to return to your mother, don't you?"
S-06: Oui.
105: Then you.. [S-06 begins to sob] "Oh, for Christ's sake. I'm sor-

[ASSOCIATE 105 PAUZED THE RECORDING]

105: Well, let's try this again. What happened before you got here?
S-06: I was spying on a Seer. He then entered this basement underneath one of the abandoned buildings near our tower.
105: Spying? Why?
S-06: Somebody I knew disappeared about a week before. And he was acting weird. So, I followed him.
105: Did you tell anyone?
S-06: It was more a spur of the moment thing. I didn't think I would find anything. But then he left the door open. That is how I snuck in.
105: What did you find?
S-06: Just a dusty basement. But he was building something. He had all these weird constructs I never saw before. Really, small. Probably Revisionist designs. And he had this noisy machine that smelled of gasoline. I think it powered whatever he was building.
105: What did he build?
S-06: I dunno. It looked like a man-sized portcullis or something. Didn't look like anything special"
105: Did you go through it?

S-06: **... Oui. I mean, it looked like a garden ornament. So, I just. I- was just fooling around. Then everything went black. And then I fell... And that is how I got here.**

[END OF FRAGMENT]

WORLDVIEW AND KNOWLEDGE:
Due to her age and particular view of the world, Associates are advised not to discuss certain topics, technology in particular. S-06 is convinced her abilities are magical and believes engineers, mechanics, etcetera, are Arcane Smyths, capable of building magical machines. Apparently, this is what all the children on her Plane of Origin are taught, which is believed to contain Tier V civilizations.
To ascertain her knowledge and skill, S-06 was asked to aid Special Committee Antiquarians with electrical Tier IV devices recovered in the field. During these tasks, S-06 displayed an adequate knowledge of disassembly and circuitry to guess the function of these devices. However, circuitry are confusing her, as the components do not posses the 'Arcane' layout required for proper 'Mana-flow'.
To demonstrate, S-06 created her own circuit. The layout of the wiring and conduits she arranged in symbolic shapes and patterns. The device is functional but far larger then is required.
She was also asked to preform several chemistry experiments, during which she demonstrated adequate knowledge of chemical processes and solutions. But while she performed her task, she recited various incantations and performed other symbolic gestures to ensure success.

What follows is Dr. Benedictine's evaluation of S-06's performance:
Watching S-06 work is just as fascinating as it is frustrating. This girl has a good understanding of Tier IV electronics and decent analytical ability to understand their function. Probably better than I do, as she grew up surrounded by technology like this. It must have been - magical.
That being said, while an engineer would admire its efficiency, S-06 complicates it. She evaluates circuits like an art critic would judge a brush stroke on a canvas. She opens the device and looks at its guts just how an auger from Ancient Rome would look at the innards of a sacrificial animal. As she looks for meaning that isn't there, she mutters about "Ley Lines" and "Mana Flow." The purity of the conductors and that the "Gems" are not properly purified. The fact that it just works seems to be of little significance to her. Imagine being surrounded by people, philosophizing about the significance of two cogs connecting, rather

than exploring their potential. Suffice to say, a task which could be performed in minutes can take her hours. Not to mention her chemistry tasks. Oh, dear. Again, her knowledge is impressive for a girl her age. But before every action, she starts chanting like one of those New Age charlatans. In fairness, some of her incantations seem to have a proper length for a reaction to take place before adding the next chemical.

HEALTH EVALUATION:
S-06's handlers are concerned for her well-being. Her overall demeanor is melancholy that is only elevated when practicing "magic." Her other activities mostly include drawing, writing, sky-gazing, or sleeping. S-06 does seem to desire interaction with the other inhabitants of the Sanctuary but prefers to observe them from a distance, often engaging in other activities like drawing. She rarely communicates, but this could be due to the language barrier.

EXCEPT FROM A PERIODICAL EVALUATION, BY DR. JENEVER:
S-06, down below referred to as Angel.

Dr. Jenever: Hello Angel. How was your day?

S-06: I spend most of the time with Mr. Brass today.

Dr. Jenever: Good. You like him, don't you?

S-06: He is ok, I guess. We don't really speak.

Dr. Jenever: Tell me Angel. Are there people like him in your world?"

S-06: Oui, but I am not allowed to speak to them. They are bad people.

Dr. Jenever: Why is that?

S-06: Papa told me they only make people that way when they do really terrible things. I mean, they do look like Mr. Brass, but they don't think. They are Golems that
just do the things they are made to do."

Dr. Jenever: Like slaves?

S-06: Non, slavery is illegal. A Seer told us it is their way of repaying their debt to society."

Dr. Jenever: You seem troubled.

S-06: It's just... They are golems. They're like tools. Sometimes when nobody was looking, we would throw things at them. You know, see if we could get a reaction out of them.

Dr. Jenever:	**You talk about them like they are not human.**
S-06:	**They're not. I mean, I don't know any other humans who behave like that.**
Dr. Jenever:	**What about Mr. Brass?**
S-06:	**He is not like them... Well, first I did think he was a scribe golem. But he isn't. He gave me some paper to draw on.**

ADDENDUM S6-7: CONCLUSION ON THE MATTER OF S-06'S RETURN HOME

The matter on S-06's return remains unresolved for the foreseeable future. This was determined in a meeting with a dignitary from Plane 07 in 1868.

This meeting happened after Associate 167 vanished near the Carnec Monument, a few days after S-06 initial discovery. He was missing for 35 days until he reappeared in the town of ██████ wearing similar outlandish robes like those worn by S-06 on the day she arrived.

Associate 167 has been debriefed on his stay on "Plane 07" and has statements with other material are being logged and processed.

A day later, a Traveler arrived from Plane 07. An older man went to a nearby city, dressed the same way as S-06. He rented a room at a tavern and walked about town like a tourist. The day after his arrival the same Associates who detained S-06 confronted the "Wizard". The Wizard proclaimed he expected them earlier and agreed to come willingly under the condition to parley. The Chair agreed.

The Wizard was transported to site ██████ where Dr. Jenever entered the conversation with the Wizard, assuming they were negotiating S-06's return home.

	[BEGINNING OF FRAGMENT]
156:	"Let's start with how you got here."
Wizard:	"As she did of course."
156:	"We found no Rift."
Wizard:	"And you won't find it, ever. We have cloaked all portals leading into our world. How that fool stumbled into this one is beyond me. It's a good thing we have increased security since the incident."
156:	"That lab she found was yours?"
Wizard:	"My lab? The area she disappeared from was an officially restricted area of the campus, I'll have you know. A place in which she had no business being!"

156: "She told us she was looking for a missing student."

Wizard: "My goodness, non! Some servants dropping off new equipment left the door open, despite clear instructions not to! Blatant disdain for sacred equipment. She just wandered in - like a child. I looked at her record. Multiple trespassing incidents, fights with other students. Acting contrary to instruction during class. A classic example of a misfit. She probably would have been - removed, at the end of the year."

156: "What does that mean?"

Wizard: "None of your concern... However, this is not the first time I have interacted with outsiders. Let's address the beast in the room."

156: "And what would that be?"

Wizard: "Our people don't know the distinction between magic and what you call, technology."

156: "Do you mean, you teach them there is no difference?"

Wizard: "We teach them what you call, Tier V technology. It is sacred and should be revered as such. Of course, these devices are but mere tools, however. Mankind is capable of destroying itself in a breath's notice. After the Great Calamity, humanity was at the brink of extinction and society reverted to those of hunter-gatherers. Only a small number retained their knowledge and restored civilization over the course of countless generations. Wizards were revered as gods. Some even started to believe they actually were. Others started to arm savage tribes and conquered their own kingdoms. It was only
the other Wizards who could stop them.

"This is why we decided it was better to secure our technology. Teach the populace and our own children of its sanctity until the day comes that humanity on our world is mature enough to wield it on a worldwide scale."

156: "So, you created a caste system?"

Wizard: "Call it what you like. We have protected our world from all interference and tyranny. We observe planes like these only to ascertain if these are any threats."

156: "Are we?"

Wizard: "Non..."

156: "But?"

Wizard: "But nothing."
156: "I think you are afraid we'll undermine your precious religion."
Wizard: "You would do that, Associate? You would destroy the foundations on which an entire society is built. Why? A philosophical dispute?"
156: "You are manipulating language to control the masses."
Wizard: "Are we? Or do we teach them to respect the power technology brings? Do you trust half your society with a gun, Associate? Do you believe your industry is used wisely? Have you smelled the air outside?"
156: "Progress is messy, I agree. But we improve."
Wizard: "You improve? How many must suffer so your elite can learn from their mistakes? How many tyrants will you allow to rise?"
156: "At least we learn, Wizard. If you treat people like children, they'll never grow up. Never learn what makes your precious 'magic' so sacred to begin with."
Wizard: "Ha, ha, I see. I hope our little discussion makes it Apparent why we cannot allow you to come back to our world. Please refrain from investigating the portal any further. You don't bother us; we don't bother you."
156: "We can agree to those terms I suppose."
[The Wizard gets up]
Wizard: "Good, I am glad that is settled. I'll take my leave then. Please don't give me a reason to return."
156: " That is fine... So, you take her back, I presume."
Wizard: "Who?"
156: " The girl!"
Wizard: "Non."
156: "No? Then why are you here?"
Wizard: "To tell you to stay away... As far as the girl is concerned, this is the lawful punishment of her transgression. There is nothing I can do about it."
156: "She can't stay here!"
Wizard: "I am aware of that."
156: "She is a child! And your responsibility!"
Wizard: "As far as our administration is concerned, she is already dead. If you want to take care of her, you may... Good day."

[END OF FRAGMENT]

ADDENDUM S6-7-1: POST-INTERVIEW AUDIO-LOG BY DR. JENEVER

"I am recording this because I don't want to think longer on this subject then I have to. How do you explain to a child she has been abandoned? She barely understands reality. I don't know what will be more painful. That all she was taught is a lie or that she has been orphaned because she made a mistake. Maybe she can outgrow her belief in magic, the same way normal children do. But the pain of being banished like that. People have been scarred by less. At this point, it might be best to keep her ignorant of her situation. Make her comfortable. Potentially, she could make some friends that can support her. I just don't know how long I can keep up the lie. As for the practical concerns, the Sanctuary is our only humane option. Maybe when she is old enough, she can become an Associate. But I can't imagine. No matter what, she'll never belong any-"

[A DOOR OPENS, AND SOMEBODY CAN BE HEARD ENTERING THE ROOM.]

"What is going on?"
"I am sorry to interrupt, ma'am, but S-06 just piled up a bunch of crates in one of the alleys and climbed on top to peek through the window. She said she is looking for - the funny golems. But I think she may have seen - our guest."
"Oh, for f- ...I'll be right over."__

CHAPTER SEVEN

16TH OF MAY, 1875, 14.56 PM

Ol'Barrow had taken the long way around as he walked back home. He had a lot to process, and even more questions. But right now, he was looking forward to a moment of rest.

When he opened the front door to his cottage. His mouth fell open.

Mrs. Appletree, still wearing her coat, looked at him, her face frozen in a dismayed expression.

Igraine stood before her, with a hammer clutched in her hands, and black stains on her cheeks. There was a broken chair in the corner. Disassembled lamps on the table, and wiring hanging from the ceiling. Even her dress had a tear.

In the back, the mutt walked out of the room, sensing the outburst.

"What the-," Ol'Barrow barely managed to control himself. "What happened?"

Mrs. Appletree clasped her hands together. "I'm sorry, David. I was only gone for a few hours."

"I just wanted to fix the bed," began Iggy, girlishly. "But then I found out your wiring is wrong... Then I broke the chair... Then, uh... I'll have it done by tomorrow," she attempted to reassure him.

"What did you do to my home?"

"It's a - fire hazard," answered Igraine softly.

"It's what?"

Ms. Appletree walked up to him. "She's just trying to help. Just come. I'll make you some tea."

He looked at the dusty wires Igraine had pulled from their nooks and crannies, as Ms. Appletree walked him to the dinner table. "Iggy, clean this place up," she told the girl. "We'll fix all this in the morning."

"What did she do to the bed?" asked Ol'Barrow dismayed.

"Just sit down. You have bigger things to think about."

"Like what?"

"Like, have you decided what you'll do?" she asked with her hands on her waist.

"What do you mean?"

She raised her voice. "Your mother?"

"She is not my mother," Ol'Barrow snapped. But then, he sighed and shrugged his shoulders. "I don't know," he groaned. "I have no idea what to do about it."

"She raised you for a good ten years. She even left the house to you."

"It was my father's house to begin with," he protested.

"Oh, come on. When was the last time you saw her?"

"The last time I met her was on the train to London. I was still a constable back then, so that was a long time ago. We talked briefly, but it ended up in a row. Just as it always did. She is just incapable of normal conversation."

Ms. Appletree tilted her head as she gave him a dismissive glare. "Do you remember what you were like?" she asked, sternly. "You acted in the same way you are doing now. Like a brat!"

Ol'Barrow heard Igraine giggle at the remark, but she pretended not to listen when he looked in her general direction.

"Go see her one last time," Appletree insisted. "You won't get a second chance. I'll go with you if you want... Sleep on it."

He sighed reluctantly. "Right."

Then she whispered. "Before you turn in. Do you know a certain Christopher?"

A tingle went down his spine. "Uh, I used to. Why?"

"Igraine asked about it."

Blast, Ol'Barrow thought, assuming he must have been talking in his sleep. No wonder Igraine looked so perplexed when he woke up. "He is a colleague who died of cancer," he said with a low voice. "That was ten years ago."

"Oh, I'm sorry."

He grinned awkwardly. "Well, the best ones go first... I'm going to turn in now."

"All right. Don't make a choice you'll regret," she warned gently. "Bye now."

And with those words she left. Now, Ol'Barrow realized why he kept Diane at a distance. She always had this way of dredging up the past. A tether, as it were, that reminded him where he came from and who he used to be. Ol'Barrow didn't like who he used to be either. But he was stuck with that version of him. And that was all he could do.

By the time Ol'Barrow awoke from his after-dinner nap on the sofa, the sun was already setting. The sight of Iggy doing the dishes in her underwear annoyed him. She probably wanted to keep her robes dry, but still.

Ms. Appletree put on her coat. "I'm leaving, Mr. Ol'Barrow."

"Right... Thank you for dinner."

"You're quite welcome," she said smiling. She was such a dear.

Still sleep drunk Ol'Barrow sat down at the table. "Iggy, put some clothes on!" he cried over his shoulder. "You'll catch a cold."

"But it's still drying on the lines," she said. "Besides, it's warm."

"I would like to remind you, you are a guest."

She frowned her lips at him.

Ol'Barrow sighed. He should send her away, but... Ol'Barrow looked up at his wiring but still needed reattaching.

"I'll fix that tomorrow," Igraine argued.

"You'd better."

"You should have gotten a proper electrician to fix it. And you chair. And b-"

His disgruntled stare shut her up. "I'm serious," she said, softly while drying off a bowl.

Ol'Barrow looked back at the wiring. At the time he had done that in a hurry. It was by coincidence a power line ran by his house, and he jumped on the opportunity to get that electrical lighting. He knew it needed rearranging, but he had just never got around to it... And Bigsby had been right about electricians; They were in short supply. "A fire hazard, ehj," he mumbled.

"Did you say something?" asked Igraine.

"Should I light up the fireplace?" he asked. "You'll catch a cold dressed like that."

Her gloomy expression disappeared. "Can I do it?"

"No," he said as he got up. "Let's keep those clothes clean."

After lighting the fire, he poured himself some perno, and sat down at the table. This was his guilty pleasure. Perno was not as good lukewarm as it was ice cold. But it would do... *Those cool boxes would come in handy for this*, he thought while taking a sip, and let the strong aftertaste fill his mouth. It was the small pleasures.

Meanwhile the girl stared at the fireplace, as if hypnotized.

"I suppose you don't have a fireplace back home," said Ol'Barrow as an observation and question at the same time.

"No..." she murmured. "The air ventilation can't handle it."

"Hm?"

"The last time I saw a fire like this was when Doctor Jenever took us to the Christmas Fair in the city. There were bonfires everywhere."

Christmas? Ol'Barrow thought. *Half a year ago*. "I suppose you don't go out very often."

"It was the last time I did anything with her," she said. Then Igraine suddenly reached for her bag on the table and took out a plain eye patch. "I always need something like this for a disguise," she said, smiling ironically and put on the patch to cover up her crystalline eye. "First, I was let out every week, but then there was an incident... Only special occasions," she added, melancholy.

The room fell silent. The ticking of the clock and the crackling of the fire competed for who was the loudest.

Sipping his drink, Ol'Barrow noticed Igraine's eyes shifting from left to right, while resting her chin on her palms. "You have something you want to say?"

Like the flip of a switch, her eyes fixated on him. "Did you find anything?"

He put his glass on the table. "Not really. Did the doctor ever tell you about being involved with the Signalites?"

"Non. We only talked about... My situation," she answered, evasively.

Ol'Barrow grabbed his hook pedantically. "What is your situation exactly? How did you end up here?"

"I told you, I just wanted to be away from that place."

"And, with that place, do you mean another Plane?"

"N-Non," she mumbled. "It's an Association facility. That is where I met Doctor Jenever."

"But you are an Outsider, right?"

She was reluctant to answer the question.

"Right," Ol'Barrow shifted in his chair. He didn't want to treat this as an interrogation, but what was he supposed to do? "So, how long have you known the doctor?"

"Three years or so."

"Was she behaving differently the last time you met?"

"I told you. She said she would be back in a couple of weeks. Then... Somebody told me she would never be coming back. And I should not ask any questions."

"Did they now?"

"Yea. Now, you find anything about that C-33 file?"

Ol'Barrow squinted an eye as she changed the subject. "I suspect it might have infected an actress. Maybe that cult is infecting more people."

"So, we're going after the Signalites?"

Ol'Barrow ignored the determination behind that question. "I will talk to my boss tomorrow and tell him what we discovered. And you should think of going back home."

She looked at him for a moment with a cold pedantic expression. Then she finally responded. "You'll need me."

He glanced at her as he considered his options. "Maybe," he admitted. "But you're too young to get involved in such dreadful business."

"I'm sixteen! I don't need looking after!"

"Alright, fine then," He got up and directed her to the stuffed closet bed in the wall. "How about you clean out that bed in the morning. I'm tired of sleeping on the floor."

Tick *Tick* *Tick* *Tick*

17TH OF MAY, 1875, 9.45 AM. DOVER POLICE STATION.

There was a restless atmosphere in the precinct that day, and the air was heavier than usual.

Tick *Tick-Tick*

As he sat hunched over his desk, Ol'Barrow 's poor typing skills didn't attract the usual mockery of his colleagues.

Tick

On the keyboardless Index-Typewriter, after he used a stylus to choose a letter from an index-plate, Ol'Barrow pushed down the black key again with his hook to type the selected letter on the paper. He was never good at typing, but this model allowed him to work at the same frequency as he was used to. Letter by letter, he summarized his findings for the higher ups. He struggled with the amount of urgency he should add to his statements. like, "To reiterate", or "We were alarmed by". Ol'Barrow stroked his fingers through his hair while rereading his last sentence and muttered, "Is this even proper English?"

Preoccupied with his work, Ol'Barrow did not notice the superintendent walking up the half landing until he raised his voice to his colleagues on the floor. "Please, listen up everyone!"

The floor fell silent, with only some soft murmurs at the far corners of the room.

"There has been a policy change regarding street gambling," he announced while shifting the gaze from one end to the other. "The council has ordered the policing of any games on the street that involve an ante of any kind. These are now forbidden within the Borough, and offenders are to be apprehended, and fined."

"What? Like, all of them?" one officer asked, abhorred.

"Yes, without exception!" The superintendent reiterated.

There was a disapproving ruckus among the officers. "Like we don't have enough to do. We barely patrol our beats as it is."

"They are not gonna take it. We already closed some of the gambling dens. Where are they gonna go?"

"They're just going to do it at home. You know, where we can't see it."

"Yeah, that will solve the problem," another responded sarcastically.

The superintendent raised his voice again. "Listen! Talk with the neighborhood watches in your beats. We will relay to the press that the new policies will be enforced within the next three weeks. This new power that has been entrusted to us should make it easier for us to bring order back to the streets," he tried to assure them.

"Humbug!"

"They'll just move elsewhere!"

The superintendent put his fists in his waist. "You have your assignments! This is your job as long you wear your uniforms," he reiterated, and walked off.

There was a dissatisfied murmur going around. It was not just the announcement. It was a frustration that was mounting for years now. Every time the constables found a way to deal with changing circumstances, be it within or without, the rules were changed once again.

The inspector refrained from getting involved in the conversations. This is what happens when you stir a hornet's nest. The workers become restless, and all they do is complain about a situation outside their control. As a result, nothing gets done. Not until they are bored of complaining and tolerate the new situation instead. So, Ol'Barrow focused on finishing his report. When that was done, he went up the stairs to the Chief Inspector's office.

Mayfair sat behind his desk writing his own letters when Ol'Barrow came in. He gave Ol'Barrow a quick glance before getting back to his own work. "Ah, David, do you have anything to report?"

"I do... What is all this about going after gambling all of a sudden?"

"The reform commission deems it a societal ill that needs to be done away with," he responded without looking up from his desk.

"This isn't a solution, Arthur. This is just bowdlerizing the problem so they can pretend it doesn't exist."

Mayfair put down his pen and looked at him. "What do you want from me? It's not my decision, but the commissioner's." he said. "Listen, this will go as it always does. We enforce whatever rules they make up for a couple of months. The folks get used to it. It becomes less of a problem overall, and then we forget about it."

"Assuming people will comply."

Mayfair just shrugged. "Sometimes they do, sometimes they don't."

"Do you really think they'll just stop gambling?"

Mayfair grinned. "Hell, no. The certified gambling houses will just start raking in more money. That is all," he stated cynically. "Anyway, did you get some rest, David?"

"Some," Ol'Barrow began cautiously. "I have been pondering over the discoveries we made yesterday." He handed the chief his report. "It was quite revealing."

The chief scanned the document. At first he nodded, but then his eyebrows rose up like he received an outstanding bill. "Lantry?" he exclaimed, abhorred. "The actress and the Signalites?"

"Yes, Liggit believed they were experimenting on paupers, to whom he referred to as lab rats."

"Do you have any proof apart from Liggett's claims?"

"Not yet," Ol'Barrow admitted.

Mayfair lay down the file and folded his hands against each other. "David. The Signalites have friends in high places. One mistake and your career is over," he warned. "Focus on the train station murders."

"The train station?" He cried out dismayed. "That is what led us to them in the first place!"

"Yes. Sure," he responded diplomatically. "But don't you think you are a bit... widen your scope before you start making accusations against a person who can sink our department."

Ol'Barrow let the response sink in for a moment. "This is about the budget cuts, isn't it?"

Mayfair raised his eyebrows. "Ol'Barrow! S-36 is an Outsider! What could she possibly have to do with the Signalites?"

"It's bloody obvious!" Ol'Barrow responded. "They are taking orders from some outside force."

The chief inspector gave him an unsettled stare.

"Don't look at me like that! You've known about those rifts longer than I have."

Mayfair seemed at a loss for words.

Ol'Barrow sighed. "Listen. Let me bring in Lantry for interrogation. At least to ask about her relationship with Liggit"

"Liggit was obviously paranoid. You wrote that he put bars in front of his windows, for Pete's sake."

"Para- He was murdered, Arthur! And we handed their bodies over to the Signalites, without informing the families, I might add."

"The answer is no."

Ol'Barrow changed tactics again. "What about that meeting? The philanthropy ball we have been invited to?"

"We?" Mayfair grabbed the decorated envelope that Lantry had given him from a drawer and held it up. "I have been invited. And even then! No," he said and dropped the invitation in the rubbish bin beside this desk.

Fresh out of ideas, Ol'Barrow stared blankly at the letter between the peanut shells and other waste.

There was a knock on the door.

"Come in!" cried Mayfair.

It was the superintendent who looked from behind the door, addressing the chief. “A word, sir.”

Ol'Barrow got up. “I'll go.”

“No, you stay!” ordered Mayfair. “I am not done with you.” Then the chief walked outside with the superintendent.

Ol'Barrow got up to stretch his legs a bit and paced back and forth to try to come up with arguments to apprehend Lantry. But then, inside the bin by his feet, he noticed leaf gold glitter in the lamp light. He stopped and stared at the envelope stuck between the balls of crumpled paper and peanut shells.

"*Get the ticket*," he heard his father's voice in the back of his mind. The phrase from his dream stirred up his frustration.

Ol'Barrow grinned. “No,” he said, shaking his head.

"*Get the ticket.*"

“What would I possibly do with it,” he thought out loud.

"*Get the ticket!*"

Ol'Barrow quickly looked over his shoulder to see if his superior was still distracted by the superintendent. “Oh, what harm could it do,” he thought out loud, and quickly reached inside the bin, opened the envelope with his hook, and pulled out the contents. After placing the envelope back as he found it, he stuffed the invitation inside his vest, and feigned innocence when the chief returned.

“Fine then,” the chief groaned as he sat down. “I want you to take the week off. That's an order. I'll figure out what to do with you in the meantime.”

“Understood, sir.”

The chief raised his voice at him again. “I mean it! You're dismissed.”

The inspector nodded and like an obedient schoolboy, he got up from his chair, walked out, and calmly made his way toward the exit. But inside he was that thrilled; he had difficulty feigning his depression. He had a ticket. He wanted to say it out loud. I have a golden ticket!

...

His triumph was followed by a moment of contemplation.

"Now what?"

19TH OF MAY, 1875, ON THE OUTSKIRTS OF CANTERBURY 7.37 PM.

The setting sun painted the leaves of the trees a rustic amber, as when a church bell ran in the distance. Ol'Barrow was holding Igraine by her cold hand as they walked beside an unpaved forest road, just outside of Canterbury. Ahead, the sound of chamber music could be heard from behind the trees. However, the orchestra was in fierce competition with the restless murmur from the guests attending the charity ball.

He looked at Igraine for a moment. She looked rather uncomfortable in her green dress, with white ruffles around the edges, matching pelerine, and a sash tightly wound around her waist. It was easier to pass her off as a boy. Her neck long hair was unlike any girl her age, and she insisted on wearing an eyepatch to cover her crystalline blue eye. But Igraine assured him it would make sense in a place like this, because the cult's main targets were invalids. And the short hair could be explained away with a recent lice infestation. How irresponsible, he thought. But her insistence on joining this clandestine infiltration frustrated him, and he was in no position to lecture anyone about responsibility. And truth be told, Ol'Barrow needed the help. Igraine had already proven herself to be quite the infiltrator. The ease with which Igraine came up with these fabrications worried him though. Then again, she spent years among people accustomed to speaking in weasel words and half-truths, so what could he expect? At least she was motivated.

They finally reached the manor's property. Ol'Barrow had heard a lot about the lifestyle of the rich and famous, but never witnessed it up close.

The estate was surrounded by freshly painted walls, crowned by decorative spikes, to discourage trespassers. The front gate was wide open to let the coaches drive in unhindered. There were even some electric carriages. These looked like pony carriages, minus the ponies, and they barely produced any sound. Although he appreciated the practicality, in the big picture: If engines could replace beasts of burden, and machine parts human limbs, what do they even need nature for?

The moon was barely on the rise, but the chiseled stone road up to the manor was illuminated by electric lamp posts, driving away the shadow between the trees. Although Ol'Barrow had grown accustomed to light bulbs he was in awe of the glowing spirals bent into the shape of musical notes trapped inside.

"That's incredible," he muttered.

"It's OK, I suppose," Igraine whispered while keeping her eye on the ground.

"I suppose, it's nothing like what you got back home," he responded.

She remained silent as the festive white noise became louder with every step they took.

"Did I say something wrong?"

Igraine looked at him with an odd stare. Something about her seemed different. A deep buried wisdom perhaps, that only someone in her situation could possess. Whatever it was, it unsettled him. "I know what you are trying to do," she said. "Please don't. I am here to find the doctor. That is all." Then she looked away.

The pebbles underfoot cracked under their weight as they strolled on. Ol'Barrow did not know how to respond, apart from scolding himself for getting her involved. He should have known better. For a distraction he focused on the front of the manor that was lit up with light projectors. Its grandeur made the century old building seem like a modestly sized palace. The architecture included Italianate features. Like a dozen or so sashed windows in arched frames, arranged in three neat rows on top of each other. Each of the windows was lit up brightly by big fluorescent light bulbs hanging behind the colored glass panels of purples and greens. The manor's two symmetrical wings were separated by a tower, with a tiled roof and an arched doorway in front. The steps leading inside were covered by a red carpet and decorated with ornate grated fences on either side.

One carriage after another pulled up in front of the entrance to deliver the guests, some of whom even Ol'Barrow could recognize. Local politicians, factory owners, and even known celebrities from Kent, dressed according to the latest fashion, walked up the steps of the mansion. Ol'Barrow was amazed how these women managed to exit the vehicles while wearing such wide dresses.

And there he was, an unknown police officer, dressed horribly out of date, with a young girl wearing an eyepatch. But they were not here to show off, or so he kept telling himself.

Somebody pulled weakly on his sleeve. "Are we going inside?" Igraine asked, finally breaking the awkwardness.

Ol'Barrow sighed, think he should send her home, wherever that might be. But they were in front of their destination now. No way to go, but forward. Ol'Barrow straightened his jacket and stroked his hair back with his one hand. "Yes."

Ill at ease, they walked up the red carpet. He wasn't sure what was more intimidating. The manservant, clothed in velvet uniform, checking the visitor's invitations at the door, or the members of the local elite, who seemed to have some repulsive aura of upper-classness around them.

As they walked up the stairs, the manservant's delightful expression turned when he saw them approach. He seemed somewhat puzzled by the awkwardly grinning inspector. But then the doorman looked at Igraine and bent forward with a wide smile. "And what brings you here, little lady?"

*Blast!*Ol'Barrow became nervous.

"I really like Miss Lantry's voice, sir," Igraine answered, with an excessively girlish voice. "I've listened to 'When the Songbirds Leave for Winter' on the Wavecaster. She really helped me through the days when I was stuck in bed for my operations."

"Well, that is great," the man responded, patronizingly. "Miss Lantry has a gift to make people very happy. Well then. Enjoy your evening."

The moment the doorman looked away, Igraine looked at Ol'Barrow and stuck her tongue out, along with a disgusted expression on her face.

Ol'Barrow smiled at her and breathed a sigh of relief as they entered the reception area. The hall was lit so brightly, the marble floor, the mirrors on the wall, the crystal chandelier, everything reflected the warm lamp light to excess. Yet, he felt like he could not see where he was going. In his mind, David was back at that luxurious train station from his dream. But this time, he was already on the train. "Time to meet the fellow passengers," he thought.

The entrance hall flowed in three directions from here on. Four if he counted the Imperial staircase going up the first floor. In front was the theater, large enough for dozens of people, and to his sides the hall ways leading into the manor's wings.

The inspector was not in his element. Guests were everywhere, talking, dealing, spreading gossip. Servants offered drinks, including alcoholic beverages, and decorated bonbons. There was just so much temptation in the world of the elite. Speaking of which... He noticed Igraine reaching for a glass of wine and pulled at her wrist. "You're not old enough!"

Disappointed, she grabbed a glass of squeezed orange juice instead.

"Just too much temptation," he mumbled as they walked into the gallery.

On the first and second floor, there were balconies with a full view of the main stage, complimented with countless ornaments. But Ol'Barrow noticed an absence of human depictions, statues, paintings or otherwise, that were fashionable. Instead, there was a collection of antiquities arranged beside the walls. Like old prosthetics, including a 16th century one once owned by a mercenary captain of sorts who served in Italy. Books on artificial life, with crude sketches of golems. One such drawing attracted him in particular: one of a small leprechaun-ish man who seemed to live inside a sperm cell.

"It's a homunculus," Igraine explained when she noticed him eying it. "They used to think sperm contained small humans who received a soul from the woman after entering the womb."

"I, see," muttered Ol'Barrow, a tad embarrassed. He turned his attention to an old Wavecaster on a pedestal. His eyes grew wider when he recognized it. It was the same device he had seen in the harbor the night of S-36's attack. "What the hell?"

"What's wrong?" asked Igraine.

"That Wavecaster. There was one just like it at... Well." he struggled to finish the sentence.

"You mean that old U-K Mark II? Robert Mozellian used a modified version of one such radio to receive the Signal for the first time."

"Mozellian?"

"He is considered to be the founder of the Signalites. You didn't know?"

"I have been very busy. Beside, my interest is in Lantry."

"Don't you think it's important?"

"That's enough sass from you, young lady."

She reached closer to his ear. "I can get inside the manor's wings," she whispered eagerly.

"What are you planning?"

"It will take a few minutes. The mansion is not that big. If anybody asks, tell them I am in the lavatory."

"No," he protested

Instead, she turned away from him, and reached for the nearest glass of wine.

Aggravated by her disobedience, he stopped her again. "What did I tell you?"

She pulled herself free and stamped her foot like a child. "You never let me have anything!" she cried. Then she ran off and disappeared into the hallway before he could respond.

Multiple pairs of eyes stared at him as he stood there, wondering if *Igraine had planned this?*

He smiled like he had a toothache at the onlookers. "Children, ha."

Annoyed he was bested by the twerp, Ol'Barrow moved to another part of the gallery and took a sip of his glass. A servant approached him from the side. The blood in his veins froze as he recognized the smug grin of the man who offered him a drink on a silver platter. It was William Macarthur, the former convict, and the last man Ol'Barrow wanted to see.

"Some wine, sir?" Macarthur asked with a false smile.

Ol'Barrow glanced at his glass that was clearly full. "So, you are tending drinks now?"

"All part of the job, inspector," he answered cordially. "The funny thing is, the Signalites aren't allowed to drink alcohol, yet here I am. Offering the elite the opium for the people."

"I suppose some people believe the rules do not apply to them."

"They have an odd obsession with the wellbeing of the brain. Alcohol limits their potential for ascension."

"I see... How - interesting. So, it's not a matter of principle."

"Look at these people. You think they have principles? You think they care about the wellbeing of poor amputees? No," he concluded . "The moment they can replace their limbs for a dime, that means they can be put back to work. If they don't work as indentured servants, maybe they'll work for less pay."

"Well, it's good to hear you still have the revolutionaries' language down, comrade," Ol'Barrow sneered. "But what are you trying to prove with your little social commentary, exactly? You clearly do not believe in their cause, just like you didn't in the great revolution. What are you up to?"

"I could ask you the same thing," Macarthur responded smugly. "Still, I should have expected you to show up."

"And why is that?"

"Because you are a rabid dog," he said. "You don't let go."

"Well, unlike some, I have changed a lot over the years," Ol'Barrow said, dismissively.

"I'm sure you have,"Macarthur remarked. "So, what brings you here, inspector? Gaining our Society's trust for a proper new hand?"

"Who knows," Ol'Barrow responded overly friendly. "I know little of the Followers of the Signal at this point. But I've heard a lot of good things."

"Oh, too bad. No cops allowed."

"Really? Are our brains too dull for ascension?"

"You are operatives of the Hierarchy. We can't have members serving two systems."

"I'm sorry, but I have no idea what you are talking about."

Macarthur leaned in closer. "Then let me put it this way," he whispered. "There is going to be a reconstruction, inspector. It will make men like you obsolete. A complete revamp, not just of society," he declared. "But humanity itself."

"Reconstructing humanity? So, you did abandon the revolution."

"The revolution abandoned me, remember? Tossed me aside like a useless tool. It's because of them you broke my legs."

Aggravated, Ol'Barrow lowered his glass. "Oh, please. You never gave a rat's arse about their revolution."

"I gave my legs for the revolution!"

Ol'Barrow stepped closer. "No, you didn't. You just wanted to burn things to the ground. That's why they turned you over!" Ol'Barrow prodded Macarthur's chest with his hook. "Ten years, and you still can't get that through your thick head?"

Macarthur just looked at him with those venomous eyes of his, and said, "I will not argue with a guest. But I'll end with this. The revolution died that night. But soon, it will be superseded," he said resolutely, and turned away.

The moment Macarthur turned his attention to the other guests, his entire demeanor changed, as if the argument hadn't happened. How typical.

When taking another sip, the inspector realized he had emptied his glass during the confrontation, and promptly decided to have another drink. On a large table there was a crystal bowl filled with punch. Fresh fruit drifted on the surface that looked irresistible.

As he poured himself a glass, with an excessive amount of fruit, a man leaned with one hand on the drinks table beside him. After pouring the remaining contents for a glass inside his gullet, the man reached for a full one on the table. His artificial shins were exposed. These prosthetics were so polished they reflected the light on the carpet around him. A bit atypical for a drunk... But not for an Utter-Krapp employee, who wore the compagny's logo on the vest of his three piece suit..

"*Of course,*" Ol'Barrow thought to himself. "*Who else could provide the Signalites with such technology?*"

The man noticed Ol'Barrow eying him. "Well, good day," the salary man said, slightly slurring his words. "I don't think we've had the pleasure."

Ol'Barrow quickly changed his demeanor. "Well, I'm here on police business," he responded evasively.

"Is that so? Oh, where are my manners." Ol'Barrow stepped back as the company man invaded his personal space. "I am Jonathan Peal. I didn't expect any representatives of the police to be here."

"I noticed," he grinned. "I'm just not clear on why people seem to have it out for me."

"The Signalite's anti-establishment position is well known," he said, and took another sip. "I even heard rumors that any member needs to resign their state position if they seek to join."

"And here I thought they had members in every position in society."

Peal looked around for a moment. “As you can clearly see, they do.”

Ol'Barrow glanced at a man he knew was on the city council.

“Like shepherds, they guide their sheep,” Peal said with disdain oozing from his voice. “But every shepherd needs a dog who keeps the flock in check, if you catch my drift.”

Ol'Barrow shook his head in ignorance. “I'm not sure I do.”

“Oh... You are a cop, aren't you? Have you ever received complaints about barking dogs? You know? The ones behind a garden fence, just barking at everything for no apparent reason?”

“Yes, sure.”

“Does anyone ever ask you why they are barking?” he asked, inquisitively. “Or do they just want them to stop?”

Ol'Barrow nodded. “I think I see your point. But who are the dogs in this little metaphor?”

Peal put his finger on Ol'Barrow's chest. “You!” he said. “And me. Well, my employer to be more precise, but no one believes us. Oh, don't get me wrong, I've been asked to muzzle some dogs myself, if you know what I mean... Don't answer that! But in this case,” Peal finally got to the point, “We have been trying to warn them. About Lantry, in particular. Except, we were already too late.”

Ol'Barrow shook his head. “What do you mean? Too late for what?”

“They already put their finger in every pie!” Peal said, raising his voice. “They have henchmen on every level.”

“Really now? They have infiltrated everything?”

“Infiltrated?” he repeated, dismissive. “Don't be so dramatic. They were taken on like every bureaucrat. New government agency here. Some public works there. An uncle gains a position, he takes on a nephew. A Signalite gets a prestigious function... You get the idea. Surely nobody will ask any questions. Many of them are not even aware of what they are doing. When your boss asks you to misplace a file regarding a member of the congregation. Surely, there is no harm in doing so.... But even useful idiots expect to get something in return.”

“If this is such a big issue, why has nobody done anything about it?”

"And take responsibility for something that has been festering for decades?" Peal rolled his eyes. "People's political carriers are at stake."

"Hpf. So, how is Utter-Krapp any different from the Signalites?" Ol'Barrow asked, skeptically.

Mr. Peal grinned. "A good question. But for another time."

"And how about yourself? What has brought you in their good graces?"

Peal took another sip from his glass. "I'm just here on business. Our company has extremely strict guidelines on, uhm. Religious organizations."

Looking at Peal's feet, Ol'Barrow asked: "Are these legs your own company's design?"

The corners of his mouth curled up. "Oh, yes. I am not bragging when I say that our company has been involved with every technological breakthrough in the past fifty years."

"You don't say."

"Let me put it this way," He pointed at the display cabinet. "Take that radio over there."

"The Wavecaster Mark II?"

Peal gave Ol'Barrow a surprised glance. "Well, yes. Without that device, there would be no Followers of the Signal."

"But they developed their prosthetic technology by themselves, correct?"

"That is what the judge has decided, yes," Peal replied scornfully. "That is why they invited me, you see. To rub in their victory in the courts."

Ol'Barrow looked at him for a moment. "No Humbug, Mr. Peal. Are the courts right?"

Puckering his lips, he shrugged. "Well, based on the patents I've seen, they merely made some modifications to our designs."

Ol'Barrow stepped closer. "Allow me be blunt and make some off the record statements."

The salesman raised a concerned eyebrow. "Alright."

"I know how Utter-Krapp is using the rifts to acquire their technology," Ol'Barrow stated. "I have been through one located inside one of your company's properties."

"Well, excuse me, inspector. But I will neither confirm nor deny that."

"It doesn't matter to me whether you will or not," said Ol'Barrow. "I still know that you do."

"Is this going anywhere?" asked Peal, bored with this line of questioning.

"In your humble opinion, as an expert," started Ol'Barrow. "Do you think the Signalites could have gotten their technology on their own? Without outside-" Ol'Barrow emphasized with air quotes. "Help?"

Peal bit his lips together as he looked around and said, "If I were a conspiratorial man, I would say... it depends on how you look at it. They make no secret of it that the Signal is their teacher. They'll do as the Signal commands. What I wonder is, what do the broadcasters want in return?"

Ol'Barrow paused. He hadn't considered that all. Then again, till a while ago the Signal was just an esoteric concept. But now, it was becoming a recurring topic of conversation as something very real. "You know the answer?" asked Ol'Barrow.

"Please, this is not the place," said Peal. "And I'm not drunk enough yet to discuss these matters. Besides, it looks like the main performance is about to start."

As if on cue the lights dimmed, and spotlights lit up the stage as Lantry walked up to the sound amplifier, accompanied by the loud applause from the attendees. Ol'Barrow studied how she responded to the praise and basked in the attention of the most influential people in Kent. Peal applauded as well but did so without any enthusiasm. But did it matter? Was he not signaling his support for this prophet, even if he cared nothing for her ideas?

As the noise toned down, Lantry began with the typical, "Thank you all for being here," spiel. But Ol'Barrow had to confess, would more public figures speak with such a sultry voice, people might be more interested in the wellbeing of their city.

As for the rest, Lantry's speech was what he expected from any activist, or proselytizer. She talked about the deplorable state of society and the injustices, etcetera. Surely, not things Ol'Barrow disagreed with; Grievance is an easy sell. But he heard it so many times before. He didn't know what was worse, the speaker, or the elite members in the audience who wouldn't touch the downtrodden with a ten-foot pole. They would rather talk about how the poor ought to behave, or how the state should be charged in taking care of the people. As long as they didn't have to do it themselves. The speech therefore was as mind-numbing as it was frustrating. It was like being in church all over again, but the audience seemed to eat it up regardless.

Dramatically, Lantry raised her voice as she began to preach. "They'll tell you that humanity cannot, nor needs to, improve. That we must accept the cards nature has dealt to us... But Mother Nature doesn't not care about us. We are but one of her children, of which she has had millions. And that is not a tragedy. That is by her design. Our species is supposed to go defunct. If we trust in natural selection, our species is destined to disappear, and all our achievements will be for nothing. If we are to believe these Darwinists, we are nothing but a branch on a tree." She paused as to let the futility of existence sink in. "I believe that," Lantry continued. "We have the creative potential and intelligence to avoid the destiny Mother Nature has intended for us. The Signals have told us how. But we need to start now... And that is what we do here. We improve humanity, with knowledge passed on to us. It is but the first step in the great scheme of things..."

Assistants entered the stage to move the chandeliers, and other items, off the podium.

"Tonight, I want you to meet Ada. A successful dancer at the Royal Opera House. But a collision with a carriage crippled her. After her accident, doctors had told her she would never dance again. Of course, they were no Signalites. We did not just repair the limbs, we replaced them with something superior, and improvable... This will be her first public performance since her accident. Please, welcome Ada Joffrey and Paul Burns."

The noise of applause vibrated between the walls as the dancers revealed themselves. A man with an intricate hand, dressed in a tight-fitting burgundy torero costume, and a woman with prosthetic legs, wearing a slender Flamenco-like dress. Her skirt was open in the front, so her shins were clearly visible for the occasion. Ol'Barrow recognized a sense of pride and nervousness in the woman's face as walked on stage.

As light on the audience dimmed, the dancers took positions opposite each other. Everyone held their breath as a shared sense of awe and wondrous curiosity fell over the attendees. The orchestra started. Lantry parted her lips and sang with her clear voice that reverberated through the gallery, awakening a swell of emotion in her listeners. With a few simple steps, the pair started their performance. A bit of awkwardness at first, but swiftly they lost themselves in the moment. They serenely waltzed on the melody of the music, unhindered by the mechanical limbs that bent and twisted without fail through the succession of complex motions. Watching the locomotion of the prostheses' cylinders and springs were as fascinating to behold as the dance itself. And on and on it went. Even Ol'Barrow was intoxicated by the spectacle, despite himself.

Then they finished their performance. The dancers assumed their final position. The music stopped, and then among the audience erupted a thunderous applause.

Lantry congratulated the dancers and handed them flowers, as was customary for a hostess to do. Yet, Ol'Barrow couldn't help but sense the malice behind Lantry's smile. Did she really feel happy for these invalids? Or was she just parading them on stage, like circus animals, to attract new followers?

He barely finished his thought when suddenly Lantry's face contorted like she was in pain. In the middle of the stage, she started to hunch over as if she lost control over her facilities. Dumbfounded, Ol'Barrow watched as Lantry fell to her knees, pressing one hand against her temple.

Gradually, the murmur of concerned and curious voices grew into a mild panic. "My God. Miss Lantry seems to have been taken ill."

Some of the servants surrounded the stricken woman, blocking her from sight, while others told the attendees to stay calm and keep their distance from the stage.

Ol'Barrow slowly made his way to the exit. With everyone distracted, it seemed a good moment to find Igraine.

Some moments earlier...

Hiding in the shadow of the staircase, a pleasant shiver spread through Igraine's chest when a servant walked her by unawares. He was so close she could have grabbed his trousers if she had wanted and given him a good fright. Instead, she showed mercy and let him pass unmolested. Lower lip clenched between her teeth, Igraine peered around the corner into the hall of the east wing that was sparsely lit by the lights coming in from the adjacent rooms.

The murmur of the attendees had just died down for some reason, and now there was an odd silence, apart from an echoing voice in the background, that she could barely make out. She figured the main presentation was now in progress and couldn't wish for a more suitable diversion.

With gentle steps, she sneaked through the corridor, moving from one door to the next. Peeking inside of each chamber, Igraine lifted her eye patch and activated her analytical view. Her vision turned her surroundings from an gloomy library to a grainy green world accentuated by white and dark lines. Glancing over the walls and floors, she scanned the interior for any discrepancies. But after a few seconds, something inside her head started to strain, as if her nerves were being stretched like a rubber band. When the sensation became too strong, she turned the mode off, and her nerves relaxed. It had not always been that way, but recently it had gotten worse. And yet, it was a mild inconvenience compared to her after afflictions.

Shaking off the onset of depression, Igraine continued her investigation. But despite her effort, she had no luck finding anything. Rather, it was a noticeable lack of things that surprised her. For example, plants, or images of picturesque landscapes that the people here seemed to enjoy so much. Then again, what could be expected from a Signalite who was repulsed by human biology? It only made sense that Lantry hated the rest of nature as well. In that regard, this building must have been like an oasis within the wilderness to them.

Then Igraine found a room with an overabundance of things. The master bedroom; Lantry's most private domain. From the door post, Igraine could see the glints of various valuables. But the real eye catcher was the bed. Its reflective panels were sleek, with curved angles, and devoid of ornamentation - as was the rest of the furniture. But despite its minimalistic design, it looked luxurious, and not all that different from what she was used to on her home world.

On the vanity by the bed stood a single small standing mirror, instead of a large one that she would expect. Odd, because beside a commode there was a display of brooches, rings, ear hangers and so on. She also had various wigs on display, made of some advanced nylons - Well, advanced for this world's standards at least. There was also an array of perfumes, in wonderfully ornate flasks made of crystal and precious stones. No pearls or ivory though. No, Lantry was consistent in that regard.

Igraine opened a couple of flasks, for research of course, and took a huff. Unfortunately, her nose was not trained enough to smell if these were made of natural extracts or not. One flask, made of crystal, contained a substance as dark as licorice. Igraine liked licorice, so she picked it up to try it. But after removing the lid, she immediately retracted her nose. "Oil?" Of course, Lantry needed oil, but to store it in such a container.

Adjacent to the bedroom was a bathroom. The floor was still wet when Igraine entered. The tub inside was arranged like it was made for an invalid, surrounded by beams and other aids so Lantry could get in without her prosthetics - or so Igraine assumed. She was surprised however by a pile of small rough sheets, akin to sandpaper, on a stand beside the tub. If Lantry didn't bathe with her legs attached, what were these for? Her skin? Then Igraine figured it made sense. She heard people use dried sea sponges to scrub their skin clean, but if you do not want to use natural products, what do you use? But if so, how clean did Lantry want to be? There was a pile of the stuff.

Apart from the array of oddities on display, there was something off about this room. The dimensions didn't match up compared to the layout of the other rooms. The most obvious explanation would be the water works - very advanced for this society. Especially when so far removed from the town.

Igraine inspected the faucet and used her sight to follow the pipes until she found what she was looking for. Behind the paneling, she spotted power lines beside the service pipes. The wires became brighter as she approached, until she could make out its destination. Up close, she made out the outlines of a lock, hidden behind a resin disk made to look like a part of the decor. She studied the intricate lock that, when switched, would activate the wheels that rolled a hidden door sideways. The lock was so similar to what the Association used, she suspected there was no way the Followers came up with this on their own.

By using her manipulator, she turned the various components of the mechanism. It used to be like manipulating anything with her fingers. But it had become more straining as of late, like when her fingers refused to do what she wanted after hours of drawing. Then there were the headaches, and finally the seizures. Igraine took a deep breath and redoubled her efforts. Time was running out, and there was no point in feeling sorry for herself.

Finally, the switch set the wheels in motion. Smoothly the wall panel moved aside, revealing a staircase that ran down into a utility tunnel.

Down in the humid shaft, few light bulbs hanging the from power lines overhead, lighted the way. The plumbing and wiring had remained fully exposed, as she came to expect. The philosophy of these people seemed to be "out of sight-out-of-mind" and only bothered to refine the spaces they presented to their guests.

On her own Plane, even the common components were revered as essential parts of the arcane networks. By now, Igraine realized that magic was a foolish notion. In this world, however, the wiring wasn't worth more than the copper it was made of. Although this made fabrication easier and available to anyone, these people were wasteful and very eager to destroy what was deemed to be of no further use.

Further down the passage, Igraine traced the cables back to a crudely dug hole through the brick foundation. From there, the power lines pronged toward both ends of the tunnel. This type of conduit wasn't usual for a household on her world, let alone a primitive manor like this. Whatever Lantry was hiding, it required a substantial amount of power.

With no way to go but forward, the girl pressed on toward the end. There, past an archway, she noticed rows and clusters of blinking lights in the darkness. It was a room filled with the buzzing sound of electric machinery, and the rumbling of a generator.

Strained to her limit, she activated her eye for just a second. It just gave her the vaguest impression of what was waiting for her in the dark. But it was just enough to spot a switch, and she turned on the lights.

The interior lit up. What was revealed could either be a laboratory, or a workshop, containing a turning lathe, drill press, and other machinery not typical of this world - at least not yet. But what really grabbed her attention was a curtain concealing a corner in the back. Walking up to the obscured section, she glanced at workbenches. There were unfinished prosthetics, primitive radios, crudely made switch boards and other machine parts she couldn't identify at first glance. Despite all she saw, she failed to puzzle together a clear vision of what they were doing here.

Then she reached the curtains. Pushing aside the cloth, Igraine peeked through the crack. It was dark, making it hard to make out anything in detail. Convinced the coast was clear, she grabbed the cloth.

The curtain rings shrieked as she yanked the fabric aside.

What was revealed made the girl freeze in place.

Holding the curtain inside her quivering grip, Igraine stared at the lifeless expression of a finely dressed woman, seated on a nearly horizontal surgical chair. Igraine barely managed to contain a girlish squeal, and yet, the woman gave no response. Her eyes blinked, but she didn't flinch a single muscle.

Nervously Igraine just stood there, her feet nailed to the ground. "H-he-hello?"

She waited for what felt like a minute, but the woman's mind appeared to be as vacant as her expression, blinking her eyes mechanically at regular intervals.

"A-a golem?" Igraine thought. After more hesitation, she stepped forward to investigate the woman up close.

She was dressed like some villain from an audio-drama-poster, and her skirt lacked all the ruffles, and other decorations, the women of the land fancied so much. She also wore gumshoes. Regardless, she looked beautiful with long silver manes running down her shoulders. The spotless skin of her neck was covered in small tattoos, some of which had been struck through, confirming Igraine's suspicions - this was the assassin who attacked Mr. Ol'Barrow.

Igraine didn't dare to strain herself any further, but even with the naked eye she could determine the excessive amount of augmentation the assassin went through. If anything, the human body merely served the augmentations, rather than the other way around. Igraine bent forward to look at the back of the headrest. Through a hole, a plug went into the back of the lady's head, connecting her to a machine that was beset by neatly arranged incandescent lamps that flickered at random intervals. Behind the lamp-panel was a network of interconnected circuits with cables plugged in. She imagined it as some improvised type of switch board. But what purpose could it serve? While skimming the surface of the wire work, it dawned on her it could be a router of sorts, managing and transmitting information. But from where to where? Igraine possessed some knowledge of the Association's primitive digital systems but wasn't aware of any others in this world.

"Ptssssss-ssssssssss"

Igraine jumped back when the nearby radio started to make deep droning noises, like it was hit by an electric charge. Shocked, she stepped off a cable she was standing on. If that disturbed the Wavecaster, this place had to be a fire hazard.

But the radio kept producing strange noises, like it was cycling through various channels at a high pace, producing a constant sloshing sound. "Thjuhthjuhthjuhthjuhthjuhthjuh."

Freaked out by the noise, Igraine stepped up to the device and looked for the off button.

“Don't touch - that, dial” cried a mechanical voice that sounded like outtakes from various broadcasts stitched together to make a full sentence.

Igraine pulled her hands off the device. That was a single phrase uttered by three different voices with random sounding inflections. “What?”

"ThjuhthjuhSurprizzzed? Thjuhthjuhthjuh”

She nervously backed away from the machine.

“ThjuhthjuhDon'tthjuhleavethjuhthjuh"

With her eyes fixated on the Wavecaster, Igraine backed away toward the exit, but stopped when her back collided with something. Releasing a girlish scream, she turned around in a flash. Then, Igraine froze. Her feet felt glued to the floor as she was looking up, petrified with fear.

The golem had awoken and was staring down on the girl with a malicious glee.

Instinctively, Igraine raised her left hand at the assassin, but the woman grabbed her by the wrist and yanked girl's arm in the air.

“Auw!” Igraine was dancing on her toes as the woman pulled her up just high enough to strain the arm-muscles under the weight of her small body.

“What’s this-Pebble?” came from the Wavecaster.

Igraine noticed the woman eying the manipulator in her palm.

The assassin lay her hand on Igraine's face and with her thumb forced her left eyelids apart to inspect her one blue eye.

“Let me go!”

“No... Why are- you - here?”

“I was just curious.”

“You are Traveler.”

“So, what?”

“Did the, as-sociation. Take you too?”

Another shiver spread through her chest. “You know of-” Igraine now understood what the numbers on the woman's skin meant. “They'll come looking for me!” she threatened, but her voice quivered too much for it to make any impact.

“That's-What, I, am counting on. The - - will-ll, be pleased.”

“No!” the girl cried when the woman forced her arms behind her back.

Suddenly, the radio vomited a flood of beeps and boops that Igraine recognized as a arcane transmission when received by analogue systems. The cringe inducing noise even made the golem pauze whose smile faded like a shadow touched by the sunlight.

What could that be? Igraine barely finished the thought when the woman threw her head back. Then she convulsed as if she was suffering a stroke, pushing Igraine against a table in the proces. With terrified fascination, Igraine watched how the golem paced mechaniclly around the room, swaying her arms as if she were fighting off a swarm of bees.

Igraine covered her ears when the woman started screaming. Her cries sounded like the high pitched creaking of a thousand rusty hinges, while the golem was knocking over solid metal objects like they were made of cardboard.

Then she just stopped. Her body was stuck in an odd position, like a marionette suspended from its threads.

Afraid to startle her, Igraine shuffled to her left, hoping to make a dash for the exit. But then, as she was about to make a run for it, the creature lifted her head and turned to face the girl.

As if trapped by the gaze of the basilisk, Igraine's body felt like it had turned to stone by those silver eyes devoid of emotion. Then golem lunged, squeezing the girl’s head between her hands.

Feeling as if her skull was trapped in vice, Igraine has squeezed her eyes. Waiting for the end. But nothing happened.

“Angel,” spoke a distant woman's voice.

Tears flowed down her check when, Igraine peeked.

Those silvers eyes, were staring right at her with urgency.

All Igraine could do was stare back, shaking all over.

“Angel,” spoke another voice.

Igraine's eyes shifted in the direction of the Wavecaster, then back at the golem. “Doctor?”

“Janes - machine - factory.”

"W-What?" Igraine managed to squeeze past her dry lips.

"Johns - saw machine - factory."

"What do you mean?"

The golem's eyes were rolling inside their sockets till Igraine could see the white of them. Growling, she stumbled back, wildly reaching behind her neck like something was attacking her. Then she jerked her head forward again, whilst grabbing something beneath the silvery mane. Then she jerked again, and again, till something snapped. With one last pull the golem ripped the outlet from the back of her neck and fell on her knees.

As the golem sat on the ground, Igraine finally shook off the paralysis, and fled back into the tunnel, as fast as her legs could carry her. She jumped up the steps, ran down the hall, and dashed past surprised visitors and servants who were already in a state of turmoil. But Igraine didn't care as she was storming out of the manor. She just kept on running, past the fountain and down the pebble stone road. But when the gate was coming into view, the world started to blur.

Non. Not now!

Her lungs refused to take in any more air, and her throat was parched. Out of breath, she leaned against the outer wall. The world was swirling around her now, and she could feel her limbs growing weak. As her awareness was fading, and all feeling flowing from her body, the last thing she saw was a tall figure closing in.

CHAPTER EIGHT

19TH OF MAY, 1875, 8.56 PM. LANTRY ESTATE, NEAR CANTERBURY.

The thrashing of pebbles barely drowned out the sound of Ol'Barrow's breathing, as he raced to the gate. "*What the hell got into that girl?*" he thought, imagining Igraine having another fit. The light of decorative lanterns cast shadows all around him, as his legs were going numb, and his throat felt like it was on fire. But he kept on going, until he finally reached the perimeter. Out of breath, he slowed down, and looked around the juncture. At first, he saw nothing beside the shadows between the trees. But then he spotted Igraine, leaning against the outer wall, gasping, and looking pale as a blanket. "By Jove! What the hell happened?"

Startled, Igraine looked at him with swollen eyes. "I - saw - her," she answered between breaths, while her voice quivered as if she were about to cry.

He swallowed, convinced she was on the verge of having another seizure. "Let's get a move on." He picked Igraine up, which is harder with one hand that he first assumed. But finally, he managed to lift the girl off her feet and carried her in his arms down the road.

"B-but," she muttered with a soft voice. She clearly wanted to be let down, but her intention didn't translate into motion.

"Let's get you home first."

"But..."

"This was stupid," he thought aloud. *What now? Walk to Canterbury?* Igraine was small, but not so small that he could carry her all the way. "Stupid," he repeated.

"But I heard her," she kept insisting.

"Who do you mean?"

"The - one you are looking - for. S-"

He stopped dead in his tracks. "S-36?"

She nodded. "Down in the basement. But Dr. Jen-"

He turned to the manor, from which a dismayed murmur reverberated over the trees. "Dr. Jenever? What about her?"

"I heard her over the wireless. She said something about..."

"Go on."

"John's or Jane's Saw Machine Factory?"

"Sawing Machines?" It didn't ring any bells. "What about it?"

"I don't know. Just..."

Shaking his head, he continued walking. "We'll look into it tomorrow."

"But she's down there!" cried Igraine.

A shiver went down his spine. He almost forgot about S-36. This was not at all what he expected to discover. He knew Lantry was involved, but this. "Yes... All the more reason to get out of here," he said to put Igraine at ease. But how? A directionless torrent of concerns streamed to his mind. *Damn it! I just had to get that ticket, didn't I!* Meanwhile he kept walking on like he was on rails. There was no other option. But his legs couldn't handle the additional weight. "Can you walk?"

She nodded.

The veins in his legs felt relieved as he put her down. Igraine too struggled to stand up straight, but eventually they started their walk, be it like an elderly couple with arthritis.

As Ol'Barrow stretched his back for a moment, there was a rustling of leaves. In a flash they turned to face the origin of the sound.

"Somebody there?" Ol'Barrow cried out, using his best constable voice.

After a brief pause, a man walked from between the trees into the middle of the road. He was thin, wearing a trench coat with baggy trousers underneath that seemed two sizes too big . He pulled at the working-gloves he wore to tighten it around his fingers and straightened his flat cap that was covered with fresh seeds sticking to the wool.

Ol'Barrow looked at the wall to his right. There was no entrance into the manor ground to be seen. He concluded the stranger either climbed the perimeter, which was unlikely with those decorative spikes, or had been laying in wait.

The man came up to him with a rather uneven tread as if he were intoxicated. But he had a sober, rather suspicious look in his eyes that was focused on them.

"Uh, hello," Ol'Barrow began. "Are you lost?"

"No," he answered with a nasally smoker's voice. "I'm looking for a girl," he answered bluntly. "She stole something."

"Oh, my. Well, good luck with that," Ol'Barrow responded aloof. In a different situation, he would have walked away, but he didn't dare turn his back.

"They said she wore a green dress, and had an eye patch," he continued. "Just like the one beside ye."

That made Ol'Barrow pause . "You must be mistaken, sir. My niece has been drifting in and out of sleep all evening. But she was really looking forward to seeing Miss Lantry."

The stranger looked anxious but persisted regardless. "Listen. I don't want to start a scene, all right. Why don't we go back and get this sorted out? That's fair, right?"

"Listen, sir. This lady is not well, and needs her rest."

The man swallowed as his expression grew increasingly tense. "I'm afraid I-" He seemed distracted by something.

From down the road, a buzzing sound approached, like that of an electro motor. One of electric carriages leaving the manor probably - or minions giving chase?

Ol'Barrow wasn't sure if they should run for it, move out of the way, or hail the driver.

The stranger looked uncomfortable as well. The inspector had seen that expression many times before. It was that of a culprit who was deciding he should fight or flee.

Thus, they were standing there like ghosts in the nights as the buzzing sounds came nearer. The vehicle's lights appeared from behind the bend now. It was like playing a game of chicken, and both parties refused to budge as the approaching light casting increasingly longer shadows in front of them.

"Look out!" cried the driver. The buzzing receded as the carriage pulled to a standstill. The driver stood up behind the wheel and raised his head above the windshield. "What the hell are you doing in the middle of the road?" As the pair turned to face him, the driver leaned sideways from behind the glass for a closer look. "Is that girl alright?"

"Well, to be honest..." Ol'Barrow muttered.

The enclosed cabin opened, and a man popped his head out of the doorway, holding on the brim of his top hat. "Jared? What is going on?" he asked, in a posh accent.

"The poor lass doesn't seem to be well, my lord."

Ol'Barrow recovered his composure and addressed the noble. "My niece. She just collapsed. I hoped to encounter a carriage along the way to town."

"Well sir, you found one," the noble man responded happily.

Ol'Barrow wasn't sure about this. It could be a trap. But the stranger seemed just as uncomfortable with the situation as he was.

"I- um," began Ol'Barrow hesitant.

"Please, sir. I couldn't live with myself if I left a sick child by the side of the road like that."

"If you insist."

Awkwardly, the pair entered the vehicle as the stranger observed them silently. As he was about to shut the door, the stranger raised his hand. "Safe travels."

Ol'Barrow gave him a friendly nod, uncertain if the man was being sarcastic.

Ill at ease, the odd pair sat down on the shallow bench opposite to the aristocratic couple. The cabin was just like that of a horse cart. Opposite of Ol'Barrow, the nobleman was so tall that he had to fold up his legs in a seemingly uncomfortable position to make room for their guests. Meanwhile, the lady sat smiling next to his lordship, with her hands on her lap. A small woman with rounded cheeks, giving her a bit of a doll-like appearance.

"Thank you so much," Ol'Barrow said, breaking the ice somewhat.

"Don't mention it. I'm Reginald Carlston. This is my wife, Clarissa."

“Pleased to make your acquaintance,” the lady said.

“Uh, I am Connely, my Lord,” Ol'Barrow answered as naturally as he could. “This is my niece... Iggy.”

“From where do you hail, Mr. Connely?”

“Dover, my lord.”

“I thought I recognized the accent. That's a bit out of the way.”

“My niece really wanted to see Miss Lantry, my lord.”

“Our children wanted to come too,” Lady Carlston responded. “They are big admirers of hers, you see. I hope Miss Lantry is going to be all right. I've never seen anyone faint like that. On stage in all places!”

“It can happen to the best of us,” Ol'Barrow muttered.

“Probably for the best the children weren’t there to see it,” Lord Carlston said. “The news will drive them wild. Should we tell them when we get back, dear?”

“Better to hear it from us than from the news,” the lady said cynically. “God knows how they'll sensationalize it.”

“Yes,” the lord sighed, admittingly. “Celebrities are like saints to them. They struggle to remember a single bible verse, but they can talk hours about the worlds in these dramas. Lisa, what do they call it again?”

“The lore, dear.”

“Right, lore.”

“I used to have such a... Colleague,” Ol'Barrow brought up.

“Well, I can imagine what that is like. What do you do, Mr. Connely?”

“I-um.” he looked at his hook. “I used to be a soldier. I won our tickets at a veteran's raffle.”

The happy couple's faces clouded.

“I see,” the lady whispered, saddened.

“For what it's worth,” the lord began. “I thank you for your service.”

“It really isn't necessary,” Ol'Barrow respond politely, convinced he made a mistake. Pretending to be a factory worker would have been just as credible.

They talked some more to pass the time. Within moments, Igraine had fallen asleep, and rested her head against his arm. A rare moment for the Inspector who never imagined taking care of a child. Or just have a conversation with people that didn't involve work. So many types of human interactions that many take for granted were a rarity for him. It was a strange experience, but overall a pleasant one.

A couple of minutes had passed when suddenly the wagon shook violently as if something had fallen on the roof.

Before anyone could react, there was a scream from the driver, and the roaring of the engine rose to high pitch buzz as the carriage accelerated, and just as suddenly changed course. The passengers screamed as they were tossed around in the cabin as they ran off the road, and the vehicle started to keel.

Metal creaked and wood snapped as the wagon toppled sideways while sliding down a slope. The cart had ended up wedged inside a ditch, leaving a more foot or so between the door and bottom.

Moments passed while a battered Ol'Barrow leaned on his arm against the side of the interior, mindful not to crush Igraine who lay curled up in the corner of the bench. "Hold on," he groaned while clenching his teeth. "We'll be out of here in a moment."

After some uncomfortable twists and turns, they managed to open the door that folded down like a latch.

Finally, the couple managed to emerge from the turned vehicle, looking like a pair of rodents squeezing themselves through a hole at the same time. Then they crawled, dressed in their fineries, through the rancid, porridge-like mud on the bottom.

Ol'Barrow followed suit and dropped down in the black porridge that smelled of open sewage. From underneath the carriage, he saw Carston's boots as the lord helped his wife up.

"Help," squeaked Igraine above him as she reached out to him. Blood ran down the side of her face from a gash near her hairline.

As Ol'Barrow helped her climb out of the wreckage, he noticed different steps sink into the mud. There was another sound, but his battered brain couldn't recognize it.

"Hello, we-" Lord Carston's voice just stopped. "What are -"

There was the sound of a blunt impact, followed by Lady Carston's dreadful shriek. Ol'Barrow recoiled as the Lord's body fell in the mud. The lady's voice was quickly silenced as someone squeezed her throat followed by a gurgling death shriek that made Ol'Barrow sick listening to it.

He clenched Igraine to his chest as the lady dropped in front of them – dead .

Metal feet, not resembling any human's, sank into the mud beside her. With every motion, its joints zoomed like a foot-cranked sewing machine.

Ol'Barrow held his breath as the creature bent forward, resting one metal claw in the dirt. Eyes, burning like red-tinted lanterns, peered beneath the wreckage.

Quickly, the two survivors crawled from beneath the other side of the carraige. But as Ol'Barrow struggled to get up, muddy boots were barring his way.

It was the man they met on the road. He didn't wear gloves this time now, revealing the intricate prosthetics hidden underneath - skeletal hands devoid of any decorations.

Ol'Barrow pushed Igraine away, hoping she would make a break for it. Then he crawled to his feet, as quickly as his battered body allowed. Hook raised, he waited for the stranger to make the first move.

Instead, the man looked him dead on, the corner of him mouth twitching. "You should have just listened," the stranger sneered. "All she wanted was the girl."

"Shut up," cried another man, who sounded like he had a bad case of miner's lung.

Ol'Barrow's feet sank deeper into the mud as he stepped back the moment the second assailant emerged from behind the wagon. A homunculus; an amalgamation of mechanical parts and human flesh, built for a single task . His left hand was replaced with something resembling a cleaver and his legs were steel frames in the shape of some animal's hind legs. Even his feet had been rebuilt resembling a bird's. "Just kill him and get it over with."

The stranger seemed uncomfortable. "This is your own fault," he reiterated softly, and grabbed Ol'Barrow with one hand while balling the other one into a fist. Serrated nails pierced Ol'Barrow's flesh as the metal fingers gripped his shoulder like a vice. The automaton raised his fist, lunged, and then…

His arm suddenly halted.

Ol'Barrow gasped when the automaton's joints seemed to have frozen in midair. The stranger's attempts to move were like those of a mime pretending his arms got stuck.

The other homunculus walked up to them and looked at Igraine laying on her belly in the mud. Her left arm was stretched all the way out, aiming the glowing marks in the palm of her hand at the stranger. "It's the girl," he said bemused, looking down on Igraine. "Isn't it?"

Igraine looked at him defiantly, maintaining her grip on the stranger's arm from a distance.

In a sudden motion, the homunculus kicked her in the side. The stranger's hand was released immediately as Igraine rolled over like a plaything.

"Now, finish him, brother," the homunculus commanded. "I'll take the girl back."

Still the Stranger hesitated as the big one walked toward Igraine.

Ol'Barrow watched how his three toed foot sink beside him into the mud as the mechanical man walked him by like he wasn't even there. Just as S-36. This was like Bigsby's murder all over again.

After another step, the homunculus stopped. With his glowing eyes he looked down on Ol'Barrow, and smirked. "Not so mighty now are ya, peeler."

Ol'Barrow blinked. "Not a thr-" he could barely speak.

The homunculus stepped forward to have a closer look. "What's that?" he asked giddily. Unlike his hesitant companion, he enjoyed this. Just as Ol'Barrow had come to expect from Lantry and her ilk. Suddenly, the inspector was filled with a onset of disgust as Macarthur's gleeful grin flashed before his eyes, making determined he could not give them the satisfaction. Mustering his strength Ol'Barrow roared as he swung his hook in a wide arc at the homunculus' knee. Sparks flew as he lodged the tip of his peg in his medial compartment and pulled. Just like that, the leg gave way and the homunculus toppled over. When the homonculus lay on his side, Ol'Barrow crawled on top of him.

But the creature pushed him off with ease. Rising to his feet, the homunculus looked at his brother with frustration. "Don't help, or anything," he sneered with contempt. "You get the girl then! I've had about enough of this wank stain."

"I'm sorry," he apologized. "I didn't want to get in the way."

"Oh, forget it!" The Homunculus grabbed Ol'Barrow by the collar and lifted him up as if he was a mere child. "You wanna play, meat sack?" he smirked with a crooked grin and threw him aside.

Landing landed nine feet away, the shock of the impact knocked the air out of him when Ol'Barrow slid through the mud leaving a deep trail in his wake.

As the inspector was laying there, the homunculus approached. The glowing eyes looked straight at Ol'Barrow, blinding him with their light beams.

A flash lit up the trench as a gunshot sounded, unannounced.

The automaton stepped several paces back while struggling to maintain balance. As the assassin regained his footing, he looked down at the wound in his side.

Ol'Barrow rolled over to see.

There, on the precipice stood the Associate; the man who saved him at the harbor from S-36. Fumes still drifted in front his green lit glasses as the Associate aimed his heavy revolver.

Realizing his position, the homunculus raced toward the Associate, kicking up patches of mud as he leapt through the air.

But the second shot forced the machine-man back with tremendous force, crashing him right on top of the cart wreckage.

In his panic, the stranger reached for Igraine to spirit her away. The Associate hesitated who to aim his gun at as he raced toward the tree line with the girl under his arm..

"Never mind that one, get the girl!" cried Ol'Barrow, still sitting in the mud."

As if struck by inspiration, the Associate dashed after them.

Ol'Barrow could hear the brushing of leaves when the Associate disappeared between the trees.

As Ol'Barrow struggled to get up, there was a shot. And another.

Ol'Barrow, held his breath. "No more?" he muttered, uncertain what the silence meant. He was about to walk past the vehicle when there was a sudden racket.

The inspector staggered back as the homunculus emerged from the wreckage like a corpse that just broke free from its coffin. Blood flowed from its mouth while splitters the size of railway spikes stuck out of the fleshy parts of its body. It muttered some inaudible profanities as he grabbed Ol'Barrow and reigned him in with jerking motions.

Ol'Barrow noticed how the creature still attempted to dislodge its cleaver from the wreckage, giving him a flash of inspiration. Ol'Barrow leapt toward the creature holding him, and leaned his whole weight down, slashing his hook at the homunculus' shoulder.

The creature tried to push him away, but it was already too late.

The hook had caught some exposed wiring, and as the creature stretched out his arm sparks erupted from the severed plugs.

The moment the mechanical arm went limp, Ol'Barrow recovered his footing, and flushed with rage he confronted the murderer. His sense of fear, pain and humiliation had turned into an unrelenting surge of fury then demanded to be sated. He bit his lips together as he struck the thing with a broken beam. It felt good. The euphoria of turning the tables was exhilarating. The homunculus was crippled now, defenseless, and whining pathetically. This thing that was murdering so gleefully just minutes ago was now at his mercy. Ready and able to finish this, Ol'Barrow raised his hook, ready to strike the abomination right across his throat when a sudden cry broke the spell.

"Non!"

Strikken, he swung around.

Above him, Igraine stood beside the Associate, hand pressed against her mouth like she was embarrassed, or horrified. The Associate however simply raised his gun, aimed, and pulled the trigger. The Homunculus jerked aside violently, slammed against the wreckage, and collapsed like a broken doll.

There was sudden uncomfortable silence. Even the noise from the manor was gone. All that remained was the accelerated beating of his own heart.

Flushed with shame, Ol'Barrow looked at the lifeless husk of the thing too embarrassed to look in Igraine's direction. All this time he convinced himself he had changed since his abuse of Macarthur. He had been wrong, and Macarthur was right.

Behind him, the Associate holstered his gun and wiped away the blood from Igraine's face. "How long have you been away from Sanctuary?" he asked her in an excessively gravelly voice.

She muttered something unintelligible.

Ol'Barrow pushed aside his shame and turned. "What is Sanctuary?" he asked.

"We don't have time for this," the Associate grumbled, and reached down to pick up Igraine.

Ol'Barrow was shivering as he stepped forward. "Where are we going?"

"We?" the Associate snapped. "You can go to hell as far as I care. I'm taking her somewhere safe."

"But, what about-"

"Just stop!" the Associate cried with a clear voice. Then he put on his theatrical voice again. "You outlived your usefulness. Take what is left of your decency and retire."

Too shaken to move without falling over Ol'Barrow reached out his hand. "But-" he wanted to protest, but the Associate had already disappeared among the shadows between the trees.

Left behind in the ditch, bruised and mentally depleted, Ol'Barrow fell to his knees in the mud. Behind him lay five dead bodies. If it weren't for him, none of this would have happened. And why? Because he didn't get his way?

Even then, how could it possibly have gone so wrong?

Among the unknown variables, there was only one certainty now. This was the point of no return. He was going down a train track with an unknown destination, and it was doubtful there was a station along the way.

How could things have gone so wrong?

Then, just as he intended to collapse, a high pitch scream broke the silence, followed by a manly, "Fire! Fire!"

A dancing ember rose above the trees. It must have come from the manor. Ol'Barrow just dropped himself to the ground and rubbed his face against the grass. "What the hell is happening?"

CHAPTER NINE

"Good morning Dover, I am Frank Dimbleby of Dover Public Broadcast. On the line this morning is Henry Coquelin, well known for his appearance in Electric Bob's Big Black Ostrich. Well, sir. I am sure all our listeners were shocked to hear what happened to actress Clara Lantry prior evening."

"Thank you, Tom. Yes, what happened was nothing short of an attack! A targeted action taken by a man we have confirmed works for a local police borough. We knew for a while now; certain members of the elite consider us a threat to their power. And as we have seen the past few weeks, they are ramping up the harassment."

"I see. There are rumors of a child accomplice. Is there any truth to these claims?"

"This is true. She is yet to be found. That is why we offer a reward for anyone who can provide us with the information that will help us apprehend this delinquent."

"With Lantry incapacitated, who will lead the Followers of the Signal, Mr. Coquelin?"

"There seems to be a misunderstanding. The Perfect is the official leader of our organization."

"But surely, he has not made public appearances in ages. People are wondering if he is even alive. He has not even responded to last night's events."

"The Perfect is occupied with far more important matters."

"More important? An attack on one of your most prominent members surely has priority?"

"The Signal has intensified its transmissions the past few months, and translating it is of the utmost importance."

"Well, what does the Signal say?"

"I'm afraid I am not privy to that information. Even then, much of it is very fractured. That is why the interpreters do not make the transcripts public. And even so. Who knows what the ruling classes would do with that information? Everyone has a right to join the Ascension. The upper classes would keep it to themselves. That is why they orchestrated this attack. In order to intimidate us and make us submit!"

"Yes, I understand, Mr. Coquelin. Thank you for calling... Well, dear listeners, this is all the time we have for now. Next up, a single by Jack Urby. The Lights of London..."

THE PREVIOUS EVENING, 19TH OF MAY, 1875, 8 PM, DOVER...

The twilight already darkened while the ringing of the doorbell was sinking in the rushing of the sea behind the Associate. 321 was waiting in front of an elegant door at Marine Parade in the shadow of Dover's White Cliffs. The Theodore household lived adjacent to the beach's promenade, making in stand in stark contrast to the squalor of the working-class quarters he visited a few days ago. Behind the windows glowed a hospitable light, giving the home a cozy feeling in this cool weather. The American had underestimated the difference in temperature between day and night and felt the need to rub his arms constantly.

A maid opened the door unassumingly, until she looked up at his face. "Oeh!" The maid jumped back out of fright the moment she saw him.

"Good evening, miss," he said, ignoring her reaction. "I have an appointment with the master of the house."

The young woman needed to recuperate from the fright. It wasn't the first time white folk got scared of him in the dark. He wasn't sure what to think of it. But experience taught him awkwardness, in this situation, was the best he could hope for.

"Uhm, yes," she said. "You must be Mr. Wilkins... I sorry, they didn't-"

"I must confess I didn't tell them. However, my time is scarce. So, if you please."

The maid nodded apologetically and let him in.

They walked down the hall, into the living room where Mr. and Mrs. Theodore were sitting, tending to their young child. It was a comforting sight. Unfortunately, it reminded 321 of his own life's choices. Ambitions he chose out of vindictiveness. Others out of a strange sense of obligation that he didn't really understand himself - not beyond the single principle: "If not me, who else?" With envy, he observed how the proud father, Stephan Theodore, struggled to take his attention off his newborn and stand up to greet him. "Sorry. You must be Mr. Wilkins?"

"That I am," 321 answered reassuringly. "I apologize for the late hour. However, I-"

Mr. Theodore's entire demeanor changed as he stuck his hand inside his pockets. "What has she done now?" he asked exhaustedly. Even his wife looked at her husband with concern.

Caught off guard by his demeanor, 321 said, "I'm afraid I cannot talk about that. But I hope you can help me understand some things."

He directed the Associate to the door. "Please, accompany me."

They moved their conversation to the smoking room at the other side of the hall which served both as a lounge and a modest library. In the corner the Associate spotted an old Wavecaster, hidden away between two closets. An odd place to be sure. "Why don't you have the Wireless in the living room?"

"I don't think it's appropriate for children to be exposed to non-stop commercialism. Not to mention all the slander and gossip that is called news these days. It makes me just want to leave the country. And I want to keep our daughter away from such things as long as I can manage it." Theodore reached for a box on the side table between the chairs and opened it. "Cigar?"

"Don't mind if I do," 321 said as he picked one up. He recognized the watchtower on the cigar label right away. "Ah, Chesapeake Bay. Forget those Cuban cigars. This is where everyone should get their tobacco."

"You know your cigars."

"I better. I grew up on one of their plantations."

Mr. Theodore froze at the statements. "I'm sorry...I-"

321 ignored his muttering, cut off the tip of the cigar, and struck a match. Red embers shone brightly as he inhaled deeply, and the bitter taste of tobacco filled his mouth. After enjoying the aroma, he blew out a thick circular ring of smoke, while the embarrassed host observed him

performing the ritual. "Ah," said the Associate delighted. "Did you know that sweet-scented tobacco has its origins in Chesapeake Bay?"

"Can't say I do," said the man, flustered.

"Yes. For a long time, it was the only place to get it. The demand was such, not only did it fuel the entire colony, but they also needed to import labor to harvest the crop. Growers would pay colonists to cross the Atlantic, only to make them pay it back by working on their plantation. When that didn't suffice, they imported my people."

Theodore just looked at him, still holding the box in his hand.

The Associate lowered his cigar. "I'm sorry, I didn't intend to embarrass you. I don't often get to talk about..." he stopped and changed the topic. "Mind if I ask you a few questions?"

"No, no, please have a seat."

As he sat down, 321 rested the cigar in the ashtray on the table. "You are a Catholic, correct?"

"I am."

"And how long had you and Clara Lantry been together?"

"About three years."

"Why did you divorce her?"

Theodore sighed deeply. "We were happy. However, we had no children. Not for a lack of trying. We looked for a cause, and... We assumed it was me." Theodore paused. Or rather, his mind retreated somewhere. Then his body shivered, like he forced himself back into reality. "Carla convinced me we could fix it. We tried a variety of things... Then it started to dawn on me, it might have been something else. You see, my doctors couldn't find anything wrong with me... So, it might have been... She said that wasn't possible because she had a child, but it had died."

"I had no idea."

"You won't find it in any newspaper, unlike any other detail about her life," Theodore said ominously. "Regardless, I believed her. As I believed most things she used to say."

"You mean, she didn't have a child?"

"She had it aborted," he stated bluntly.

"Because it was out of wedlock?"

Theodore shook his head. "She never admitted that treatment made her infertile. But that is not the reason we parted." Blinking his swollen eyes, he inhaled deeply. "It was the lies," he hissed. "We could have adopted. We cou- No... It wasn't good enough for her. Even when I found out, she insisted she wanted to help me. Insisted that if I only got proper treatment. Lies," he hissed like a snake. "Just more lies!"

At that point, 321 wasn't sure if he was having conversation with a man, or some spiteful spirit residing inside his mind.

"And when she got that deal at Utter-Krapp, she was gone," Theodore concluded.

"Was that the soap commercial?"

Theodore nodded. "I had to send her divorce papers so I could marry my Maggie." He paused. "Still. Even though Clara is out of my life, her venom is still running in my veins."

You don't say, thought 321, but he kept that observation to himself. "What about her involvement with the Signalites?"

He shook his head again. "She uses people and throws them away. She'll stay with those useful idiots until she needs them no longer."

"What do you think she wants from them?"

He thought about it for a moment. "Adulation?" he murmured. "No." His mind seemed to dwell again.

"It must be hard for you to hear her voice through the ether," 321 said to get his attention.

An involuntary smile appeared around Theodore's lips. "Yes," he admitted, glancing at the wireless, tucked away in that far off corner of the room. "I prayed for her. Tried to find it in my heart to forgive her. But I can't," he said, shaking his head mechanically. "I can't forgive her for what she turned me into."

"I see."

"I wish she could just disappear..." Theodore recovered himself. "To finish my answer, I don't know what she is after. All I know is what I heard on the news. She replaced her legs; did you know that?"

"I do."

"I can't be surprised. Her obsession with her appearance goes further than mere vanity. I don't know If I believe the story about the abortion either," he said as if he was thinking aloud.

321 tilted his head. "What makes you say that?"

"One of the reasons we went well together I think, was um... Neither of us enjoyed physical contact that much. But frankly, I think she is repulsed by it."

"You think she..." He struggled to find a decent way to describe the situation.

"The idea of a child growing inside her..." He didn't finish the sentence. His consciousness seemed to be confined to the darkest recesses of his mind now. The place where Lantry left him. How else could he have come up with such dark fantasies - or were they? After all, the woman cut off her own legs to be more like the Signalite's leader- Wait! 321 sat up straight. "How does she feel about leadership?"

"She loves it, as long as she's the one in charge. Why?"

321 rose to his feet. "I think you provided me with enough information. Thank you for your time."

Theodore hesitated. "Before you go, can I ask you a question?"

"Of course."

"How do you do it?" he asked. "How can you stand us?"

The Associate swallowed. He wasn't quite sure himself, or if he should. "I think you Brits are alright," he finally answered. "I served in the royal navy chasing down slave traders on the Atlantic. I don't think it's so much a matter of not being able to stand the white men. In your words, it's about who they turned me into."

Theodore looked down. It was hard to tell what was going through the man's head. Maybe he too struggled to reconcile his feelings with a world that at its foundation seemed unjust.

"Unfortunately," 321 continued. "I don't have a single person to blame. But a system that helped create it together. It's just that, some are more to blame than others."

20TH OF MAY, 8.45 AM, DOVER.

When 321 left his hotel that morning, he felt a strange energy in the air. Upon reaching the front of the police station, it became obvious what happened the night prior.

A boy with rosy cheeks and rough hair was standing on a small cart screaming everyone's ears off. "Extra! Extra! Get the Daily News! Signalite charity lit on fire!" The Associate was cupping his ears as the newsie went on. "Actress Clara Lantry in hospital!"

The Associate reached for some pence in his vest right away. "I'll take that!"

An hour later, 321 was striding past the cells inside the police station. The tapping of his cane on the brick floor reverberated through the barren hall as he walked behind the constable on duty. The gazes of a handful of drunks and prostitutes, sitting idly behind the bars, followed him curiously. Even after all these years, it was an odd experience for him to see whites in captivity.

"So, you actually locked up an inspector," 321 remarked.

"He's an inspector no more, sir. Quite frankly, he has always been an iffy one. Quite a temper. I heard they promoted him so they could keep him behind his desk."

"Is that so?" said the Associate, surprised.

The constable shrugged while checked his keyring.

As the guard was opening the cell door, Associate 321's shadow was cast on the ground beside the prisoner's bunk.

The haggard man was laying lay on his side, peering down his shoulder as the Associate stood there in the door opening. His clothes were dirty and torn, and his face bruised like he had been in a bar fight. No wonder they kept this disgraced officer out of sight.

Taking off his hat, 321 walked in without asking. There was a barred vent in the wall that allowed fresh air to come in, but it still reeking of sweat and mold. The Associate unclasped the bunk on the opposite wall to Ol'Barrow's and guided it down. Groaning, he sat down and leaned on the cane planted between his feet.

The inspector's gaze silently followed the Associate's movement, while lying there like a hangover drunk.

321 sniffed his nose and began. "Well, this was unexpected."

"I have a knack for disappointing people," Ol'Barrow answered dejected. "But you already knew that."

"Are you referring to your career?"

"If you can call it that."

"As I understand it, you were a hero at one point."

"You can't believe the media," he said, and rested his head on his pillow. "Not even then."

The Associate cleared his throat. "So, I've been told... David, I-"

"Are we on a first name basis now?" Ol'Barrow interrupted him, surly.

"As I see it, you are running out of friends, I thought."

"Friends? Don't speak to me about friends."

A few hours earlier...

"Why the hell did you do it?" Chief Inspector Mayfair bellowed, red faced, back inside his Dover office. "Was there anything else you've been doing behind my back I should know about? The bodies aren't even cold yet, and already I have their lawyers crawling up my ass!"

Mayfair's voice seemed to come from two rooms down the hall as Ol'Barrow was fighting to stay awake in the chair during the chief's tirade. He hadn't slept for twenty-four hours, and his mind was drifting between the now and then.

The night before, people fleeing from the fire found him by the wreckage. They assumed it was an accident at first. But upon discovering the homunculi, they were bewildered, as were the police officers who arrived to fight the fire.

Then came the witness statements claiming a man and a girl had fled the building just before the fire was detected.

Ol'Barrow had no proper excuses for being there, so all he could do was proclaim his innocence. But the mysterious events sparked his interrogator's imagination. Not only did they connect him to the fire, but they were convinced he had poisoned Lantry somehow. But on the matter of the Carlstons, whose children were now orphaned, they didn't have an obvious answer. Nor did they know how to handle the dead homunculi, beyond keeping it out of the press.

It didn't matter. Whatever the outcome, it would be a political one. They didn't even care about the strange girl who was missing, nor the man who had gunned down the Nyctolar, as they started to call the homunculi after some French made audio drama about an augmented detective who could see in the dark.

"Do you even care what damage you have done to our reputation?" Mayfair concluded.

Ol'Barrow barely managed to look him in the eye, and replied hoarsely, "I did not light any fires."

"I-don't-care!" Mayfair reiterated every word with another slam on the table. "And neither does anyone else! There were members of the city council present. Everything! Everything indicates it was you, and that girl, that caused all this. Regardless of who lit the match."

"What about the... Nyctolar who attacked us."

Mayfair was pointing out of the window as he looked down on him. "You expect us to go out there, and tell the populace a mechanical freak did this?"

"There are more of them beside the ones you got in the morgue."

Mayfair just looked at him.

"You can't hide it forever, Arthur. You refused to take a stand against the Signalites, so I had to."

Mayfair's eyes bulged in rage. "Are you saying this is my fault?"

What followed was a moment of agonizing silence.

Mayfair tapped his finger on the table. "Your badge."

Ol'Barrow felt a shiver running down his limbs. "Excuse me?"

"Do it, now!"

Ol'Barrow felt an emptiness growing inside him. His fingers barely felt anything as he reached inside his vest and nearly failed to grab hold of the wallet containing his shield. Whatever energy he had left, he had to spend it all to lay it on the desktop.

Mayfair lost patience and grabbed it from his hand.

At that moment, Ol'Barrow felt the chief might as well have taken it from his cold dead fingers. The force had been his life. The one thing that kept him going. What was he going to do now?

Mayfair was fidgeting with the badge as he stared at it. "I should never have let you have this to begin with," he said, holding it to Ol'Barrow's face. "I thought you had changed. Maybe you are right. I only have myself to blame really." He tossed the object in the bin. "Now get out," he warned. "I cannot even entrust my garbage to you."

The former inspector hadn't even closed the office door behind him when he was approached by two of his colleagues.

He sighed. "I am not in the mood, Williams."

"I am sorry, sir," began the chief constable. "But you are under arrest."

Ol'Barrow looked down from the staircase onto the floor for a moment. But everyone was looking away, not even granting him an accusatory glance. He couldn't blame them. How many disgraced officers before him had walked down these steps in shame? To be honest, he should have done the same years ago. Rejected and powerless, Ol'Barrow limply offered them his left arm. "No point in shackling the other wrist."

"...I got a sense that is what happened," responded the Associate. "It appears the borough police don't want anything to do with this case anymore."

"Yes," Ol'Barrow sighed, reminding himself of what Mr. Peal told him. He was a barking dog now, and they wanted to muzzle him so he couldn't tell the world all those uncomfortable truths. Or worse. Confront his fellow peelers about them. How often had he ignored injustices? Like the girl buying bottles of gin, while she should be buying bread. Ol'Barrow felt a waft of shame submerged his mind. What a difference could he have made if he just explained to the girl it didn't have to be this way. Maybe it would have sparked a single act of rebellion against her lot... Maybe. But in the end, it was a fact that he hadn't even tried.

"There is little I can do for you, legally," 321 said. "But I can offer you a way out."

Ol'Barrow looked at him. "I am not looking for a way out," he said. "I want to make those murderous bastards pay. And Igraine... I need to make sure she's all right."

"You will," 321 assured him. "If you become an Associate."

Ol'Barrow's jaw dropped. "Really? Me?" He showed him the stump where his hand used to be. "Look at me."

"It didn't stop you from defeating a Nyctolar."

"Well... Yeah, but..."

321 groaned as he rose to his feet. "Would you join us, Mr. Ol'Barrow?" the Associate asked formally. "And finish what you have started?"

Ol'Barrow didn't need to think about it. "I can't."

321's demeanor changed. "Excuse me?"

"I can't," Ol'Barrow repeated.

"Why not?"

"I just caused a major incident, and you want to take me on? Why?"

"I can't tell you unless you accept."

"No."

There was a moment of silence. "I see," said the Associate. "That's unfortunate."

"Is it? Is it really?"

The Associate released his usual grunt. "I understand your actions did not have the desired outcome," he said. "But we can't live being afraid of the consequences."

"Well, I'll take my chances with this decision."

"So be it." The Associate knocked on the door, and the guard opened up. "I suppose this is goodbye then."

"Yes... goodbye," said the prisoner, and prostrated himself on his bunk.

"Sleep well, Mr. Ol'Barrow."

"I will."

And with that, the door was closed once again.

Ol'Barrow shivered when a chill ran down skin. Was he waking up in his own sweat again?

No. It was worse than that.

When he awoke, Ol'Barrow was shuddering all over on a wet coarse surface, surrounded by nothing but blackness and the freezing cold. There was no sound but the drum of his own erratic heartbeat. His legs were folded up. His quivering hands were stiff and grazed by the icy bed on which he lay. Desperately, he reached out his numb fingers into the darkness, only to find walls in every direction.

It became harder to breathe all the while.

In a panic he raised his feet and kicked upward against the lid. And again. And again, and again, till finally, the top popped loose.

After one final thrust, the cover flew off.

Gasping for air, Ol'Barrow sat up straight. "Thank God!" he cried. Hastily he climbed out of the icebox and proceeded to brush off the ice crystals the best he could. Catching his breath, he attempted to rub himself warm as he looked around in the dark room.

His breathing started to follow a rhythm. The rhythm of a train engine that ran on unaffected by his distress.

He cringed as the high-pitched screech of grinding wheels against the train tracks pierced his ears.

"I'm back on the train?" he concluded out loud. His eyes widened as the realization sank in. "Oh, no. I'm back on the train!" The same train. The same cargo hold in which his father had locked him up. Ol'Barrow's legs felt like rubber as he lost his balance. Leaning on a crate he told himself it was the same dream again. So, there was nothing to be afraid of, really. Right?

Still rubbing his arms, he wandered past the piles of cargo, as he explored the wagon. At the end was a door, surrounded by an ember light, which irradiated a comfortable warmth that made his body thaw just by standing near it. Checking the exit, he discovered it was unlocked, and opened it. The scent of burning coal made his eyes water as he looked straight into the locomotive. In front of the console, in which the oven burnt brightly, a mechanic was shoveling more fuel into the firebox.

The man turned around and took off his goggles.

Only then did Ol'Barrow recognize him. "Mister Wilkins?" The soot on his cheeks was so thick it was hard to make out 321's already dark complexion. "What's going on now?"

The machinist looked at him with confusion as if it should be obvious. "Everything is fine, sir," he reassured him. "We'll reach the next station soon."

"Right... What station would that be?"

"Are you afraid you are on the wrong train?" the mechanist asked sincerely.

Ol'Barrow nodded. "That's one way of putting it."

"I suggest you head back to your cabin. You are not supposed to be here."

Ol'Barrow nodded again. "Also aptly phrased."

Suddenly, the speakers produced an ominous beep. And again, the melody of "Roses in the Rain" started playing, followed by a message. "Next stop. Station Thirteen. Station Thirteen is the next stop."

"Thirteen? Are you serious?"

"Yes, sir," the mechanist answered. "It's the first stop since we departed. Are you all right?"

"Excuse me," Ol'Barrow said. "I need to get off."

A moment later he was back in a passenger car, standing in front of the exit, hoping the train would stop soon, worrying his father would come around again. He slapped himself against the cheek. "This is a dream. Stop it! You know what? Stop dreaming all together."

It did not work.

With a metallic screech, the train gradually came to a standstill, until the engine vocalized a relieving hiss.

The one-armed conductor of last time, Slober, opened the door for Ol'Barrow, and for just him.

As he stood in the door opening, there was nothing but pearly white steam obscuring his view, which made Ol'Barrow wonder if there was a station at all.

"Are you getting off, sir?" the conductor asked, suggestively.

"Sure," Ol'Barrow mumbled. "I wasn't supposed to be on there to begin with." Descending the train steps, he squinted his eyes while moving through the haze of water droplets. Carefully, Ol'Barrow reached out his toes until he touched the ground. Wood cracked as he shifted his weight on the terminal floor, and he advanced a few steps until he cleared the steam. There was but a single ramshackle door in front of him, with a covered-up hole. Ol'Barrow knew the sight all too well, having kicked in a couple of such doors during police raids.

The landlords couldn't help it their tenants were criminals, so instead of replacing doors they patched them up like this.

Ol'Barrow clenched his teeth when the conductor blew his ear-deafening whistle. Then the train started its forward motion, and within moments, it was gone.

Turning his attention back at the door, Ol'Barrow considered there was something oddly familiar about it. When opening it, he revealed the narrow apartment floor. Just a corridor with dusty windows at one side. Doors on the other. This was nothing like the squalid labor-lodgings, but it wasn't far removed. A cold shiver was running down his spine upon realizing he had been here before. He didn't remember a train track running through the hall, though, that bent off underneath an apartment door.

With no other way to go, Ol'Barrow walked up that very door marked with a stamped metal sign, displaying the number 54. So here he was, again. He wasn't sure about that number, but he knew the last time he stood here was about ten years ago.

After some hesitation, he knocked.

There was no response.

Ol'Barrow then reached for the handle and opened it effortlessly. Careful not to trip on the tracks as he walked, he entered the bachelor's apartment.

It was as he remembered it. Dust, dirty dishes and laundry, and a police uniform's coat and top hat lay messily on the chair by the table. Even the stench of a filled chamber pot permeated the air. He recollected it all, except for the rail that ran across the floor.

In front of Ol'Barrow, in the middle of the track, stood a bed. Inside it a lay person wearing a woman's pinkish nightgown.

"Mother?" he cried, dismayed. "Is that you?"

The patient turned around its entire body to face him. His corpse-like complexion and bloodshot eyes made Ol'Barrow take a step back. "Christopher?" So, it was James Christopher after all, just as sick and miserable as the last time Ol'Barrow had seen his colleague alive.

THE EVENING OF SEPTEMBER 14TH, 1857, DOVER.

Ol'Barrow hadn't known Christopher too well. He only learned his name about a week prior when they were temporarily assigned to the same beat. Dover was in the grip of a string of arsons, and people were getting restless.

During one of their nightly patrols there was another fire at the Black Horse tavern, in the shadow of Dover Castle. They were the first at the scene, but the fire inside had already spread through the entire ground floor, and panicking guests were already climbing out of the windows overhead.

People were passing each other buckets of water from the water pump. Not to save the tavern, but to keep the fire from spreading to the nearby buildings.

"Please, has anyone seen Tiffy?" cried the old proprietor. "Has anyone seen our maid?" His cries fell on deaf ears as people were too distracted by the guests trying to jump down into the blankets people were holding up in the street.

The old man grabbed Ol'Barrow by his coat. "Please, sirs. Please look for her."

Ol'Barrow looked inside. One side seemed clear of flames.

"You can't go in," Christopher warned.

"I'll just have a quick look," said Ol'Barrow. "Just in case."

"You'll choke!" Christopher called out to him.

But Ol'Barrow ignored his warnings, threw a bucket of water over himself, and stepped inside. As he stood in the doorway, he could feel his eyebrows singe away in the crimson glow of the flames. "This is the police! Anyone still insi- *Cough*'

The smoke was already getting to him, and tears rolled down his face as his eyes watered fiercely. At that moment, he wanted to evacuate. But then, through the roaring of the fire, he could make out the sound of desperate knocking.

"Help!" Cried a voice over the roaring of the flames.

He located the source of the noise coming from a door, barricaded by collapsed floorboards. It would not take much effort to clear, but because the boards were stuck it was impossible to open the door.

"Help me!"

"I'm coming!"

With a broken beam, Ol'Barrow wedged away the burning debris. But as he did, one of the smoldering boards pivoted in an unexpected direction. Ol'Barrow's eye widened as he saw the burning end of the beam come at him. But it was too late. Desperately he turned his gaze away, so the board landed on the side of his jaw. Terrified, he knocked the beam aside, but the smoldering embers already set his sideburns alight. He felt the embers burn into his skin as he covered his cheeks up to quell the flames. Once done he picked up the pole again. "I'm nearly there," he cried, forcing the last beam aside.

There was no reply.

"Open the door!"

Still no response.

"Come on!" Ol'Barrow coughed as he rushed for the door while embers rained down on him. A cloud of black smoke escaped the room as the woman fell toward him and rested limply against his shoulder. Without giving it any more thought, he dragged her out of there and dashed for the exit, carrying her over his shoulder.

An astounded crowd received them, cheering as he emerged from the smoke. Never had he seen so many people so pleased to see him. Or seen people pleased to see him, period. Not out of uniform at least.

But it was to no avail. Tiffany Carbonkel might have been alive by the time he carried her outside but died before she got to the hospital. She wasn't the only one, but it was her death that wounded him. He hadn't even noticed his facial burns till later.

The scars on Ol'Barrow's cheek were itching when Christopher said, "It didn't matter, Davie. You were a hero that night."

Ol'Barrow noticed a newspaper article pinned to the bedpost. , read the headline. "It was nothing like that," Ol'Barrow hissed. It even included a sketch of a constable running out of the flames carrying the damsel in his arms. Something about that image offended him. Something he couldn't quite explain, but he wanted it to disappear. He pulled the article off the bedpost and tore it in half. "Lies," he hissed like a steam exhaust, while shredding the paper with his quivering hands. "All fuckin' lies!" He kept tearing until nothing but flakes remained. "You knew! What the hell is the matter with you, Christopher?"

The sick man made some unsavory gurgling noise followed by several coughs "You remembered my name," he said short of breath.

"Of course, I have!"

"Of course? Did you know who I was before we were assigned to the same beat?"

"Well, no," he muttered, surprised by the aggressive questions. "No, I suppose I did not. I'm sorry about that."

"You're sorry? No," he said, shaking his head. "You had no reason to know me. Quite frankly, I didn't know you either."

"Yes, that's right. We didn't know each other. That's why I never understood why you did what you did? But it's not-"

"Not important? Then why did you come and see me?"

"To convince you not to take the blame for my actions. To admit to the higher ups it was I who did that to Macarthur."

"No, you didn't," Christopher sneered sneered. "You wanted me to tell you he deserved it. That you did nothing wrong. You didn't even know I was dying before you walked through that door."

"No, but-"

"No buts. This isn't about me. This is about you, and your desire to believe it was his sacrifice that changed you."

"His?"

"You know as well as I know where we are!" Christopher yelled. "I'm wearing your mother's gown, for Pete's sake."

"Y-yes."

Christopher slammed his fist on the mattress. "Dammit it. Now I forgot where I was going. Oh, yeah," he said before continuing. "You haven't changed a bit."

Ol'Barrow puffed his chest. "Yes, I have!"

"No, you haven't. You've been on rails your whole life. It was your father's fault; it was your mother's fault. If anything, if Christopher hadn't kept you on track for a time, your life would have derailed otherwise. Admit it," he sneered. "If you really cared about what you did, you would have resigned."

"But. But if I resigned then..."

"His sacrifice would be for nothing? What exactly did he sacrifice? He was a cop, sure. But did he ever stick his hand into the fire? Did he go above and beyond? No, he was like you. Doing whatever he felt like. Just. Like. You. Sure, he disgraced himself so you could keep your job. It's sad. It really is. He found out he was a shite by the time he was already dying. But then you, for once, stuck your head out. You went inside that burning building, lit by Macarthur. That made Christopher think you cared about those inside. He really did. But we all know what it's really about. It's what nearly got Igraine killed."

"What?"

"And Bigsby... Yeah I'm going in deep mate. It's that thrill you get. Going into the unknown."

"No."

"Ye-es," he sneered. "You're always looking for that next fix, ain't yea?"

"Igraine was my fault, yes. But not Bigsby! How could I have known? How could we have known?"

"Do you realize who you are talking to?" Christopher asked pedantically. "They are never gonna let you go, mate. No matter what path you take, they'll be traveling with you."

"W-what are you saying?"

The ground beneath Ol'Barrow's feet started to tremble. Then there was the blowing of a train whistle in the distance. He turned to face the door. It irradiated an aura, switching between red and green, while the sound of an approaching engine was getting louder and louder.

"Train's here looks like!" cried Christopher. "Are you going to get on?"

"But how do I? I mean-"

"You've always gone in without thinking of the consequences. Why start now?"

"Because... Every time I do. I.... Wait, what about you?"

"Christopher is dead, mate. He made sure you could board the train that was about to hit him."

"But that makes no sense," Ol'Barrow pleaded.

"Life makes no sense. That Lantry woman is right about that. Christopher knew it was about to crush him all those years ago. But he could make it count. Even if it was a futile attempt. Maybe even a mistake. Still, you remember him for what he was,"

The boards beneath Ol'Barrow's feet were trembling, as the train was right outside the door. Objects were falling off the walls and the nails were rising from the floorboards.

"Don't end like him, is all," remarked Christopher a matter of course.

The train came smashing through the door, steaming right at Ol'Barrow who jumped out of the way.

There was a sudden dull crashing sound.

When Ol'Barrow looked over his shoulder, the bed was gone. Just the train that was racing by. Christopher had done it again.

Laying on the ground, Ol'Barrow saw the wheels rushing by. There only seemed one thing he could do now. There didn't seem to be any other way to get out of this place. He had no other reason, just this instinct that he needed to get on. He imagined it could make things worse. But if he didn't- He didn't want to be stuck in this dump for longer than he had to.

The tail end of the train was in sight now. Ol'Barrow got up and raced for the track. It would end here. He jumped up the steps and attached his hook to the railing at the back of the railway car. But he could not keep his balance and clung on for dear life to grating, his feet hanging in the air. The train disappeared into a dark tunnel. There was nothing but a single lamp lighting the rear of the trail while Ol'Barrow tried to pull himself up, while wind and gravity was forcing him off the train. This was real. Very, very real. Something about this made it more real than anything he had experienced before. His hook was the only thing that kept him from slipping away.

The carriage door opened. An obscured figure emerged from the doorway and stood by the railing as if nothing of note was going on as he produced his smoking pipe.

"Uhm, hello," he yelled over the wind .

The figure looked at him. "Oh, hello," the stranger remarked, and continued to light his pipe.

"Excuse me," O'lBarrow insisted.

"Yes?"

"I could use some help."

"Oh," the figure put his pipe away. "Why didn't you just say so," he said, reaching out a hand.

Ol'Barrow hugged the grating as he stretched out his arm and let the stranger reign him in. Out of breath Ol'Barrow crawled up the deck as his heart drummed at the rhythm of the tracks below.

"Tu-tum tu-tum tu-tum"

The white noise of the train wheels reverberated all around Ol'Barrow when suddenly, there was the gnashing of a key being turned inside its lock.

It felt like a ball was being bounced around inside his skull as he awoke in his prison cell.

The light from the hall was blinding him as two men entered, dressed as typical London gentlemen. "Good day, Mr. Ol'Barrow. I am Associate 233. My companion is 411. I think you are already familiar with our organization."

"I already spoke with 321. I have nothing more to say."

"321? Yes, we need to have a word about that. But not here. You are being transferred."

"But why? I want to speak with a lawyer. I know my rights."

"I'm sorry, but when it comes to Rift Related Activity, the normal rules do not apply," the Associate said somewhat gleefully. "Afterwards you can direct your complaints to a Regulator of The International Committee of Rift Related Activity"

"Or 'RA' as most people call it," said 411.

He could barely process what the men were telling him. "And how does this information help me now?"

"It doesn't."

CHAPTER TEN

20TH OF MAY, 1875, 3.05 PM, DOVER POLICE STATION.

Ol'Barrow had been sat down at a table in one of the interrogation rooms. He'd sat at this table with suspects many times before. Of course, then he was the one doing the interrogating.

Two associates with disdainful glares peered down on him. 233 was crossing his arms arms, while 411 held a leather doctor's bag by his side.

"We have some questions about the girl," said 233.

"Well, I don't know where she is," responded Ol'Barrow, bluntly.

"But you know who took her," said 411.

"A masked associate. I don't know who, or where he is either."

411 put the bag on the table. "Mr. Ol'Barrow. Our time is precious, so I suggest you answer our questions."

"What do you have there?" asked Ol'Barrow.

233 walked around the table. "A piece of evidence, we believe it might help you remember," he said while taking position behind him.

Meanwhile, 411 unclasped the lock on the bag and opened slowly, almost ritualistically.

"What do you think you are doing?"

As 411 was reaching inside the bag, 233 leaned in closer "We know exactly what we are doing. But do you fully comprehend the consequences of your actions?"

There was a sudden noise by the door that attracted the Associate's attention.

Without introduction a man stormed in, and he raised his finger into the air. It was Mister Peal dressed in his black and white company suit. He took a deep breath and cried. "I demand to have a word with my client!"

Right away, 411 pressed the bag shut with a caught look on his face.

"Who on earth are you?" asked 233.

"Marcius Peal, attorney at law, this man's attorney, to be exact. And I know this man is innocent! I know because I was with him that very moment the fire was lit."

233 was grasping his throat as he stuck his hands inside his pockets. "Mr. Peal, you have the wrong idea. This has nothing to do with the fire-"

"Irrelevant. This man should have his lawyer present. I was given permission by the chief inspector himself."

"I appreciate your candor, sir. But our investigations are on a need-to-know basis."

"I am his representative," Peals interrupted again. "It is my job to know. Or maybe I should call my acquaintances at RA and ask their opinion on these unlawful proceedings."

The two Associates looked at each other. "Again, this is not a criminal investigation."

"Is that so? What's in the bag?" Peals asked suspiciously.

"Just some evidence we wanted to show to the eyewitness. I'm afraid-"

"Need to know," he said, nodding sarcastically. "I get it. In that case I demand to have a word-"

"That will have to wait, but I'm afraid we can't continue until you vacate the room."

"I'm not leaving till I've spoken with my client," Peal protested.

The suitcase suddenly moved, like a rodent was crawling around beneath the heavy leather.

"That is some kind of evidence you have there," sneered Peal.

"Its contents are not meant to be seen by Utter-Krapp employees!" said 411, about to carry away the bag. The moment, however, he attempted to lift the luggage, it shook violently as if in protest. Leaving the item on the counter, 411 took his distance as if for a angry dog.

The men watched in anticipation as the bag was seesawing on the desk's edge.

Ol'Barrow got of his chair. “What's in the bag?” he asked with increasing concern.

Everyone jumped back when the doctor's bag toppled down the ledge, and landed with a muffled thud on the floorboards.

The men held their breath as the bag was shifted by what sounded like a beeswarm trapped inside. Then there was the humming of an electric drill and the shredding leather. Within moments, a rotating awl emerged from the side. Before Ol'Barrow could make sense of the situation, a coppery snake-thing slithered out through the hole. The alien looking automaton crawled around on the floorboards, seemingly in anger, while buzzing like a wound-up toy. Around its serpentine body were fins, making it look like a fish swimming in circles, be it at remarkable speed. Ol'Barrow immediately concluded it was a C-33. Or at least, that was the only thing that made sense to him.

The thing kept slithering around from one corner to the other, crawling between the men's feet as they jumped around like squeamish maids. Finally, it stopped in the middle of the room, curled up into a spiral and raised its drill-shaped head like a cobra. The blade-like appendages shimmered as they spread out, buzzing threateningly like large insect wings, and the conical drill unfolded into four pincer-like jaws. It observed Peal for a moment, before swinging its head in the direction of the next person. The automaton continued measuring up ever man in the room, until it noticed Ol'Barrow. The C-33 paused. Then, it pressed its head against the floor and dashed toward the former inspector.

In a panic, Ol'Barrow climbed on the table as the machine came at him. He looked down from a top the counter as it slithered beneath the chair. It did not help that the thing's carapace gleamed like that of a cockroach, as it peered up at him from underneath the furniture. Wrapping its serpentine body around the paw, it scaled the chair with ease, forcing the inspector back on the floor.

Ol’Barrow swung around as the door behind him opened. “What is bloody going on?” cried the constable, who leaned with his head through the door frame.

233 gestured him to stay away. “Close the door!”

But Ol'Barrow made a dash for the exit. “No, let me through!”

Caught off guard, the officer toppled over as Ol’Barrow forced him aside, followed by the two Associates in his wake. “Stop! Stop them,” yelled the constable, as Ol'Barrow ran down the hall. Behind him, he heard the buzzing of the snake-thing closing the distance. Running ran past the corner, he spotted the janitor mopping the floor. Realizing he could not outrun the damn thing forever, Ol'Barrow yelled at the janitor, "Give me that mop!" Alarmed, the clueless janitor held out the shaft. Still running at full velocity, Ol'Barrow grabbed hold of it, tumbling to the floor as he did. Sliding across the slippery surface on his ass, armed with nothing but a wet cleaning implement, he saw the C-33 slithering toward him at great speed. Clenching the shaft under his arm, Ol'Barrow aligned the end of the mop like a jousting knight of old, while the drone was strafing from left to right as it was coming closer and closer.

Once in range, the automaton lunged at him through the air.

Seeing the drill come toward his face, Ol'Barrow closed his eyes, and swayed the mop to his right. The creature produced a high-pitched buzz as its drill got entangled within the strands of the mop. Surprised he caught it, Ol'Barrow struggled to hold on to the pole as the machine jerked its tail around. But with its head thoroughly entwined, spun its serpentine body around its own axis while lashing its tail on the floorboards.

"Can somebody get me a bucket!"

20TH OF MAY, 1875, 3.25 PM, DOVER,

321 was enjoying a cup of coffee across the street of the police station as he listened to the music playing over the speakers. One of the things he came to appreciate most in England were the store's wavecasters playing his favorite music, not caring if he had heard them all a thousand times before.

Thinking of the other day, the Associate he still felt rejected. He was fairly sure Ol'Barrow dismissal of the offer hadn't been personal. Maybe he had been wrong about the inspector. Or maybe... Maybe his own intentions weren't as pure as 321 had made himself believe.

As in a daze he sang along. "And every day I would look by the tree to see you there..."

"You like that song, sailor?" A young lady stood beside him. Her skirt was a tad too high and her bust too low. "What brings you here, sailor?"

"My sailing days are behind me, madame."

"Merchant ships?"

"A fishing boat for a while. But mostly the navy."

"American Navy?"

"And the West Africa squadron," he added.

Her eyes grew larger. "Really? The anti-slavery patrols?"

"Yes."

"I met some of you before. They say it is extremely dangerous."

"Highest attrition rate in the Royal Navy," he boasted. But the fact of the matter was most had died of malaria and other diseases that plagued the African coast. Catching slave traders was a glorious cause, but those in service perished in the most inglorious ways.

"Then why risk it?"

"Catharsis, I suppose."

"What do you mean?" She asked, puzzled. "You were a slave?"

"I still have the scars on my back, madame."

Her soft palm caressed his hand as she looked at him. "I don't mind," she said. "I can make you forget about them for a while."

She is good, he thought with contradictory emotions. Soliciting adventuresses was anything new for him. But the best know how to tear open the wounds and then promise to mend them. 321 began to laugh.

"What's so funny?" she asked, caught off guard by his behavior.

"I appreciate the offer but I'm afraid I can't."

There was sudden unrest in front of the police station across the street. For some reason, constables were sending people out of the precinct in a hurry, including the administrative personel.

"What's that?"

"Duty calling," said 321.

The moment the Associate emerged from the café; a sergeant approached him. "Oh, sir. I am so glad to see you. We need your help right away." The sergeant requested the Associate to follow him inside, and led him up to the double staircase.

The puzzled Associate heard shouting from upstairs, and suddenly a lashing sound cut through the turmoil like the cracking of a whip. There it was again. The lashing pierced the dark corners of 321's mind, dredging up the memories of lashing he received. And those whippings he witnessed on either side of the Pacific.

"You alright, sir?" asked the sergeant. "They said they have it under control."

"Forget it," he muttered. "I'll find it from here, sergeant." 321 then walked up to the first floor, where a hallway was congested by a crowd of onlookers. It was an uncanny sight for him to see white men in uniform watching the spectacle, while the snapping sound of lashes cut through the excited cries. 321 forced his way through the group of unnerved constables and saw David Ol'Barrow holding down a serpentine creature inside a bucket, with the mop.

Dark soapy water splashed on the two nervous constables who held the bucket in place while the machine thrashed about like a trapped eel. "Why won't it stop?" complained one after evading another lash of its tail-end.

Ol'Barrow didn't respond, as he was too focused on his new nemesis. It didn't even seem to occur to the man he was fighting a monster with a cleaning implement. Neither did he notice Associate 321, looking at the officer's attempt to drown the robot.

Ol'Barrow looked at 321 and grinned in that involuntary, boyish way of his. "Oh, Associate. We wondered where you were."

Ignoring the question, the Associate stepped up, advancing his cane. Without taking his eyes off the C-33, he detached the top of the cap stick and, to everyone's dismay, unsheathed a baton that was concealed inside the shaft.

With a rising pitch, the baton activated, sending faint blue sparks running down its rod.

"Let go of the bucket," 321 warned. The moment the constables backed off, 321 jabbed the prod into the vessel. Violent shocks cracked, and sparks flew as the machine thrashed about even more erratically. It wouldn't last. When the fiendish device had finally stopped moving, the Associate reached in with his hand and lifted the C-33 that was curled up in an awkward posture like a dead snake.

Some of the men backed off when they saw the thing in his grasp. A worrying sight, to see Dover's finest recoil from a small thing like this. But then he realized the men policed by consent and didn't carry weapons apart from an occasional baton. A principle that lay at the foundation of their work. A principle they had to abandon if they were to fight this threat.

321 handed the defunct C-33 over to a constable. "There you go, officers. I regret to say you might encounter more of these."

Nodding, the officer looked at the thing as if he was holding a week-old cadaver. Was it a reluctant confirmation of 321's concerns? He wasn't sure. He knew the Dover police were in no state to deal with this threat. But, for that matter, neither was anyone else.

The atmosphere within Dover's police station had changed in a short couple of hours. The incident of a worm attacking a former inspector greatly upset the constables, and emotions ran high. Many already talked about the need to arm themselves. And then old rumors of monsters and other strange sightings were brought up. Most still believed these witness accounts were hyperbolic. However, such claims now held credibility, where previously there was none.

That mattered not to David Ol'Barrow, however. Nothing mattered. He was just looking at the toes of his shoes, which were in dire need of a polish. He had made a feeble attempt to wrap his mind around all these past events. Even though he defeated an outsider, he didn't feel any sense of triumph. Rather a sensation of fatalism. That continued struggle was pointless, and the department was powerless against a creature that fit inside a doctor's bag.

Meanwhile, his self-appointed attorney, Mr. Peal, just ended his legal rant against the chief inspector that had lasted for... Ol'Barrow had lost track of the conversation a couple of seconds in. "Therefore, his actions were in self-defense," insisted Peal. "And holding my client in for arrest could be considered-"

Mayfair slammed his fists on the desk. "Enough!"

"Excuse me?"

Mayfair got up from his chair and took a deep breath. "I'll release Mr. Ol'Barrow," he announced as politely, and subdued, as possible. "For the time being. Now, please. Get out of my office."

"Well, my job here is done," Peal announced. "For now. We'll be in touch, Mr. Ol'Barrow."

Ol'Barrow shrugged. "Thanks?"

Mr. Peal folded his hand into the shape of a pistol. "Tsk. Don't mention it."

When Mr. Peal closed the door behind him, there was a moment of awkward silence in the office.

321 straightened himself and cleared his throat. "I suppose, I should congratulate you for stopping a hostile infiltration."

"Uh-huh," grumbled Mayflower.

"Those C-33's are no laughing matter."

"Um-huh."

"It confirms some suspicions we had for a time now. Those associates, who are some of the Signal's followers, have abused their authority."

"Hm-hm."

"And when we confirmed this connection, we can investigate the Signalite's cult for being involved in unauthorized rift related activity. Maybe we finally can get their Perfect to talk. This is a major breakthrough, Chief Inspector," he announced, encouragingly.

"Yes-s," Mayfair growled, displeased.

"Of course, the attack on your station is a separate charge that needs to be investigated. By your department."

Mayfair slammed his hand on the desk. "Yes, fine! I get it. I must take on some of the most influential people in the county. Starting with the commissioner himself."

"Did somebody call?" said a deep voice from behind the glass.

The chief inspector was sweating bullets when the door opened. It was Commissioner Chandler, in dress uniform. "By Jove man, I could hear you on top of the stairs." His face was already red with frustration.

"S-sorry, sir," muttered Mayfair.

"Sit down." The commissioner turned to the Associate. "You must be 321 I heard so much about."

"Yes, sir."

He gave Ol'Barrow a peculiar look, but without acknowledging him and went straight on with vocalizing his displeasure to Mayfair. "I was looking forward to a peaceful week with the grandchildren for the first time in a year," he started, "Instead, I am dealing with stolen bodies, killed cops, burned mansions, murdered aristocrats and an assault on my station!" He pulled his jacket straight. "Dover ain't what it used to be… You, Associate. What does your Chair expect to do about this?"

"Why, commissioner. The Chair won't do anything unless the city of Dover would request measured escalation of the Association's operations."

"Measured escalation?" repeated the commissioner. "You have your headquarters in the city, and you need to escalate?"

"They what ?" asked Mayfair and Ol'Barrow in sync.

"Shut up, both of you," he snapped. "Tell me you have absolute proof these traitors were working for the Signalites."

"We can provide it tomorrow. I would suggest you arrange a meeting with the council in the meantime. And if you have some way for me to get in contact with their leadership, that would be greatly appreciated."

Ol'Barrow and Mayfair were holding their breath, as the commissioner nodded while grinding his teeth. "You better," he growled softly. "I'll also contact the garrison at Dover castle," he announced.

"With all due respect, Commissioner," responded, 321. "I do not object to putting the garrison on standby. But be careful. Based on recent events our suspects are behaving erratically. Military presence might provoke them to do, something rash."

Commissioner Chandler paused. "I'll consider it," he said and addressed the room. "Find me that evidence." And with that he left.

The men in office waited till the Commissioner was out of sight.

"What did you just agree to?" groaned Mayfair. "You are putting the reputation of this department on the line, you know that?."

"That is the idea," answered 321 bluntly.

"But we have the proof," remarked Ol'Barrow. "There is nothing to worry about."

"No," corrected 321. "We have two Lost Numbers who could have recovered that C-33 from anywhere. They could be working for Jenever, for all the council cares. And considering how uncooperative those bureaucrats have been up till now, we either need the Lost Numbers, or other concrete proof."

"But they-" Ol'Barrow conceded his point.

After Mayfair rubbed his eyes, he crossed his arms. "Fine then. I'll ask the chief constable to get everyone on active duty."

"All right, but what about Igraine?" asked Ol'Barrow. "They are hunting her too."

"I'm afraid she'll have to wait, inspect- Sir," 321 corrected himself. "I'll be outside. Don't be long now."

The moment 321 shut the door behind him, the temperature seemed to drop.

Ol'Barrow looked at the floor to avoid Mayfair's gaze. "So..."

"I cannot reinstate you," Mayfair stated.

"Well, that's not, ehm-," David muttered. He wasn't even sure what he wanted to say. Finally, he managed to bring up the question. "Why did you let Peal in?"

"Why do you think?" said Mayfair. "You saw how he was talking my ears off. And I didn't see the harm."

"That's it?" Ol'Barrow exclaimed.

"Alright, I didn't trust those Associates either."

Unsatisfied with the answer, Ol'Barrow nodded regardless. "Fair enough, I suppose... You do realize I am not going to stop my investigation."

"That's what I am counting on. You are a bloodhound like that."

Ol'Barrow grinned involuntarily. "Funny. Somebody mentioned that to me a day ago." His smile disappeared quickly when a thought occurred to him. "Oh, dear, the dog."

"What dog?"

"I need to go home," said Ol'Barrow heading for the door. "Good talk."

"Don't think this is over!" Mayfair yelled as Ol'Barrow walked out. But Ol'Barrow didn't care about any of that at this point. He just wanted to go home. Unfortunately, when he closed the door behind him, 321 and Peal were waiting on the half landing. "What is this about?" he asked.

"Well," Peal beg an, as if he were about to hand him a bill. "I managed to set you free for now. But the charges have not been dropped."

"You think I care about any of that right now?"

"The Dover police will treat you as a flight risk," Peal warned.

Ol'Barrow lowered his shoulders. "Ah, bloody hell."

"Consider the constables watching your house as personal security," said Peal. "Worked for me in the past."

"He has a point there," said 321.

Ol'Barrow nodded. "So. You really believe the Signalites are- "

"Allegedly," interrupted Mr. Peal.

"To answer your question. Yes, I do believe it was them. But do I think they are interested in controlling your mind for the sake of some grand scheme? No. They were aware you were dismissed."

"So, this was just for revenge?" Ol'Barrow concluded. "If Macarthur is involved that makes sense... Well, with that cleared up, I'm going home."

Before he got a chance to walk away, 321 called out to him. "Before you go!" Reluctantly, Ol'Barrow turned to face 321 who gave him a sincere look. "Have you reconsidered my offer?" the Associate asked.

"Is this some type of recruitment tactic?" asked Ol'Barrow cynically.

"Did it work?"

Ol'Barrow gave him an accusing glare. "I want to discuss the terms and conditions first. But I have other things to do now."

"So, do I." 321 sighed as if he were about to take on a great burden. "There might be a man who can help me track down 411 and 233. If he doesn't kill me."

"Why would he do that?"

"Well... In the eyes of some, I might be considered to be a Lost Number myself."

Ol'Barrow gave him a glassy look. "Oh-kaay."

"Go home. Take a bath," 321 insisted. "You reek of sewage."

"That must be the mud... I'll be going now."

"Yes, enjoy your afternoon off," said 321 nodding.

"I'm serious."

"I know."

"So-"

"Just, go man!"

20TH OF MAY, 1875, 5.45 PM. OL'BARROW'S HOME, DOVER.

The rain was gone, and the air was smelling unusually clean with a hint of tree blossom.

Ol'Barrow's swollen joints had eased up somewhat when he got home, and he was looking forward to some time for himself. He just hoped the dog hadn't wrecked his house in the meantime, accepting the poor thing had most likely polluted the floor.

The moment he opened the door there was a loud bark, followed by the three paws running toward him. "Hello... You?" he said, but to his surprise the dog ran past him, through the door and stopped right outside. There it looked around, seemingly in confusion while squealing unhappily.

He sighed. "Sorry, boy... She is not here."

The animal just looked at him with a sad look in its eyes.

Ms. Appletree emerged from the living room. "Where have you two been? Where is Iggy?"

Completely unprepared for this encounter, all he could mutter was. "Oh. Well..."

"Don't tell me you lost her," she asked, half-jokingly." And why do you look like you rolled off the staircase and back again?"

"Diane, this might not be-"

"You lost her?" she blurted out.

"No... She is back with her family," he lied.

"Oh, don't think I believe that story for a moment. You really think I am that thick?"

"It's none of your business, alright?" he said sternly, and walked to the kitchen.

"You made her my business, remember? You asked me to watch her."

"You could have said no," he protested, as he started to wash his hands.

"Oh, listen to you. Mister, I can do it all by myself. Look at you! You are a wreck! She's a lot like you, you know that? Fixing your house in that condition. You both need serious help."

"She's back with the people who..." He wasn't sure how to describe their relationship and finally settled on. "Foster family."

"Really? What happened to Edward's cousin? Or whatever it was."

"It's none of your concern, alright?"

"Then why do you lie to me?" she snapped. Her shrill voice pierced his eardrums, prodding his brain like a hot poker.

"It's just my way of saying she'll be fine! Alright!"

"You don't believe that."

He threw up his hand in frustration "Will you stay out of it, woman! I'll resolve this. Just, leave me be!"

"If you send me out that door, I am never coming back!" she said, resolute.

He spread his arms wide. "Well, what are you waiting for?"

"Fine!" she said, stamping her foot.

"Fine," he called after as he watched her walking away in a huff.

She was about to grab the door handle when he reached out to her. "Wait!"

She had already opened the door. "What?"

"I'm sorry."

Tilting her head , she answered sneering. "Hm?"

"I'm sorry... Please, don't go."

"What for?"

"I-" He sighed. "It has been hell the past few weeks... I know… I might end up working something like the night shift at the train station."

20TH OF MAY, 1875, 7.05 PM, PROMENADE, DOVER.

The streets emptied as night approached. The scent of fish drifted on the sea breeze when Associate 321 walked down a backstreet, not far away from the city's promenade. Music from the restaurants reverberated through the alley while groups of intoxicated sailors wandered the streets. After some searching, he finally found the White Tower pub. A refuge for many wary sailors, eager to feel the ground under their feet again and, most importantly, get drunk.

As he walked in, the murmuring chorus of deep voices, and eye watering scent of tobacco reminded him of his navy days. In particular the many visits to the bars and gambling dens of the African ports. Walking by various tables, he heard Polish, Spanish, even some Dutch. Places like this were ideal for anyone who didn't want to stand out - Someone just like the man 321 spotted by the billiards table.

A red-haired man, wearing green pants and matching waistcoat, leaned over the table with a cover worn thin in places. From beneath a pronounced brow ridge, he peered over his cue like a marksman aiming down his barrel as if he were studying the ball for any sign of weakness. His thick arms were going back and forth, taking his time aligning the tip. Then, he took the shot. The white cue ball collided with a red one, scattering it seemingly at random across the bed. Score-wise the shot hadn't achieved much, but the grumbling of his opponents at the impossible angles between their targets, brought a smile to the tall man's face as he observed them.

321 didn't doubt for a moment that the man with massive arms was the one he was looking for.

As the tall man moved away from the other players to chalk his cue, 321 approached looking him straight in the eyes. “Good evening, sir. Do you happen to be the gentleman who goes by the name, Mr. Lotto?”

The man turned his head with a crooked grin around his lips. “Depends on who's asking,” he answered with an Irish accent.

“Did you kill a man named Jack Eisenberg?”

He frowned to feign insult. “That's a bit of a straightforward question.”

“Number 45.” 321 continued relentlessly and awaited the assassin's reaction. As expected, glancing around the room the Irishman licked his lips. “Well, if you know his number... Why you wanna know?”

“Did you interrogate him?”

“No mate. My job was to dispose of him.”

"The police found his body frozen in a container, at the local train station.

Lotto nodded with a smirk on his face as if he were very pleased with himself.

"So, what inclined you to break his leg?"

"He did that himself," answered Lotto, coldly. "Idiot broke the chair he was sitting on in his futile attempt to liberate himself."

"What had he done?"

"They guy was a terrorist. He was one of the people who drowned the town of Saint Augustine back in Spain a few months back."

"Well, that answered that question. But I know there is more to this. What was his relation to S-36?"

Mr. Lotto turned away as if insulted. "Oh, for Pete's sake."

"It's important! I need to figure out what she is after."

Leaning on his cue, Lotto blew out a long puff of air from between his puckered lips as he looked at the floor. "Many years ago, Eisenberg, 45, tried to solve a murder of a retired Associate. 115." Lotto stopped and shrugged his shoulders. "Listen, it's a long story."

"Tell it anyway," insisted 321.

"I'm in the middle of a game."

321 pulled out one of the cigars. "I brought some refreshments."

His eyes lit up. "Brightleaf cigars?"

His observation brought a smile to 321's face. "A man of culture, I see."

"I get around." Lotto said, and rubbed to roll under his nose as he took a deep hiff. "Ha… Fine then. Get yourself a drink."

THE DISCIPLES OF DISCONTENT

Spring 1875, somewhere in France.

Moonlight shone down through a hole in the barn roof when the man awoke to find himself blinded and restrained. His senses struggled to adjust to the dim light that shone through the burlap and the faint smell of mold that it irradiated. As feeling returned to his body, he noticed the restraints around his wrists that were tied behind the backrest. Confusion turned quickly to panic when he realized his ankles were bound to the chair legs, and he started to jerk his body in a futile attempt to pull himself free. Wood creaked as the chair moved from its place, but his restraints refused to budge. He must have shoved the chair full circle when one of the legs succumbed under the strain. As it snapped, he keeled forward, landing on one knee while the cleft of the same leg got caught between the floor and the seat carrying the brunt of his weight.

It happened to be his bad leg. A rupturing sound was rippling down his cleft as if something got hold of the muscle and snapped it like a twig.

Screaming, he attempted to lay on his back, but his bond with the chair prevented him from finding relief from his torment. Laying there whimpering, he heard a door open.

"For Pete's sake, can't they make chairs like they used to?" a man complained, with a growling Irish accent.

"Who's there?"

Untouched by his suffering, the stranger's steps came closer. Groaning, his captor pulled him up and replaced the missing chair leg with a crate to support the weight.

Once the prisoner was vertical, he addressed the Irishman. "Who are you? What am I doing here?"

The Irish man was occupying himself with other tasks as he responded. "We know damn well what yea are doing here, mate," he replied absentmindedly.

"Who are you?"

"I go by many names. But you may have heard of Mr. Lotto."

The prisoner, recognizing the name, was stunned.

"That's right. I am here to say yea your number is up, 45."

"Do you know who you are working for?" The prisoner asked, aware of the danger he was in. "What they have d-"

"Oh, come on! Always with the what about-ism," he complained indignantly. "I am not here to judge yae, mate. That verdict has been passed years ago."

"They are in no position to judge me! Listen! They set Aqrabua free!" his prisoner pleaded.

"Ai." Mr. Lotto took his time before he continued. "I have 9's number as well. I just never got to meet him. But you have, didn't yea?"

"Yes..."
"How did ya meet?"
"I found him. Found him on Plane 22."
There was a moment of awkward silence till the Irishmen responded, "Go on."
45 sighed, considering what would be the best place to start. "It must have been October of 1863 when I visited a former Associate to find out what he knew about a certain Construct. C33-1..."

He lived in one of those guild-run rural communities that produced apple juice, of all things. He was a stubby man, not all that happy to be visited by strangers. The least of all Associates. But he allowed me into his cottage. A bachelor's home, with clothes hanging to dry in the middle of the room and empty cider bottles on the table.
"Ask away, but make it quick," he said, uncorking a fresh bottle.
I asked him if he heard of Associate 115.
"I might have," he answered, sitting down with one foot on the tabletop.
"She retired a number of years ago. Since then, she seemed to have lived as a homemaker near Madrid. Two children."
"How nice for her."
"They are all dead," I told him bluntly and observed him in anticipation of a response.
He adjusted his position in the chair. "That's terrible."
"They were murdered. No," I corrected myself. "Butchered."
"Well, that's even worse. Not sure why you have come all the way to tell me so."
"You were on an expedition to Plane 22 with Associates 9, 54, and 115. That happened nine years ago."
"Can't say I recall, mate. I am horrible with numbers."
"How about Construct 331."
His eyes flinched. "What about it?'
"According to the files I retrieved from the Association's Library, your expedition attempted to track the origins of a number of parasitic constructs, did you not? Automata, to be specific."
A forced smile appeared on his face. "Oh, I think I am starting to remember now. Yeah, we tracked down a bunch of them to someplace in France. An instance of C- I don't remember the number. Snake like-things that like to drill inside people's spines."

"C-33," I said to jock his memory. "They enjoy going after people active in mass production companies."
"Yeah, they had targeted some young industrial town in Southern France. We dealt with it."
"How?" I asked.
He sighed. "We found the infected and let the authorities handle it. The usual."
"What about Rift 22?"
He hesitated. "Yeah... Yeah, we found it. But we aborted the expedition after one of those things caught 9. A Fascinator jumped on his head. They're smarter than they look."
I shook my head in ignorance. "Fascinators?"
"Yeah, C-44. Look like walking hats. Jump on top of somebody's head and just turn them into some mindless automaton. A terrible fate, I can tell ya that much."
"You left him behind?"
He smiled like a simpleton. "Ha! There wasn't much choice."
"Hmm." I reached into my pocket and produced an old telegram I recovered in the Association's archive and proceeded to read its contents. 'This is the last message I sent - I must return. Found a way to triangulate the signal. If the source is correct, this will sever them from the control unit. Instructions follow." I looked at him. "What did he mean by that?"
The former Associate stared back at me with dim eyes. "Tell me, mate. Does the Chair know you are here?"
Now I hesitated. I couldn't admit I wasn't authorized. And it was obvious at that point I wouldn't get any useful information out of him. So, I thanked the man for his time and left without learning anything new, just confirming certain assumptions of mine.

My personal investigation started two months prior, during my stay in Madrid. While visiting the local lodge, I was informed of a horrible murder of a family, a husband and wife and their two children. It was remarkably savage, which made police suspect Outsiders were involved. But it wasn't the apparent horror of the case that made it stand out to me. It was the fact it was an isolated incident. It didn't set off alarm bells until a fellow at the lodge from Madrid admitted the mother was a former associate.
The woman in question had retired from the cause years ago, and there didn't seem to be a motive for murder. For all intents and purposes, it seemed random. But that answer didn't satisfy me. Something about this event worried me, and I feared more associates might be in danger. Throwing

myself into the case, I investigated her past activities as Associate 115. She had been very active during her time. Her final expeditions involved several Associates: 9, 54, and 61. 54 had already deceased: A suicide. 61 was the gentleman at the apple farm. And the frontman of this group, Associate 9, had disappeared. I mean, he had vanished from the records, all together. I discovered this when I requested information at the Association's central library. But all I got were some old telegrams from which I managed to decipher Associate 9's final destination: Rift 22.

I found this unacceptable, however, and addressed the error to the library's clerk. An odd red bearded man wearing a top hat with a stovepipe sticking from the side, indoors. As a matter of fact, his whole right side had been heavily augmented, including the eye, arm, and leg. And the Bone-saws had done a terrible job of it, as he moved around like a cripple, throwing the weight of his prosthetics around with every step. But when he stood still, he irradiated a sense of dignity about him that seemed inconsistent with his motions.

"I am sorry," he answered bluntly with a deep voice. "But these entries do not exist,"

I pressed my finger on the paper. "But these are noted right here!"

"Maybe these were reported by Associates but never deposited," he retorted. "The old guard wasn't very keen on the paperwork, you see. These days we have envoys to collect the files from the various lodges, but not then."

"And these files have not been retrieved since?"

"That's the problem with acting too late. Done damage is done, sir."

"All right... Who was supposed to 'deposit' these files?"

He slowly lowered his gaze down at the register. "Associate 9... Of course, this is an old record. The gentlemen could have retired since then."

I started to lose patience with him. "How about this?" I said. "Deliver me all the entries regarding Associate 9 from... two years before and two years after this item was filed."

His left eye stared at me from beneath the ridge of his thick brow to emphasize his displeasure. "That will take time," he growled. "Come back tomorrow."

So, I did, and once the files were provided, I searched the documents for any valuable entries. But Associate 9 seemed to have disappeared from the face of the Earth. No reference to him retiring from the Association or going missing. Just cases that he had worked on before and some correspondence. There was a theme in his work. He had a keen interest in automatons. In particular, C-33 and C-44, which he believed were related to each other and suggested a force was creating unwilling sleeper agents through parasitic machines. He referred to these agents as Nyctolope. It had something to do with an odd glow in their eyes that could be seen under certain low-light conditions.

Then, I encountered an obscure reference. Construct-331. I searched the pile for the entry with this number but could not find it. Realizing it was missing, I looked in the librarian's direction. At that moment, he glanced back at me. Abruptly he staved off his gaze, pretending to be distracted by a piece of paper. Feigning ignorance as well, I turned to the files in front of me. Despite sensing all this paper was but a distraction, one entry caught my eye—a telegram containing Associate 9's final message.

"I must return. Found a way to triangulate the signal. If the source is correct, this will sever them from the control unit. Instructions follow."

Of course, as far as the archive was concerned, these instructions never arrived.

A week after I visited (former) Associate 61 at the apple farm, I arrived in the French town that Associate 9 had visited last. A planned city in which every street, building, and lamp post had been predetermined. The settlement had been a reformer's dream to house the labor population of the then-new factories. But by then, it had become another failed community in the country's south. The remaining working-class families lived in dilapidated tenements on either side of the narrow streets. On my way to the police station, the odor of stale garbage drifted on the dank autumn breeze as I walked past the boarded-up shop fronts. I had seen no young or healthy men or women. Just the poor and destitute. Parentless children running amok. Elderly, too worn out to walk straight. And a housewife sitting beside a pile of empty bottles, undoubtedly waiting for a check from her husband, who worked half across the country.

A statue in the city square was maimed to a point only the torso and legs remained, postured like that of a military officer in the prime of his life. What little splendor the city possessed had faded away or was painted over with cries for revolution or denunciations of society at large. In front of the police station, a bust of a man in uniform was smashed. Some pieces of its face still lay neglected at the feet of the sepulcher. It didn't make sense to me. They had all the opportunity to make something of this place. Yet, it appeared they rather reveled in misanthropy.

Inside the police station's reception area, an older man in an antiquated gendarmerie uniform sat at the desk. Another one leaned backward in a chair; his legs prostrated on top of a table as he slept.

The officer looked up, surprised to see me, and greeted me with a hoarse voice. "Can I help you?"

"Bonjour, I need information regarding an incident that occurred nine years ago."

Straightening himself, he looked me up and down in suspicion. "Are you a journalist?"

"Non. But I am an investigator. It might be related to a recent murder of a family in Spain."

"Mon Dieu!"

I showed him a picture of Associate 115 from a few years prior, after the birth of her second child.

The old gendarme nodded. "Oui, she was here when..." He stopped as his mind seemingly drifted away.

"When, what?"

Embarrassed, he replied, "Strange things were happening at the factories. Some workers had been murdered. Then... The Maltoux family was killed. They owned most of the factories here. It was the youngest son. He lost his mind. It is suspected he was responsible for the other murders as well."

"Then he took his own life, didn't he?"

He nodded with watery eyes. "Oui. Shoved his head between the spokes of the watermill."

As was typical of individuals infected with C-33; they destroy their own heads. "That is when she came?" I asked.

"Yes. Paranormal investigators, they called themselves." He was smiling ironically. "It all started when they uncovered that ancient burial site about a month before the murders."

Paranormal investigators. The statement would have made me laugh under other circumstances. Obviously, it had been a cover, but not that far from the truth either. Even funnier was that they confused an automaton with an evil spirit. But I could appreciate the metaphor.

"Merde!" he cried as he slammed his fist on the desk. "The mayor had told them to bury that thing! But it would be good for tourism, they said."

"The burial site?"

"Oui! They discovered it when they were constructing a new factory building. The town was doing great back then. But once the Dolmen got revealed, it was all over. The Maltoux family had visited the site when the entrance was cleared. But once inside, they left the basement in a huff. They had seen something inside. And the son, Frederique. He had never been the same since. He started acting odd. Reclused in the manor. And if he left their estate, he was always at the factory..."

"I need to see this burial site, monsieur ."
"Monsieur. You should leave this place. It has driven this town mad, haven't you seen it?"
"Exactly. That is why you need to point me there right away."

Walking by the roofless factory walls of the construction site was an odd experience. But this was the location of the Neolithic dolmen that I was looking for. At the edge of town, the ancient relic sat there at the bottom of the grass-covered trench, surrounded by crumbling brickwork. It seemed rather idyllic despite the decay. But when I descended, my suspicions were once again confirmed. The chamber underneath the massive stone slabs was supposed to be sealed by a metal door. Unfortunately, it was forced out of its hinges, its padlock still hanging off the door bolt. Whatever had done this had been powerful enough to break the entrance open with such force it had shattered the stone holding the door in place.

Lantern in hand, I went down the stairwell into the ancient structure. Descending the slate steps, I realized this tomb was larger than the exterior suggested. Down in the cellar, I finally found it. Rift 22, drifting just above ground like a faint shadowy flame.

A question in the back of my mind made me hesitate. What did I hope to achieve by traversing this gateway to the other world? But vanity, and promises to myself to solve this mystery enticed me to place the lantern on the cobblestone floor, and I stepped inside the rift. I waited for my vision to blur. The sense of non-existence took away any doubt I had about what I was doing. Then I felt my feet again, walking on a softer surface. After raising my eyelids, my sight adjusted to the light, and the new world revealed itself to me. That is when I gazed into the precipice right in front of my feet. Peering unwillingly at the dirt below, my heart seemed to skip a beat when I took my distance from the edge and looked around in bewilderment on the lookout for any other way to get myself killed. But no. I just happened to stand at the edge of a man-made ravine.

From the precipices, I overlooked the strip mine that reached beyond the horizon. A massive excavation machine had unearthed an ungodly amount of land, leaving a trench of sixty feet deep reaching for miles. But it wasn't just the earth itself that had been moved. The nearby city had entire districts scooped out of it, including the sewage systems, as if they intended to remove it from the geological record entirely. However, for whatever reason, the work had stopped. The enormous excavation wheel was stuck in the side of the pit of its own making, buried underneath a clock tower whose foundation it was scooping away. The Gothic arches that were caught inside the wheel were strained under the weight of the crumbling monument. But they bore its weight, just as they had done for hundreds of years. And they seemed intent on doing so for another century. The behemoth itself was now serving as a nesting ground for birds flocking around the rafters connecting the main body with the caterpillar tracks, from which plants had sprouted.

My direct vicinity consisted mainly of overgrown mounds of dirt leftover from the excavation works. But at some places, I could spot buried remnants of walls and other man-made debris. Curiously, I went looking for any hints of the world's fate. I discovered ditches that included recently turned earth. Upon inspection, my estimation of this place being a buried junkyard turned out to be correct. The ground was rich with all matter of items. Metals, resins, and even materials are often described as plastics stuck out from the ground. If I weren't mistaken, the Association would describe this as a tier IV civilization, one that further developed than our own and, therefore, of great interest. That was not sufficient reason, however, to remove knowledge of its existence from the archives.

Venturing into the city, I explored the overgrown streets of the outer districts, where traces of the chaos still remained. Between the working-class houses, all manners of household objects and random luggage were wasted away underneath the foliage. Even though the families that lived here disappeared, it felt like they were still present in spirit.

While conceptualizing what could have transpired, I found a clue beneath a spoke wheel of a crashed carriage. An object that stood out even in this futuristic environment. It was a spider-like contraption with a hat-shaped shell that seemed out of place in this world. One of its legs broke off as I studied it, but I was certain. C-44; A monstrous device that attached itself to its victim's head, turning it into a mindless automaton. I knew more planes succumbed to swarms of these things of unknown origin, but I'd never seen one. This specimen was deactivated for months, if not years, but that didn't put me at ease, for it wasn't making any sense. What I had seen in those crime-scene photos and reports was nothing if not the work of a sick mind. Not that of some soulless automaton.

It dawned on me that nothing here had anything to do with the murder. But something had come through the rift!

Could it be the man at the apple farm was lying? Had they left Associate 9 behind in his hour of need? If 9 had survived, he could be craving revenge even after all those years. But I discarded the ridiculous notion. Even if it were so, Associate 9's body would have crumbled to dust after a month. Thus, I continued my search.

The inner city's houses, venues, and public buildings were but barren shells of their former splendor, circumvented by the same sensation of dread I experienced in the previous districts. These monumental buildings were not destroyed by war or machines, however. I found no craters or bullet holes. No shell casings or abandoned military equipment. Instead, I discovered the burned remains of furniture and books inside pyres used to set buildings alight. Defaced and dismembered statues, graceful decorations, and even the spandrels had been vandalized. Whatever the identity of the city and its people happened to be. It was all turned to rubble and ash. Though it was clear the city was to be wiped off the face of the earth, this destruction did not feel consistent with the land-moving machine. Instead, somebody had attempted to finish whatever the excavators had started. But why? Didn't they want future generations to see their achievements? To read the wisdom of their ancestors or hear the melodies that have been passed down the ages? What could drive anyone to destroy in days that took civilizations countless generations to create? And what would they replace it with?

On the vertical surfaces that weren't destroyed, they had scratched or painted hollow phrases like Unite. Ricke-tick-tick. Find-the-transmission. Nothing-to-lose, and rig-the-world. That had been their contribution to this place. Instead of building it up again, they turned it into an altar to resentment. But resentment against what?

The red of the encroaching sunset appeared in the sky, and I decided to go back while the light lasted. I was unsatisfied, however. It seemed too obvious that whoever remained in this place couldn't be responsible for the murders. But why did the Association hide it? What had they attempted to achieve here?

Then, I stopped. A statement clad on a wall froze the blood in my veins. My gaze scanned the six feet tall letters and translated the jagged symbols smeared across the brickwork:

"Triangulate the Signal!"

A mixture of bewilderment and terror overcame me. Was this left here by Associate 9? Did that mean he was still alive? Impossible. Even if the survivors hadn't killed him, Travelers Disease would have.

My contemplation was interrupted by a gong-like drone reverberating through the empty streets. Turning to the source of the dreadful sound, I realized it came from the collapsed clock tower leaning against the Excavator. So, the survivors were still here.

Searching out the tower, I noticed a faint noise. A rhythmic sound like that of horse hooves coming down the street. But as the noise coming from ruins behind me appeared, its rhythm sounded more akin to the systemic ticking of numerous grandfather clocks. As I turned about, they had appeared. Three of them. Automaton-like humans vaulted from behind the walls and rubble. Their skin was pallid and scabbed. Their prosthetics, though far less elegant or sophisticated looking than those on the crippled librarian, were more agile and articulated in ways alien to humans. Their posture was akin to those of hyenas, while their heads ticked like pocket watches and the joints rattled as springs being wound over and over again.

One was female, wearing something resembling a tattered undergarment, patched together so much I doubted anything of the original fabric had remained. Her limbs were all prosthetics, the arms being unusually thin and frail-looking while her thighs were thick, their joints arranged like those of a turkey. Beneath matted braids of hair lurked the crazed eyes of a beast, eager to lash out at me.

The second one, on the other hand, had the appearance of a peaceful giant, augmented from the waist down and fitted with limbs too large for his head and chest. From behind a curtain of dark hair that reached down his back, glowing eyes were staring at me with a mixture of contempt and curiosity.

The last one, a man with a metal scalp, seemed to be the most sentient of the trio. Like the others, his legs were rudimentary prosthetics resembling the back legs of a bird. His arms were human, marked with countless surgical scars. His head twitched mechanically as if a spring forced him to look to the side.

Despite their apparent differences, each had cylinder-shaped devices sticking out the back of the skulls, arranged like a cluster of insect eggs.

Once the one with the metal scalp managed to control his spasms, he gradually turned his gaze to me and spoke out with a throaty voice that pierced my eardrums. "What does it do here?" he said to nobody in particular. I believe he was thinking out loud.

Holding my hands up in front of me, I pleaded with them. "I mean you no harm. I am just exploring."

"That tone," he remarked with suspicion. "It came through that Portal."

"Uhm, yes. Yes, I did."

The automata looked at each other. "You are a follower of the Ish-tar?"

Surprised by the question, I hesitated. How did it know of us? It must have been something that happened all those years ago, and I decided it was better not to take any chances and said, "I am not sure to what you are referring."

"They promised," he screeched. "They promised! They would reconnect us!"

"I still don't know what you mean," I insisted, but he seemed deaf to my pleas.

"The Ishtar condemned us to this!" He pressed the palms of his hands against his temples. "Gears grinding to the interior of our skulls, going ricke-tick-tock! The Signal takes it away. Ends the noise! Reset the Signal. Reset the Signal!" He seemed to get stuck in a loop and repeated random phrases like a broken gramophone. His odd companions, coming closer, groaned in sympathy, judging me to be the source of his suffering. Like pack predators, they surrounded me.

Before I could turn away, the woman had leaped behind me, barring my way. That is when the giant grabbed me and lifted me up like I was a mere child. Its oversized hands squeezed the air out of my chest, and I could feel my ribs being strained under pressure. I couldn't breathe, and my sight started to fade to black. It was the closest to death I have ever been.

"And sometimes, I still feel his grip choking me."

Mr. Lotto nodded in approval, be it with a sarcastic grin. "Great story."

"You know nothing," 45 moaned through the burlap sack. "Men might already fear the cold rationality of the machines who care nothing for their suffering. But how about machines who revel in our pain?"

"How about men who act the same?" Mr. Lotto retorted.

"How dare you compare us to them!"

"Ah, hit a nerve there, did I? For where I am sitting, you Invictus blokes are no bloody different."

"We do it for the sake of the world!"

"Oh, of course, you do."

"Listen!"

"No, no. I heard it all, mate. Lived it. Got the bloody commemorative pin. I have done all the things you've done. I just didn't get thousands of people killed by blowing up a dam because you suspected some C-33 infestations."

"Suspected? They were out in the open!"

"So, maybe they were. But thousands? Those were just the deaths. That city has stood there since antiquity. And you wiped it away with the same ease you empty a chamber pot."

"You do not understand..."
"Care to explain, then?"
"I was getting to that!"

In the midst of strangling me, the giant froze. Astonished, I saw his head being jerked back. Releasing his hold on me, he reached for the collar that had suddenly wrapped around his throat. As the giant stumbled backward, the other two automata froze the moment the creature cast its long shadow over us. A hooded mechanical centaur, its upper body draped in moldy leather robes, wielding the man-catcher that enveloped the giant's neck. Its torso was slight to the center of the scorpion-like frame, so two legs were in front of its chest.

Petrified, I observed how it dragged the giant, ensnared between the pole arm's prongs, besides its arachnid-like body with the same ease I imagined the Grim Reaper wielded its scythe. Agile as a woodlouse, it traversed the debris and swung the giant through the air like a fisherman throwing out a line. With a thrashing sound, the mechanical homunculus landed somewhere out of sight in the rubble of the ruins.

Then the centaur turned to face us. "Dunn tousiem!" it bellowed, with a voice that vibrated like a tuba. "Iaief use fur this specimin!"

The duo recoiled with a mixture of fear and awe. It only took a moment before they ran off and disappear inside among the crumbling walls.

Caught in its shadow, I hesitated to look at the centaur. When I did try to make out its visage, all I could see was a cluster of lights where a face should be.

"Thank you," I said.

The centaur tilted its head awkwardly.

"I said thank you," I repeated.
Straightening itself, the creature reached behind its back, searching for something inside its cloak. Finally, he retracted his hand and threw something in my direction.
I caught the object resembling a telegraph horn.
"Speak," he commanded.
I held the speaker to my face. "Like this?"
"Yeahs."
"Em, thank you for saving me," I whispered into the horn.
The moment I spoke, the creature brought its man catcher to bear. "Are you Ishtarian?" it bellowed, coming toward me.
"How did you... Never mind. What did they mean by ` 'they would reconnect us'?"
"Hmmm. You know nothing, do yea?"
"No, sir- What's your name?"
"Aqrabua," it growled. The automaton's body hinged, chirped, and rattled as it bent its scaled frame in the opposite direction. "Fullow me!"
Left with no other option, I followed it to a dome-shaped structure on a hill, like an observatory. The hill might have been a park one time, but now it was littered with junkpiles, scrap, and discarded prosthetics. I paused when I noticed a pile of human bones.
"What is this place?"
""My workshop ies inside," it said. "After the Connection was severed, most of us regained..." he hesitated to say it. "Loneliness..." It continued. "We were all alone since then, with the noise inside our heads. Most succumbed to the madness. But I augmented myself. Changed my auditory system. I have been improving myself. Made me more efficient. Made others more efficient. Prepared others to unite with the network. Yeash."
"Have you changed the auditory systems of others as well?"
"No-oh."
"Why not?"
"They would lose their sense of purpose. Become aimless. Or try to improve themselves, making them my enemies."
At that moment, I realized I wasn't just talking to some horrific engineer. This thing was something that kept his fellow automata in a state of permanent suffering because it suited its ends - whatever those might be.
Holding open the door, it bid me to enter the dome.
Against better judgment, I did.
When I traversed the doorway, the interior was vibrating with the humming of machinery. The observatory had been converted into a dreadful

amalgamation of greasy tools and surgical instruments. Cables ran up the partially disassembled telescope like creepers, and the opulently tiled floor was covered by a mixture of oil and dried blood. In front of the telescope's base stood a cage that might have housed birds once, but its contents were now hidden beneath a moldy carpet.

Without saying a word, Aqrabua walked past me and grabbed the tapestry. Pulling it away with frightening ease, he revealed a cadaverous-looking woman in haggard clothes, sitting motionless in a fine, be it weathered, baroque chair surrounded by dead plants. She was staring lifelessly into nothing while cables were hanging down her shoulders from beneath her nest-like hair. On top of her head sat the corroding contraption. It was again a version of C-33, its legs buried inside her skull, possibly for many years. She did not seem to mind, content with sitting there like a soulless fairy tale princess.

"That ies the last Original," he explained. "Thies unit is still in contak. The Ishtarian used iet to sever the connection, and only he knows how to reset iet."

It all started to come together. Associate 9 came here to break these automata. But instead, he returned their consciousness to them, turning them into the monstrosities I had witnessed that day. No wonder the Chair didn't want anyone to find out about this place.

"Ever since the connection got severed, the madness spread," he continued. "Now they know of the portals, they go, and seek out the Creators. Thies ies a problem for me. Ief the Creators find out what happened, they might return to terminate us."

"Who are these, Creators?" As I uttered the phrase, the irony of their title hit me. Were they not the ones who built the excavator?

He ignored my question and simply said. "Ia need yea to speak to the one who did thies. Ask hiem how I can reset this unit. Yea can find hiem inside the Cathedral."

"Why don't you ask him your-" Then I looked at the horn in my hand that allowed us to communicate, and I changed my question. "Is he the Ishtarian, you mentioned?"

"Yeash."

"That should not be possible," I retorted. 9 should have turned to dust years ago.

Towering over me, he anticipated my explanation, but I couldn't give it to him without confirming my identity - if he didn't know that already.

"The Cathedral, you say. And what will I get in return for this favor?"

"Ia let you live," he stated bluntly. "And maybe I won't send the others after you when you are done."

Left with no choice, I made my way toward the Cathedral.

At this point, I had gotten tired of being pushed around by parties with hidden agendas. The Association had tried to hide the atrocity Associate 9 had committed, and now I was a pawn in one of this monster's games.

The night was vast approaching as the low droning noise from the tower made the debris quake beneath my feet. From a bedroom window inside a dilapidated hotel, I watched as dozens, if not hundreds, of the monstrous automatons were leaving the Cathedral. A genuine medieval building, frozen in time during the moment it was about to be dug away by the excavator like a sandcastle. But what could they possibly be worshiping? Maybe the automatons simply didn't know better.

I watched glowing eyes pass by in the twilight while they mumbled random words and plain gibberish, supported by the constant rhythm of clockwork. When the last ones left the Cathedral, I hurried down and sneaked through the ruins until I finally reached the front gate. As expected, saints were torn down, their faces smashed. The stories and depictions that once held meaning were painted over with more meaningless jargon.

The cathedral's interior was in a similar condition to the outside, yet it was more than that. What I found was nothing short of a morbid reliquary, lit up by collections of tubular lamps attached to the age-old chandeliers with glass crystals at its center. Amongst the light fixtures, strung up 30 feet above the choir area, I spotted his remains. Associate 9's arms were spread wide like angelic wings, while his torso was suspended from numerous steel cables and tubes attached to the incomprehensible tangle of rafters above. Little else of him had remained. But how? How come his body had not been turned to dust? The tubes! It was hard to say from this distance, but the secret must have poured through those tubes! Could it be that they found a countermeasure for inter-planer entropy?

The hairs on the back of my neck rose when a shrill, obnoxious voice of an old man vibrated through the nave. "Who's there?"

As if frozen, my soles stuck to the ground as I looked up in fright.

"Hah! I can see you scurrying about. Yeah! You!"

I turned my gaze in the direction of the corpse.

"Don't be shy! I hang here for your entertainment," he cried as if it were a big joke to him. "Who are you, young man? A new believer? Nooo-ow, you are not here to hate on me. Are you?"

"No." I answered, finally knowing how to respond. "I am here to... Undo a mistake."

"Huh." He sounded like he was about to suffocate. "An Associate then?"

"Yes! Yes, I am an Associate. Are you number 9?"

He smiled with a toothless grin while making a sound as if something were broken. "Heh, heck, heck, heck. I used to have a number!" He proclaimed in a way that conveyed both pride and malice. "Yes! That is how I got strung up here."

"So, it is true then," I said. "You did this to them!"

"Yeessss. It's because of me!" He cried again with that ominous tone that filled me with dread. "They hated me. They wanted to tear me apart, but now I am the object of their veneration!"

"Why? What did you do?"

"Look at me! Is it obvious? I freed them. Heck, heck!"

"How did you do it? Did you do it by reprogramming one of these things? Tampering with its receivers?"

"Reprogram?" His voice broke. "Hah. They turned me into this to torment me like the gears in their heads that go ricke-tick-tock. Ricke-tick-tock. He started to sing, but the melody quickly turned to cries and wails that echoed from within a pit of regret and self-pity as he kept repeating the mantra. "Ricke-tick-tock! Ricke tick-tock! ricketic-tockricketic-" The old man went berserk like a gramophone that got stuck on a loop as his body started to jerk back and forth, faster and faster, with such ferocity it caused a wave in the drapes of cables behind him. "Ricketicktockricketick-Ricketicktockricke tickricketick-"

"Stop it!" I cried, attempting to shout over his intense ramblings. "How did y-"

Before I could finish the question, an ear-rupturing metal sound made the ground shake.

Stopping abruptly, the old man looked up at the rafters in anticipation.

I pleaded with him. "Quickly! Tell me, what did you do?"

Another surge of steel grinding against steel followed by the ticking of gears turning. Still looking up at the ceiling, the helpless old man started to ascend while the cables were tightening, lifting him up.

"Tell me!"

He looked down at me one last time. "Start by triangulating the Signal," he cried, and then he repeated it with a contradictory tone of triumph. "Triangulate-the-Signal!"

That is when he rose up in between the crisscross of steel beams, chains, and cables until he had disappeared from sight.

Through the white noise of colliding objects and screeching metal, I could already hear the sound of approaching clockwork. I fled the Cathedral, then the city, and made my way back to the edge of the pit where the Rift home awaited me. I didn't think of anything else other than getting out of this hell hole.

During my final dash for the Rift, as the moonlight illuminated the wrinkles between the mounds of trash, my foot stepped on a plate. The last thing I heard was the clenching of metal as my leg got stuck in a bear trap, whose rusted teeth bit me all the way to the bone. Searching the foliage in my vicinity for anything of use, I discovered even more traps. I had been a fool to think that Aqrabua would let me get away this easily. Cutting my hands on countless objects, I dug out a rod and pried my leg free for the iron maw.

Bleeding, I staggered the last distance to the R ift that was in arm's reach. But I had cheered too soon. The Rift flickered to life. Like a specter emerging from the water, somebody came through from the other side. It was the man I met at the apple farm, former Associate 61. The moment he saw me, he drew a revolver and pointed it in my general direction. "I am gonna have to stop you there, mate."

I allowed myself to tumble backward, too exhausted to stand. "So, you lied to me! You knew what they did to 9."

He looked at me, baffled. "What are you on about?"

"I saw him hanging in the Cathedral. Still alive and untouched by Travelers Disease! Is this what you are trying to hide?"

He raised an eyebrow. "You are making a bigger deal out of it than it is."

"Then why is he still hanging there?"

"Why? Politics, that's why. In case you haven't noticed, those freaks aren't exactly the sharpest tools in the shed. If the Chair and the Oversight Committee committed for once, this city would have been cleared within the week."

"Then why? They already killed 115! Aren't you afraid they are gonna get you too?"

"You have no proof it was one of them. In fact, I suspected it was you. Who could have figured out what her number used to be? She was too thorough in letting anything happen to her family!"

I paused to consider. "Unless the Chair wanted her to be found, so nobody would know about your secret."
That made him pause, but then he shook his head. "You are really overthinking this."
"Am I? What certainty do you have that they are not going after you next?"
He seemed puzzled by that statement. I let him mull it over before I said something stupid. Then he lowered his gun. "Fine," he said, offering me his hand. I hesitated, for after all that, I wasn't sure I could trust anyone. But if I were to expose the Association, I had a need for allies.
So, I decided. Straightening myself, I reached out to him. But before we could shake hands, trash sheared past me as something rose from the ground. 61 screamed as he was lifted off his feet by the beast that had become all too familiar to me. It was Aqrabua who had been waiting to ambush us. He scooped up 61 with his man-catcher, who lost consciousness almost immediately. It all happened so fast. Awestruck, I looked up at Aqrabua's illuminated gaze as he hung 61 over his shoulder.
"You served me well, little one," he said. "Better than even I anticipated. I have been waiting for these to return. Number 115 wasn't as cooperative."
"So, it was you?"
"By proxy, yeash," he admitted. "Now go! We're done here!" And with that, he left me behind.
I don't know what became of 61, but I think I have a fair guess.
Since then, it has become clear to me Aqaubua isn't just any freak. He has been dispatching his agents all over our Plane till this very day, using the same stratagem as the Creators of C-33 and C-44. They create their minions on our Plane with the help of various factions, the Association included.

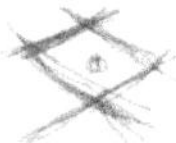

"So, you see. It's not just the C-331-s that the Chair is trying to hide," 45 proclaimed to Mr. Lotto. "Aqrabua is out there, sending his agents out to destroy our world."
Mr. Lotto shook his head in disbelief. "So, that is what this is all about. Your personal guilt for leading 61 to him?"
"No! Don't you see? His agents have infiltrated the Association! They found a way to neutralize the effects of Travelers Decay. They even have a safe house code-named Sanctuary where they keep all manner of Outsiders! Look for it!"
"Okay, mate, I think it is time to put you out to pasture."
"If you are not with us, you're against us. Atlas Invictus!"

"Mate, I don't care whose side you think I am on. I am here to kill a man who committed treason," Lotto said, hanging the noose around 45's neck and tightened the knot.
"We did it to save the world, you prick!"
"Yea, great job you've done," Lotto rebuked him. "No matter what you do, you are always on the right side of history. Trust me, I've been there, mate. I know how good it can make you feel. That's why I volunteered myself to rid the world of the likes of you."
The man shook his head. "How does that make you any different?"
"Like I said. I don't pass judgment. I am just an executioner who enjoys his job. Bye!" And with that, he opened the hatch that was underneath the chair. The traitor died swiftly as the fall broke his neck. Lotto wouldn't have minded if he had lasted a bit longer. It was just a shame the giant didn't end him, for generations will suffer due to his actions. But done damage is done. He picked up the telegraph and contacted his employers.
"Did you complete your objective?" asked a distorted voice from the other side of the connection.
"Yea, mate. I hung the garbage out to dry. I will prepare the body for the autopsy tonight."
"Good. Your payment will be transferred as usual?"
"Yea, that's fine... But tell me, did you try to cover up what Associate 9 had done?"
There was just the noise of static.
"Did you copy? Did you-"
"I'm sorry, Lotto. The signal seems to - br- up. Could you repeat that last message? Over."
Lotto sighed. "Just make sure my payment is transferred. Over."

"... Then, as instructed, I packed his body and had it sent to Dover for collection," the assassin concluded.

321 gawked at Mr. Lotto, who took a long drag from his cigar. Unsettled by what he had hear he had trouble standing straight. But that was more likely due to the drinking He wasn't exactly sure how much ale he drank, but enough to struggle vocalizing his thoughts to the hitman. "So, what you suggesting is... The Chair had been aware of the events which transpired on Plane 22, and their unwillingness to engage the Signalites is because this would expose the truth behind our current predicament."

"If 45 was thruthful, yea."

"And who was this contact you mentioned who was reluctant confirm your suspicion?"

"Could have been RA. Could have been the Chair."

"RA. The Committee for Rift Related Activity? Are you in their employ as well?"

He moved his face closer to 321's. "Listen. Our arrangement is quite simple. I don't ask questions, as long as I know the hits are legitimate." He took one final drag from the cigar and pressed it out on the tray. "I'll tell you this. The hit was set out only recently, right after the attack on Saint Augustine."

"That could be for any reason," 321 concluded. "But... What baffles me is that 54 reportedly ended her own life?"

Mr. Lotto nodded. "Yeah, if memory serves me right."

"Then why does S-36 still recite her number."

"I just work through my targets, mate. I don't keep track."

"Please, this is important. S-36 wrote the numb er forty-five above 45's body, inside the crate lid."

"Maybe it was a mistake. Happens to the best of us."

"Humans make mistakes, Mr. Lotto. She is..."

"She's what?"

321 raised his finger when he had an epiphany. "S-36 only announces the number of her current targets," he thought out loud. "That must mean 54 is still alive!"

"Maybe she is just misinformed."

"What if she is not?"

"Well," Lotto said as he slapped him on the shoulder. "I wish you the best of luck with that mate. Now, I have a game to play."

Intoxicated, 321 pulled his jacket straight. "So do I, it would seem."

Relying on trusty his cane, 321 made his way to the door. Meanwhile, his clouded mind processed what he just heard. More and more it was dawning on him that this entire situation could be the result of Association's meddling in other-worldly affairs. The Chair had a rule about that. Don't interfere unless the events posed a security threat to Atlas. Any other actions taken had to be greenlit by the responsible coordinator, or sometimes even the Chair itself. Now, this disaster occurred in the early days of the Association and was likely the impetus for such regulations. Regardless, 321 imagined the Association wouldn't want this to become public knowledge, and was likely what got 175 killed. Whatever the reasons, all 321 knew for certain, he needed to find Dr. Jenever.

Grumbling, 321 pushed open the door with his shoulder. As stumbled into the street, he failed to notice another pedestrian coming from the side. When he bumped into him with his heavy frame, he pushed the man to the ground.

"Oh, I'm terribly sorry," 321 apologized, and reached down to help him. But when he bent over, the man started to flail his arms around like a toddler throwing a tantrum. "Noooo! Get your hands off me!" he cried drunkenly. "I don't need your bloody help. Haven't you done enough!" 321 took his distance, dismayed by the man's infantile whining that attracting the bystanders' attention. "Everyone treating me like I'm a bloody doormat," he whined as he crawled to his feet. "Sod off all of you!" His shouting reverberated through the street as swung fists in random directions.

321 tried to appease him. "Sir, I want to-"

"You think you better than me don't ya? All you bloody tars are the same!" he said, stamping his feet. "Huh!"

"I just wanted to say, I'm sorry."

"Ohhh, you're sorry... Well, that makes it all all right, doesn't it? I hope y'all feel better." He swung around, vocalizing some utterings as he walked down the street like being prodded with a pitchfork.

"Well, somebody is havin' a bad day," one sailor remarked, followed by ironic laughter from the other bystanders.

Squeezing the collar of his coat, 321 walked away without saying anything. To him it seemed, everyone was having a bad day.

CHAPTER ELEVEN

20TH OF MAY, 1875, 9.05 PM

It had been quite the evening at the Ol'Barrow house. Diane was pouring warm water over Ol'Barrow's shoulders as he sat naked in the tub. He didn't recall the last time he had a decent bath like this. As a matter of fact, he had taken little time for himself as of late. Diane had to make him. So desperate not to upset her again, Ol'Barrow even took his clothes off when she demanded he'd take a bath. Another thing he hadn't done for at least a few weeks. When he observed his murky reflection in the condensed dressing mirror, a bruised face looked back at him. A bump on his forehead shimmering through chestnut strand stood out like a blue boil, and the scar on his cheek looked more pinkish than usual. He groaned, with a mixture of delight and fatigue, as Diane was soaping his shoulders. Her hands might be soft, but her firm grip was just what his aching muscles needed.

"You've gotten thinner," said Diane softly. "And stiffer."

He looked up at her. "Hm?"

"Not like that!"

He chuckled as he lowered his gaze. "Yes. I guess the Signalites are right in that regard. Our bodies are just filthy weak machines created by an uncaring creator."

"You're not getting philosophical on me, are ya?"

"Well, it's just... Never mind, I don't know where I was going with it."

"That's you. Always starting things without thinking."

He looked up into her dark blue eyes. "Like getting on a train, not knowing where it is going?" he asked.

"That's one way of putting it," she said while her hands approached his neck. "Then again, you could just be standing there in the terminal. Just waiting for something good to happen."

"Yeah... Yeah, I guess."

"It reminds me of how I met Gerald," she continued whimsically. "I was supposed to go to London that morning, but I overslept. Not even that long. But I saw that train disappear into the distance. And Gerald was standing there, struggling to carry three suitcases." She sighed. "Typical Gerald. Always trying to pick up more weight that he could carry."

"Explains why he married you," Ol'Barrow responded in jest.

"Oh, David!"

"It's true. You were always hard-headed. I was quite frankly surprised you found a man who could handle you. Auw!"

Diane squeezed the swelling where his neck met his shoulders. "Speak for yourself," she sneered, massaging the stiff muscles. "When was the last time you gave yourself some rest? This behavior ended Gerald, you know. When he worked at that place where they made the stuff of asbestos, he said I shouldn't concern myself with those rumors. Even after he got sick in the lungs. Even then. It still boggles my mind how people can defend what is obviously bad for them."

Ol'Barrow looked over his shoulder. "Can I ask you a hard question? Would you have married Gerald if you knew what would happen to him?"

She stopped what she was doing. "Gee, I don't know... I would have told him not to work at that place. Don't know if he would have listened, though. And even if it isn't one thing that kills yea, it's another. In the end, there is only one certainty in life."

"Would you want to live forever?" asked Ol'Barrow. "Without all that getting old stuff. Or need to eat. Or make money."

"Are you talking about heaven?"

"Yeah," he responded, somewhat puzzled. "It kinda sounds like that, doesn't it? But what if life could be like that? Without a body to take care of?"

"Gee," was her only response. She worked the swelling in his shoulder. "I mean. Wouldn't it be boring? What would be the point of taking care of each other? What do we complain about? What would be the point of children? Or growing up? What would we do with all that time? Dance around the Maypole? And you said, without a body? So, you'd be alone with your thoughts then." Her face became more severe with every passing moment. "That doesn't sound like heaven at all," she waxed philosophically.

"Ya," he whispered, leaning his head back, and stared at Diane. "There was an attempt on my life today," he confessed.

Her hands froze. "What? How?"

Reaching for a towel, Ol'Barrow rose from the water. "It's too long a story... My point is, I might have done something that exposed them."

"Who?"

"Well, I am no longer a cop, so... The Signalite cult."

"The one with the celebrities?"

"Yes. Innocent people died. Iggy disappeared. But I feel, somehow, it needed to happen..." he looked at Diane. "Does that make sense?"

She blinked sheepishly. "I suppose a lot of bad happenings lead to positive actions in the long run. I mean, when that tavern burned down ten years ago, we finally got a fire department. They've done a lot of good. But she's still a child."

His mood changed when she brought up the fire at the Black Horse. "Did you really have to use that example?"

"But it's true," she reiterated. "It-" She stopped herself.

"Did it do me a lot of good?" he asked, annoyed.

"I'm just saying, that's life," said Diane. "Things often get worse before they get better. I mean, at times like that, heroes are made."

Well, some hero I turned to be, thought Ol'Barrow. "I was just doing my job."

"Really? How many of you were there?"

"Just me and Christopher."

"Did he try to save that woman?" asked Diane.

Ol'Barrow froze for a moment and then shook his head as an odd sense of realization surged through his body. "No... No, he did not," he admitted, pondering if he had gotten Christopher all wrong.

"Do you think you could have saved her if he helped?"

He raised his finger at her in indignation. "Now, hold on!"

"Or anyone else, for that matter?" she continued.

He lowered his hand. "Risk two lives to save one is just..." Meanwhile, Ol'Barrow considered the possibility he had misunderstood Christopher all those years. He assumed Christopher did what he did to save Ol'Barrow. But now he wondered if he ruined his own reputation out of guilt for not helping the woman.

"That is not the point," Diane continued. "The point is that you tried. That's more than anyone else had done."

"I wasn't thinking at that moment."

"Well, maybe that is what we need more of then."

"But that's exactly why I am in this situation. It's why Igraine is not here."

"Did you force her to go along?"

"N-no."

"See. You two are exactly alike. Like a couple of scheming children when I was looking the other way." She smiled. "Now, get some clothes on."

"Cu-coo..! Cu-coo..! Cu-coo!"

21ST OF MAY, 1875, 8.00 AM

The bird in the grandfather clock never sounded that clear on any morning. When Ol'Barrow awoke, sloughed on the couch, he found Diane's head resting on his shoulder, and on the table stood an empty bottle of wine. Gently, he moved Diane aside, got up, and clumsily rearranged his clothes. Blinded by the orange sunlight, Ol'Barrow walked up to the sink and poured himself a glass of water from the teapot to hydrate his dry mouth. As he looked down, the mutt sat by his feet with his nose in the air, squealing anxiously. "I suppose it's time for your walk."

The dog's bark overloaded his intoxicated brain.

"Alright!" Ol'Barrow groaned while massaging his eyes. "I suppose there is no harm in walking you to the station."

A moment later, Diane blinked her light-sensitive eyes as she awoke. "Wha- time is-it?" she yawned. "Wait. Where are you going?"

"To the station," he said while leashing the mutt.

"But you're fired."

"I'm still responsible for Igraine. And I no longer need to follow orders."

"What do you mean by that?"

"It means this concerned citizen is going to assist the borough police in the search for a missing child."

She sighed, obviously too tired to argue before her morning tea. "Just-bring her home safely," was all she said.

He nodded, holding the mongrel's leash. "I will."

Despite it being an ordinary workday, there was an oppressive calm in Dover's streets. There were fewer children out, and pedestrians seemed to be in a hurry to get home when they left the stores. It even affected the mongrel, who was walking beside him on his best behavior, as if he were afraid of being scolded for the smallest infraction. Ol'Barrow figured the news of the Nyctolar had reached the masses and wondered how the authorities would spin this debacle.

On one street corner, a boy yelled: "Extra! Extra! Lantry Manor Arsonists still on the run!"

"Read all about it," cried another. "The Nyctolar are comin'. Are they a government project run amok?"

In front of a store, people had gathered around a wavecaster, listening to the shrill voices that were shouting at each other through the ether.

One voice, young and well-articulated like a public speaker, yelled at his opponent. "This was an orchestrated attack, I tell you!"

An older, angrier voice responded whose words drowned within the ether because he spoke under his breath like a bulldog. "You can repeat the statement all you want. Those mechanical freaks of yours killed three people."

"There is no evidence."

"No evidence? Two of 'em were found dead at the scene of the crime."

"Obviously they were planted there."

The crowd in front of the radio laughed, nodding and commenting as if it was a boxing match. They all knew this was a farce. But at least it was entertaining.

"I mean..." muttered the young man. "Who could have even killed them at the time of the incident?"

"That's a very good question, ain't it? I suspect it was that peeler you are tryin' to lock behind bars."

Ol'Barrow kept his eyes in front, ignoring all the slander and misinformation until he reached his destination.

Inside the police station's reception area, it was busier than usual. Strangely enough, the citizens were conversing in hushed tones. It almost felt like a funeral. His attention was drawn to a chiseled gentleman with a black eye. He was sitting in the main hall, where Ol'Barrow's desk used to be, amidst the humdrum of officers and clerks. The downtrodden man nodded at a constable, who tried to console him. The man seemed shaken indeed. A victim of assault, Ol'Barrow guessed. Surprising. The man had a military vibe to him, confirmed by the metal hand he possessed - one with adjustable fingers.

Meanwhile, a small man in baggy clothes was leaning on the front desk counter. "And that's when I saw 'em!" he said to the constable on duty and held his hands together like he was holding binoculars in front of his eyes. "Right in front of my window, peering inside with its red eyes. They said I had too much absinthe. But I know what I saw!"

"Of course, sir," sighed the old constable, who looked like he was at this all morning.

Ol'Barrow recognized the officer and called him out. "Huette, is that you? I thought you retired for good?"

"Oh, hey, Boss," he said warmly. "The lads are all out in the street taking interviews, trying to put a lid on this new hysteria. So, I thought I'd assist as a clerk. It's just like with those bloody revolutionaries from ten years ago."

"That bad?"

"You haven't heard?" he asked, surprised. "The Luddites, sir. Since they got word of the murders, they are spreading rumors of a machine uprising led by the Signalites."

They might be right about one, but Ol'Barrow decided to keep his predictions to himself.

"I'm just here to help, but uhm..." Huette whispered. "I heard what happened. Should you even be here?"

"I am just a citizen now," said Ol'Barrow. "Concerned with a murderous group of terrorists and a missing child."

"If you say so, sir..." Huette rose as something attracted his attention. "Oh, dear. She's still at it?" he muttered with mild annoyance.

Ol'Barrow looked over his shoulder. A constable came in together with an old lady who looked like she'd been living on the street for a long time. Her thick coat was dirty and worn. Her hair was unwashed, and her potato-shaped nose red.

"Remember," she said, with a surprisingly posh voice that sounded only half lucid. "I came here voo-lun-taa-rily," she reiterated, overpronouncing each vowel.

"Yes, Mary," responded the constable, aggravated. "Now, please have a seat here. Don't fall off. Yes, yes... Alright, Mary, can you tell me again what you saw at that factory?"

"I told you. It was a machine man. You wrote it down when I told you days ago," she insisted.

"Yes, Mary. I'm afraid they lost it in the archive."

"That reminds me. Did you find those Red Caps I reported?"

The constable rolled his eyes while penning down her statements. "I'm afraid they are still in hiding, Mary. Can we get back to the machine-man?"

"Yes, you see, I was walking by the River Dour when I spotted him near that closed-down factory."

"No shortage of those. Which factory, Mary?"

"The one with the sewing machines."

A light blinked on behind Ol'Barrow's eyes when she mentioned the sewing machines. "Johnston's Machine Company?"

"You know it, Boss?" asked Huette.

"Yes, they made various patented machine parts that they licensed from foreign companies. They closed down about a year ago."

"Yes!" Mary said. "Strange folk have been squatting there for a while now."

"What kind of folk?"

"I'm not paying attention to them. More machines, I'll wager. They seek their own kind, you know?"

"I'm sure they do," said the constable. "Thank you, Mary. We'll look into it."

"And don't forget about those evil Red Caps."

"Thank you, Mary! You may go now."

"Oh, and remember Prince Albert? I saw him again at..."

"Yes, yes," he interrupted her, gently pushing her toward the door. "We keep an eye out for him as well."

When the constable had rid himself of Mary, Ol'Barrow addressed him. "Why was I not told of this machine man before?"

"Mary comes with these types of stories all the time," he responded dismissively. "Jewish wizards, monsters in the river. And Red Caps," he added, shrugging his shoulders. "I never heard of the Nyctolar before. Not until the Lantry Manor burned down."

Ol'Barrow sighed, admittingly. "So, are you going to investigate?"

"It's one location of many, sir. After the word got out, everyone claimed to have seen one or two. This morning a gentleman with a metal hand prosthetic was physically attacked."

"Oh, damn."

"Yeah, you're lucky you still have a hook still. Any amputee with something more mechanical in appearance is a suspect now. Anyway, we'll get to check that factory. Before morning, I'm sure."

"Before morning?" responded Ol'Barrow, dismayed. Then again. He couldn't be surprised. It was hard enough to maintain order without killer automatons at large. "Well, I suppose I'll be off then," said Ol'Barrow donning his hat.

"Wait," said Huette. "You're not going there, are ya, boss?"

"Well, it is my duty as a concerned cit-"

"Alright, get out of here, you nutter," shouted Huette. "Just don't do- Oh, why do I even bother... Next!"

Standing outside, knew exactly what he was going to do. He looked at the mongrel who was still walking beside him. "What do you think, old boy? Want to find Iggy?"

The dog barked, enthused.

"That's what I thought." He looked at him one more time. "I should give you a name... How about, Old Boy?"

The dog gave him a glassy look.

"Yeah, that's stupid... We'll think of something. Come, boy."

And so, they walked through the downtown street. The old factory wasn't that far out, on the west of Dover. But there was a foreboding atmosphere that didn't sit well with him. The silence before the storm.

20TH OF MAY, 1875, 4.20 PM. AN UNDISCLOSED LOCATION IN DOVER.

The loud clanking of metal hitting the pavement reverberated through the empty building.

Igraine blinked her eyes. Feverishly, she moved her fingers about the mattress: a canvas stretcher inside a dilapidated room with soot-covered brick walls smell of wet charcoal. When moving, her side ached fiercely. As she reached down, she felt the imprint of the golem's foot on her right flank. She was lucky he missed the ribs, but barely.

"You are awake?" asked a familiar woman's voice.

She turned her head. "Doctor!"

Doctor Jenever was standing at the door opening. Her lavender dress was protected by an oil-stained leather apron with square pockets with fine tools sticking out of them. Her already jaunt face, covered in days-old makeup, looked thinner than Igraine remembered. Jenever approached the girl and crouched down by her bed. "Shhh. Lay down," she said as she stroked Igraine's hair.

"But doctor. I-" She couldn't finish her sentence as it hurt to breathe sitting up.

"Igraine. You shouldn't excite yourself."

"But."

The doctor deepened her voice. "Be quiet now, Igraine!"

Hurt by the remark Igraine, watched the doctor rise up. Her searching for Jenever now felt like a waste of time. All the things she had wanted to say. Words of gratitude she replayed many times inside her imagination had gone like an extinguished flame.

"I'm occupied," Jenever said. "I'll bring you something for the pain later."

The pain? Igraine hadn't come here for medicine! As the doctor walked away, the girl wanted to reach out to her. Speak her mind. But weakness and disappointment prevented her from doing anything.

The masked Associate, who had saved Igraine the night prior, appeared in the doorway. "Everything alright here, Doctor?" he asked with a gravelly voice that sounded like a character from an audio-play.

Jenever walked him by. "Make sure she does nothing stupid," she said and disappeared into the hallway.

Angry, Igraine laid herself down.

"So... How are you feeling?" the Associate asked, maintaining his act.

"What happened to Mr. Ol'Barrow?" she asked, her eyes fixated on the ceiling.

"He's been arrested," the Associate stated bluntly.

She turned her gaze toward him. "Why?"

"Worry about yourself. If it wasn't for the doctor, you might have died. Do you realize that?"

"I want to see the doctor. I need to speak to her."

"Are you even listening?"

Despite the pain, Igraine slowly rose, lifted her feet off the mattress, and got up.

The Associate walked up to her. "What did she just tell you?"

"I don't care!" she cried. Her body ached, and her tread was uneven, but she kept on going.

The Associate stepped in front of the door, barring the way. "Get back to bed!"

"If you don't let me through, I'll-" She suggestively held her left hand in a grasping posture.

"You'll what?" he asked, unfazed.

Just thinking about using her manipulator made Igraine's head hurt. But she had no time to think about that.

"Let her out!" Jenever yelled reluctantly from a distance away.

Both of them were quiet for a moment, but then the Associate relented.

Sunlight shone through the algae-covered skylights as Igraine entered the factory hall that had been picked clean of any valuable parts. All that remained were the crane rails overhead and the large flywheels, which were used to set the machines in motion. Remains of rusted anchor bolts lodged in the floor testified that this was once a place of industry. Now, the hall was just an empty shell. This could not have happened in her world. But not because of their reverence for technology. But because nothing ever changed. Based on the building's condition, this had been in use not that long ago. But this world's insistence on progress had made it obsolete.

Only a single corner had been occupied, walled-off by crude barriers of suspended cloth and crate panels. Amidst electric devices emitting high-pitched tones and radio murmur, Doctor Jenever was sitting on a high stool in front of her worktable.

Thin plumes of smoke rose as she sat hunched over her project. She was working on a crude circuit board by the illumination of a lamp suspended from a swivel arm. The component was covered in carefully arranged wires, reminding Igraine of what she found in S-36's lair beneath the mansion, be it cruder and made of reused parts. Igraine walked up to the doctor, who acted undeterred by her presence. Jenever's fingers moved mechanically as she soldered wires into place. Iggy had never seen the doctor work on any devices. Nor had she ever made any comments on technological matters apart from Igraine's augmentations.

"What is all this?" asked Igraine.

"It's a machine that allows me to receive and transmit information."

"So, it is a router?"

The Doctor inspected the circuit critically. "It's an apt comparison. I suppose I should come up with a name for it. Some would call it a Nexus Node. Or at least an imitation of one."

"Why do you and S-36 both need them?"

The doctor froze when she mentioned it. "Oh, child."

"Stop that. I am not a child! I already spot three possible improvements just by looking at it."

The doctor put down her work. "But you are far from mature," she said sternly. "You still have to learn the limits of your abilities."

"Well... You just left me," Igraine retorted accusingly.

"I left because I- I thought I knew somebody who could fix you."

Igraine froze. "Quell?"

21ST OF MAY, 1875, 9.12 AM. LIGHTHOUSE ROAD, DOVER.

The howling sea winds terrorizing the White Cliffs were once again trying to discourage Associate 321 from leaving the confines of his transport. But he had no choice. Holding on to his bowler, he left the carriage and walked toward the Watch Tower Tavern. The moment he was out, the coach driver signaled his horses and drove down Lighthouse Road. Even though it was a half-hour drive from the city center, the violent sea wind made the tavern appear to be a safe haven amidst the perceived desolation of the White Cliffs.

Inside the tavern, there was barely anyone apart from the barkeep and an elderly gentleman sitting at a table, with his back toward 321. It was a strange sight to see the man enjoying his meal all alone in the dining hall. The news of the recent attacks may have discouraged people from leaving the populated areas.

The barkeep, meanwhile, acted as aloof as usual as he rearranged his inventory of expensive liquor bottles.

As was his habit now, 321 approached the bar. "I would like a room without a view," he said.

The barkeep, however, did not respond and kept rearranging the bottles.

321 tapped the tip of his cane on the floor to get his attention. "Excuse me."

Sluggishly, the barkeep turned around. "That's an unusual request," he answered, more performative than usual.

321 cleared his throat. "Well... The sea frightens me. You never know if there is a-" He heard the front door being shut. "Monster..." When 321 turned around, a man in plain clothes barricaded the front door behind him with a beam.

"What are you doing?"

The man crossed his arms as he looked him straight in the eyes. "I got me orders, sir."

"Orders?" It was a sign this man was not an Associate.

When he looked around, two more men emerged from the doors on either side of the room.

321 turned to the old man who was still sitting at the table cutting his rare steak, unfazed by what was transpiring around him. 321 raised his voice. "What is going on?"

Gleefully chewing the steak, the gentleman took his time to swallow it down. "321, I assume," he spoke with a mouth full without looking away from his plate. Once done, laying down his utensils, he turned to face the Associate. "I wished you'd come five minutes later." His voice was as rough as his squared frame. With a napkin, he wiped his long silvery beard containing faint traces of reddish hair. "I looked forward to eating that steak in peace," he complained. "My house servant insists on cutting the fat off, every time... Bad for the heart, she says. As if fat will kill me."

321 carefully unscrewed the knob of his cane. "You know my number," he said, composed. "Who are you?"

"I used to have a number," the man groaned as he got from his chair. But now, you'll address me as Chief Regulator."

The Associate hesitated, uncertain whether this man was friend or foe. "You're from Ra?" he asked. "So, are you involved in the Signalite affair?"

His lips frowned at the mention of the name. "They are one reason I transferred to Ra. And then I discovered they have their supporters there as well. But..." He looked behind him and gestured for somebody to come in.

A slender man in a seemingly featureless dark blue suit walked in wearing a blank mask adorned with nothing but the all-seeing eye of Ra. He was followed by 122. 321's ally didn't look at all happy and avoided eye contact.

"Perspective change," continued the Chief Regulator. "The pieces are falling together, and time is running out."

"Thank you, regulator," said the masked man courteously with a somewhat effeminate voice and addressed 321. "Thank you for your service up to this point, Associate."

321 tried to relax his posture. "Well, much obliged. Now, please tell me. What the hell is going on!"

The Chief Regulator chuckled. "We are, like yourself, in the process of figuring it out."

"Suffice to say, I am both a RA employee and a Follower of the Signal," said the masked man. "I always have my doubts about Lantry's proselytizing. The Chief Regulator convinced me I could no longer be passive in this matter."

321 could sympathize with his position, but still. "Alright... I still have no reason to trust you. Does the Chair know about this meeting of ours?"

"The Chair knows its place," said the Chief Regulator. "They have a job to do. We inspect rather they perform that role in accordance with international treaties."

"Are you... Aware of what happened on Plane 22?"

The masked man had no direct response. "I'm afraid I am not."

"How about you, Regulator?"

"Are you bating me, sir?"

"I am talking about what the police now call Nyctolar. The ones killed near the Lantry manor."

The Regulator nodded, dismayed. "So, you know about that, do you? Who told you?"

"As an Associate, I am allowed to be discreet about my sources."

The masked man looked at the regulator. "How is Plane 22 related?" he asked him.

"Just tell the Associate what you arranged," the Regulator demanded impatiently.

"Yes. I have communicated with Druid's Isle. The location of the followers' prime receiver."

"Their main temple?" asked 321.

"It's not a temple, sir. It's a community center," the masked man corrected him.

321 sighed. "If you insist."

"Regardless, the Perfect has agreed to meet with the Association. I would have gone myself but-"

"Why me?" responded 321 directly.

The Regulator slammed his fist on the table. "Because most of the Association is still oblivious to what you are doing."

122 finally spoke up. "It's true. They are blind-sighted by Dr. Jenever's disappearance and the C-33 specimen at the police station."

"And the two lost numbers?"

"They are still fugitives?"

"Do they know about S-06 and Ol'Barrow?"

122 shrugged. “I they don’t already, Associates might suspect she was he girl at the mansion. I expect to figure it out any moment now.”

“You can tell them it's her. The Signalites are looking for the girl.”

“Why?”

“I have no idea. Maybe her implants are a curiosity to them.”

The Regulator looked uneasy after his remark. “A curiosity, indeed. Well, maybe the Perfect can shed some light on things.”

“Well, yes. Except,” began 321. “How do I get to Druid Isle?”

21ST OF MAY, 1875, 11.12 AM. JOHNSTON'S MACHINE COMPANY, DOVER.

Footsteps reverberated across the court as Ol'Barrow and Old Boy entered Johnston's factory ground. He happened to know the abandoned factory used to buy the rights to produce patented machines, such as Singer, and other known brands. Cheap knockoffs, people called them. Others considered them the affordable alternative for the working class. It did not matter, for the factory closed down regardless. The large building, and associated storehouses, were useless brick and mortar now. The old chimneys, which cast their long shadow in the morning sun, looked like they could topple at any given moment. One of them even wore a nest as a crown, guarded by a single stork. The animal stood on the edge, frozen like a statue, staring into infinity while crows and other birds flew by.

Observing the stork made Ol'Barrow wonder what that bird saw that was so intriguing it didn't care about anything else.

As they traversed the concrete court, Ol'Barrow heard the distant prattling of a generator from inside the main building. So, Mary was right. These were no ordinary squatters. Still, he spotted no signs of occupation.

Silently, he approached the gate leading into the factory’s terminal. Old Boy licked his nose nervously as Ol'Barrow peeked past the massive doors. It was a storage area, separated from the factory floor by a brick wall and some utility rooms.

To his astonishment, Ol’Barrow then found what he was looking for. Near the corner of the doorway stood the very carriage that was used to steal the Signalite bodies from the morgue. One wheel was still crooked from colliding during their escape. This was all the proof he needed to get the police involved. However…” He looked down at the dog. “What do you think, Old Boy? Should I go in?”

Staring at him with foreboding eyes, the dog kept licking its lips.

"You know. Maybe we should check if Igraine is really in there. I mean, we both know the excitement isn't good for her. So, if a dozen peelers storm the place. Or, maybe, the police will attract unwanted attention." Ol'Barrow imagined the sound of a train in the distance, blowing its whistles. "I'll check. Just in case." The mutt was squeaking nervously as Ol'Barrow unhooked his leash. "Stay here, alright."

Old Boy lay down with a questioning look in his eyes.

"Don't worry. I won't do anything stu-. I won't be long."

The thumping of the generator became louder as he entered the storage room. The large sliding doors to the factory floor were slightly ajar, allowing him to peer inside.

The hall was mostly empty, but one of the far corners was suspiciously obscured by wooden boards and cloth like a makeshift wall.

The rooms to Ol'Barrow's left allowed him to walk around the hall, concealing his approach. As he Sneaked inside the dilapidated chambers, the remains of date commercial posters, and imprints of removed furniture, were staining the walls. This place used to be some office, most likely the foreman's. Now, these were but empty cells, smelling of damp charcoal and covered by obscene graffiti.

He snuck through a corridor connecting the various spaces. Peering through a dusty window, he still had no clear view of what was happening in the obscured corner of the hall. The generator's buzzing, however, was getting louder was nearby.

"Good," he whispered, confident the noise would drone out his movements. Encouraged by this stroke of luck, he followed the wires secured to the wall with porcelain knobs until he reached a doorway. Inside the chamber from which the lines originated, he found an emergency generator.

Someone had been tinkering with it recently, for the tools were left behind inside a rusty bucket.

Ol'Barrow stopped when he noticed a discrepancy in the generator's rhythm. He cupped his ear, when realizing the noise wasn't from the machine.

There it was again—a metal sound, like a water pump being cranked.

Carefully, he sneaked to the door and crouched. Like a child in hiding, he peered around the corner into the hall. Nothing.

Convinced it was time to go, he walked on his toes back to where he came from, wishing he wore rubber soles.

Sneaking through a doorway, he noticed a glint past the corner of his eye—a reflection within the dark.

"Who's there?" Ol'Barrow whispered.

There was no reply. But as Ol'Barrow's eyes adjusted, the asymmetrical gestalt of a man wearing a top hat unveiled itself in the blackness of the shadows.

There was the hissing sound of venting steam. Before Ol'Barrow could react a mechanical hand reached out to him.

Ol'Barrow was too late. His windpipe was clenched shut when the mysterious figure grabbed him by the throat. Lifting Ol'Barrow off his feet, the stranger pressed his back against the wall. Metal fingers squeezed the trespasser's neck as the man observed him with his one eye. The other was covered with an intricate monocle that was fitted with a small telescope, long enough to stab somebody in the eye. "What are you doing here?" he growled with an eastern European accent.

"I-can't..." Ol'Barrow squealed pointing at his own neck. He gasped for air as the strange man released his grip just enough for him to breathe.

Catching his breath, Ol'Barrow inspected the stranger, whose arm was large and seemingly unwieldy, as was his bulky leg. The telescope grafted to his right eye socket was impractical. Stranger still, on top of his gaunt face with thick reddish sideburns, was a top hat with an angled stove pipe coming from the side. Yet, despite his asymmetrical deformities, the man still managed to acquire a well-fitted frock coat, be it with a single sleeve.

"I-eh," Ol'Barrow muttered, still gasping for air. He wasn't sure what he was looking at. This man could be a Nyctolar, but he seemed too dignified and nervous.

"I'm looking for..." Ol'Barrow squealed. "A girl. She's missing, you see. And I got a tip that she might be here."

The strange man squinted his eye in disbelief. "A missing child?" His gravelly voice sounded educated but with a Slavic undertone.

"Yes. Red hair. About this tall," he muttered.

"Hmmm?" he growled suspiciously.

"Two different eye colors."

"Uhm."

"Her name is Eh-graine..."

The stranger stared at him, waiting for an indication.

"Uh, she stayed at my place for about a week."

Ol'Barrow's jaws clamped together as he was lifted off his feet again. "That was you?" he bellowed. "She nearly died because of you!"

"Y-yes, but-" Powerless, Ol'Barrow tried to reach the ground with his feet, but the man's brass grip was unyielding. "P- Please," he muttered as the cold digits tightened around his neck.

They were interrupted by small animal feet racing toward them. It was Old Boy coming at them at high speed, leaping with every step.

The man jumped back when the dog grabbed him by his trouser leg.

"What is this? Get away," the figure cried, struggling to shake his leg free.

"It's Iggy's dog," squeaked Ol'Barrow. "You wouldn't hurt a girl's dog, would you?"

The brass man looked at Ol'Barrow with disdain but lowered him on his feet - be it reluctantly.

Ol'Barrow tried to calm the dog right away. "Down, boy!" he said, hooking his prosthetic behind Old Boy's collar.

"Why should I trust you?" the mechanical man said.

"Well, how about by the fact I didn't report your location to the police or the Association when I found your carriage."

The brass man didn't respond right away. "Then, why didn't you?"

"Because I wanted to know if Igraine was Okay."

"Well, she's fine," the brass man said and pointed at the exit. "You can take your leave."

"No! You, people, owe me an explanation! Men died! And I lost my hand!"

A woman raised her voice. "Screaming won't help!"

Ol'Barrow looked sideways.

There, in the middle of the hallway, she stood. Dr. Jenever's pale face looked even more emaciated than the last time they met .

Ol'Barrow rearranged his clothes. "Well, hello, doctor. It has been a while."

"You have a lot of nerve to come here," she said, unwelcoming.

"Says the woman who stole bodies from the police morgue," he retorted. "All of this happened because of you. But please. Do tell me why I am being inappropriate."

"That's enough. What do you want?"

"I want to see Iggy."

She took a quick breath. "Fine."

"And the truth," he added. "All of it."

She crossed her arms. "You don't know what's at stake."

"Well, then, you better explain it to me. The authorities are about to mobilize the army and who knows what else. I can go back to the station and tell them this place is empty. If I don't return, well, they know where I am," he gloated. "So, you better have a damn good reason why I shouldn't report you right this instance."

She gave him a toxic glare.

The brass man faced her. "If this is true, maybe the Chair is willing to listen," he remarked smoothly.

She looked at him, insulted. "Do whatever you want," she said and walked away.

Ol'Barrow observed the doctor pace through the hall. "That was..."

"She's tired," said the brass man. "That's all."

"And you are?"

The stranger looked at him as if he didn't know how to respond. "Mr. Brass," he finally replied.

Ol'Barrow offered him his left hand. "Pleased to make your acquaintance. I'm Ol'Barrow."

After some hesitation, Mr. Brass accepted. Ol'Barrow cringed when he shook him his firm grip. "Please follow me, Mr. Ol'Barrow. But no funny business."

Mr. Brass took him to Igraine's room, where Old Boy raced toward the girl as fast as his three legs allowed.

"Doggie!" Iggy was delighted but didn't get off her stretcher. "No, don't jump- Auw!"

Ol'Barrow pulled Old Boy off the helpless girl, who was groaning in pain be it through smiling lips.

After getting the dog under control, he finally managed to address Iggy, who was still lying on her back. "How are you doing?"

"Alright. I just have some bruises."

"Really?" he asked, skeptical. "Just bruises?"

"And tired, I guess."

"So, are you glad you finally found the doctor?"

Her eyes flinched for a moment. Then she nodded hesitantly. It didn't seem all that genuine. Maybe it was just the stress. Jenever didn't seem like very good company, either. After a moment of conversation, the girl wasn't all that talkative, and Ol'Barrow figured it was best to let her rest and returned to the workshop.

Jenever had retreated into the back, where she was standing in front of a console, plugging and unplugging various wires into an array of sockets.

"So, what is all this?" Ol'Barrow asked as he approached her. "A secret lab? Were you working on all this with Liggit?"

"He helped me with some experiments," she answered curtly.

"Listening to the second signal?"

"Yes."

He nodded, pouting his lips. "Any luck?"

She sighed. "We extracted a crucial component from the body we recovered."

"Stole from the morgue, you mean?"

"We now can properly separate the two lines of code," she continued to explain. "However, it is a two-step verification process. For that, we need their cipher."

"A what?"

She turned to face him. "OK, imagine a difference engine, in which you enter a string of numbers. Then it will put out letters, or words, instead."

He was stunned for a moment. "That thing in his head was a different engine?"

"Close enough," she said, trying to be patient with him. "However, those words still have no meaning to us. We need a cipher to translate it."

Ol'Barrow started to pace around, wagging his finger pedantically. "Let me put this together for a moment. Associate 45, who we found in the freezer at the station, was a terrorist who flooded a Spanish town. Is it fair to assume..." Ol'Barrow thought aloud. "He was being controlled by this machine in his head?"

"Manipulated is a better word," she corrected him.

"Fine... Where do we find this -cipher?"

"It might have been in the Lantry manor... Well, that was burned down. The only other place I can think of is Druid Isle."

Ol'Barrow rubbed the back of his neck. Druid Ilse. He knew where it was. In the Thames Estuary. But it was private property, off-limits to everyone. Still. "I might be able to help with that," he said.

"You can?"

"Well. Maybe my connections with the Association can. Some of them might be more willing to help you. More than you think."

"I wish it were that simple."

"Then make it simple!" he demanded. "What makes you so special compared to us common mortals that cannot comprehend it?"

"You're out of line."

"I'm out of line? My lady. I have been left in the dark for weeks. I lost friends. My hand! Yet here I am. At your service!" He said, red-faced. "I think I have earned the right to know... Why?"

Igraine was rudely awakened by a continuous ringing in her ears. Even the dog looked at her, alarmed by her sudden movements. And then the noise was gone. All she heard was the murmur of distant voices coming from down the hall. She clenched her arms to her chest out of habit, missing her doll, Anwin, very badly. She was one of the few things that gave the girl comfort. Despite being a replica of the original that she brought from home.

In a childish act, Igraine had put Anwin out of reach of the Pendleton Field that kept her alive all this time. By the time she came to collect her, Traveler's Decay already had taken its hold. As she held her cherished friend in her arms , Anwin had fallen apart like burnt sheets of paper into dark flakes drifting on the wind.

Afterward, Dr. Jenever made her a new friend. A new Anwin that wouldn't fall apart. It was the only thing of home she truly came to miss. All other recollections of her world just confused her now. Even if she could go home today, Igraine would do so with the greatest reluctance. Not only would it be like coming back from the dead, but she also brought knowledge from the here-after. A world that brought her a different perspective. One that would not be welcomed.

For better, or for worse. Iggy would be better off staying- even if that meant being trapped inside a habitat akin to a snow globe. A world the Association had built just for them. For some, it was a cage. For others, a sanctuary. She couldn't decide which of them was closer to the truth. Igraine had long conversations about it with Anwin. The only "person" who spoke her language and understood her worldview. And she needed somebody to talk to very desperately.

She was snapped out of her contemplations when a familiar voice shouted through the factory.

"Yet here I am. At your service!" bellowed Mr. Ol'Barrow furiously from down the hall. "I think I have earned the right to know... Why?"

The question piqued her curiosity. That was what she had been wondering. The doctor hadn't been upfront with her either. Dr. Jenever always had a way to skirt questions, and eased Igraine's uncertainty with promises of hope. Promises that would always be adjusted to something more realistic.

"Stay here, boy," Igraine said to the dog as she rose clumsily to her feet. But before she could move a single foot, there it was again. A burning sting spread through the front lobe of her brain. The sight in her left eye just disappeared, as if somebody flipped a switch. The dog barked, alarmed, as she fell on her knees. The stinging sensation spread like a growing ring of fire through her head. Meanwhile, her eye was still defunct. She had lost control again.

She lost awareness of her body. But Igraine knew, that by the time she would regain consciousness, new bruises would be covering her body. Even though she lost all physical control, her mind was all there. Most of it was darkness, interrupted by an unending series of glints, like the sparks emitted by Mr. Ol'Barrow's faulty wiring. A blackness interrupted by flashes, images from her memories. These were the hardest to deal with. Like visions of her mother. Or at least a vague recollection of those she left behind. Their faces had faded a long time ago into generic representations of human appearance. But this was her mother. She was the only person that gave her this feeling of warmth and security.

The memory was rudely interrupted by the blazonry of her home city of Breizh against a doom-spelling blue background.

CRITICAL ERROR, the message spelled out across the emblem.

"UNKNOWN FAILURE. IMMEDIATE SCRYING IS REQUIRED. SUBMITTING ERROR TO THE LEY LINE... ERROR. LEY LINE NOT FOUND. ERROR. SUBMISSION FAILED... ERROR... REMOTE SCRYING FAILED... PLEASE CONTACT CYBERMANCER... COMPOSING ERROR TRANSCRIPT... ATTEMPTING RESTORATION... RESTORATION COMPLETE. PRAISE BRASENNUS."

The horrible sensation of returning to reality.

"Mo-ma..." The hoarse cry for help was out before she knew it.

Meanwhile, the dog was barking and jumping limply in front of the doorway.

Dr. Jenever stormed in and bent down near Igraine. Out of breath, she went through her usual routine to see how bad the damage was this time. With a napkin, Dr. Jenever wiped the saliva off her face while Mr. Ol'Barrow, the stubborn old man, looked down on her with pity. Igraine hated that expression. Igraine, a genius compared to these creatures, was reduced to being pitied like a harmless, sickly child.

While they moved her back on the stretcher, their voices sounded like they came from a well. She couldn't answer their questions. The desire was there, but her mind couldn't comprehend the words anymore. Finally, the adults gave up and hoped things would get better. But they, just as well as she, knew it wouldn't. But instead of letting things run their course, they clung to hope that there was a cure for her condition.

CHAPTER TWELVE

21ST OF MAY, 1875, 1.24 PM. DOVER POLICE STATION.

By the time Ol'Barrow got back, the precinct was perpetuated by an increasingly intense atmosphere. The entrance hall was still occupied by people who sought to report sightings of Nyctolar, making Ol'Barrow fearful that the sensationalism had unleashed hysteria, posing a greater threat than the Signalites themselves.

From behind the front desk, Mr. Huette raised his hand. "Oh, Mr. Ol'Barrow! You're back."

"Yes, constable. No need to be surprised. The Nyctolar are too afraid to attack me now."

"I'll bet they are. I heard how you trashed one with a mop," he boasted. "Speaking of which, the black gentleman is here to see you."

"Most excellent!" said Ol'Barrow.

He was about to walk away when Huette stopped him. "Wait, sir! Did you visit that factory?"

"Yes. Yes, I did."

"Find anything?"

Ol'Barrow raised his shoulders while contemplating his response. "Uhm, no," he said amicably. "Well, apart from traces of vagrancy."

"Ah, good," said Huette reassured. "That is one location to take off the list then. Thank you, citizen."

"Anything to help the community," Ol'Barrow said, tipping his hat, and left.

As he entered his former office, Ol'Barrow was experiencing an uncomfortable sensation as if he were trespassing. The officers with whom he had worked for so many years ignored him like they would an ordinary citizen. It was probably better this way. How many of them defended him when he was arrested? One could argue they were just doing their job. But what about principles? Did none of them dare to stick their head above the parapet when his arrest was obviously part of a cover-up? His frustration with the injustice done to him was mounting again. Anyone could deduce he didn't kill that couple, and Mr. Peal had provided a rock-solid alibi. Undoubtedly, Mr. Peal's generosity was self-serving, but enemies of my enemies, and such...

Ol'Barrow snapped back to reality when he noticed Associate 321 standing in front of a frame hanging in the far corner of the hall. Enclosed behind the glass pane was a newspaper article. The paper had yellowed, but the letters were clearly legible. "Hero in blue faced the fire."

Hand inside his pocket, Ol'Barrow approached the Associate who was still studying the text.

"This is you?" 321 asked, pointing his cane at the front page. It was a sketch of a constable running from the burning building with a young woman in his arms, leaving a trail of smoke in his wake. "I read about it in your report, but I hadn't noticed the headline."

"It's, well..." Ol'Barrow wanted to say that it was something anyone would have done. But it wasn't true, was it? "A single act doesn't make one a hero," he declared instead .

"I agree," 321 said to Ol'Barrow's surprise.

"You do?"

"To be a hero, one doesn't need to step forward," he began rambunctiously. "Everyone else just needs to step back."

"Well," mumbled Ol'Barrow. "That is one way of looking at it."

321 tilted his head with a questioning glance. "Are you alright, Mr. Ol'Barrow?"

He tried to shake off the effects of Mr. Brass' chokehold. Last night's wine didn't help in that regard. "I apologize... It is nearly afternoon. Are we any closer to finding this evidence we were looking for?"

321 sighed reluctantly. "As a matter of fact, I have an invitation from the head of the Signalites himself."

Ol'Barrow's jaw dropped. "You? From the Perfect?"

"Yes, but we need to charter a boat nearby to get there. This whole thing is a big embarrassment for them, you see."

Ol'Barrow shook his head. "No, I don't."

"It appears there is a bit of a schism within their organization," 321 explained. "Between Lantry and... Well, the supporters of the Perfect who appear to be dwindling in numbers."

"Ah, civil war?" Ol'Barrow deducted. "I never heard of this."

"One side has lackeys broadcasting themselves over the ether. The other consists of a bunch of recluses who study wireless transmissions like bible thumpers. Who's side of the story do you think you've heard?"

"Huh, I see your point... So, we are going to Druid Isle then?"

"With haste."

"But I haven't even had my tea yet."
"You'll live..."

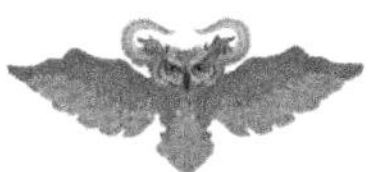

Ol'Barrow and 321 caught a cab to the town of Withstable, with the intent of catching a ferry to cross the Thames Estuary to Druid Isle. An island beside the Isle of Sheppey, so inconspicuous that even the sailors who frequented the port of London might never have noticed it. For centuries, Druid Isle had been used as a private hunting resort in between periods of disuse but had always been closely associated with the local folklore. So, when an esoteric order built a temple there, it surprised no one. Now it served as the headquarters, or rather the main temple, of the Followers of the Signal.

Ol'Barrow nervously rubbed his eyes while trying to stop fidgeting on the uncomfortable carriage bench. They hadn't even left Dover's main streets, and already his patience was wearing thin. He was about to meet the Perfect. A man who, unlike his vocal supporters, avoided the limelight. Writers, reporters, none got to meet the Signalite's leader before. But now, Ol'Barrow, a disgraced police officer, got to meet one of the most mysterious people in Kent.

"Get the cipher!" The command echoed through his mind. But how? Ol'Barrow glanced at 321, who sat opposite of him. How was he going to explain this to the Associate without giving away his arrangement with Dr. Jenever? Or maybe he should. But Ol'Barrow knew so little about the Associate from Africa, wondered why he had come all this way?

He noticed 321 observing something in the passing cityscape. Following his gaze Ol'Barrow noticed the old Norman church. It triggered a sudden sense of urgency inside of him. "This is St. Andrew's Church," he thought aloud. Faint memories of his father's funeral so long ago flashed by. It was the most terrifying experience of his life and his first confrontation with death.

Ol'Barrow had understood what it had meant when constable Huette came to his home to inform the family about his father's demise. When he heard the news, his first sensation was that of unreality; a feeling that something wasn't right. Throughout the day, he kept telling himself that it was a case of mistaken identity and his father was just patrolling his beat. But then, more and more, the awareness started to sink in that his father would never be walking through the front door again.

Ol' Barrow contemplated their final moments together. The very moment when he announced his hatred for his father. He had never forgiven himself for that. When Ol'Barrow saw his father's lifeless body inside his coffin, words were pressing against his lips. But his father looked so serene. Never before had he seen his father this peaceful. It was just that he couldn't speak. He had left this world, and all its baggage, behind. Whatever message Ol'Barrow had for him, his father couldn't have cared less.

"Excuse me, Mr. Ol'Barrow?"

Shaken, Ol'Barrow looked at 321, who leaned closer to him with a puzzled expression.

"This is St. Andrew's Church," Ol'Barrow muttered again. "It's where we held my father's funeral service. I was never that terrified of entering a church."

The Associate nodded, uncertain how to respond. "I can't imagine what it's like. But you have my sympathies."

Ol'Barrow nodded. Then he decided his priorities and swallowed his pride for just this once. "Uhm, sir. Mr. Wilkins," he muttered like a shy boy. "I know this is poor timing on my part, but I need to make a quick stop."

"Not for tea, I hope."

"No, it's... My mother, you see," he said apologetically.

"Has she taken ill?" 321 inquired.

"Worse than that. Dying, sir... I won't be long. I promise, sir."

321 stared at him for a moment. Then he looked over his shoulder, knocked on the panel behind him, and shouted. "Driver!"

Five minutes later, the coach halted on the cobblestones in front of a two-story house adjacent to Park Avenue.

Associate 321 looked up at the two-story Tudor-style house, with its dark oak ribs set between plastered walls and triangular roof gable. "Nice place," he complimented.

"Is her son Herald's," Ol'Barrow explained.

"You brother's, you mean?"

"Foster brother. We were never much of a family." Ol'Barrow then opened the door and stepped outside, sighing. "Let's get this over with."

After taking a deep breath, Ol'Barrow rang the doorbell. Counting the footsteps coming down the stairs on the other side of the door, he prepared for the inevitable confrontation with his brother, who he had not seen in-

A man his age opened up. He was a plump, tired-looking gentleman with a dark retreating hairline, dressed in a red flannel robe with mismatched pants. He raised his heavy eyebrows in surprise when he recognized him. "David?"

Ol'Barrow tried not to come across as too apologetic while greeting his stepbrother. "Hello, Herald."

Herald Oltoak's demeanor was a mixture of concern and inconvenience. "I'm sorry. I wasn't expecting you."

"Uhm. Neither did I," Ol'Barrow confessed.

After an awkward silence, Herald stepped aside. "Please! Come in."

Before Ol'Barrow set his first foot through the door, he heard a loud, obnoxious coughing of an old woman, followed by more coughing, but this time even louder. He looked nervously up at the staircase as if he were expecting a monster to rear its head. "How is she doing?" he asked softly.

"Worse every day," Herald said and added, "TB."

Ol'Barrow swallowed the lump inside his throat. "You are by yourself?"

"The maid is with her. Richard is in the backyard right now. Not that he is of much help."

Ol'Barrow expected as much, but he was in no position to judge Richard. "Is he, um, still fishing?"

"He does, near Whitstable. Days on end."

"I don't have much time," Ol'Barrow insisted. "Official business, you see."

Herald nodded. "Yes, of course. Follow me, please."

Together, they walked up the steps. Meanwhile, the worst of the coughing had passed. Silently, the two men entered the bed chamber, careful not to disturb the patient.

Inside the bed, Mrs. Oltoak sat upright in a fetal-like position while a middle-aged woman sat beside her. The maid held a bowl between their mother's knees as Mrs. Oltoak rasped her throat and coughed up what sounded like a horrid amount of fluid. When the fit had finally passed, she panted hoarsely in a way that Ol'Barrow could feel the phlegm stuck in his own throat with every audible breath. Mrs. Oltoak's dilated eyes turned toward him. "David?"

"H-Hello," he muttered, surprised.

Smacking her lips, she looked away as if she had lost interest. "What are you doing here?" She asked surly.

Ol'Barrow swallowed again and took a deep breath. "I have come to say goodbye."

"O-oh... Well," she rasped her throat again. "Goodbye."

Herald stepped forward. “Mother. Do you know who David is?”

“Of course, I know,” she said. “He is the Fergersons’ child.”

“No, mother.” Herald quickly turned to Ol'Barrow. “She knows who you are,” he admitted, embarrassed.

“Are you going to leave now?” she asked.

Herald exhaled heavily as if he was breathing out his mounting frustration. “Yes, mother. We'll be in the next room.”

“Is Fredrik there too?”

“No. Mother. He's in Paris for work.” He turned to Ol'Barrow again. “She knows where Fred is.”

Ol'Barrow nodded and addressed her for the last time. “Well, it was good seeing you, Mrs. Oltoak. I'll be going now.”

By then, she had already turned away and gone to sleep.

That was it then. Ol'Barrow walked out of the room with his head down, telling himself that he had done what he came to do.

Herald closed the door behind them. “Let me get you some tea,” he said.

Ol'Barrow looked up in surprise. “I, uhm.” he wanted to protest, but his throat was parched.

“It won't be long,” Herald assured him. “The kettle is already heating up.”

“If you insist,” Ol'Barrow said, too polite to refuse. “But I can't be long. Somebody is waiting for me.”

“Ah, police business,” Herald responded, somewhat excited.

Ol'Barrow nodded sheepishly. “Something like that.”

A moment later, they sat down in the kitchen. Based on the fully furnished interior and hand-pressed wallpaper, it appeared Herald had done quite nicely for himself.

“Your family is not home?” asked Ol'Barrow.

Herald was arranging the cups. “Thought it would be best to keep them out of the house till... You know.”

“I see... So. How is Fredrik?”

“Working himself to the bone, as always,” answered Herald. “But he's trying to help the best he can. His wife and children came by this morning to see her one last time.”

“So, it's...” insinuated Ol'Barrow.

“She's been gone for years now, David. I wish it could be under better circumstances. But now, it's for the best. Everything has been arranged. The letters are ready to be sent out.”

The kettle whistle blew, and Herald got up to serve the tea.

"Tea's done?" Bellowed a voice, as rough as sandpaper, from the yard. A moment later, a bear of a man with a silvery beard entered, a pipe clenched between his teeth, and wearing a heavy woolen coat with a tall collar. He froze the moment he saw Ol'Barrow sitting at the table. "Davie? Where have you been, mate? Are cops that busy these days? And what the hell happened to your hand? You look like you escaped from Treasure Island."

"Actually, I lost it in the line of duty," Ol'Barrow corrected his brother, Richard. Being the eldest of four sons, he tended to be the man in the house while their father was on the beat. He had done so with reluctance. And the moment he was free to go, Richard chose a rather lonely occupation of captaining a fishing barge.

"And you didn't tell us?" Richard responded, dismayed.

"I-" Ol'Barrow looked at his foster brothers. The thought had not occurred to him. Neither had he expected them to care? "Maybe, I should have," he admitted. "But... I was astonished when I received the letter about Misses Oltoak."

"You had thought we had forgotten about you?" asked Herald.

"You really think that after all those fights I had to get you out of, we would have left you hanging?" added Richard.

"I mean," Ol'Barrow muttered. "It's been years."

"Well, to be honest, we didn't expect any response from you," said Richard.

"Rich!" interrupted Herald, embarrassed.

"No!" Richard raised his voice. "This must be said. She raised you as her own, despite what a little cocksheit you were. And you never wrote any of us."

Herald, at this point, pretended he wasn't in the room.

"No, you're right," Ol'Barrow confessed. "I have been ungrateful. But for what it's worth, I am here now! And - And I'll go up there and apologize."

Without further delay, Ol'Barrow got off his chair and walked up the stairs to her room. The maid was cleaning up when he came in. "Would you mind, miss? I want to talk to Mrs. Oltoak."

"Of course... I'll be downstairs if you need me."

After thanking the maid, Ol'Barrow looked at his mother, who lay on her side facing the wall. "Mother?" he called out, hoping to get her attention.

There was no response.

"Fine then. You don't want to speak to me. I get it. So, I'll just say..." He was looking for the right words. "I want to thank you. Thank you for taking care of me. Even after dad died. And let me keep the house. And... everything." He was fighting to hold back the tears. "Uhm, but most of all. I, am, sorry. I apologize... Being a terrible son." He faced away. Afterall, what was there left to say?

"David..?"

He froze when hearing her voice. After a moment of hesitation, he looked over his shoulder. She was looking at him with a renewed clarity that seemed unthinkable a moment ago. "Yes?" he muttered.

"You were never sorry for anything," she said without judgment.

He stepped forward, fell to his knees beside the bed, and looked her straight in the eyes. "Well, I am now!" he insisted.

Her eyebrows rose as she stared at the hook. "What happened to your hand?"

"I'm a- I am an inspector now. And-"

The corners of her mouth curled up. "Oh! Your father would have been so proud."

"You think so?"

"Of cour-" the high pitch of her enthusiasm caused another coughing fit.

"Are you- I'll get help," Ol'Barrow assured her as she curled up, whooping horrendously, and he hurried off to get the maid.

A moment later, things had gone quiet again. The poor woman lost consciousness as the maid attempted to keep her from choking. Again, he felt this overwhelming sense of helplessness. Not so much for the inevitable moment that she would pass away. But this horrendous awareness there was little, to nothing, he could do to make her more comfortable.

"Feel free to go," said Herald. "We have things under control."

"She said dad would be proud of me," confessed Ol'Barrow. He couldn't believe she would say such a thing.

"Be grateful," said Herald encouragingly.

"I should be."

"Don't be too hard on yourself."

"You don't understand... I-"

"Yes?"

"I had several brushes with death as of late," Ol'Barrow confesse'd. "It makes a man reflect on his life. I'm not sure I like what I am seeing."

"You weren't dealt an easy hand," Herald responded. "Don't you think you made the best of it. Lesser men wouldn't have made the decisions you did."

"You make it sound like that was a good thing."

"Come on, David. You are a peeler!" said Herald. "Don't tell me you haven't seen what people have done to themselves. How many drunks and gamblers did you bring in?"

"I suppose there is a lot of temptation in the world."

"Mr. Ol'Barrow!" cried 321 from downstairs.

Looking down through the staircase, Ol'Barrow saw 321 standing by the door. "I understand this is a difficult time, Mr. Ol'Barrow. But we need to catch a boat."

"Yes. Yes, you are right..." Ol'Barrow had a sudden burst of inspiration . "One more minute." He hurried down the stairs and raced to the kitchen where Richard was having his tea. "Rich, you still have your fishing boat moored near Whitstable, don't you?"

"Yes. Why?"

"I need you to do me- No. The Empire a favor."

"The Empire, you say? Can I at least finish my tea first?"

321 raised an eyebrow as he entered after Ol'Barow. "Mr. Ol'Barrow, what are you on about?"

As Ol'Barrow looked over the Thames Estuary from atop the fisher trawler, the sky above was turning to a monotone gray. He tucked up his coat's collar for protection against the obnoxious squeaking of seagulls and the wind blowing in his ears that carried the London odor of sewage mixed in with the sea air. Ol'Barrow still found it hard to believe the capital of the Empire could produce a smell that made the scent of Richard's fishing barge seem timid in comparison.

Richard, or rather captain Oltoak, was standing in the small cabin right in the middle of the deck, gloating as he turned the steering wheel of the Persephone. The steam-powered fish trawler was his brother's pride and joy. "They called me mad," he told Ol'Barrow. "When I proposed getting it, they told me it would blow up. I had problems finding a crew. The only ones who would crew her were foreigners. Only Ramos here stayed on for longer," he said. "But when the fish left the estuary, I was the only one who had a ship capable of effectively fishing further off the coast."

"The fish left the area?" asked 321, surprised.

The captain eyed the muddy surface of the water. "See any?"

Leaning over the railing, Ol'Barrow looked at the rippling surface. The water was so murky it was hard to see anything. But his brother persisted. "You used to see them swim all the time, up till 'they' arrived," Richard said, nodding his head in the direction of Druid Isle. "First, I thought it was the noise of construction. But they never returned since. Now you might see some lost jellyfish from time to time."

"Really?" responded 321, surprised. "What were they building up there?"

The captain pointed at the mast rising from behind the vast hedges surrounding the interior of the island. "That bloody pole, or whatever it is! One brainy type said it was an 'antani', or something."

"Antenna?" Ol'Barrow corrected him.

"Yea, whatever." The captain blew out a long plume of smoke. "Sometimes I got some of those pencil necks from the universities, asking me if I encountered any 'unusual' species of fish. Told them it was a better use of their time to see what those freaks were up to. I've seen them on the island, parading around on those fancy metal legs of theirs."

Meanwhile, hissing and puffing, the boat approached Druid Isle. Ol'Barrow observed the wonderfully kept hedges that obscured the island's interior. The only feature that rose above the vegetation was a vast mast rigged on all sides with cables. An antenna for sure, but that was all Ol'Barrow knew on the subject. Bigsby might have known. He had been more appreciative of modern advancement than he was. Ol'Barrow couldn't help but wonder what Bigsby would have thought about these technological achievements if he had learned about their other-worldly origins. But right now, he had bigger concerns.

Standing by the railing, Ol'Barrow asked 321. "I have to wonder, sir. Do we have the same intentions going into this meeting?"

"Do you have specific objectives? " 321 retorted.

Ol'Barrow looked him in the eyes and asked. "Do you trust me?"

"How do you mean?"

"There is only one way I can mean it," Ol'Barrow insisted. "Do you trust me? Do you believe we are working toward the same end?"

"If you put it like that, yes."

"Can I trust you?" he asked, friendly yet provocative.

321 turned to him in a flash. "What?"

"Don't be difficult, man!" Ol'Barrow scolded him.

Leaning on the railing, 321 depressed his head for a moment. "I suppose I never told you how I got wrapped up in this."

"Now that you mention it. You know everything about my past, but I know little of yours."

"What can I say? I was a slave, Mr. Ol'Barrow. I escaped when I was sixteen, and I joined the navy."

"Is that all?"

"You sure you want my life story?" 321 asked, skeptical.

"I do," responded Ol'Barrow bluntly. "You know mine. It's only fair."Fora moment, 321 stared across the estuary. "Very well then..."

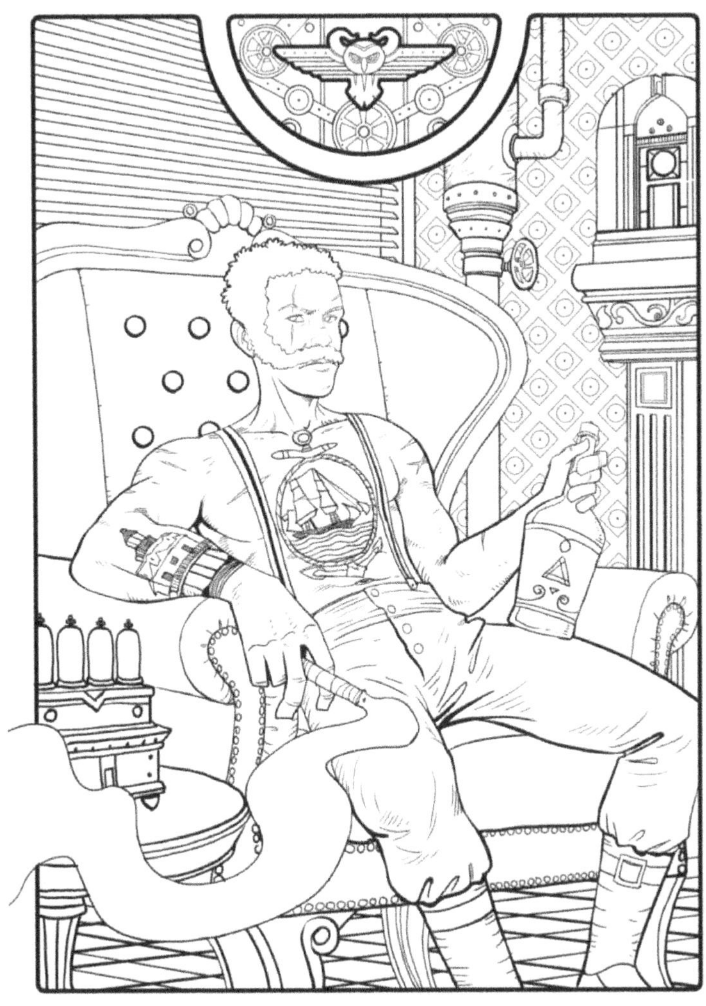

I grew up in Chesapeake Bay, on a tobacco plantation near the Appalachian Mountains. My mother died when I was young. So, on Mr. Krudd's plantation, I was a loner. But the Thompsons looked out for me. Probably because I played with their children from time to time. I had known no other life than that of a slave. But Mr. Krudd made sure we learned to read. A proper protestant should know how to understand the Bible, he said. Through books, I learned about life outside of the plantation.

I would say that Krudd wanted the best for his slaves, but he did execute corporal punishment. laziness in particulaire. Wake up too late, you'd be whipped out of bed. For dallying during work or taking a nap. Lashes. And so on. All I can say about that is he never gave the impression he enjoyed the punishments, even if he would attend as often as he could. But his foremen did. And did they ever. Especially when Krudd wasn't watching. I have seen slaves emerge from the tobacco fields, running for their lives to Mr. Krudd and begging for mercy. If they could find him or his sons. I had it happen to me when they caught me dozing off on a warm afternoon. Whipped me right in the face, as you can see right here.

Two days later, I was with a group in the field gathering hay for the stables, including Mr. Jeremiah Thompson. That is when the foreman fell asleep under a tree.

"We can make a run for it," one suggested.

My eye was still swollen from the abuse, and I wanted out. But not Jeremiah, who shook his head. "I got a family to take care of. I can't run off in the woods like that."

"You want to be a slave forever?" I asked him.

"I'd rather raise my kids like slaves than be a dead freeman, if you don't mind."

"Then let 'um be slaves, brother. Come with us."

"I'm not leaving 'um behind," Thompson insisted and couldn't be convinced otherwise.

So, we ran off. But in the woods, our group was spotted by hunters who chased us for sport, I suspect. That's when I lost sight of the others, and I have no idea what became of them. But I managed to stowaway on a train to Pennsylvania near Richmond. I had to hide away in a crate for much of the journey. Of course, I was ill-prepared for the ride and lost consciousness somewhere along the way. The first thing I remember was waking up when somebody opened my container.

In a panic, I jumped up, scaring the man stiff. Before I could comprehend what had happened, I was standing in the middle of a marketplace, surrounded by a crowd of whites gawking at me. In a moment of self-awareness, I threw my hands into the air and cried. "I'm free!" My cheer was followed by thunderous applause. At the time, I assumed seeing white folk clapping for a negro was the strangest thing I'd ever witnessed.

Some abolitionists took care of me after that. I didn't have many skills, so I joined the Navy. That was the only branch that didn't have restrictions on colored folk joining. That was right after the annexation of Texas in 1845. I was just in time to partake in the war with Mexico that started the year after. My ship was involved in various actions near San Francisco and Los Angeles. I even got a commendation.

By the time the war was over, I had saved quite a bit of money and considered going to Liberia. A colony on the African Pepper Coast, just like the colored from the United States. It sounded implausible. Too good to be true, some might say. Well, I'll tell you about it later.

I remember visiting the ACS office to discuss my repatriation. My case officer had a box of Virginian cigars marked with the light tower. He told me the story of his grandfather, who came over from Europe to Virginia to work as a serf on a cotton plantation. He then gave me the box of cigars. His grandfather always said it was important to remember where you came from...

321 produced a box of cigars from his coat pocket. A watchtower in gold leaf was portrayed on the lid of the cedar wood box. "Do I ever?"

When I left for Liberia, I was optimistic. In the states, even when in uniform, I couldn't walk across the street without getting stares from some of the whites. At times, I wasn't even allowed to talk with white women. It was very clear I wouldn't be free until I was back in Africa. Or so I thought. But the moment I set foot in Liberia's capital, Monrovia, I couldn't believe my eyes.

Now, I wasn't expecting yurts, teepees, or carriages pulled by rhinos. But when I disembarked, it was like walking down the streets of Richmond again. Even the manors were built in a similar Greco-Roman style common in Virginia. The familiarity was nice at first until I met the native population. Just like the buildings, the Liberian Americans dressed very similarly to the white folk in the American South. They looked like a vague recollection of what the southern planters dressed like, fringing on parody. This was made even worse when they stood beside their native servants. In particular, the men who wore nothing but a loincloth. Many of the native women I saw wore western style servant clothes. Yes. In a city without white folk, I could easily separate the black natives from the black colonials.

Before, I held no illusions there was no such thing as black slave owners. I knew there were a couple back in the states. But this city was full of them. And few of them cared about the obvious irony, considering it a part of the human condition.

This place wasn't as open to me as I expected, either. The Liberian Americans, as they called themselves, were tight-knit and weren't eager to employ a man from the States. As for the menial jobs, these were done by slaves. Finally, I managed to find work on a fishing boat. It was hard, but it paid the bills.

"I knew it!" Richard cried from his cabin. "I bet you were a sailor! Pencil pushers don't grow hardy hands like that!"

"Rich, would you mind!" cried Ol'Barrow over the engine's noise.

"What happens on my boat stays on my boat!" he retorted.

"Please, continue," grumbled Ol'Barrow, embarrassed.

One day I met Janny again. I knew her from Krudd's plantation, where I grew up.

I couldn't believe my eyes when I walked inside her small guest house in Monrovia. She built herself a new life here. And, of course, owned a female slave who performed many menial chores while Janny took care of business.

"How did you get here?" I asked Janny.

"With the help of the ACS. They paid for our passage here after the manor burned down."

"The manor burned down?"

"And some of the cabins too..." She said, admittingly.

"Whose?"

"The Thompson's. Those in the manor didn't make it either. It probably started due to the drought and all. After the fire, the ACS came by. Bought us free from the family, and the rest is history."

"Are the others here too?"

"Most of 'um I think. I suspect some of them are either dead or have returned to the States. I know Martin has an estate near Plantation Hill."

"A plantation. With slaves? Are you serious?"

"Yes. He's doing quite well for himself. He used to lead militia expeditions into the bush. That is how he got his slaves."

"And you? How did you get her?" I asked, looking at her servant.

"Oh, Akeelah? Well, I once tried to do business with a native man," she explained. "He would deliver me fresh game for some tobacco from the States. But he said he needed the tobacco up front to pay the hunters. I suppose you could say she was collateral, and he would take her back when he returned with the game. Except, I never saw him again."

"So, you kept her?"

"What was I supposed to do? Send her back into the bush, naked? I clothe her. I feed her and provide a roof over her head. The least she can do is help with the chores around here."

That is how many, maybe even most, looked at the situation. In their eyes, the natives were either children or ruthless savages. Don't get me wrong. The natives aren't much better. Life in Liberia is hard enough without wars with the native tribes. Fortunately for the colony, they fought each other as often as they fought the colonists.

I myself nearly relented. After spending more weeks fishing, the prospect of getting some slaves and starting a plantation became more appealing. Now, I know how to grow crops. I could even manage some people. But I wasn't big on the business side of things. So, I reached out to Martin Krudd. And what do you know, he responded, inviting me to his estate.

That very night, I told Janny about my plans. But she was less than enthused. "Don't trust Martin, Ross," she said. "I don't think the fire back in Virginia was an accident. That's all I'm sayin."

At the time, I thought she was being hyperbolic. But in hindsight, Martin was a known scoundrel. Always had been. He stole food and personal items from the estate. The older slaves, and those with children, saw him as a bad influence. But the younger, more rebellious, saw him a hero, myself included. His heroic status became apparent when his actions invoked the wrath of the overseers, who would punish anyone else if they couldn't find the real perpetrator. And Martin let them. And those accused refused to give him up. On the plantation, we allowed such things to happen. At the time, I saw it as an act of rebellion. But looking back at it, we might have been afraid to speak out.

Mr. Thompson wasn't afraid of Martin. Even though he was a gentleman, he scolded him many times. At the time, I sided with Martin. But, I never dared to admit this to Mr. Thompson.

Finally, I visited Martin's plantation near a place called Prospect Hill in Mississippi in Africa - Yes, that is what they call it. When I arrived, it felt like coming home to a Virginian cotton farm. Men in loincloths and women in western dress harvested the rows of cotton plants. I was shocked when one of the women looked at me. Her gaze pierced my soul. Her eyes were the same as those of my fellow slaves, that looked at me as if I were a white man.

Then, Martin walked off the veranda of his manor to greet me with open arms. "Look, the one who got away! Ross, how have you been, brother? Did I hear right? You're a Navy man?"

"Yes... I heard you were freed after a fire."

"Oh, yeah." He slowly shook his head. "That was tragic. I couldn't stand the scent of tobacco for a year after. Speaking of which... you happen to have some cigars, Ross?"

"Yeah, I do." I took the pack from my jacket and offered him one.

He stroked the cigar against his nostrils and smelled it indulgently. "Doesn't have the same scent as cotton, does it?" He cut off the tip and lit it up with a gasoline lighter - which was no way to light a cigar. Then he proudly showed me his house, which was the spitting image of Mr. Krudd's home, all while dressed in similar attire to Mr. Krudd.

We were sitting down for a drink when I changed the conversation. "I met Janny in Monrovia," I began. "She said the fire wasn't an accident."

He tugged at the cigar and blew out a plume with a glib expression. "Now, why would Janny say a thing like that?"

"Did anyone know the ACS wanted to buy the folk on the plantation before the fire?" I asked.

"Sir, I don't know what you are implying. But if it were up to Mr. Krudd, he would never have given us up."

"Right... I heard the Thompsons died as well."

"Oh, that Jeremiah..." I caught Martin repressing a smile. "Probably for the best. He loved Mr. Krudd." He put the cigar back to his lips. The embers burned brightly as he inhaled extensively and blew out a long thick plume. "He really did... It's fitting, you know. Like with the kings of old, he got burned along with his master," he proclaimed with an ironic smile.

"Yeah... Very fitting."

"Jerimiah was the example of a natural-born slave," Martin continued. "Harmless... Forget freedom. What the whites took from us is our ability to forge our own destinies. But men like Jeremiah... Take life as it comes, my ass," he honed. "He's like a doormat. Grateful for anyone to walk all over him. If the ACS had bought his freedom, he would have tried to sell himself to the first plantation he'd come across." Martin had a hearty laugh over his own joke and stuck the cigar back between his lips.

"Maybe he would have worked for you," I said in jest.

He nearly choked on the cigar as he laughed at my statement. "No way, man! Ha-haa! No way. Ugh-Ugh." He put down the cigar. "I get depressed just thinking about him. Liberia doesn't need people like him. It needs more men like us!" he boasted. "People who see possibilities and act on them."

"Well. We'll see. It appears all the jobs are already taken. I tried the militia, but they are not hiring Americans right now."

"You don't want to work for the militia!" He laid his hands on my shoulders. "I need a new foreman, Ross," he said with that pearly smile of his. "And I can't imagine a better man for the job."

I was speechless. I still have no words for what went through my mind at that moment. Looking over my shoulder, I observed the slaves in the field. It was just like the life I escaped from... In some sense even worse. I looked at Martin. "I can't help but think what the ACS would think of us, setting you free only so you can enslave people."

He laughed heartily. "The ACS. Come on. Do you really think those white folk care? They are happy to get rid of us!"

"I could think of easier ways for them to do so."

"They are afraid of us, Ross. The only reason there hasn't been a large-scale revolt is that there are too many Jeremiahs over there. That would change the moment they realize they have to fight for their lives. So, they just..." he pointed a finger away from us, "send us back."

"Maybe that's true," I muttered. "For some, certainly. But I don't see-"

Martin became defensive. "Look at them," he said, pointing at the slaves working in nothing but a loin cloth. "These are people from the bush, Ross. There was nothing when we came here. The Kru and Greb were occupied by killing each other until we arrived. Then they wanted to kill us instead. Hell, Ross. These people sold each other as slaves. They would have sold us back into bondage if they got the chance. But instead of destroying them, we are teaching them how to farm, read, and pray."

I was stunned at his sentiment.` I can't say he was an exception in Liberia. But to hear it in his words, so bluntly, broke something inside of me. All I could say was, "You sound like a white man."

It was a statement he didn't take very well. He challenged me to a duel that would take place two days later... That is right. For calling him white, he challenged me to meet him with pistols at dawn for calling him white. We even used American-made flintlock pistols.

We started facing away from each other. At the mark, we turned. I fired my pistol without aiming. Right before I felt his bullet hit me in the leg. Writhing in pain, I rolled through the dust. But when I recovered from the initial shock, it turned out I had shot Martin in the stomach.

He passed away the next day.

Martin Krudd's passing sent waves through the colony, and the moment I heard the news of his death, I fled back to Monrovia. It so happened a vessel of the Imperial West African Squadron was inside the harbor, delivering liberated slaves to Monrovia. The West Africa Squadron was under orders to hunt slave traders. It's also one of the deadliest posts in the British Empire, mostly due to the climate. So, when I reported to the steamer HMS Hydra with a bullet wound, they didn't ask many questions.

I stayed with the British navy for some years. I didn't know what else to do other than hunt slave traders. The worst thing was, when we managed to capture another ship, we would drop off the liberated slaves at Monrovia or Freetown. And some of them would end up owning slaves themselves. Nothing was learned.

When the American Civil War started, I considered going back and joining the Union fleet. But if Liberia failed to live up to the dream of creating a slave-free society, what hope did the States have?

I stayed with the squadron, but after the Civil War ended, politicians disputed its necessity. Besides growing weary of my thankless job, I feared I would end up without a cause worth fighting for.

Then, one day in 1865, we caught sight of a Portuguese slave trader heading for South America. The Sao José. She was a fast ship, but the Hydra was a steamer. Unable to outrun us, the Sao José sailed into one of the bays of the Salvation Islands.

We were more powerful, but we didn't want to sail straight at her broadsides. Instead, we waited for nightfall, and under cover of darkness, we landed with a sloop on the island to scout out her position. To our dismay, we found the Sao José stranded on the beach, without lights or other signs of her crew.

A few of us boarded the ship while the rest stayed on the lookout for the slavers. On board, the top deck was empty, and the sloops were gone. No moans, cries, or rattling of chains. Yet, for some reason, the entrance to the lower decks had been bolted shut. We took out some tools and pried it open. Man, the stench of human filth and death that rose from the depths was nauseating.

We went down with lanterns lighting the way. Down there, we found the emaciated prisoners still chained to their cots. Some had already perished in the tropical miasma. Those who were still alive just sat there motionless, like frightened children, not even begging to be released. They just stared at us with frightened hollow eyes.

I reached out for the man closest to me. "Listen, brother. We are here to set you free."

He shrank away as if he was afraid to be touched.

"It's alright. We are here to help."

He refused to look at me, staring into the darkness of the lower deck. Boatsman Sumption walked further down the hold. Then he jumped back! "Oh, dear Jesus!"

When I looked in his direction, he illuminated what got him so riled up. In front of him hung severed limbs from the chains bolted to the rafters.

Lighting up the hold with the lantern, we noticed the trail of blood heading toward the hatch leading down to the lower level.

I immediately produced my colt and asked the prisoner. "Who did this?"

All he whispered was. "Ninki Nanka."

It's not a name you often hear. Ninki Nanka is a monster from African folklore. An amphibious dragon-like beast stalking the marches of the West coast.

"He must mean some large animal," grumbled Sumption. The boatsman never had much patience for things that didn't make sense to him. Of course, none of us had ever heard of the Rifts before.

Four of us went down into the darkness of the lower decks. As we climbed down the ladder, we heard a thrashing sound. It came from a walled-off section of the ship, from the same direction as blood leading straight through the door in front of us. Yet, we felt compelled to follow. The room beyond looked like a stable, including a cage littered with human remains. All the while, the noise of something being slammed against the boards got louder.

As we went to the back of the stable, we caught something in the light of our lanterns. It was the body of a black man lying lifeless on the boards. His lower regions were obscured behind a corner as he lay there, blissfully unaware that something was tearing at him. We immediately assumed it was the Ninki Nanka, hidden behind the wall, as it fed on the body. While it was engrossed by its feeding frenzy, we closed the distance. Whether it was some ill sense of justice or morbid curiosity that drove us, I do not know.

I walked behind Sumption, aiming my pistol over his shoulder while he moved in closer with his rifle, bayonet mounted and ready.

Suddenly, the corpse was shoved in front of us, its lower body enveloped by dark snail-like flaps. The light of our lanterns revealed the front half of the thing, which had the posture of a crocodile but an elongated neck that fanned out into pedal-like jaws with which it used to ensnare the victim. But instead of swallowing its victim whole as a snake would, it tore off pieces of its trapped prey. Its bony scales covered its back and folded outward when it spotted us. Vomiting, the beast spat its victim's remains at us with alarming velocity. Sumption and I managed to dodge the carcass, but the man behind us got hit in the head, rendering him unconscious.

Sumption fired several shots in the dark, as the creature produced wretched cooing noises as if the sound reverberated through a poorly tuned trumpet. It continued to vomit, covering Sumption with the rancid remains of its victims.

We fired at the thing, but it only made it angrier, if anything.

My last companion lost his nerve. "Run, man! Run!" he cried, running back to the ladder.

I fell back when the monster launched its tongue at me. The rubbery tendril pierced my leg like a harpoon. Then it just reigned me in. Desperately, I just emptied every chamber on the beast at point-blank range, and with every shot, the flashes of my gun lit up the star-like jaws of the thing. Before the vapor of my gun had settled, it was apparently dead. I severed the tendril with my knife. Then I woke up the other survivor, and together we left without looking back.

Ol'Barrow looked at him, intimidated. "Was that thing an Outsider?"

"Yes. Of course, I only learned that later."

"What happened then?"

"We got the survivors off the boat, and we burned the Sao José."

"Why do you think they transported the creature?"

"That is what I wanted to find out."

With my captain's permission, I interviewed some of the liberated slaves and investigated the documents recovered from the ship. The clues led me to a small harbor town in Peru. Unfortunately, the admiralty refused to investigate. Therefore, I resigned from my commission, gathered my savings, and left for Peru.

There I found Sante Dane, an old settlement on the fringes of the Amazon from the early days of colonization, located at a swallow bay with many plantations in its vicinity. Despite being the gate to a river running deep inside the Amazon, I couldn't find this waterway on any maps.

"It hasn't been mapped, senior. Many tried but never returned... Some say monsters are lurking in the river." It was one of the few answers I got out of these folks. Most claimed they knew little of the town's origins. The people were friendly enough, but one couldn't help but feel otherworldly affairs were at play here. Its church had altars dedicated to saints I couldn't recognize. Its houses, adorned with spiral-like motives foreign to all other places I passed through, bore great resemblance to the ancient Meso-American civilizations and were.

Then there was a steamer moored inside the dilapidated harbor. A big one, coated in fresh white paint and a golden figurehead of what seemed to resemble a goddess from antiquity.

I was asking around town about the steamer. But the townsfolk were tight-lipped about them, and it didn't take long before I attracted unwanted attention.

When heading for my lodgings one night, I was greeted by two gentlemen in the street. "We're told you've been asking a lot of questions, meu amigo," one of them said while concealing a weapon behind his back. We came to blows, and after a short struggle, we were at something of a stalemate when one of them drew his machete. But at the moment he made to lunge at me with the blade, he was shot.

A man concealed by the shadow of a tree fired at him with a revolver. Then he shot the other with the same ease.

I crawled to my feet when he stepped out of the darkness. "Don't go anywhere now," he warned. He was an older man with a silvery ducktail beard, dressed in a white suit with a matching hat tainted with sweat and dirt stains. "So, what do we have here? A lost negro stirring up a hornets' nest?" he said, with a strong southern accent. "What in tarnation do you think you're doing making an enemy of one of the most powerful families in Sante Dane?" Needless to say, this type of man was exactly the reason I wanted to get out of the States.

"Well, I'm sorry, sir," I answered. "I am grateful for the rescue. But that's none of your business."

"What's with the smug language? You one of those uppity negros?"

"Like I said, sir. It is none of your damn business. Now it's best for the both of us to part ways right now and pretend this never happened."

"Oh, I'm sorry," he responded, feigning insult. "But listen well, boy. You are not going to leave this place alive after tonight. Not without my help."

"I'll take my chances."

"I don't think so. I've been watching these dogs for weeks now. And just exposed myself to save your black ass," he said and cocked his revolver. "And don't think it wouldn't be a pleasure to blow it apart regardless."

Left with no choice, I turned around. "What do you want with them?"

"Well, preferably, I'd blow them away. But I was asked to adhere to protocol, and I am a man of my word."

"Protocol? Who do you work for?"

"Now, listen here, young man. For this to work, do not ask me questions I have no intention of answering. My offer is simple. I need help with haste. Now the folk's lips here are sealed tighter than an Alaskan whore in winter, and we seem to have a common target."

"What makes you think that?"

"Don't insult my intelligence, boy! Running your mouth the way you have can only mean one of two things. Now, if you were the type of idiot who came here to die, you would have done something stupid already. So, that makes you an idiot who is after the Cyprians. Now, I don't know what your beef with the Cyprians is, and I don't care. But I am in need of an idiot, and it would appear the Lord has provided."

I had no choice, so I agreed to this southerner's demands and joined him in his misadventure. That man was Associate 175.

"Wait," said Ol'Barrow. "That bigot is the man you want to avenge?"

"I said no such thing," protested 321.

"Then, why?"

"He was an Associate!" 321 snapped resolutely. "And he likely died by traitors' hands. And if there is one thing I can't stand, it's traitors!"

"You made it sound like you wanted to kill him yourself," said Ol'Barrow, observantly. "Anyway, what happened then?"

"175 send me a message from England."

"No, I meant in Peru," said Ol'Barrow.

321 started to laugh. "Well, that's Association business. And considering you are not one, you are not privy."

Ol'Barrow squinted his eyes. "You are just being spiteful, aren't you?"

321 kept his eyes facing forward. "We're near the island."

"Alright... So, what happened to 175?"
321 sighed.

When I was in Freetown, he sent me a telegram, claiming he needed assistance. A few weeks ago, when I arrived in England, he told me to meet him at the Trident tavern. I waited there for an hour or so before he finally stumbled in. He seemed intoxicated or something. I had seen him drunk before but nothing like this. He was making a scene with his antics, like he lost control of his faculties, bumping into people and making a general nuisance of himself.

I had no choice but to step forward and take hold of him. "What the hell do you think you're doing?"

"I'm doing just fine," 175 said casually and handed me a note. That is when I noticed the fresh burns on his hands. As for the message itself, all it showed was gibberish. Letters and illegible symbols drawn over each other, as a toddler would.

Meanwhile, he prodded my chest. "I need more jenever," he said. "Get it. I need jenever."

"They only have gin," I answered, overwhelmed by his behavior.

"I don't care about gin," he whined. "He's a prick. I need you to fetch me jenever!"

I started to understand what he was getting at. "Let's take this conversation outside."

"No, no, no Hobgoblins are there."

"What are you talking about?"

"You don't understand. They told me what he was up to on the radio."

"Who? The goblins?"

"I tuned in, and there was the sound of crickets drowning," 175 answered. "So, I started looking for the puddle."

"What in tarnation is wrong with you?"

He Ignored my question and continued. "Spirits are trying to contact the mothership, you see. So they can... Sa- Sa-see," he mumbled as a crazy man. "It tha ra-tu--ure."

"Rapture?"

His eyes widened as if my statement was a revelation. "Yes... You get it now!"

"Why-"

Again, he ignored me. "Need to go. Ponies are waitin'."
"I'll take you to your room," I suggested. "Where are you staying?"
"No... They watch. Can't see us together. Goodbye." And having said that, he left in the same fashion as he arrived. A day later, he was found dead on Dover's beach.

CHAPTER THIRTEEN

21ST OF MAY, 1875, 5.15 PM THAMES ESTUARY

321 looked across at the murky waters of the Thames as they approached Druid Isle.

"Dover beach?" muttered Ol'Barrow in disbelief. "I don't recall a body being found."

"It was an Associate who reported the body, and the disposal was handled covertly. Associate 122 claimed he was supposed to meet 175 on that beach. Something about finger rings and toy bears."

"You believe him?"

"If you are asking me if I believe 122 killed him. No, I do not. 175's skull was smashed in by something solid and remarkably fist-shaped."

"So, the Nyctolar then?" Ol'Barrow concluded.

"Who else?"

"I say..." Ol'Barrow was stung by a realisation as the bruises around his neck began to itch. He did know somebody with a hand like that... But he kept his speculations to himself.

As the steamboat followed the bank around the island the obscured levee of Druid Isle came into view. It was the only vantage point from where the isle's interior could be seen. Featureless statues of bronze guarded the archways leading into the central square. Beyond its pointed fences was the Signalite's main temple, which, to the ignorant, might as well have been an alien spaceship. Its polished brass exterior was trapezoid in shape, like a Meso-American pyramid, with streamlined corners and devoid of any decoration. The facade, covering the gable surrounding the entrance, was like abstract art. The outlines followed the trapezoid shape, but within its boundaries, horizontal beams fanned outward like ribs inside a ribcage, perpendicular to which was a wide vertical column resembling a spine. Ol'Barrow couldn't help but squint his eyes as he looked for the tip of the antenna high up in the sky. It looked like a granite needle seemingly in perfect alignment with the facade's central pillar and the top of the pyramid.

"Incredible," Ol'Barrow muttered.

"I told you those blighters are up to no good!" cried Richard.

Ol'Barrow spun around. "Rich... could you-"

"You won't even know we are here," Richard interrupted him, making a mockery of his concerns. "Now, gentlemen, please move out of the way so the lads can anchor the ship."

Hands inside their pockets, the investigators observed the crewman prepare the ropes.

"So, before we dock," Ol'Barrow whispered to 321. "I need you to trust me."

"This again?" sneered 321. "What are you talking about?"

"I found Dr. Jenever," Ol'Barrow said with a straight face.

321's eyes grew wide. "You did?" He bit his lips before continuing. "You're- Alright, fine. What did you find out?"

"She's trying to make sense of the Apocryphal Signal that Liggit wrote about. She believes the Perfect has the cipher we need to translate this Signal."

"So that is what this is about." He harrumphed. "Very well. But you will take me to her when we are done."

After the boat was moored and the investigators had disembarked, somebody emerged from the cabin overlooking the area. A sturdy man with brown sideburns, brushed off his well-kept overalls as he approached them with a roused expression. His resin incased shins, and steel knee-joints squeaked lightly as he paced toward them. "What's this?" he called out with a gravelly voice. "You have no permission to be here!"

"Actually, we do, sir," 321 answered reassuringly. "We are invited by your secretary, Miss Hardy. We are investigating a string of murders, including those of your members."

Although the statement diminished the tension, the man remained suspicious. "Did she now? Fine then, but I am keeping an eye on you. Basic procedure, sirs. We like to protect the privacy of our members."

"How thorough of you," replied 321 skeptically.

"I didn't get the impression your members are very discrete," said Ol'Barrow in jest. "Them proselytizing on the Wave and all."

The man glared back at him. "Those hypocrites?" he said, insulted. "Don't compare 'm to us."

"Then I won't, sir," Ol'Barrow apologized. "I was just wondering."

"Cheerio," the groundskeeper grumbled. "Please follow me, sirs."

321 and Ol'Barrow strung along through the archway. The plaza beyond, usually a place to show off one's exotic flowers, was devoid of life. It had some of the elements one expected inside a fashionable garden, like paved walkways running past arches and even gazebos, but that is where the

similarities stopped. The space was entirely symmetrical, with smooth tiles crafted from different materials that strongly contrasted with each other. But it was the copper rib cage around the entrance that dominated the space.

The grinding of metal could be heard all the way to the manor as they walked.

"How did you get your legs, sir?" Ol'Barrow asked the groundskeeper.

"I lost them to gangrene in India," he explained. "The Dragomen agreed to fit these prototypes in return for keeping the grounds secure."

"Who are the Dragomen?"

"They are the highest tier members. I guess you could call them the executive committee."

"So, they provided you with legs and a job?"

"That's right. I'd be on the blob if it weren't for them."

"I see."

The groundskeeper remarked softly to Ol'Barrow. "They do have something for that hand of yours."

"Here on the island?"

"Neh. We have clinics on the mainland."

"If that is so, what are you doing here?"

The squeaking stopped as the groundskeeper stood in place and pointed at the mast behind the manor. "That right there. That is the antenna that transmits the Signal across the country and beyond." He pronounced the word *Signal* with an unnerving reverence. "The Signal is received most clearly here on the Island. From here it gets repeated to the outside so Decoders at our various chapters can record the codes and pass it on to the Dragonmen who record it into the scriptures."

"I assume the Decoders are another tier within your organization?" guessed 321.

"That's right. I prefer to stay a simple Cog myself. I have enough responsibilities."

"A Cog? Like in a machine?"

"The most common part in the perfect system," he replied proudly.

"I see," Ol'Barrow was a bit unnerved by the statement. 321 did not look comfortable either, especially when they approached the entrance that could have been built by beings out of this world. And the motifs did not stop there. Ol'Barrow was impressed with the interior that looked both organic and mechanical simultaneously. The walls were furnished with ribs curving up and across the ceiling. Impressive, but Ol'Barrow couldn't shake the feeling he was walking through the insides of a whale.

The spaces between the vertical ribs were used to exhibit various items, ranging from lavish artificial limbs to drawings of worlds with mechanical people. The Signalite's perfect world, Ol'Barrow imagined.

Inside a reception area at the end of the hallway, a lady behind a gleaming counter was waiting for them. But Ol'Barrow's attention was drawn to a model of a mechanical man with bat-like wings dangling from the ceiling above. Beside it hung stuffed seagulls, giving the impression the mockup was soaring through the skies. Ol'Barrow imagined this was the future the Signalites were aspiring towards. It appeared to be very promising for amputees like himself. Yet, he could not help but wonder if humanity would ever be capable of living a fulfilling life like that. If the human body could be replaced with anything, where does it end?

In the meantime, 321 approached the woman behind the counter. "Miss Hardy, I assume?"

She was a proper lady, wearing a practical bustle dress, and her black hair was styled in tightly pinned plaits running along the back of her neck. "Yes. You are with the Association, I take it," she said, unenthused. "The Perfect is expecting you. Please, follow me, gentlemen."

Their eyes grew wider when she turned around. The dress' hindquarter was open, exposing her back, which was supported by a mechanical carapace wrapped around her midriff like a corset. She wore ballerina-like shoes due to her bare legs being braced with a cage-like contraption. They couldn't help but stare, too embarrassed to ask questions.

They followed the secretary through a wide trapezoid door and entered a massive chamber where they were surrounded by the sounds of sparks and the gentle hum of an electric generator.

The visitors were stunned.

"Please wait here, gentlemen, as I fetch the Perfect," Miss Hardy said to the men who were standing there with their mouths agape. She left through a double door tucked away in the far corner, leaving the duo to drink in the strange environment. The room looked like a combination of a chapel and a laboratory. Beneath an elaborate web of wires and cables, buzzing with activity, stood a pulpit in the middle of an operation theater consisting of resin steel-enforced benches. Behind that lectern, two massive wireframe cylinders of brass and copper wiring stood on either side of a huge console that was fitted with dozens of meters and gauges, whose needles were swaying erratically from left to right. Behind the machine was another secluded area, barred off and obscured by plain synthetic curtains. Attached to said bars was a sign that read: "Danger, High Voltage!" in red, lighting-shaped letters.

"Where did we end up?" asked Ol'Barrow with a mixture of amazement and dread.

"Well, I guess you could say it's from another world," 321 said in jest.

"You don't say?"

"I have seen stranger things."

They were interrupted by a door opening, followed by Miss Hardy entering the chapel.

Then, the Perfect appeared.

Ol'Barrow squinted his eyes to see if he wasn't mistaken.

"Now, I stand corrected," 321 whispered to Ol'Barrow.

At snail's pace, an enormous buttoned-leather chair rolled toward them, humming like an electric car. Inside it sat the Perfect, unnerving the investigators with his uncanny visage. He, or rather it, was sitting motionless in a wheelchair: a machine onto itself that included a built-in phonograph and a horn that rose from behind the seat. To say it sat there like a doll would be redundant. Because it was one, taking the form of a mannequin that wore glossy human skin. Either they had attempted to make it more relatable, or it was a macabre parody of a man wearing a red smoking jacket with black pantaloons. Ol'Barrow couldn't tell.

But its eyes. Its eyes looked even more alive while trapped behind those metal eyelids. They shifted in their sockets, curiously looking their visitors up and down, unaffected by their abhorred expressions.

From the horn sounded a hollow mechanical voice. "Welcome, gentlemen. I_appreciateyou_coming_all_this_way," it said. The intonation of every word was wrong.

"We_hope_tobe_of_any_help_in_regards_to_this_dreadful_affair."

Ol'Barrow had trouble adjusting to this situation. "Pleased to meet you, sir," he began, uncertain if he needed to address the horn or his face. "Yes, we have some questions regarding..." He didn't know where to start.

Aware is his hesitation, 321 stepped forward. "Let's start at the beginning. What is your relationship with Miss Clara Lantry?"

"Lantry..." he began. Even the poorly tuned machine couldn't hide his disdain. "That _ woman _ has _ undermined _all _ we _ are _ attempting _ to _ achieve while _ accusing _ us _ of... A _ lack _ of_commitment. She _ came _ to _ us _ like _ so many _ others. She _ used _ her _ considerable wealth _ and _ popularity _ to _ buy influence. By _ the _ time _ we _ realized _ what happened, many _ were _ already _ led _ astray."

"Are you aware of Mr. Liggit and Miss Boerhave?" asked 321.

"We _ are."

Miss Hardy joined him. "Few of our siblings dare to stand up to Miss Lantry. But the few who do have informed us of certain events."

"Mr. Liggit claimed in his diary there was a dispute within your organization about the validity of an Apocryphal Signal," remarked 321. "Is this true?"

"That _ is _ unfortunate. Yes _ it _ is _ true."

"What is this Apocryphal Signal?" Asked Ol'Barrow.

Miss Hardy turned grim as she looked at the Perfect.

"Its _ a _ transmission _ by _ forces _ who _ attempt _ to _ distort _ its message _ and _ desires _ to _ guide _ us _ astray."

His claim was conspiratorial, but Ol'Barrow figured he had no choice but to go along with it. "What forces are you speaking of?"

321 interrupted him and addressed the Perfect. "I don't want to waste any more time. Are you familiar with a being named Aqrabua?"

Ol'Barrow raised an eyebrow. "Who?"

"I'll explain later... Perfect, do you know what Rifts are?"

"We _ do."

"Are you aware of similar creatures to those who were killed outside of the Lantry Manor, existing on other planes of existence?"

"We _ are _ aware _ of _ a _ False _ Shepherd. Yes. If _ this _ is _ the _ being _you _ call _Aqrabua, we _ can _ not _ say."

321 leaned his hand on his cane. "This Shepherd, I assume, is the Apocryphal Signal? And you never thought of reporting this to the Association?"

"Actually, we assumed you were already aware," responded Miss Hardy, seemingly surprised by his statement. "An Associate visited us a month ago."

321 seemed stunned by this. "A member of yours?"

"No. An _ obnoxious _ man _ from _ the _ United _ States."

321's expression turned from surprise into a state of nervousness. "His number?" he asked.

"175," answered Miss Hardy.

Ol'Barrow looked at 321. "Wait. Isn't that...?"

"Yes," 321 answered in awe of this revelation. "175 was murdered, presumably by a Signalite. One with a prosthetic hand."

"We _ assume _ it _ must _ have _ been _ one _ of _ Lantry's _ minions."

"We don't have any other suspects," admitted 321. "Do you think his death is related to his visit here?"

"We _ are _ not _ sure _ what _ you _ are _ implying."

"He implies nothing," intervened Ol'Barrow, annoyed. He was quite accustomed to dealing with lawyers at this point, and it was obvious the Perfect wanted to derail the conversation. "What was 175 doing here?"

This time Miss Hardy responded. "He was investigating the disappearance of an Associate. He claimed it had something to do with the flooding of that town in Spain."

"Is that so?" muttered 321 and tapped his cane on the ground. "What brought him to you?"

"I told you. A missing Associate who happened to be a member of ours," said Miss Hardy. "But it was from years back, so there was little information on this person."

"What was his number?" asked 321.

"54?" guessed Ol'Barrow aloud. As 321 was looking at him in surprise, Ol'Barrow immediately wanted to apologize for the assumption that escaped his lips. "My apologies, I didn't mean-"

But 321 ignored Ol'Barrow's mutterings and turned to their hosts. "It was, wasn't it?"

"I can't say. But 175 believed so."

"And?" began 321 impatiently. "What did you tell him?"

"He _ accused _ us _ of _ allowing _ Outsiders _ into _ the _ world. We _ showed _ him that his _ claims _ were _ incorrect."

"How?"

The doll went mute for a moment. "No _ point _ in _ hiding _ it _ at _ this _ time. Very _ well." The Perfect turned his chair toward Miss Hardy. "Sister. Please open _ the _ door _to _the _ Vault."

Not questioning his orders, she the led investigators to the back of the chapel . Her mechanical movements however, while producing the keys betrayed her reluctance.

As Miss Hardy unlocked the bulky latch in the bars, the Perfect explained. "It _ is _ one _ of _ the _ big _ mysteries _of _ our _ cause." After been provided acces to the obscured area, he continued. "We _ believe _ it _ contains _ a _ Rift. But _ we _ haven't _ found _ a_ way _ in. At least, till _ now."

"How do you mea-" The moment the investigators caught sight of the Vault, they were stunned. On top of a round podium stood a dodecahedron-shaped structure that looked like abstract art. The surface, composed of a greenish quartz-like compound, coarse and sharp, was unlike any construction material Ol'Barrow had ever seen. Suspended above the podium was a brass ring bearing copper spherical cages containing crystalline blue prisms. As it turned gently around it own axis, rainbow-colored light beams could be seen from particular angles.

"What are those contraptions?"

"There _ are _ valuon _ crystals _ inside. Perfect-lee _aligned _ so _ they _ create _ a _Pendleton _ Field."

Ol'Barrow harumphed. "W-What' s a Pendleton Field?"

"I thought these were hypothetical," responded 321. "But there is a rumor that a Pendleton-Field allows any Outsider to remain where they are without-"

Igraine! Ol'Barrow realized, finishing 321's sentences in his head. *The Association had kept her in a Pendleton Field all this time!*

In the meantime, 321 continued. "This field is here to keep that thing intact?".

"That _ is _ our _ assumption."

"Your assumption?" questioned 321, dismayed.

"It _ was _ finished _ after _ Mozillian _ died," explained the Perfect defensively. "We _ don't know _ the _ identity _ of _ the _ builders. Despite _ his _ many _ public _speeches _he _ did _ not talk _ much _ about _ his _ many _ projects."

321 stroked his chin. "Was he the one who ordered the destruction of his body? b"

"Yes," the Perfect confessed. "Mozellian _ explained _ his motives rarely. We considered _ often _ what _ he kept _ in _ the _ Vault. But _ the _ more _ we thought _ about _ it, the _ more we _ suspected _ he _ wasn't _ trying _ to _keep _ us _ out. But _ keep something _ else _ in."

"And he left you no instructions?" asked 321 skeptically.

"Correct."

All the while, Ol'Barrow attempted to read the Signalites' motives. But he had a hard time telling if they were lying or were as ignorant as they claimed. "In summary," began Ol'Barrow. "You have no idea what is on the other side of that Rift?"

"Correct."

Ol'Barrow growled inwardly as he sighed. He wanted to confront the Perfect about so many things. But he could not find any contradictions in their statements. "This is all very interesting," he grumbled. "But this is getting us nowhere. Lantry is already out of the picture, as far as I can tell. That leaves her henchmen."

"We _ have _ no _ control _ over _ her _ followers," the Perfect reiterated.

"Can you at least *guess* what they are up to? What about this Ascension you keep going on about?"

"That will do, Mr. Ol'Barrow," interrupted 321 sternly. "But I am curious as well. What caused the rift between you and Lantry...? No pun intended."

The Perfect lifted his hand mechanically off the railing, like an automaton at a carnival. "Like _ many _ actors, Lantry _ has _ her _ head _ filled _ with _ radical ideals _ about reshaping _ society. To _ her, Ascension _ is _ merely _ a _ means to _ an _ end."

321 leaned forward, leaning on his cane. "Ascension sounds pretty final to me. What could possibly be her goal?"

"You _ misunderstand _ us. Ascension _is _ the _ carrot _ she _ used _ to _ hold _ in front _ of the _ horse."

"You have to understand, Associate" added Miss Hardy. "Lantry and members of the bourgeoisie were supporters of the Frankfurt Commune in '71."

"The what?" asked 321, ignorant of the event.

"It was an uprising in the city of Frankfurt," answered Ol'Barrow. "It happened in the wake of the Franco-Prussian war, during which a revolutionary council took control. It lasted for weeks, until it was put down by the French army, was it not?"

"Yes," confirmed Miss Hardy. "But after reports came out of mass executions and other crimes, internationally, revolutionaries became more divided on their politics. Lantry was very much on the side of the Communards."

"I'm sure it has not made her immensely popular with the moderates," pondered Ol'Barrow.

"Not at all. Not even with the more radical types. She-"

"Rome _ was _ not _ built _ in _ a _ day," bellowed the Perfect. "But Lant-tree _wants _ ascension now. She _ knows _ she _ cannot _ have _ it, for _ our _ work _ will _ take generations _ to _ complete."

321 rubbed his chin again. "I have a dark suspicion this is where the Apocryphal Signal comes in."

"Correct."

"Yes... Lantry claimed to have cracked the code, making her able to translate the Signal herself. That's when she started to proselytize for the False Shepherd."

"Like _ mindless _ sheep, they _ believe _ her _ promises _ of _ swift _ ascension _ and the _promises _ of _ a _world _ without _ want _ or _ need."

Ol'Barrow crossed his arms in disbelief. "Don't you believe the same things?"

"Yes," admitted Miss Hardy without shame. "But the first essential step is dismantling the Chaos Engine."

"The what-now?"

Miss Hardy inhaled somewhat reluctantly and explained. "It is what we call the system that created the universe."

"This _ endless _ cycle _ is _ the _ cause _ of _ mankind's _ suffering. For _ each _ virtue, it _ created _ a _ vice. For _ everything _ that _ gives _ us _ joy, it _ finds _ a _ way _ to _ make us _ suffer_ for _ it. Humans _ made _ their _ existence _ bearable _ by _ deluding themselves _ that _ there _ is _ such _ a _ thing _ as _ balance _ between _ pain _ and pleasure."

321 uneasily fidgeted with his cane. "Are you talking about - nature?"

"A _ politically _ correct _ term _ to _ obscure _ its _ cruelty. Through _ the _ centuries we _ have _given _ it _ the _ faces _ of _ men _ and _ women _ to delude _ ourselves, thinking _ it _ could _ be _tamed. That _ it _ was _ on _ our _ side. Instead _ the _ Engine turned _ us _ into _ masochists incapable _ of _ imagining life _ without _ pain. The Signal _ is _ showing _ us _ otherwise. A _ system _ free _ of suffering, hierarchy _ and vice. But _ before _ we _ can _ build _ the _Ascension _ Engine, we _ must _ first reconstruct _ the _ human species _into _ machines _pure _ enough _ to _ forge _ its components."

Ol'Barrow was somehow compelled to listen to it all, despite the sheer lunacy of the message. He couldn't help but sneer. "And you call Lantry a radical?"

But the Perfect went on regardless. "Since _ the _ Fall, our _ species _ has _ been denied _ our intended _ destiny _ and _ are _ left _ to the _ invisible _ hand _ of _ evolution. The _ Nephalim _ were the _ last _ of _ the _ great _ people _ who _ could _ have _ revived the _ Forgotten _ Empire, but _ they _ intermingled _ with _ lesser _ breeds, giving _ rise to _ modern _ men _ instead. The _ Great _ Flood _ then _ washed _ away _ all _ their achievements, leaving _ us _ to _ crawl _ in _ the _ dirt _ like _ worms."

321 swallowed nervously. "Are you referencing the Old Testament?"

"A _ record _ distorted _ by _ trivial _ pursuits _ and _ the _ ambitions _ of _ emperors. But _ it _ will _ do as _ a _ frame _ of _ reference. It's _ all _ that _ remains _ of _ the Great _ Age."

"Until Founder Mozilian discovered the Signal, here, on this very Island," added Miss Hardy.

"A very intriguing story, but!" proclaimed Ol'Barrow impatiently. "Why are the criminally insane of Dover forming an army? And knowing Macarthur, he intends to start a little commune of his own. Not to mention her ally, S-36. Is she one of your creations?"

"We _ do _ not _ know _ of _ whom _ you _ speak."

Ol'Barrow showed him his hook. "This! The one who did this. Killed at least four civilians and an inspector!"

The Perfect seemed unfazed by his outrage. Instead, it responded with. "We could _ assist you _ with _ your _ hand."

The former inspector looked at his expressionless face. He couldn't help but feel the automaton was mocking him. "I'm serious," he warned.

"Forgive _ my _ enthusiasm, Mr. Ol'Barrow. Remedying _ the _ elements _ of _failing _ biology _ is _ a _ passion _ of _ ours. Too _ often, people _ assume _ their _ flaws _as _ incurable. I discourage _ you _ of _ doing _ the_ same."

Ol'Barrow bit his lips together. "Can we please get back to the topic at ha-" Ol'Barrow concealed his hook behind his back and started anew. "You said Miss Lantry decoded the Apocryphal Signal. So, how does one translate the Signal?"

"You see..." began Miss Hardy hesitantly. "And please be discreet about this. Before his death, our Mozilian left us something. A decoding machine used to decrypt what the Recorders are passing on to us."

That got his attention "Like a cipher?" asked Ol'Barrow, intrigued.

"Yes."

"Do you happen to have it here?"

She seemed somewhat puzzled by the question. "Yes. Obviously."

"We need it."

"It _ is _ not _ meant _ for _ the _ likes _ of _ you."

"Alright," said Ol'Barrow casually and continued to think aloud. "If we can't take it, what if... We bring our expert over here?"

Miss Hardy seemed appalled. "Excuse me?"

The Perfect, however, remained eerily silent.

"Yes," continued Ol'Barrow. "He gets whatever we need to discover what Macarthur is up to, and you get to expose Lantry's heresy. Everybody wins."

"And _ if _ we _ do _ not?" insinuated the Perfect.

Ol'Barrow looked at 321, hoping he could pose them an ultimatum.

Instead of answering, 321 directed his cane at the monument. "I suspect there is more to this vault and that antenna," he said. "Perfect, I would like to recommend to the Chair of the Association and armed detachment to the island untill this blows over. In that regard, I think it is best we send an expert as well. You can supervise, and assist in her operations."

Miss Hardy turned to the Perfect, who sat silently in the chair. "And _ so it begins," he said after a brief pause. "There _ is _ little _ we _ can _ do _ to _ stop _ you."

"I'll interpret that as a yes."

The scales of her corset rattled as Miss Hardy raised her voice. "What do you expect will happen?"

"That's just it, Madame," said 321 foreboding. "I don't know. If there is information you withheld from us, now would be the time to tell us."

The mannequin , however, remained perfectly silent.

Walking back to the Persephone, Ol'Barrow reflected on their conversation. The whole thing had left him unnerved. He assumed that the Perfect was insane and knew their dreams of utopia would never come to be. But there was a reason for his madness. Were humans just so accustomed to entropy that they were afraid to let go of it? He turned to 321, who was walking unevenly beside him. "Do you think he's right? Are we just that afraid of change?"

"On the contrary," 321 answered resolutely. If that were true, we would still hunt in animal skins. There is a distinction to be made between human innovation and a desire to change people's nature. The thing about innovation is, it's spurred on by suffering and chaos."

"How do you mean?"

"War. Disease. Crisis like these are forcing nations to innovate, for the alternative is to succumb."

"The alternative..." Ol'Barrow muttered. "Easier said than done."

"But never impossible," he retorted. "As long as people believe there is a chance of a better future, no matter how minor or unlikely, they find a way to overcome."

"You are talking about hope?"

321 shrugged, pouting his lips. "If there is no perspective of a better life, what is the point of even trying?"

"Hmp."

"Something wrong, Mr. Ol'Barrow?"

"Just surprised to hear that from a man with your past."

The Associate stopped. "What do you mean by that?"

"Never mind," Ol'Barrow said, wishing he had kept his big mouth shut.

"Actually, I do mind!"

"It's just," Ol'Barrow was looking for the right words. "A lot of people are born in the gutter, and that's where they die."

"That is not what I am talking about," protested 321.

"I know!" responded Ol'Barrow. "As long certain groups do well, who cares about those in the ghetto, right?"

321 became impatient. "Is there a point to this?"

"There are a lot of people who have no prospects. And instead of getting the help they need, get prosecuted. Oh, they are gambling their money away. Let's ban gambling! As if that helps anyone. Well, apart from those who have their moral sensibilities hurt."

321 just shook his head in confusion. "And what does this have to do with me, exactly?"

Not able to find the words, Ol'Barrow just put up a big smile. "My apologies, sir. It escaped my mind."

The investigators were approaching the pier now. Ol'Barrow looked around, mindful of any Signalites. When he knew the coast was clear, he asked, "Do you think the Perfect is involved with the murder of 175?"

"You are the inspector. You tell me."

"No, I don't," answered Ol'Barrow. "Look at this place. One guy on stilts guarding the gate. The Perfect is a recluse. What do you think?"

"I am an adviser. I spend most of my time interacting with colonial administrators and slave traders. This is the first time I have attempted to mind-read a puppet."

"But you didn't fight those administrators, did ya?"

"I hate to disappoint, Mr. Ol'Barrow, but in order to achieve results, I need to apply tact." 321 grabbed his cane with both hands, squeezing it. "But I was tempted... But more importantly, we need to inform Dr. Jenever of our new course of action."

"Cheerio. She is going to be a barrel of fun then?" muttered Ol'Barrow, following him.

Ascending the ship's ramp, Ol'Barrow called out to his brother who was getting the engine started. "Rich! Can you get us back to Dover?"

"Oh, sure. We have nothing better to do... God save the Queen and all that."

"I'll see to it you are compensated, Captain Oltoak." 321 assured.

"A black man paying me?" boasted the captain. "Now I have heard everything."

"A matter of fact, captain, we would like to hire you for another errand. A lady needs a lift back."

Richard frowned, intrigued. "A lady, you say?"

"Surely, you can manage a woman?"

"I don't worry about that. I can manage more of 'um than you can imagine."

"I'd rather not," responded Ol'Barrow, curtly. Sighing, he turned around and leaned with one elbow on the railing. "So, Associate. What about these guards you mentioned?"

"Leave that to me, Mr. Ol'Barrow. I would like to remind you, these matters are none of your concern."

"Still angry about me not joining, ey?"

"Not angry," 321 assured him jovially. "As a matter of fact, in this case, it might be somewhat beneficial that no one in the Association knows you. For now, at least... Still, I would prefer it if you wouldn't comment on Association affairs."

"You're hiding something, aren't you?"

"Me? No," 321 said, aloof. "But I am not going to lie. I am getting quite tired of the smoke and mirrors as well."

"I bet you are," mumbled Ol'Barrow. "But we need to apply tact."

CHAPTER FOURTEEN

21TH OF MAY, 1875, 8.30 PM. JOHNSTON'S MACHINE COMPANY, DOVER

"Was it really necessary to stop by your house?" 321 complained as the investigators exited the cab in front of the abandoned factory.

"It was," Ol'Barrow insisted. "And this time it only took me a moment."

"It took us valuable time. I had to be back by seven."

"Don't worry about it. I just hope it will convince the city council to get off its arse."

"Languages, Mr. Ol'Barrow. Just because you are no longer an officer doesn't mean you should abandon decorum."

"Hmpf, I have been upholding decorum for so long, I think I've earned it," he retorted. "Years of service and this is how they repaid me. Like I am some useful..."

321 had already stopped listening, distracted by the loud chirping of hungry chicks coming from above. The heron stood on the edge of the nest, shifting its gaze from one direction to another, unfazed by the loud complaints from its young.

"What's wrong?" Ol'Barrow asked.

"Those birds," said 321. "Do they always make such a noise?"

Ol'Barrow shrugged. "The economy is hard on everyone right now."

A moment later, they passed the storage area, back into the main hall where Old Boy lay in a patch of the remaining sunlight shining down through the sky lights. When he saw Ol'Barrow, the pup rose up on three legs to greet them. "Hello boy. Busy guarding the place I see," Ol'Barrow teased, as the dog was rubbing his flanks against him.

Ignoring the animal, 321 walked up to the fenced off corner. There, surrounded by electronics, Doctor Jenever sat bent over her work.

Ol'Barrow called out to her. "We are back, Doctor! We spoke with the Perfect."

She straightened herself, lowering her shoulders. "Can you speak up Mr. Ol'Barrow. The neighbors didn't hear you."

"As cheerful as ever, doctor."

She laid down her work, frowning her lips ever further when she caught sight of 321.

The Associate took of his hat. "Dr. Jenever, I presume."

"And who is this?" she asked, dismayed.

"I am Associate 321, at your service," he answered politely. "I have been looking for you."

She crossed her arms. "I'm sure you have."

"We can trust him," Ol'Barrow assured her. "He helped me get access to the cipher."

"You have it then?"

Ol'Barrow tilted his head. "Well..."

"You'll have to move your operation to Druid Island," explained 321. "It is the only way we got him to agree. However, under the circumstances, it is safer than-"

"I what?" Jenever snapped, her eyes blazing like those of an angry cat. "Are you insane?"

"Everything has been arranged. Transport. Permission from the Perfect. The crew of the Persephone is preparing their boat as we speak... We'll also arrange a detachment of Dragoons to secure the site."

Putting her hands on her sides, she looked at them with a sneering smile. "So... You are delivering me on a silver platter."

"You, the Chair, and the Perfect have more in common than you think," 321 insisted. "Maybe I can alleviate your concerns if you explain some of your motivations. I understand you didn't trust the Signalites within the organization. But I cannot help but feel there is more to this."

Meanwhile, Old Boy was growling as he faced the nearest exit. When Ol'Barrow check to see what got the dog rattled, Mr. Brass emerged from the hall, dragging one side of his body like a poorly tuned automaton. "What's going on here?" Mr. Brass asked.

"Down boy," Ol'Barrow snapped at the dog. "Anyway, the Perfect will allow us to use his decoding machine. However, the doctor will need to move her operation to Druid Isle. I suppose you can join her if you want."

"Hmm," he snarled, stroking his mutton chops, but didn't answer. Instead, he turned to Jenever, who had barely moved since the conversation began. But Ol'Barrow could imagine smoke rising from her ears by the way she was pursing her lips.

"You expect me to just pack my things, do you?"

321 leaned on his cane with both hands. "Doctor, I hate I have to explain this. But we arranged this to assist."

"I didn't ask for your help!"

"You did, Doctor," corrected Ol'Barrow. "You asked me to get you the cipher. And I did."

"Yes, get me-" She held her tongue.

321 continued. "Everything has been arranged. All we need is your cooperation."

Growing impatient, Ol'Barrow changed the subject. "Well, until the doctor bedazzles us with an alternative course of action, can we discuss Igraine's return to... Wherever?"

Jenever sighed. "Yes, you can actually help with that. 321, can you please return Igraine to Pendleton Manor?"

Ol'Barrow raised his eyebrows. *Pendleton Manor? Wait, Pendleton field?* He could slap himself for not making the connection before. Although he had never been there, it was hard to miss the forested estate just outside of the city.

"Madame, under different circumstances, I would be glad to comply," assured 321. "But I cannot help feeling you are attempting to get rid of me."

"All well and good, my friend," intervened Ol'Barrow. "But can we please focus on getting Igraine out of here?"

"I'll take her back," Mr. Brass interjected. "Maybe they won't ask me any difficult questions. Not right away at least."

"Good," began 321. "I need to get back to the precinct anyway. However, I will return as quickly as possible with the crew. I suggest you get your things in order, doctor."

Jenever scowled. "You make it sound like a threat, Associate."

"Dear doctor. You have tried to hide your activities from the Chair, which I can understand to some degree. But you did not disclose any of your concerns to Ra. Not to mention the deaths of inspector Bigsby or Associate 175. Now, what's the reason for that?"

"You just said so yourself. The Signalite infiltration."

321 gave her a blank stare as he was trying to read her mind.

Ol'Barrow couldn't blame him. For some reason there seemed something off about her facial expressions. It resembled human emotions, but they seemed too … superficial.

321 continued. "I consider this matter settled then. He turned to Mr. Brass. "So, you are the librarian... I saw you at the archives when I first arrived."

"That I am," Brass mumbled.

"How did you get involved in this?"

The Brass Man raised his chin in response.

Ol'Barrow recognized this behavior. Mr. Brass was looking for an excuse.

"Certain irregularities within the archive raised my concern," Brass said. "I noticed Associates affiliated with Signalite where not filing their reports as required."

Meanwhile, Old Boy was standing at attention as if he expected something to emerge from the hall.

"Eager to see Iggy, boy?" asked Ol'Barrow. "Come."

Walking through the hallway alongside Mr. Brass, Ol'Barrow observed the mechanism of his hand. It could easily be wielded like mace, leaving a "fist shaped" imprint, as 321 had put it. "If you don't mind me asking," began Ol'Barrow. "You are not from around here, are you?"

"What gave it away?" Brass mumbled, sarcastically.

"Well..." Ol'Barrow was distracted by Old Boy who was walking dog who walked reluctantly beside them.

Then the dog froze and started to growl softly, baring his teeth.

"What's wrong, boy?"

The dog barked aggressively with his tail lowered and his ears straightened on end.

"Down boy! What's the matter with you?"

The mongrel stopped growling but kept his teeth bared. As if being repulsed, Old Boy started walking back and forth from one wall to the other, snarling and staring down the hall as he did.

Mr. Brass' eye lit up faintly as he peered into the shadows.

"You see anything?"

"I do not. Maybe rats? Place is swarming with them."

"Fine, be that way," Ol'Barrow told the dog.

When they walked into the room, the girl lay face down on the stretcher, breathing heavily to the point she sounded like a overweight man snoring.

Stepping closer, Ol'Barrow spoke softly not to startle her. "Iggy, you awake? How are you feeling?"

Without moving, she muttered something intelligible into her pillow.

Ol'Barrow produced her doll that he picked up at home and shook her gently to catch the girl's attention. "I brought your friend."

Igraine finally raised her head, unfolding her arm to reach out to her doll.

Ol'Barrow was taken aback when he got a glimpse of her pallid face that was bleached like the moon's surface with dark bags surrounding her eyes. Unsurprising, but there was something about her sick expression that unsettled him greatly. Her skin was almost translucid, as she smiled faintly with purple lips.

After receiving the doll, she pressed it lovingly to her chest. But she did so with strange feral movements, and a slight manic expression, proving to Ol'Barrow there was something horribly wrong.

"Can you get up?" he asked encouragingly, hiding his concern. "We are going to take you home, miss."

The girl's smile disappeared, and her eyes filled up with suspicion. Holding her toy tightly and she folded herself up in a fetal-like position.

Ol'Barrow kept up his fatherly act despite himself. "Iggy? What's wrong?"

The girl shook her head. "I don- wanna g...," she whispered inaudibly while fidgeting like a small child.

"Speak up, lass. What did you say?" Ol'Barrow asked, closing in on the sickly girl who kept her distance. "Iggy? Should we get the doctor?"

"I don't wanna go!" she cried.

He froze. "Are you serious? Iggy, you need to go back," he insisted.

She opened her eyes wide in defiance. "No, I do not!" she said out loud, manically facing away.

"Ol'Barrow," muttered Mr. Brass with dread under his breath. "Her pillow."

Ol'Barrow shifted his eyes at the stretcher. Dark grey stains on the linen seemed alarmingly out of place. He looked back at Igraine's pallid skin that, the more he looked at it, seemed transparent. "Iggy. You need to go back... Now."

She shook her head again. "No, I don't."

Ol'Barrow looked at Mr. Brass, who glanced back at him with the same sense of desperation.

"Iggy, you are a smart girl. You know what is happening to you."

Clutching the doll to her chest as if it were about to fly away, her mouth quivered. "Well..." She paused to breath. "Maybe that is what I want to happen!"

Stunned. Ol'Barrow stood there, his one hand frozen as he reached out to her. He wasn't sure- no - didn't want to believe she meant what she just said.

But her eyes looked straight into his, followed by a slight but very suggestive nod.

"You don't mean that. "

Without warning, the girl sprinted out of the room, and before Ol'Barrow could recover, was running down the hall. But there was Old Boy, barring her way. Instead of greeting her, the dog snarled and barked loudly as if he were stricken by rabies. Yet, he did not attack.

Seemingly unfazed, she dashed in the opposite direction, shearing past Ol'Barrow who finally shaken off the initial shock. "Iggy!" he cried after her, as he gave chase. But his legs couldn't keep up with the youth who sprinted around a corner and out of sight.

Ol'Barrow ran as fast as he could, slowed down before going around the bend and...

Suddenly, a tall figure obstructed his way.

With no time to respond, Ol'Barrow and the stranger collided with such force it knocked him back and onto the floor. Struggling to get up, Ol'Barrow got a glimpse of the man who lay on his side, groaning as he was kicking his bulky legs. Metal legs that were reminiscent of a construction crane.

"Oh, shit," was all Ol'Barrow could mutter. Spurred on by fear, he propelled himself off the ground like an athlete dashing away at the starting line and ran back down the hall. "Alarm!" he screamed. "They found us! Alarm!"

As he made haste to the main hall, another Nyctolar emerged in front of him from an adjacent room. Slowing down, he looked for a way out.

At the end of the corridor, Doctor Jenever stood in the door opening with a puzzled expression.

"Doctor, get away!" Ol'Barrow cried before running into the stairwell to his right.

At that moment, 321 was inside the main hall when shouting could be heard from the hallway. Then Jenever came in running, crying. "The Signalites are here!"

321 sprang to attention. "We need to get into the street," he suggested. "Come!" He started to run to the best of his ability. But to no avail. The moment he turned around, three Nyctolar had already come running toward them from across the factory hall.

A shot was fired, followed by another. One of the invaders collapsed to the ground with a hole in his chest.

Above, on top of the walkway stood 212, who fired another shot with his revolver. But the assassin evaded this time. 321's mouth dropped when the Nyctolar ran up the wall and reached a six-foot ledge on the wall's support-structure with ease. From there, the Nyctolar climbed to the base of the walkway, grabbing one rafter after another like a monkey.

321 directed Jenever in the direction of the generator room. "Doctor! Go around!"

Without saying a word, Jenever ran off and fled into the corridor.

"That broad is the one we need to get!" cried one of the Nyctolar, and ran after her, ignoring 321.

Brass stormed into the hall and reached out his prosthetic hand to stop the last one from slipping away. But the Nyctolar grabbed the librarian's arm instead, and with a spin of his hips, flung Brass aside.

With clown-like movements, Brass advanced a few unbalanced steps before toppling to the ground. As he fell, Brass rolled sideways as if he just jumped off a moving train. His massive arm swung in a wide arc as he tumbled on his back, knocking over a column of radio equipment that fell on top of him.

Alarmed by Mr. Brass's defeat, 321 nervously unscrewed the cane's handle and unsheathed the baton inside, which crackled to life immediately. His assailant didn't seem that impressed, however. He flexed his artificial arms, sneering. "What are you going to do with that, Yank? Play baseball?" The Nyctolar then picked up a radio case from a shelf and raised it. "Fetch!"

The Associate barely managed to duck as the bulky device flew by and shattered against the wall behind him, spilling its individual components.

"Come on, meater. Don't hide," the Nyctolar sneered as he grabbed the table behind which 321 had sought refuge. Again, the Associate barely managed to retract his legs as the Nyctolar flipped the workbench over with ease.

"There you are! I gonna give you a good-"

There was a thrashing sound. It was Mr. Brass liberating himself from the radios on top of him. His hat was gone, revealing a glass dome through which his brains were visible for all to see. Sparks jolted across the cranium's surface as Brass threw aside the last device, rising to his feet. "You son of bitch!" he swore, red-faced, while faint plumes of heat were irradiating from his head. His movements were fluid now, and the jerkiness in his steps w as gone as he encroached on the Nyctolar.

The assailant lunged at Brass with his fist, but Brass blocked the man's punch. Sparks erupted from the inside of his prosthetic arm as he forced the limb aside, pushing his assailant off balance. As the Nyctolar leaned forward, Brass swung the back of his fist at his attacker's face.

321 clenched his teeth as he looked away. But he already saw the man's head deform by the blunt force of the impact.

When 321 looked up, Mr. Brass leaned over the lifeless body, staring at his own bloodstained digits.

"Never killed a man before?" asked 321.

Mr. Brass looked at him, shaken. "I'm a librarian!"

Caught off guard by Brass' outburst, 321 nodded. "Right... Let's find the others."

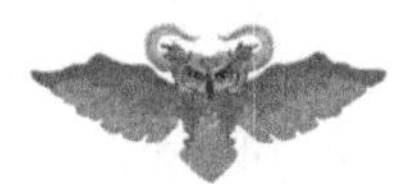

Ol'Barrow was running up the stairs, unsure what to do next. He imagined he could take a detour across the first floor and join the others that way - hopefully. Out of breath, he entered a neglected workshop with forsaken furnishing on the second floor.

When shots were fired ahead of him, Ol'Barrow froze. In the background, he heard screaming and heavy steps running across the concrete floor. "Oh, no," he muttered.

That is when 212 came running in, his back facing Ol'Barrow. In desperation, the Associate turned over a table and took cover to reload his gun with a speed loader.

When a Nyctolar on artificial legs stormed in, 212 got up, aimed his gun, and fired. The shot missed leaving a sizable hole in the wall. Evading the second shot, the creature continued the charge.

Now or never, thought Ol'Barrow and ran to intercept the thing. But as Ol'Barrow grabbed hold, the creature spun around him with an uncanny twirl, body-checking the investigator instead. As a result, Ol'Barrow rolled over the ground like a chump.

212 tried to shoot the Nyctolar again, but his assailant dodged with inhuman speed, gaining distance. Once in range, he lunged at the Associate, knocking him to the ground and sending his gun hurtling through the air. As the Associate was lying on his back, the Nyctolar raised his leg to step on him, smiling as he did.

While the Associate was struggling to keep the Nyctolar from crushing his chest, Ol'Barrow crawled through the dust. That is when he saw the revolver lying about a foot away from him. He was running out of time as the homunculus squeezed the air out of the Associate underfoot. With his hook, Ol'Barrow reeled the revolver in at the trigger guard and grabbed hold of it with his left hand. The weapon felt remarkably like his service Webley, but while pointing it in the creature's general direction, it was far heavier.

When the Nyctolar looked sideways, his sneering expression turned to panic as he looked down the massive barrel. His expression made Ol'Barrow hesitate, and his hand was already getting tired. But the creature sped towards him, he pulled the trigger. To his horror, it refused to budge. The Nyctolar was upon him now, twisting his hips as he ran at him like a soccer player, ready to kick his head off. Ol'Barrow roared as he squeezed the trigger again. The gun flew back as he fired, nearly striking Ol'Barrow in the head.

The Nyctolar, however, staggered back, bleeding as he struggled to remain upright.

Ol'Barrow fired again, cocking the gun outward to stop himself from getting struck by the recoil. As a result, his arm swung backward in an unnatural arc, followed by a tearing sound coming from his shoulder. His body was locked in place, and his arm refused to move. Ol'Barrow knew this pain. His shoulder. It dislocated. He should have known. His body shivered and turned until finally... Release! With an audible pop, the joint snapped back into place, releasing the tension on muscle and sinew.

"Oh-faa-" he gasped. "Haaaa..."

"I-h...Inspec-?"

"What... Who said that?"

The Nyctolar lay lifeless on the ground.

He had won? They had won?

Several feet away from him lay 212 moaning on his back, breathing heavily.

"Associate?"

212 forced some pathetic grunts across his lips, while his chest was barely moving.

After crawling toward him, Ol'Barrow inspected the man up close. "I think-' Ol'Barrow prevented himself from speaking out. But he suspected his ribs might be bruised. "Take it slow. I'll get the Doctor..." If he could find her. Despite the silence, he could only hear 212's audible gasps from behind the beak-shaped mask. Ol'Barrow began removing the goggles and the padded helmet. When it was time to remove the face guard, Ol'Barrow was stunned when he recognized the young man's face. "By Jove... Constable Derby?"

The constable, who went missing all those days ago, looked at him blankly. So, this is how they managed to infiltrate the morgue. But Ol'Barrow had no time to waste. As a matter of fact, it had become forebodingly silent.

After running downstairs into the factory hall, Ol'Barrow found 321 beside another dead Signalite. "Where is Jenever?" he asked, figuring 321 would be okay.

When 321 had directed him to the generator room, Ol'Barrow found her.

"By Jove," was all he could mutter while standing beneath the doorpost.

There was the Doctor with her back toward him. Her sleeves were torn and blood-stained while she was standing in between three dead Nyctolar. From between the ripped crimson ribbons of her cuffs stuck long triangular blades shimmering in the twilight.

"Doctor? How did you...?"

Glancing over her shoulder, she looked even more glossy and dark, with expressions even more lifeless than before. "Never mind that..." she said, aggravated. "Where is Igraine?"

CHAPTER FIFTEEN

21ST OF MAY, 1875, 8.41 PM. JOHNSTON'S MACHINE COMPANY, DOVER

Strands of dark fog drifted all around her as Igraine ran across the courtyard with Anwin clenched against her chest. Her imagination was running wild, bringing harrowing hallucinations to the life she had trouble rationalizing away. The world was in a violent state of entropy. She was running through as storm cloud of volcanic ash as everything around her was being ground to dust. This is what the world looked like when suffering from traveler's decay. Igraine had studied the documentation on the affliction, but nothing in the files could have prepared her for this experience. Every waking moment, she had to decide if she was imagining things or if the sky was really on fire.

Dizzy and out of breath, Igraine was slowing down while the bricks beneath her feet were turning to sand. But she needed a quick breather before Mr. Ol'Barrow managed to caught up. She looked at her precious friend for comfort. "Where shall we go Anw-"

In horror, she observed how the doll's clothes were turning gray and shriveling up like the petals of a wilting flower. That's when the stitches around her mouth came undone.

"What’s wrong?" spoke the doll as her mouth moved a like that of a sock puppet.

Screaming, the girl dropped Anwin as she backed away in fright, telling herself it was but a hallucination.

But then Anwin spoke again. "Iggy? Where are you going? Don't leave me in this place."

Igraine rubbed her eyes, hoping the horror would go away.

Instead, another shape emerged from the fog. That of a slender woman wearing a wide-brimmed hat.

Igraine froze as she recognized S-36. Her silvery manes reflected the dark red hue of the burning sky as Anwin began to sing. "I'm just sitting watching roses in the rain. Feel the power of the rain. Making the petals bloom..."

In the red light of the setting sun, Ol'Barrow was kneeling beside the Old Boy.

Squeaking, the dog was thrusting his nose against Igraine's cherished toy that was soaking up water in a shallow puddle.

Jenever walked up to them, looking like a ghost in a tattered dress. She had retracted her blades and stared stricken at the doll. "Igraine would not leave her behind like that," she said softly, with barely any emotion.

Ol'Barrow was not moved by her sudden concern. "How much time do we have left, doctor?"

"The symptoms have just manifested, so... four days under normal circumstances."

"Normal? Because she lived inside a Pendleton Field all this time?" Ol'Barrow deduced.

She nodded, crossing her arms as if she were freezing.

"What happened during her stay there?" asked Ol'Barrow. "Why is she having fits?"

Jenever gulped uncomfortably. "We tried everything to help her. We negotiated with her people. We even stunted her growth so she wouldn't outgrow her implants. But she is becoming more irrational, and the seizures-"

Ol'Barrow interrupted her. "You're sure she is just angry because of the implants failing?"

"Everything that we did was in her interest. Sir," she said mechanically.

"I see..."

"Doctor!" cried Mr. Brass from down the hall. "You have to come quick!"

As they returned to the workshop, they were greeted by the eerie notes of a distinct song being broadcast through the ether. Ol'Barrow recognized it immediately. The melody of Roses in the Rain, followed by a string of numbers: 8, 54, 68, 122, 321.

Before nightfall, the borough police had arrived on the scene, attracted by reported gunshots. The crew of the Persephone had also come with a cart to load all the lab equipment under the strict gaze of Doctor Jenever, who, for some reason, also insisted on bringing the bodies of the Nyctolar along. She seemed to have a sudden strange fascination with them that was rather unsettling.

Fortunately, 212 was walking again. Ol'Barrow's shoulder hurt, but could still move. It was obvious. However, both men were in worse condition than they wanted to admit. Brass, however, stared blankly at the darkening sky in contemplation.

As the constables were occupied with the crime scene, Ol'Barrow was walking Old Boy around on a leash. The dog was confused, squealing one minute and barking the next, as Ol'Barrow was maneuvering his shoulder to keep the blood flowing.

The tapping of 321's cane reverberated through the yard as he walked up him. "How are you doing, Mr. Ol'Barrow?"

"Feeling older by the day."

Resting his hands on his cane, the Associate gave Ol'Barrow a pedantic look. "You look like a man who is in over his head."

"I suppose I am," Ol'Barrow admitted. "But I have to see this through."

"If this is about S-06, you better make sure you are still alive when we get her back."

"When..." Ol'Barrow sneered, but then he curbed his cynicism. "Yes. Yes, I suppose you are right."

321 lowered his shoulders with a shrug. "I realize our Association has not given you a very good first impression," he conceded. "But once mobilized, we can bring down the wrath of the sky goddess upon them, unlike anything you have seen before."

"And yet, you didn't manage to catch S-36 all these years?"

"Things are different now. If she has taken the girl, S-36 is bogged down, making her vulnerable."

Ol'Barrow pursed his lips as pessimism got hold of him, and he looked up at the sky. "Perhaps... But how did they find us?" he pondered aloud.

321 looked at the gray heron on the chimney. "212... Shoot that bird."

After the Associate drew his gun, an ear rupturing short echoed between the chimneys. The heron toppled over like a statue and dropped down like a brick. As Mr. Brass picked up the carcass, mechanical components spilled upon the bricks. "That says it all, doesn't it?"

As the stood around the automaton, an angry cry broke the tension. "What on earth is all this!" It was chief Mayfair, coming at them from the street, red-faced. "What was that shot? You nearly gave me a heart attack." His expression changed when he saw Brass holding the broken heron. "What is that? What are you?" he asked Mr. Brass. "What's with the bird mask? What's inside the factory?"

"One question at the time, Arthur," responded Ol'Barrow.

"Don't Arthur me, sir. Why is it that every time I see you, there are dead bodies on the floor?"

"Did you sleep at all last night?" Ask Ol'Barrow, genuinely concerned.

"Don't you start!" Mayfair warned him.

"Chief Inspector!" interjected 321. "The Association has the situation in hand."

"You call this- You are supposed to be an adviser!"

"Well... You see, during our investigations, we come in contact with...let's just say our secondary role is espionage."

"Spies? Oh, that is just wonderful..." He looked at the crime scene and held out his arm. "What am I supposed to do with this?"

"We were already working on a plan until we got interrupted. I suggest we continue, starting with relocating Doctor Jenever and her equipment to Druid Isle. I hope you can arrange a convoy for the doctor?"

"Who?"

"Miss Boerhave," he corrected himself. "She was working against Lantry all along."

"So, you have proof Lantry is involved?" he asked, hopeful. When 321 gave him an angry glare instead, Mayfair passed the look on to Ol'Barrow.

"Don't look at me. I don't work for you anymore."

"Alright," Mayfair seceded. "Convoy, you said?"

"Please," 321 insisted. "Time is sparse."

"What about us?" asked Mr. Brass.

"A very pertinent question," began 321, and gave a quick look around. "212, Mr. Ol'Barrow, would you excuse us?"

Ol'Barrow raised his eyebrows "I thought we talked about this," he said. "And I think after all this, I deserve to know what's going on."

321 looked past the corners of his eyes. 212, on the other hand, left without saying a word. Now they were left alone. 321 stepped closer to Mr. Brass. "Answer me, librarian. Did you kill 175?"

He looked at the crushed bird for a moment and nodded. "175 asked me to do it," Brass confessed.

321's jaw dropped. "He what?"

"I think he went quite mad... His reasoning was that no one would have believed if he told what happened."

321 cocked his head. "What happened?"

"He was investigating an old case. When he asked for certain files I... Well, I was aware of their contents."

"Did these files describe the events on Plane 22?" asked 321.

Brass was silent for a moment. "So, you do know."

"I don't," Ol'Barrow interjected. "What are you talking about?"

321 looked over his shoulder. "We'll cross-examine that later. Brass, why did you agree with this?"

Brass nervously shifted from one foot to the other as he glanced around. "Alright, I was the one who was tasked by the Chair with the expulsion of the evidence regarding what happened on Plane 22," he admitted. "If you are as informed as I am, you might have figured those Associates might be responsible for this whole situation. And God knows what else happened because of it. But I did secure what I could in the Bunker."

"Why did you not speak out?"

"I don't have the luxury," Brass growled. "The only reason I didn't end up on a dissection table was because of the Association. The same goes for other outsiders in their care. RA might treat the Association as a necessary evil at the moment, but not all feel that way. If given half the chance, they would abolish the Association and appropriate all its assets, including us," he said, pounding his chest. "Is that what you want?"

"No, of course not!" 321 responded. "But RA already knows."

"The-They do?"

Ol'Barrow, who listened intently, stuck his hands down his pockets. "So, this whole thing is just over some people refusing to communicate?"

"Yes, and no," sighed 321, frustrated. "175 just created a situation so nobody could ignore it any longer... For the small price of his own life." He took a deep breath. "I am not even surprised."

Ol'Barrow cleared his throat. "Sooo, how does this information help us in our current predicament?"

321 thought about it for a moment. "None," he said. "You are excused, Mr. Brass."

"Will you report this to RA?" Brass asked, concerned.

321 looked on as two groaning constables carried away a Nyctolar on a stretcher and took a deep breath. "175 got himself killed to inspire action. Not to start arguments on who's to blame... Maybe, when we'll get through this." He looked at Brass. "Maybe some good men will step forward and demand that they be held to account for their own actions."

Brass swallowed.

"See if you can help the crew load the wagon," 321 suggested.

"Very well, Associate," he said, and walked off with his head down.

"So, do you think he'll confess?" asked Ol'Barrow.

321 looked him in the eyes. "Would you?"

Ol'Barrow paused to reflect . "I suppose I would not."

"It doesn't really matter if he will or not. Brass is but a part of the machine. It is the desire of every cog to keep the machine going."

"So, he just didn't know better, huh?"

"The human condition in a nutshell," grumbled 321. "That is why a wrench needs to be thrown into the system from time to time... For better, or for worse."

Ol'Barrow followed his gaze to Doctor Jenever, who observed as the crewmen strapped the machines down on top of their cart. "Is this the right time to question her?"

"I got a wrench in my hand, and it's aching to be thrown. But, as I said, I'm afraid we need to keep this machine going for the time being."

21ST OF MAY, 1875, 10.45 PM. DOVER HARBOR.
The Persephone's searchlights were scanning the dock as the electronic hardware was loaded on board by a crane under the watchful gaze of Dover's finest.

"She's ready to go!" cried Captain Oltoak.

"Take care, Edward," said Ol'Barrow as he looked on from on top of the pier.

"You better get some sleep, Davy. You look like a Dover whore on Sunday morning."

"I will," he responded with some chagrin. "Good luck, Doctor," Ol'Barrow cried at Jenever, who was standing on the deck beside 321.

"Thank you," she said, be it reluctantly.

The boat left soon after, moving away from the dock with remarkable ease compared to any sailing boat.

"Thank God that's done," said Mayfair, wringing his hands. "Go home, Ol'Barrow. Your plan is moving now."

Ol'Barrow was grumbling over his aching body, feeling ancient compared to the spring constables moving around him. "Home? After this? They might know where I live," he suggested.

Mayfair raised his eyebrows. "Don't tell me you'd rather sleep in the cell again?"

Ol'Barrow put on a boyish grin. "Would you mind?"

Scientia mundos novos aperit

CHAPTER SIXTEEN

When opening his eyes, Ol'Barrow was greeted by the roaring of steel wheels accompanied by the rhythmic thumping on the train track. He found himself reclined on an upholstered train bench in front of a set table with fresh cakes, fruit, and a warm cup of tea.

"I see you are getting comfortable," spoke an imposing but polite voice.

Opposed to Ol'Barrow sat a man dressed in a pristine white suit, with one leg folded over his knee while holding teacup.

"Comfortable is not the word I'd use," said Ol'Barrow while straightening himself. Meanwhile, he tried to bring the man's face into focus. But no matter how much Ol'Barrow strained his eyes, his face was always obscured in shadow. From whence it came, Ol'Barrow did not know. "Excuse me, sir. But who are you?"

"Hm?" hummed the man, sipping his tea.

"What is that supposed to mean? Where is this train heading anyway?"

He put down his cup. "Why are you so concerned with your destination?"

"Isn't it obvious?" asked Ol'Barrow. "I don't know where I am... But I suppose we have no way of really knowing, do we... Look, I know this is a dream. I hope... OK, so maybe I don't know if this is real. I just want to know where this is all mounting up to."

"Wouldn't you rather stay here?" asked the man in return. "All your needs will be taken care of."

As Ol'Barrow was looking out of the window, towns and meadows, mountains and rivers, they were all passing by in a blur. In the distance, pedestrians, vehicles, and air balloons were going their merry way. The landscape looked picturesque, like a model town built to scale in which life was orderly and Utopian. A world where uniformed officers were there for aesthetics. A world in which men like him were obsolete. Ol'Barrow felt trapped. His whole life, he felt wired to fight injustice. First, the injustice is that he didn't get what he wanted. Then, he wanted to fight the wrong that he wasn't the man he was supposed to be.

As he was staring into the distance, a lone robed figure came into view. With its head down, it walked on a barren stretch of road, ignored by a horse and carriage heading in the same direction. "Igraine?" The figure had already disappeared from view, but he knew it was her.

"Why do you care so much?"

"If I won't, who will? Everyone seems to be so obsessed with what they want the future to be they ignore those who have no part in their grand design. Everyone wants to stop the Signal. I do too… But I am not sure my reasons align with theirs." Ol'Barrow observed the shadow. "I got on this train to avenge Bigsby. Now I want to stop that monster from claiming another innocent. But everyone else only cares about the monster… I can't trust people like that… Please, I need to get off."

The man sighed. "Fine then. I will grant your wish."

"Which one? If it affects the real world, I have some requests."

"I was thinking something more fundamental," the man said.

The whistle started blowing, and the train slowed down, coming to a standstill.

"It appears we are here."

Ol'Barrow looked outside. What he saw through the window was his own home.

Perplexed, Ol'Barrow got up. "I will be off then. Thanks for the tea."

"That is fine, Mr. Ol'Barrow."

He faced the man one last time. "Before I get off... Have you been putting thoughts into my head?"

"Which would those be, Mr. Ol'Barrow?"

He considered it for a moment. "Never mind," he mumbled. "Forget it."

Outside in front of his home, the front door was already unlocked when Ol'Barrow grabbed the doorknob. His house was as he remembered it, except for one thing. At the table sat a man he recognized as Nestor Ol'Barrow. His father.

Nester was reclining in his favorite chair, smoking a cigarette - a smell that Ol'Barrow wasn't missing at all.

His father blew out some smoke. "Oh, look who decided to come home."

Walking toward him, Ol'Barrow was caught off guard by how casual his father acted. "I am not a child anymore. I make my own choice now. Well, I suppose I always did, but..."

"Nobody has to take care of you?" his father added.

"No."

"Why did you want to see me?" asked Nestor.

Ol'Barrow's eyes turned moist due to the smoke. "Uhm... The last time I saw you, you left through this door. Ever since that day I..." He turned away as a tear started to flow down his cheek. "God damn it, why is this so difficult?"

"Just say what you want to say."

"Mrs. Oltoak will be joining you soon," he said. "We already said our goodbyes. I... It is my wish I got to say goodbye to you."

"Bit late for that."

"I'll have you know," Ol'Barrow started with a broken voice. "For years, when I came home, expecting to see you sitting there at that table as if it all had been a bad dream... I never let go of that dream."

Nestor gave him a puzzled look. "So, you kept living here?"

"Perhaps. I mean, this place is a mess, isn't it? It's old. Falling apart. Igraine was probably the first one to really do something about it. I suppose she broke the spell that made me believe everything was just fine. But you built it. This is your..." His old wooden hobby horse had appeared at the table, leaning against the backrest of its chair. "You didn't make my hobby horse, did you? Or build the house?"

"Did you ever see me working on the house?"

"I suppose I did not... I am not even sure why I assumed that. Did I convince myself that was true?"

"We believe a great deal of things that aren't true. For example, how often do we fool ourselves that things are fine? Like this shack."

"Well, it's my shack now... And the only thing that stayed with me my whole life."

"You say it as if it is a bad thing."

"Well... I never tried anything else," he admitted.

"Mr. Ol'Barrow," bellowed a voice from above.

"Mr. Ol'Barrow!" Huette's voice tormented Ol'Barrow's ears, which were still ringing from last night's gunshots as he woke up on his bunk bed. "Whut?"

"Wake up, Mr. Ol'Barrow! You gotta hear what is on the Wavy."

Blinking, he turned his face away from the light. "W-Why? What time is it?"

"It's... It's Macarthur, sir."

"Mac-" With a jolt, Ol'Barrow rose. "What about him?"

A moment later, Ol'Barrow struggled to put his jacket on as he followed Huette up the stairs. Inside the office, the Chief Inspector sat at his desk, listening to Macarthur's voice which was being transmitted across the ether. The revolutionary was at his most eloquent as he addressed his audience.

"We! The people are made to believe we must submit ourselves to the forces of nature. That we are but sophisticated animals, evolved from monkeys to resist the hardships of life. That our suffering is the result of sin. And if we just submit to the authority of church and government, we will be rewarded for our troubles when we die..."

"I already heard this from the horse's mouth," said Ol'Barrow. "They are at the Dover Public Broadcast building? Did they make any demands?"

Mayfair shoved his fingers together. "They took the employees hostage, including their host, Frank Dimbleby. The city council requested the Royal Army to contain the situation."

"Sending in the Royal Army?" Ol'Barrow stretched his stiff neck as he contemplated the situation. Surely, unarmed constables were no match for these creatures. Still, you don't bring guns to a fight if you don't intend to use them.

"What do you think?" asked Mayfair nervously.

"This seems something you should be asking 321."

"He is at Druid Isle."

"I see..." Ol'Barrow couldn't help but gloat, despite himself. "So, I am all you have?"

"Be serious," Mayfair hissed.

"Yes, sorry. I haven't had my coffee yet. Huette, would you mind?" As Huette left the office to get his morning brew, Ol'Barrow continued bluntly. "This hostage situation is a trap."

"Why are you so certain?"

"Macarthur. An Orator?" Ol'Barrow scuffed. "No, he is planning carnage. As are the rest of them. They despise our society... Ha, what am I saying? The human condition itself."

"Well, he is firing up the communards and reactionaries with his public speeches. The city council is considering martial law."

"Considering?" Ol'Barrow bit his lips. If it were up to him, he would already have. Then again. It might be the Signalite's intention. Then he raised a finger. "But... They are improvising," he suggested.

"They might have planned this all along, but we forced them to adjust their schedule. Whatever moves they intended to play in their little game, their paws were out of place. Now, we need to entice them to make all the wrong moves."

Mayfair leaned forward. "How?"

Ol'Barrow shrugged. "I think I'll have to go there and see for myself," he said half-jokingly. "I'll be off then."

As Ol'Barrow was walking away, Mayfair called out to him. "Ol'Barrow, where do you think you are going?"

"Do you need to ask?"

Just when Ol'Barrow was about to decent the staircase, Huette raised his voice. "Mr. Ol'Barrow! Your coffee!" he said, holding up a cup.

He held out his hand. "Thank you!"

Huette followed him to the front door. "Don't tell me you are going to the KPB building."

"I need to capture a gang of kidnappers," Ol'Barrow responded.

"You sure, sir? You barely survived last time."

"I know. But I need to be there. Even if it is just to point a soldier's rifle in the right direction. I may not be in the condition to do it myself, but I need to see Macarthur go down. Question him."

Huette shook his head. "You haven't changed, have you?"

"Well... I lost my hand."

As they walked outside, Ol'Barrow noticed two constables standing on either side of the entrance, holding guns. Sports rifles they probably took from home. But rifles, nonetheless.

"Something wrong, sir?" asked Huette.

"Do they really think it is necessary to carry guns like that in public?"

"It makes the people feel safer right now... And they did attack the station before."

"Oh, for Christ's sake."

Suddenly, Huette froze. "What the hell is that?"

As Ol'Barrow looked over his shoulder, his jaw dropped at the sight of the large, motorized coach that pulled up in front of the station.

Amazed pedestrians looked in amazement at the automobile Ol'Barrow had seen at the factory. On top, in the exposed driver seat, sat 212, wearing his mask again.

Ol'Barrow looked at him. "What do you think you are doing?"

"Isn't it obvious? The Association's presence has been requested," he responded in his gravely theatrical voice. "Now get on before I change my mind."

After taking a quick sip of his coffee, Ol'Barrow returned the cup to Huette and reached up for 212's hand.

When Ol'Barrow was seated beside the Associate, 212 pushed a lever forward, the vehicle came into motion. It was just a gentle nudge, but Ol'Barrow's senses were overwhelmed by the sudden movement combined with cognitive dissonance. Even though they were not going fast, Ol'Barrow thrust his legs tensely against the foot panel for security. While holding on to his hat, they drove through Dover's streets with unsettling ease.

"How did you get this machine?" asked Ol'Barrow.

"Association technology," he said, not bothering to elaborate.

"So," began Ol'Barrow. "What's with the whole Shade routine, Derby?"

"Right now, I am 212. If they ask, you are my assistant."

"Your assistant?" Ol'Barrow shrugged his shoulders. "Fine, dear boy. Now, let's talk about how you used my trust to get 45's body out of the morgue," he began judgmentally. "You haven't just deserted us. You committed a crime against the borough. And to top it off, the department lost a good man that day." Ol'Barrow emphasized his statement by holding up his hook.

212 was glancing sideways at the prosthetic for a moment.

On instinct, Ol'Barrow shifted his eyes to the side. "Be careful!"

When 212 pulled the brake, they nearly were launched from their seats as the vehicle to a sudden standstill. A few feet ahead in the middle of the road stood a young girl beside a dog cart filled with coal, gawking at them.

"Oi, scram!" snapped 212.

"Just keep your eyes on the road, boy," scolded Ol'Barrow.

212 just growled as he put the vehicle into motion and drove on without saying a word. His silence became quite awkward.

"You still owe me an explanation," Ol'Barrow said, keeping his eyes on the road this time.

"I noticed people were going missing in my beat," 212 responded. "That's when I heard about the Signalites recruiting people for their... Treatments."

"Let me guess, the brass ignored it?"

"So did the Chair," he added.

Ol'Barrow crossed his arms "One hell of an organization."

"We are still the first line of defense," 212 stated defensively.

We? These Associates really took this fraternity more seriously than Ol'Barrow had assumed. But he didn't get into it. They were reaching their destination anyway.

The Kent Public Broadcast building was an old factory complex converted into a broadcast station.

The royal army had already arrived. Soldiers wearing red coats and red-trimmed trousers observed the building from behind the brink perimeter wall. Inside a horse-drawn caravan sat two soldiers behind a receiver, making notes while they listened to MacArthur's statements.

From the factory hall's roof rose a massive cage-like antenna, and on the field beside it stood a fence-like construction beset with tubular, steel wire cages, interconnected by cables.

As their vehicle stopped, a lieutenant - recognizable by the single pip on his epaulet - stepped up with a rather puzzled expression on his face. "Good day, sirs. You are with the Association of Ishtar?" he asked with a measure of unbelief.

The young man introduced himself with his growly voice. "212. At your service."

"Ah, ha," the officer responded rather uncomfortably. "So, you are our adviser? What can you do to assist?"

"You'll see in a moment," 212 said. "Please explain the situation."

In the meantime, Ol'Barrow walked up to the perimeter of the station's grounds and peeked over the barricades at the entrance of the administrative wing. On its steps, beneath the gilded letters of the KPB logo, lay a lifeless man's body clad in the black and white company uniform.

On the other side of the street, Mr. Peal, Ol'Barrow's self-appointed lawyer, was impatiently pacing back and forth beside a company cart with the Utter-Krapp logo displayed on the side.

Ol'Barrow walked up to him. "Mr. Peal? What brings you here?"

"Members of our family are in there, Mr. Ol'Barrow. I need to make sure all parties act in their interest."

Ol'Barrow was shocked. "Your family?"

"The Ü tter-Krapp family," Peal emphasized without irony.

"Oh," Ol'Barrow muttered. "So, what happened?"

"Right now, the Signalites have barricaded all the entrances while they are broadcasting their nonsense into the ether. We don't know exactly how many. At least nine. There are about fifteen employees inside."

"Has he made any demands?"

"None yet."

It was as Ol'Barrow anticipated. He didn't expect Macarthur to make any either. If anything, this looked like a distraction. Fortunately, 321 had the foresight to secure Druid Isle. How, he wasn't entirely sure. Ol'Barrow just hoped it was enough.

In the meantime, Macarthur's broadcasts continued. "The capitalists send their enforcers, brothers, and sisters. But they stand no chance against the innovations inspired by the Signal."

"That bastard is having the time of his life," grumbled Ol'Barrow.

"Not my idea of a good time," mumbled Peal.

"Mr. Peal. Do you know of any ways in which they might have overlooked?"

"Just the drainpipes," he suggested. "But those were sealed off after this place became a radio station. But surely, these terrorists will make their demands known. There might not be any need for violence."

"Your company deals with terrorists, Mr. Peal?"

"We are talking about family," he responded, distressed. "Wouldn't you?"

Ol'Barrow was baffled for a moment. By reading Peal's eyes, he concluded that he was being deadly serious. "Well..." Before Ol'Barrow could formulate any response, he was interrupted by a low rumbling engine sound. As he looked behind him, a motorized vehicle of unusual size drove down the road. Astounded, Ol'Barrow's gaze followed the armored wagon being pulled by a gasoline-powered tractor. Both were fully enclosed. Even the windows were shallow and protected by bars. The caravan was a long, fully armored coach of riveted steel, crowned with a traversable turret on the front section, housing a maxim-gun of some kind. Its shadow enveloped Ol'Barrow as the vehicle came to a halt, and a ramp at the back of the caravan folded down. Two columns of soldiers, about a platoon of them, marched out the hatch and formed up facing the vehicle. Ol'Barrow had never seen such troops before. Although they wore somewhat typical dark blue uniforms, with red epaulets and cuffs, they were also equipped with lobster helmets with enclosed visors and noticeably short rifles. Or maybe there were large pistols? Ol'Barrow wasn't sure.

Two more people exited the caravan. One was a stocky, short-haired woman dressed in a similar manner to 212, with a red leather jacket and beige pants, but apparently didn't feel the need to wear a mask. Maybe because she wore an eye patch over her left eye, giving her the air of a villain who escaped from a radio-play poster. She was accompanied by a tall soldier with muscles to match, holding an unusual gun under his arm. Judging by the bulky barrel, Ol'Barrow imagined it was a shotgun of some kind, but its frame resembled an industrial tool, like a large drill.

After approaching them, the woman stood at attention and saluted. "I am Associate Soixante," she said with a commandeering French accent. "I am a liaison with the Special Committee Dragoons. This is Sergeant Bucket of the 2nd Dragoons. You must be 212?"

212, who just joined them together with the lieutenant, nodded.

The royal officer muttered uncomfortably. "You don't look like a-" he stopped himself. "I am lieutenant Arrington. First regiment foot guard."

"And you'll leave the operation to us," added Bucket sternly, and continued without stopping. "You and your men will maintain the perimeter and keep civilians at a distance."

"E-Excuse me?"

"Is there a problem, Lieutenant?"

The royal officer's eyes glided across the outlandish combat uniform and looked into his visor. "I suppose your men are better equipped and trained for these types of operations," he said, doing his best to sound dignified.

"Just explain the situation, Lieutenant."

A moment later, they were standing around a camp table, inspecting the floor plans.

"So, we are fairly sure the terrorists intend to use the old drainage system to leave," concluded Soixante.

"That's also our way in," explained sergeant Bucket. "We are arranging for the power to the building to get cut off."

"It won't stop the broadcast," Peal warned. "They have a backup power generator for emergency broadcasts."

"Understood," said Bucket. "When the power goes out on our signal, our platoon will enter through the drainage system."

"Excuse me," protested Peal again. "But we haven't even attempted to negotiate."

"That is not up to you, Mr. Peal," Soixante interjected.

"In that case, I must insist!"

"I'll try to negotiate," suggested Ol'Barrow. "I don't think he is interested in ransom, but maybe he will respond to me regardless. If he is not willing to negotiate, it might prove a valuable distraction. I doubt Macarthur can resist an opportunity to gloat."

Soixante looked at her fellow Associate.

"His plan might work," said 212.

"Bien. We have a bullhorn in the back. That should get their attention."

Ol'Barrow raised his eyebrows. "Oh, I'll get his attention."

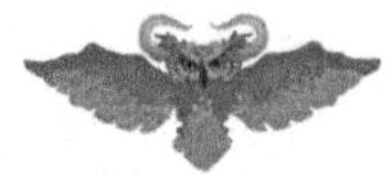

Deliberately, Ol'Barrow was walking past the perimeter wall, copper horn in hand, toward the entrance of the administrative building. Watching the speakers on the exterior wall and the windows of the first and second floor, he raised the bull horn to his lips. "Alister Macarthur! It's me. The bloodhound!" His voice reverberated between the buildings as if inside a mausoleum. "Utter-Krapp said they are willing to negotiate. They just need to know what your demands are." He lowered the horn and waited, but the speakers remained silent. Then a high-pitched shriek erupted from a wall mounted speaker. "Ol'Barrow! Ol'boy. To what do I owe the pleasure that you appear in our yard?"

"I just want to know your demands, Macarthur."

There was a lengthy pause. "Oh, a new world, perhaps. A fresh start."

"How about something more relevant to the situation?"

Another pause. "I have the voice of Kent here, Ol'Barrow. Or rather, their voice. The one that will tell-"

It was already clear to Ol'Barrow Macarthur was using this opportunity to proselytize.

"You say you care about the world so much, have you considered the people who built it in the first place?"

Macarthur ignored his question and continued, "One cannot build a world without anyone being left out. Better reshape it to our heart's desire and shatter their machine to bits."

Ol'Barrow was stunned. Such a selfish proclamation. Grinning, he lowered his head. "In other words," he thought out loud. "Create your own system of oppression." He chuckled again. There was something ironically stupid about that. But not to the fanatic. Maybe Alister was a true believer after all. Ol'Barrow straightened himself and brought the horn to his lips. "How about this? Let one of the hostages on the radio prove their safety."

It stayed quiet for a moment. "They are preparing for their next performance."

Ol'Barrow wasn't in the mood for riddles. "Bring them on the radio!" he commanded.

"I'm afraid I can't do that Dav-"

There was a cracking sound, and the transmission stopped. Ol'Barrow figured they cut the power.

Then there was a bang that sent a shockwave through the ground beneath his feet. Ol'Barrow's chest heaved heavily as he waited for what would transpire next.

A series of rapid-fire bursts, and the occasional gunshot, droned through the interior of the building. On and on it went. Ol'Barrow waited in front of the entrance with only the dead guard for company until the shooting finally stopped.

The armored wagon drove through the gate and took a position in between the various buildings so the turret had a clear view of all te entrances.

The royal soldiers following the wagon were shaken up by a loud thrashing as somebody was tearing down the walls on the second floor. Then, weapons were fired in rapid succession.

"Do they all carry Maxim guns or somethin'?" said one soldier.

"Who gives a hoot? What are they firing at?"

There was a flash behind a window on the first floor and then a gunshot, followed by a series of clumsy, unsteady thumps.

A massive shape appeared in one of the windows. Glass shattered as a Nyctolar burst through the frame with a massive body. Shards were pouring down as thing as he landed on his back. Groaning, the mechanical creature reared up, unlike anything Ol'Barrow had seen before. Only his torso and head were still in place while the rest of his limbs and body been replaced with oversized steel frames and mechanical joints. A gorilla automaton, whose armor plates were riddled with bullet holes and his eyes were bloodshot as if he were on some form of the drug.

"Surrender, or we'll shoot," screamed Lieutenant Arrington.

Instead, the behemoth roared as it was reaching for a decorative planter with Hollyhocks. Soldiers scattered as the Nyctolar lifted the stone object over his head before throwing it at the wagon. But before the stones had even shattered against the plates, the turret had opened fire. The bullets sprayed the creature and everything around it. Most impacts made a loud, steely ping in rapid succession, but his flesh was as fragile as any human's. The gorilla tried to make a desperate dash for the firing line, but a bullet jammed one of its joints. Tumbling forward, he rolled over gravel with the elegance of a trash can, littering parts in its wake until it finally came to a stand still.

Ol'Barrow was holding his breath as soldiers advanced on the Nytolar whose breathing could be heard from across the yard. The giant raised its head, grunting as it swung its arms at a soldier who managed to evade it by just a hair. The rattled soldiers then fired their rifles, shooting him like they would a rabid beast.

"Hold your fire!" cried lieutenant Arrington.

The silence was deafening as everyone stared at the carcass. No one dared to say a thing until the smoke had subsided, and it became apparent the giant had been downed for good.

Ol'Barrow studied him as a mixture of blood and oil was flowing into the gravel. Despite the mechanisms, it looked more like an animal than it did a man.

Above, Sergeant Bucket appeared in the hole where the window used to be. "All clear here," he cried.

The lieutenant's gaze shifted from the dragoons to the massive Nyctolar, then back at the sargeant. "All clear here."

Mr. Peal came running. "What do you mean, clear?" he yelled. "What about the hostages?"

Bucket squatted and addressed Arrington with a slightly hushed tone. "Lieutenant, please see to it Mr. Peal is escorted back to his vehicle."

"I heard that!" cried Peal. "Where are they!"

"Mr. Peal. Go back to your vehicle," commanded the dragoon.

Peal froze two soldiers approached him. There was a cold, unhinged look in his eyes. He suddenly dashed toward the entrance and was soon followed by the same soldiers, intent on catching him. Ol'Barrow also went inside, but only with Macarthur on his mind.

Inside, it smelled like burning. The hallways were riddled with bullet holes and other forms of damage. Some were combat related, but most were just vandalism. Planters had been destroyed. Depictions of animals and people alike had been torn up and ceremoniously burned inside trash bins. Among these items were books, but Ol'Barrow didn't check their contents.

As Mr. Peal was being dragged back toward the entrance, he was threatening to sue the dragoons who were holding him by his arms. *Poor man*, Ol'Barrow thought. He felt morally obligated to help him, but... Instead, Ol'Barrow used the distraction to look for the recording area. When he got there, the door to the studio had already been kicked in.

Soixante came from the other end of the hall as the inspector entered. "Ol'Barrow! You are not supposed to-" Soixante stopped as it was already too late. Ol'Barrow stared at the dead employees scattered on the studio floor. They were shot and lay conveniently around the entrance. It made no sense.

Ol'Barrow was rubbing his face. He had seen similar crime scenes. Mostly gang-related. But not this. Also, one of the men was probably Dimbleby. The man who owned the voice that people all over Dover heard every morning for the last decade. And yet, Ol'Barrow had no idea what he looked like. But of one thing he was certain. This massacre had been orchestrated. Ol'Barrow recognized the spent cartridges on the floor right away. They belonged to .442 and .45 caliber guns, common in the army. This was a botched frame job; one of their misplaced pawns. Ol'Barrow rubbed the back of his neck in frustration. There was nothing anyone could have done about it. Or could have predicted... Maybe, if martial law had been declared. Maybe.

"They were already dead by the time we kicked in the door," said Soixante. "And we didn't hear any shots when we entered."

"They prepared this," muttered Ol'Barrow. "They prepared this so well, they didn't know better."

Meanwhile, there was an odd radio chatter in the background. Peering through the thick glass, he studied the empty recording booth. There was nothing to see in the dark, apart from colored light flickering in the twilight.

"Did they activate the emergency power?"

"Oui. Why?"

As Ol'Barrow opened the door to the booth, recorded screams and shots resonated through the space like a macabre audio play.

"What's that noise then?" asked a Dragoon.

Ol'Barrow flipped on the light. A machine with two turning tape cylinders and a phonograph horn directed at the microphone played horrid sounds, transmitting them straight into the ether.

"Those spools have magnetic tape," said Soixante. "It's used to record-"

Ol'Barrow ran up to the machine and grabbed the spools. "Macarthur, you stinking meater, son of whore!" Ol'Barrow swore as he tore off the wheels with such violence the machine collapsed on the floor. "I'll make you pay for this!"

He got interrupted by harrowing laughter that sounded like it came from inside a tin can. Even then, Ol'Barrow recognized Macarthur's voice right away. "Bwahaha. I give to you Mr. Dimbleby's final broadcast to the world. Dying the way he lived."

Ol'Barrow looked for the source of his voice. "Where are you, you bloody rat?!"

"Welcome to the future where we can manipulate the masses from the comfort of our own home. Soon, we can broadcast our message, the truth, into every home around the world. The systems of oppression will be dismantled. A tool created by the capitalists themselves will be their undoing."

"I will find you-"

"I don't think he can hear you, sir," interjected Soixante.

"Like hell he can't!"

Then came Macarthur's final statement. "Oh, what's that sound? Can you hear the horn blowing in the mist?"

Beneath the white noise, a stream of beeps could be heard flowing through the ether. The sound was fluid, like water running down the water pipes. He heard a laugh. And another one that was a combination of a scream and honing laughter. Somebody was acting like a clown, making monkey noises and other ridiculing behavior as if it were all a game to them.

Inside the studio itself, everyone was captivated by the strange performance, until a dragoon raised his voice. "What the hell is he on about?"

One soldier standing in the doorway looked awkwardly at the scene.

"What do you want?" asked Soixante.

"Sir, we found a survivor."

The sole man who had survived the onslaught had been hiding inside an old pottery oven - a remnant of the factory. After the gunshots had ceased, he finally revealed himself. "I hid the moment those freaks got in." the technician explained.

Soixante had asked. "Notice anything out of the ordinary? Did they say anything?"

"Apart from those freaks!? Well, they were fixing those boxes to the antenna array."

"What boxes?"

MAY 22TH, 1875, 12.35 PM. DRUID ISLE.

In the garden, 321 was casually strolling from one abstract statue to the next. This was the inglorious truth of a soldier's life that it was rife with boredom. At least he felt assured by the fact a platoon of dragoons was patrolling the island. Now, they waited for something that might not come. Tedious, but if nothing happened, it was, at worst, a waste of time that could be spent on something more proactive. But according to the latest reports, there had been no indication where these Nyctolar were being operated upon or rather assembled. What does one call the transformation of living flesh into a machine? Regardless, several of the cult's hospitals were searched, but no proof of any suspect medical procedures had turned up. The doctors themselves claimed innocence.

321 studied a bronze sculpture of a cogwheel that, like a puzzle piece, was about to be added to an amalgamation of fused gears. Many of the sculptures had similar themes about parts being assembled and restructured into orderly shapes. He could see the creative soul and the artist's ability to create something out of nothing. But he wondered if the artist comprehended that his desire for order, which he expressed in his art, was antithetical to his artistic enterprise. How can one create an order from order? Or was that the point? 321 considered it. "How self-aware are these people?" he muttered to himself.

"Excuse me?"

321 swung around. It was a masked man with the eye of RA who had just left the island's edifice.

"Good day, sir. I didn't expect to meet you here," 321 remarked. "Most members have evacuated."

"I have forsaken the Perfect long enough," the masked man said. "If things happen, I should be here. Do you think that they will target Druid Isle?"

"I always prepare for the unexpected," said 321.

"Associate!" cried a Dragoon across the court. "There is a problem with the telegraphs."

321 turned to face him. "Well, get somebody to fix it."

"That is not what I meant, sir."

A moment later, 321 strode through the hall on his way to the chapel. If his legs had allowed him, he would have run. The atmosphere had grown tense in anticipation of something that was about to happen... Whatever that was.

Inside the inner sanctum, Jenever was ordering some servants about as they moved her equipment, and it was obvious her patience had worn thin. 321 had just entered, and already a persistent loop of beeps and the indistinguishable mutterings of some fool resonating through the chapel were already getting on his nerves. "Doctor, what's going on?"

"If you are talking about the noise, it's the Signal being transmitted across all frequencies," said Jenever. "It has flooded all channels."

"How?"

Sheturned to the vault, now clearly visible because curtains that had split the chamber had been removed, and the bars slid aside.

"Doctor, What is in there?"

She shrugged. "It's... From before my time."

"You mean from before when you became what you are, Associate 54?"

She stared at him with a blank expression. "So... You figured it out."

"I wondered about that number 54 from the moment I saw the photo of the crate in which they found 45. It seemed strange for a creature with an obsession for numbers to make mistakes like that... Then, I learned of 54's demise. I didn't think much of it. But then I learned the Association had tried to cover it all up. The Chief Regulator told me the rest."

"Like what?" she asked suspiciously.

He bit his lips, disappointed she didn't fall for his trap. "That you were recovered."

She walked toward the back of the hall. "Aqrabua rebuilt me as his emissary. He is the true Satan to their precious Signal."

"Are you referring to the Signalites or the Creators?"

A forced a smile appeared on her lips. "The Creators? Has the regulator told you what the Creators did to that world? Plane 22."

"I have. There is a thin line between creation and destruction. Yet, there is always some foundation that remains, even if that is just a memory. As I understand it, they tried to dig that away as well."

"They tried to wipe the slate clean," summarized Jenever. "That is how they hide. That is why Aqrabua can't find them."

He cocked his head. "They are hiding from him?"

"Aqrabua is not a "him". It's a concept. Something the Creators tried to hide away. A part of themselves." Her face contorted in some awkward expression between crying and manic laughter. "And we set it free," she said with a crooked smile. "We hoped it would leave us alone. You know, out of some sort of gratitude."

"That sounds rather naive," said 321 softly. "Why not destroy those wretches on Plane 22 and put Associate 9 out of his suffering.?"

"You can't kill an idea," she responded, insulted.

"Right... Why-" He pondered his next question. "Why did you-"

"Associate 54 didn't intend to," she interrupted him. "The report didn't lie. She went back to Plane 22 to… receive Judgment. What do you think justice is in the eyes of those things?"

"And then they built you," 321 concluded. "The original S-36."

She tried not to be insulted by his designation. "Label me how you want, Associate."

Biting his lips together, he decided to let the matter rest. "Is this also the reason why the current S-36 is targeting Associates?"

"Despite her citing my former number, I never met her," said Dr. Jenever.

"But you believe the Association has a hand in her creation?"

"I know how Aqrabua operates," she retorted. "He uses avatars to be his hands. Its prophets, or conduits. Despite being under his control, we- S-36..." Jenever corrected herself, "has some free will inside of her. It's part of their arrangement that she gets to do what she desires."

He nodded thoughtfully. "Did Aqrabua make such an arrangement with you?"

"Yes," she admitted. "And I will speak no more about it."

321 inhaled deeply as he straightened his back. “Don't worry, you don't need to. I think I am starting to understand what this is really about.”

“Excuse me?”

“This has nothing to do with what the Signalites want, has it?”

Her chest heaved as she looked at him in silence. Words were forming behind her lips, grounding her teeth, but she said nothing. Then she turned away. “Let me show you something.” She opened the door to the inner court of the complex. That was where the base of the antenna was located.

The metallic sound of the suspension cables swaying in the wind resonated through the court. At its center was a massive silvery dish fifty feet in diameter and nine feet deep, with the base of the mast right in the middle.

“What is this?” 321 asked. His voice resonated between the buildings.

“A radio telescope,” explained Jenever. “The machine that will transmit the consciousness of the faithful to the world hereafter.”

He looked up at the top of the beam reaching into the sky. “They wirelessly transmit themselves to heaven?” 321 muttered as a statement and question at the same time.

“By lack of a better word...”

“Why haven't they used it yet?”

"The _ blueprint _ of _ the _ Machine _ is _ not _ yet _ complete," spoke the Perfect as Miss Hardy pushed him into the courtyard. "Although _ the _ antenna _ is _ functional, we _ still _ need _ to _ construct _ means _ to _store _one's _ consciousness. Generate _ energy. Create _ safeguards _ to _ guarantee successful _ transfer."

Miss Hardy continued. “We are talking about city-sized storage facilities... For souls.”

“Like a necropolis?” 321 remarked.

“As a temporary measure,” Hardy assured him.

321 looked at Jenever, hoping to get some acknowledgment of the sheer preposterousness of the concept. But she gave no such thing. “Based on what I heard, Lantry wanted to accelerate the Ascension. How will she do it? Can they even transfer their minds in this state?”

"Of _ course _ not!" The Perfect's volume was louder than usual. "Not _ without our _ translations."

321 shifted his eyes to Jenever, whose expression was unmoved by the Perfect's outburst. If his assumption was correct, those

translations be damned, and these Signalites and Nyctolar were but a mere means to an end.

Still, their enemy's intentions remained a mystery, shrouded by conspiracies unrelated to mortal affairs. An uneasy feeling crept up on him as he listened to the endless stream of electric tones, wondering where a being as Aqrabua could be hiding. Then it dawned on him.

"Where do these souls go when they ascend?"

Jenever looked up at the sky. "Elysium."

CHAPTER SEVENTEEN

A crimson vortex of glowing veins spun around Igraine as if she drifted inside the eye of a whirlwind. She wasn’t afraid. Simply reminded why she wanted the pain to end. To die free. Not confined to a room until death finally took her. For the past year, every day felt like the most painful one of her life. Sketching at one moment. Waking up on the floor the next with her drawing ruined and drooled on. It didn't even surprise her anymore—just part of the routine.

Memories arose from the dark mass like soap bubbles before subsiding again beneath the surface. Most were faces of the past few years. Oh, these people, sure, they wanted to help. But all those promises they couldn't keep just turned them into liars. Lies intended to give her hope but instead reminded her that she was something to be pitied and in need of special care. She longed for danger. It is what drove her to enter the rift of this world in the first place. Igraine had wondered if, had she known what would happen, she could have stopped herself.

"Igraine?"

She awoke from her contemplations. Igraine was home again, back in Breizh. But it all looked washed out, like a pastel painting based on memories from when she was twelve.

"Where have you been?" Her mother's face was but a blur now. A generic memory of a woman with features one could consider motherly, like the image of Saint Mary.

"On the wall," Igraine said. She knew she wasn't supposed to be there: The Wardens would have taken her away if they had caught her. But she was a child, an apprentice, and a daughter of an influential Mage. So, enacting any actual punishment was not in their interest.

"Why?" asked her mother.

"I like looking at the forest. I want to know what those reed houses in the distance are like. Why can't papa take me along?"

Her mother shrugged her shoulders. "Those people are not like us. They envy us, but there is so much they do not understand."

"Why not?"

"We live in different worlds. They want what we have but don't understand what it means to have our responsibilities."

"Can't you explain it to them?"

Her mother, unlike her father, was a homebody. She didn't enjoy talking about, or for that matter thinking about, the outside world. "For that to work, must want to understand in the first place. But some of them see us as their enemies. For that reason alone, they will never listen."

"Then why does papa go there?" asked Igraine.

Her mother had grown weary of her questions. "We need them as much as they need us. Your father makes sure both parties would work together."

"What if they don't?" asked Igraine again.

"Well, that depends." she sighed. "You'll understand when you are older."

Igraine was struck by a sudden rush of despair. She was older now, and all she had learned was the meaning of boredom and disappointment. This world was not meant for her. Yet, for some reason, these people allowed her to live, despite having no reason to do so. As a matter of fact, they kept her alive at great expense. Even when healthy, she had been a burden. That's likely why Jenever was so angry with her.

"Why did you run away, Angel?" Doctor Jenever had asked during one of their regular meetings.

"I don't like to be indoors all the time," Igraine had answered. "And there was music coming from the city. And they had all these games!"

"Igraine! If you get damaged, we cannot repair your implants. Do you understand that?"

She had heard the question but didn't take it to heart. Adults loved telling her what to do, and yet they acted as if it was a burden. Still... How often had Jenever been there when she regained consciousness? Igraine would open her eyes, and there she would be, smiling and telling her, "It is going to be alright." The doctor would clean her face while her head rested in the woman's lap. "It's going to be alright."

And then, one day, Jenever was gone. Strangers, people she barely knew, would help her. But none of them cared for Igraine the same way Jenever had done. It wasn't caring but pity. Or maybe Jenever was the same way, and Igraine had fooled herself all this time. And if Jenever didn't care about her, why would she bother to say goodbye to this fake woman?

Eventually, the roaring of the dark vortex was gradually drowned out by the grinding of wheels and stomping horse feet. When Igraine opened her eyes, she was shocked to discover her head rested against the shoulder of the silver-haired woman. Gasping, Igraine looked into S-36's eyes which were staring down at her with a faint grin. Immediately, Igraine to backed away, pressing herself against the side of the cabin, and looked around.

On the bench opposed to their's lay a woman, apparently in a deep sleep. Igraine's eyes had trouble adjusting to the darkness. But after some slow deduction, the girl concluded the lady was Miss Lantry. The celebrity was hardly recognizable without makeup. Her skin appeared dry and scabbed, hardly a picture of upper-class elegance.

Iggy gulped. "What do you intend to do with her?" she asked.

"We'll _ fix _ her," sounded through the cabin's onboard speaker. "Like _ we'll _ fix _ you."

Igraine wanted to protest, but she was tired and afraid, and her mind was adrift as if the thread between her consciousness and body was approaching a breaking point. She had to remind herself to breathe as she barely registered what was happening around her, like the coach coming to a standstill. And when the door opened, the scent of salt water entered the cabin.

Without warning, S-36 grabbed Igraine and carried her outside. Holding the girl in her arms, she carried toward the piers of Dover's harbor. Among the promenade, the people on the terraces were enjoying the view of the setting sun, and noisy sailors were on their way to the bars. They were accompanied by a small host of slightly modified humans. Typical amputees with the airs of army veterans and laborers. As the group walked down the pier, some fishermen looked at them with increasing unease. Ignoring them, the Signalites walked all the way up to the end of the landing. There, they waited.

Igraine stared frightfully at the crimson sky over the Channel. In her hallucinations, the sea was like a lake of boiling lava covered by a dark miasma. She kept telling herself it wasn't real. But then Igraine noticed something gliding through the water. If she didn't know better, it looked like a boat called an Ironclad, but short and high like a tower, cutting its way through the mist.

Fishing boats were turned over as a massive shadow emerged from the sea like a whale rising from the water. The fishermen jumped back and ran off as the solid object crushed boats beneath its keel. A submarine! A vessel of such size, Igraine couldn't make out the aft. Above her, on the prow, was its name in gothic letters: Tiamat.

As the lock at the base of the conning tower opened, dozens of red dots danced in the dark. Signalites, unlike any other Igraine, had seen before, emerged from the ship. Armored, weaponized, and some postured like beasts, they advanced across the deck. Ahead of the pack walked one man dressed in a grayish chauffeur's uniform, but his pants were torn off above the knees to display his mechanical legs. Goggles-like fixtures had been grafted over his eye sockets, surrounded by still pink scar tissue. Courteous, he walked up to S-36 and bowed theatrically while taking off his cap. “Perfectly timed, Relay.” He looked at Igraine for a moment and pinched her cheek. “So, this is Davie's ward,” he said condescendingly. “And who do we have here?” he asked ironically as he bowed over the actress. “Clara?” He didn't seem impressed. “I think I prefer her when she's asleep.”

S-36 kept on walking.

“Uhm, Relay,” began one of the Nyctolar among the pack politely. Despite the impression of his heavy arms that hung sluggishly down his sides, he still sported a well-groomed mustache. “We are ready to start our attack. Unfortunately, the enemy had already reclaimed Dover's radio station, and we lost contact with... Relay?”

S-36 walked straight past the pack without even acknowledging them. The men carrying Lantry's stretcher were not far behind.

“Very well!” the mustached follower called after her. “We will do as we agreed.”

“You do that,” said the chauffeur nonchalantly.

“What was that, brother Macarthur? said the Nyctolar, offended. “I don't care for your tone, brother.”

Stopping, Macarthur took a deep breath. Igraine imagined his eyes rolling as he turned around. “Please, brother. I was just encouraging you to do your part.”

“Oh, we'll do our part. But Lantry is the Receiver. Not you.”

“Now you are just sounding jealous. No, brother. I, too, have the Relay's blessing during our sister's absence. I wish I could go with you. Unfortunately, our sister needs my help. The coming hours are going to be very taxing for her while you are the stars of the show,” he said, spreading his arms. “Paving the way for the Ascension!”

Behind him, in the twilight of the tower's interior, red lights ascended from below deck accompanied by a clockwork chorus.

“Ah, there they are,” said Macarthur.

Paralyzed, Igraine observed how the swarm of quadruped drones skittered past S-36's feet like ill-tempered hermit crabs with cylindrical shells.

"As long as the repeaters transmit, the swarms will know what to do," elaborated Macarthur. "Now get to the yard and open the remaining containers."

After entering the conning tower, the last thing that Igraine saw before the lock closed was the automatons rushing across the pier and flooding onto the promenade where the curious onlookers were now running for their lives.

The elevator was descending into the Tiamat's interior when Macarthur sighed. "Ha, I love it when a plan comes together."

Through caged construction, Igraine could only make out so much in the poor illumination. Blinking lights and glowing eyes moved through the darkness. The air was thick with fumes and the scent of burnt materials. The humming of generators was drowned out by the noise of welding machines, grinders, and heavy drills.

"So far, so good," remarked the chauffeur and looked at S-36 as if he were expecting a reply. But none came. "Anyway, final adjustments have been made to the volunteers. The Receiver should be in our hands before morning. Will Lantry still take its place?"

S-36 didn't reply.

"Just trying to have a conversation," he muttered, disappointed. "What about you, girl?" he said, looking Igraine in the eyes. "What is your part?"

Igraine shifted her gaze from him to S-36, wondering the same thing, but S-36 still gave no response.

The elevator halted with a clank, and the doors shrieked as they parted.

The blood in Igraine's veins froze as they entered the deck. The corridor was filled with heavy machines that were operating people in the same way as one would assemble a horse cart. Prosthetics were attached to patients, mechanized limbs were calibrated, and weapons were tested.

"Lay the Misses over there," said the chauffeur. "No point in sedation," he grinned as he turned to S-36. "Relay. The girl's room is ready."

S-36 carried Igraine to a small chamber where a single table, with a face-shape hole at one end, was waiting for her. Beside it stood a machine controlling a single robotic arm that leaned forebodingly over the table top while an operator in a surgeon's garb was operating its mechanical limb. It had a small array at the end, mounted with tools arranged on a revolver. She froze when she noticed one of the mounted implements was a drill. Her instinct told her to escape at all costs. And yet, she could not muster the will to flee. All her brain could contemplate was that everything was hopeless and that resistance futile. Only when the S-36 made her climb on the operating table Igraine refused. But S-36 lifted her up and slabbed her on the table like a piece of meat. They spread her arms and braced her head tightly inside the hole. As they ripped the back of her robes open, through the haze of tears and persisting fog, she saw Anwin lying on the ground. She couldn't fathom how that was even possible. Then she noticed two furry paws beside Anwin on the floor. A dog was looking up at Igraine, wagging its tail. *Old Boy?* She squeezed her eyes shut when the arm began to hiss as its manipulators came to life. Then, she waited for the inevitable as the drill started to buzz, feeling its presence in the back of her neck as it came closer. She felt the tip of the needle touch the base of her skull, followed by a warm, then cold, stinging sensation.

22ND OF MAY, 1875, 5.23 PM. WHITE TOWER INN, DOVER.
Outside, the wind was howling while Ol'Barrow was sitting in the restaurant. On the table in front, he was turning the stem of an half-empty wine glass between his fingers. He had always wondered how this place managed to stay in business but never imagined it was a secret outpost, let alone that of a spy agency.

The dragoons had brought him along for debriefing, though at times, it felt like an interrogation. Associate Soixante's shrill voice was still ringing in his ears, and Ol'Barrow feared he had developed tinnitus.

In the meantime, he learned the strange boxes they uncovered at the radio station were signal repeaters. The Nyctolar placed these devices in various counties and now flooded the ether with persistent noise. Wireless communication was nearly impossible, and telegram services had been overwhelmed. One dragoon had joked they might as well resort to smoke signals. The last word was that the authorities were tracking down these devices. While the search for the repeaters was on, officials needed to ensure the population there was no cause for panic, but they lost their conventional means to do so. Ol'Barrow imagined paperboys screaming themselves hoarse right now. Oh, the radio. It provided the population with comfort by satisfying their curiosity. Every morning, they would listen to Frank Dimbleby, the Voice of Kent. Ol'Barrow was not a big fan. But now, whenever that radio was turned on, no more Dimbleby. Ol'Barrow didn't even know which victim at the station owned that voice.

Meanwhile, the honing jibber-jabber against a background of persistent beeps unnerved everyone. The manic electric laughter was interrupted by occasional grunts and the utterances of a random phrase, like. "Ricketick-tick-. Caught the show..? Does the Shade know? Tune in! Hihihihhihi."

Leaning on the table, Ol'Barrow was pondering what to do other than waiting for the inevitable attack. There were no leads to follow up on. No clues to Macarthur's where abouts, or rather if his final message had any meaning. And what about Igraine? He hadn't dared to bring her up. Nobody cared about a dying girl during the crisis. Upon recalling her last words, he immediately put his glass against his lips.

"Penny, for your thoughts," said a hoarse voice.

Ol'Barrow looked up at the older gentleman standing beside the table. He could be a sailor with that frizzled beard or some prospector from the American frontier. Judging by his stiff motions, he very well might have been one. "Mind If I join you, Mr. Ol'Barrow?"

"Of course not, Mr...?"

"You can call me the Chief Regulator, Mr. Ol'Barrow," he said. "I'm with RA. Also, a former Associate."

Ol'Barrow gave a mechanical nod. "Two gentlemen at the police station mentioned RA. They told me to address any complaints about my treatment to you."

He grinned. "I heard about that incident, yes. Be assured, as of yesterday, these men have become Lost Numbers."

"Better late than never, I suppose... What about other malpractice by the Association?"

Groaning, The regulator sat down. "Don't get me started. I intended to get to them. But in this line of work, the past has no time to catch up with the present. And that is how we ended up here."

"In other words, everyone has been kicking the can down the road," Ol'Barrow remarked, cynical. "Speaking of which... Any luck with the telegraphs?"

"Every wireless radio in the whole London area and surrounding counties are affected... Latest news suggested some naval vessels headed south to deal with a reported uprising on the south coast. Whether this is true or not, I cannot tell," he groaned again. "People are panicking, just because they cannot listen to their daily entertainment... Do you remember the time before Wavecasters, Mr. Ol'Barrow? Have we slipped away so far we can't imagine a world without them?"

"It's a matter of normalcy, I suppose," Ol'Barrow suggested. "Like the fact that our world is connected to hundreds of different Planes of Existence."

"Normal," muttered the regulator. "I have pondered the meaning of that word. I suppose it means the things we take for granted. And to think the young assume that all the comforts they enjoy today will be there for them tomorrow."

"Like turning on the radio and listening to their favorite show?" Ol'Barrow said as both a statement and a question.

"You hate it now, but you miss it when it's gone," said the regulator pedantically.

"You're making it sound like the Signalites have a point. About nature and the world, I mean."

The regulator pouted his lips. "Well, they are not wrong."

Their conversation was caught short when a dragoon approached their table in a rush. "Sir! You gotta see this!"

They jumped up from their chairs and went outside, where the scent of cinders drifted on the breeze. Ol'Barrow put a hand on his head when he looked at Dover in the distance. "By Jove." He cried as he when saw the city's coastal district emitting a crimson glow. "What the hell happened? Do the telegraphs work yet?!"

Soixante, who was already there, shook her head. "Non. If anything, they've gotten worse."

"Sons of Bitches."

"We must hurry!" said Ol'Barrow. "The garrison at Dover Castle must be spread thin!"

"We must do no such thing," said Sergeant Bucket.

"Bu-"

The regulator interjected. "Something tells me you need to head for Druid Isle right away."

"I agree," said Soixante.

"But what abou-"

"Mr. Ol'Barrow, you are but a guest," said the regulator sternly. "You are free to defend your city if you want. However, what we do is none of your concern."

He froze for a moment and lowered his shoulders "Yes. Yes, you're right," he said, nodding apologetically. "Forgive me... Druid Isle. This is probably where S-36 is. Then Igraine might be there too."

"First the city, now the child?" said the regulator.

"She's not a child! These things. They are probably interested in her implants. They'll rip her apart to get them. But..."
"But what?"
"There is a Pendleton Array, or whatever it is called, inside the temple. They probably want that to stop her from falling apart."
"Mon Dieu, did 321 tell you everything?!" said Soixante, dismayed. "Oh, forget it. Keep trying to reach HQ. We need transportation to the isle."
"My brother," said Ol'Barrow. "He probably moored his steamboat near Whitstable."
The associate and sergeant looked at each other for a moment. "I suppose we need to commandeer a boat in order to go there anyway," suggested Soixante cautiously.
"That settles it," bellowed the Sergeant. "Everyone on the truck!"

22ND OF MAY, 1875, 5.30 PM. DRUID ISLE.

Associate 321 looked with grave concern at the smokestack that was building up on the horizon. From the levee, he could see these gray mounds of smoke appearing in every direction. He took a deep breath. "So it begins," he said as the masked man joined him.

"Looks like they started their final push," he muttered, his voice sounding as if it were about to break.

321 was wondering what was going through the man's mind while hiding his expression behind that large eye that was staring off into the distance. For a man wearing such a symbol over his face, he seemed rather short-sighted - unless he had them closed all this time. But now his eyes were wide open, observing how this destruction was brought in the name of his own religion.

"What do you think they are trying to achieve?" inquired the masked one.

"Ricketick-tick," replied 321 absentmindedly.

"Excuse me?"

He wasn't sure why he mentioned it himself other than attempting to deduct a deeper meaning from the phrase. A warning their time had come, perhaps. The Associate would like to see them try. He grinned. "Forget it," he said and tapped the tip of his cane onto the boards. "I need to see Jenever. Regulator, I suggest you take the Perfect somewhere safe."

"You think they'll come here?"

"Just do it," 321 insisted, and with that, he made his way back to the auditorium.

As he entered, 321 felt the heat irradiating from the cables running over the ground. The sanctum had been transformed into the decor from some Penny Dreadful, with the Perfect at its center. Sitting in front of the Transmuter, he was attached to the infernal machine through cables running out the back of his chair. The coils beside the stripped Transmuter sparked irregularly, lighting up the mannequin. Beside him on a table lay a lifeless Nyctolar, connected to the same console as the Perfect.

"Dear God," gasped 321. *Of Course* – It had been the Perfect who was the decoder all along.

Amidst the chaos, Jenever was standing in front of its massive consoles, operating them in a trance-like state, inspecting every gauge, adjusting each dial while lights blinked non-stop and indicators shifted erratically from side to side.

"Doctor Jenever. Whatever it is you're working on, it better be ready."

"I'm improvising, Associate," she cried over the static noise without looking back. "Unfortunately, Elysium is still out of range."

He looked at the Perfect, who sat motionless in his chair while plugged in like some defective carnival attraction. "Improvising?" He planted his cane firmly on the floor "Are you serious? What is the connection here? Is Aqrabua on Elysium?"

"It is a long and complicated story and, quite frankly, above your clearance level. I suggest you worry about keeping the cultists at bay."

He bit his lips together and turned to the Perfect. "Has the decoder at least been useful?"

She turned to face one of the consoles connected to the Perfect and reached for a lever, with a clank, a device ejected from a slit: A black square on top of a green oval disk. "This is what we pulled from 45's skull," she explained. "It's what connected him to the network remotely. It provided me with a metaphorical back door into the

system. Unfortunately, I could only use it once. Now I-" she paused abruptly.
321 cocked his head suspiciously. "Might I inquire what did you do with it?"
"That doesn't matter right now," Jenever responded evasively. "I needed these bodies so I could devise a new one, but we are running out of time."
Shrugging his shoulders, 321 looked up at the web of power lines covering the ceiling. The sight was as perplexing as the conundrum he was faced with. "So, we are going in circles?" he said as a statement and a question and looked back at Jenever. "What will the consequences be this time, Doctor?"
"Better than the alternative."
Their conversation was cut short by gunshots that echoed through the hallways.
"Oh, for the love of-," said 321. "Stay, I'll see what is happening."
His heart was pounding as he hurried outside.
The sound of distant gunfire and the scent of sulfur in the air made him feel like he was below deck again. Upon entering the plaza, two flares were soaring through the sky, confirming the imminent attack.
From behind the barricaded gate to the courtyard, the dragoons were firing at civilian ships manned by Nyctolar that encroached on the levee.
"Take positions and fire at will!' cried the sergeant as more dragoons raced to the gate. "All the civilians inside!"
Wood splintered, and metal sparked as the dragoons opened fire on the boats. They managed to hit some of the Nyctolar, but industrial steel wasn't as vulnerable as human flesh. Some homunculi leapt off the boats from great distance onto the pier and stormed the entrenched positions. Fortunately, the dragoon's rapid-fire rifles could take them down from a distance. But in the meantime, the boats were sailing into the levee, allowing more Nyctolar to disembark. Among the horde that jumped on the pier were two homunculi of obscene bulk. On their backs, they carried shells of such size that required massive arms and matching shoulders to support the weight as they were advancing on their knuckles, like gorillas.

The machine guns opened fire on the first wave. It seemed effective as the Nyctolar's armor could only protect them so much, and the heavy guns reduced the numbers significantly. The hunchbacks halted as the guns opened upon them and crouched, using their armored limbs for cover.

321 saw how the pods inside of the armor of the hunchback were ejected like spent cartridges. As canisters, about the size of a flower pot, were bouncing off the ground, mechanical appendages popped out of the bottom. *C-44,* thought 321, as the automatons came crawling toward them like drunk hermit crabs.

"Use grenades!" cried the sergeant as the dragoons struggled to hit the skittering automatons that were swarming their positions.

But before any explosives could be thrown, they were nearly upon the defenders.

Somewhere on the road in Kent, an armored vehicle drove at a great velocity in Whitstable's direction. Ol'Barrow couldn't see the landscape pass by, but he felt it. His stomach cramped together every time they would hit a bump in the road. "God darn it!"

"We are nearly there!" said Sergeant Bucket, who sat opposed to him. "You don't have to come along. The moment we find transportation-"

"I need to go to Druid Isle!" Ol'Barrow interrupted him. "Iggy is there, I know she is."

The sergeant raised an eyebrow. "The country is burning, and you worry about a gall. Strange priorities."

Ol'Barrow lowered his head. "If I won't, who will?" he asked in return. "Besides, I have been fired from my responsibilities as a keeper of the peace. Now, all I can do is what remains in my power."

The Sergeant frowned his lips as he nodded. "One way of looking at it."

Finally, they had reached Whitstable's Harbor. As Ol'Barrow got out, he was greeted by the droning of gunshots in the distance that was bouncing across the estuary's surface. "Is that coming from Druid Isle?" he asked.

"No point in worrying about it now," said Sergeant Bucket. "Where is this boat of yours?"

The question had made him nervous, afraid that his brother's ship was gone or worse. "Right... Follow me," Ol'Barrow said nervously as he walked onto the wharf. His heart relaxed when they spotted the Persephone, whose crew had armed themselves with boat hooks and paddles. Captain Oltoak held a short-barreled shotgun when he emerged from his cabin. "David. What are you doing here? Who are they?"

Ol'Barrow raced forward. "Herald! We need transport to Druid Isle."

"Davie? Are you insane?" His brother cried. "There is a-a a ship down there!" he protested. "All those things came from that submarine. It was huge... Largest of any ironclad I've ever seen!"

"Down there?" asked Ol'Barrow, pointing at the estuary.

"Yes, this massive ship that rose up from the sea. Then, those mechanical freaks came out and seized those boats to sail up the river. They killed the crews and threw 'em overboard, those bastards. Where is the bloody navy when you need them?"

"Further down the coast, I imagine," said the sergeant, "Reinforcing other coastal cities."

Ol'Barrow gulped. It was as he'd imagined. The attacks were all a distraction, and there was no way to contact any navy ships. "Please, Herald!" he pleaded. "This is for your own sake as well as that of England."

"You don't need to join us," added the sergeant. "We can sail the ship ourselves."

"Blast you!" The captain cursed, gritting his teeth as he looked around. "Fine, get on board before I change my mind!" he said and turned to his crew. "You lot! Last chance to get off."

The sailors looked nervously at each other. "We're good," said one. The others nodded in agreement, although their expressions suggested they did so against better judgment.

"Let's get this horse and pony show on the road then," muttered the sergeant and told his platoon to board with Soixante following suit.

The Associate paused to address the former inspector. "Last chance to turn back, Mr. Ol'Barrow."

But he was already climbing on board. "I made up my mind." The steam engine was hissing as Ol'Barrow observed the smokestacks at the horizon from atop the deck. "Damn those bastards."

The hissing of white static reverberated through her head as Igraine regained consciousness. Or had she? For some reason, she felt like she had been awake all this time but forgot. Meanwhile, the humming persisted as if the universe was reaching out to her, drowning out any other thoughts.

Igraine reached for the back of her neck and, with her fingers, explored the cold, slippery sockets that were now at the base of her skull. She could feel swollen muscles squeezing the rigid wires leading into her brain. Something about the Receiver, she recalled.

Igraine looked at the tattoo inside her palm. The ink had turned cloudy, and the triangles looked washed out like they were out of focus. A strange tingling sensation ran down her arm all the way to her neck. As for her sight, she was seeing various colors of the rainbow around every object now. She was obviously beyond repair and of no use to anyone. So, why?

She had expected this to happen. She'd been anticipating this for weeks. That was good. A sign her pain would be over soon. And yet, it gnarled at her, but she couldn't fathom why.

Meanwhile, the universe was roaring in the background of her mind like a Wavecaster from inside another room as if it were calling her.

"You are awake," said a familiar voice from the Wireless.

Miss Lantry? Igraine rose up from the operating table, and there she was: Clara Lantry. Her appearance shocked Igraine. It would seem the actress, known for her sensuality, cared for her biological components no longer and looked like somebody who had been raised from the dead. Her skin was dry, and her eyes were swollen. The waist-long hair reminded Igraine of a bird's nest, concealing silvery tendrils running underneath, just a chrome carapace running done her entire back. Her new eyes reflected Igraine's pale face as Lantry smiled at her. "Welcome," she said. "I am sister Clara Lantry. Who are you?"

"I'm..." She stopped to close her eyes and think. Her mind was so slow now. Of course, it was. Her implants, the source of her intellect, had broken.

"Don't worry. I know what it's like to be in a broken body," said Lantry as she closed the back of Igraine's torn robe. "It won't be for much longer... Come."

Lantry was holding her hand as Igraine carefully lowered herself off the table. She felt so small and powerless. Incomplete. No longer the girl who could move things from afar and unlock the secrets of her surroundings at a mere glance. The machines surrounding her, although familiar, now confused her. Ideas and solutions did not come to her anymore. There was that nagging feeling and a question: Why had she done this to herself?

Lantry looked at gray stuff sticking to her own fingertips. It was Igraine's. It should repulse the actress who despised biology. Instead, she stretched the corners of her lips into an unnatural smile. "Come, child," she said, rubbing her fingers together. "We must hurry. The Relay is waiting."

"Why?" asked Igraine softly. "Where are we going?"

"To the Transmuter," she said assuringly. "The time of Ascension is at hand." She inhaled with an elated smile on her face. "Then we'll truly be free."

Igraine just looked at her, petrified. It wasn't Lantry's now alien appearance that scared her. Strangeness was a mundane affair for her. But this woman's mind was terrifying. A crazy woman with whom she didn't share the same experience of reality. Lantry had wealth, fame, the admiration of millions, and above all, was free to go wherever in the world she wanted. And that wasn't good enough… Then, what in the Multiverse could possibly satisfy her?

The slushing of the propeller resonated through the submarine as they walked down the corridor. Seeing a colorful aura around every lamp, she wasn't sure if reality itself was collapsing or if these were her last fleeting moments of sanity.

Back at the elevator, a crowd had obstructed their way. Behind them, S-36 was standing there like a mannequin, accompanied by Macarthur, who was passing back and forth in frustration. He stopped when Lantry and the girl squeezed their way past metal limbs. "Finally, sister," he sneered. But Lantry didn't seem to notice. Igraine figured her mind had already ascended somewhat and lost sight of this world. Lantry did not even acknowledge the other Nyctolar following her every movement in anticipation of something. Attention? A rousing speech? Or were they hoping to become heroes today, lauded by the famous actress?

Lantry took position beside S-36 with Igraine and, facing her admirers, raised her voice. "Brothers and sisters! Until now, your lives and struggles were hidden beneath the surface. But as if reborn, you are about to reemerge, and then you'll pave the way into the future by proving Ascension is possible. Humanity will finally be inspired to rid themselves of their chains and cooperate in the Great Machine's construction. The Capitalists and their oligarchs will try to stop us and fail..."

Igraine couldn't help but cringe. Lantry believed Humanity would join their cause. Her mind might be slipping, but even Igraine wasn't convinced of such naive assumptions. Humans, be it in this world or the next, never agree on anything, even in the face of overwhelming evidence. Igraine herself had believed magic was real. When faced with evidence on the contrary, she rejected the obvious conclusions and substituted them with her own. No, even if Ascension were real, it would be turned into a hostile entity fitting a century-old narrative that had preserved their way of life.

Lantry's audience, however, was encouraged by this lunacy and gladly entered the elevator's cage in anticipation of emerging from the sea.

22ND OF MAY 1875, 6.10 PM. THAMES ESTUARY, NEARBY DRUID ISLE.

The Tiamat was submerging in the river delta while their procession headed for Druid Isle on board a captured pleasure boat. The setting sun's reflection looked like a thousand rainbows to Igraine, overlayed by the persistent chaos caused by her imagination. But it didn't seem so bad anymore as the low drone inside her head continued, calming her somehow, just like all those radio ads that had sung her to sleep so often.

While Nyctolar used their mechanical limbs to paddle tirelessly with near-perfect synchronization, putting most rowing teams to shame, Macarthur was standing in front with one foot on the ledge as if he were a character in some epic painting. Igraine observed how the others were fitted with similar sockets to her own, either on the side of their skulls or the back of their necks. But these were already occupied by antennas or tails hanging down their backs, probably interconnecting them through wireless signals.

Head hung low, she looked at her hands. They were corpse-like, and dark gray smudges had appeared beneath her skin, which she didn't dare to touch. Being disgusted by herself, she looked at the strewn-about belongings around the boat, like an umbrella, a woman's hat, and a snapped cane: the previous occupants', perhaps.

A doll dressed as a proper lady left beneath one of the benches drew her attention. Her white dress and rosy cheeks irradiated a soft, pinkish glow. After picking it up, she held it close to her chest. It wasn't Anwin, but it provided her with some comfort. The unconditional love that only a cherished toy could provide... She wondered what became of Anwin.

“You don't need that,” said Lantry, but Igraine ignored her.

Then Lantry grabbed the girl’s hand. “I'm not your enemy,” she said reassuringly.

“Is that what you told the people on this boat as well?” asked Igraine with a thick voice.

"It is as they say," began Lantry. "To make an omelet, you need to break a few eggs." Then she withdrew herself. "You'll understand when we get there."

Looking at the doll, her slow mind contemplated the metaphor. The girl who owned this doll... Was... The egg? She deduced. So, I'm an egg as well? What kind of omelet will I be? The thought terrified her, but she didn't dare to ask Lantry what they had in store for her.

When they reached the devastated piers of Druid Isle, Lantry squeezed Igraine's hand giddily.

The sound of rapid-fire and heavy gunshots echoed in the distance as the smell of sulfur drifted in the breeze. Despite Lantry's dignified posture, she was gloating as they walked side by side through the scenes of death and destruction. Enjoyment was not the right word. But something behind those reflective eyes admired the sight of bullet holes, craters, and stray mechanical parts. "More eggs," imagined Igraine as they passed a dozen or so dead Nyctolar on the dock as well as inside the courtyard. The bodies, surrounded by destroyed crab-like robots, leaked a dark mixture of blood and oil between the tiles. The corpses were twisted, both physically and, as in concept, horrifying Igraine. Never had she been more aware that she herself had been an amalgamation of flesh and technology- Just prettier. She only just realized it.

Meanwhile, they were walking into the shadow of the main complex. Beside the temple entrance, a one-armed Nyctolar leaned limply against the wall as he struggled to stand straight on a defunct leg. "Relay," he exclaimed the moment he saw S-36. "Resistance was stronger than we expected... The guards. They're not Royal troops. Maybe forces sent by the Creators."

Igraine looked at a mangled soldier just beyond the doorway. She recognized the dragoon's uniform. Advanced weapons for this world's standards, yes. But did these cultists really believe these were Outsiders?

"Has the Transmuter been secured?" asked Lantry.

"The heretics and their allies have retreated into other parts of the temple. But we almost captured the Transmuter..." he hesitated as he was afraid to continue. "We think the Apostate is there."

Lantry's expression turned as she gasped. "The Apostate?"

For the first time, Igraine noticed S-36 furrow her eyebrows together, but then the corners of her mouth stretched outward into a wicked grin. The golem stepped forward and dropped herself on all fours while arching her back like an angry cat. Her boots came apart, and her skin burst as her shins and feet unfolded into bird-like prosthetics. Blades unfolded from her lower arms as she rose with the strength of her legs alone. And off she went at breakneck speed, leaving a trail of torn fabric and synthetic skin.

Shaking, and feeling the weight of the doll increase as she watched the golem race through the hall.

"Amazing," muttered Lantry and raised her voice. "Come! The moment of truth is upon us."

As the host continued down the hallway, Igraine felt like she walked through the innards of a whale due to the red walls and bone-like architecture while shots and screams echoed through the complex.

Inside the reception area lay several of the Perfect's supporters, dead behind their barricades, overcast by a bat-like shadow swaying from side to side. The Nyctolar stared with their mouths agape at the outlandish architecture and the Da Vinci-like flying machine hanging from the ceiling. Even in their current form, the supporters were but simple men and women unfamiliar with the tastes of the rich and eccentric. Lantry, however, frowned her lips at the interior. "What time they wasted on building this place? Instead of building the Machine, they constructed a monument to themselves."

"A simple lie can be very profitable," said Macarthur, whimsical as if he was reciting a song.

They were interrupted by the loud thrashing of furniture being demolished and the sparking of electricity coming from behind the auditorium door. Everyone stepped back as the door burst apart. Along with splinters, dust, and door remnants, somebody flew backward through the entryway.

As the dust settled, Igraine gasped when she recognized the woman crawling up from the debris. It was Dr. Jenever dressed in her undergarments.

As she looked up, the Doctor froze upon seeing Igraine.

Peering into the doctor's dilated eyes, Igraine felt shame, both for who and what she had become. She was with them now, even if she didn't want to be. Even if she didn't have the power to resist, Igraine was with them, allowing Dr. Jenever to suffer like this. Only if she had been stronger. Only if... guilt was consuming her. All the effort, all of Jenever's time and energy. All the risks the doctor had taken. This is how Igraine had repaid her by wallowing in self-pity and becoming useless to the point that she couldn't speak out. And now, when the Doctor needed her most, she was a wreck. A sinking ship sent to save somebody who was drowning.

Lantry pulled Igraine closer as S-36 emerged from the doorway to charge at Jenever, who barely managed to dodge the attack. Excited, Lantry was squeezing Igraine's shoulders as they observed the fight. "I can't believe we are witnessing this," Lantry whispered, awed by the spectacle. There was something unsettling about a celebrity, lauded by millions, being this awestruck. Then again, that golem was the embodiment of a living saint. S-36 leaped through the air, cutting one of the flying machine's suspension cables, and one by one, the other wires snapped under the weight. Like a bird of prey, the flying machine glided at Jenever, who failed to dodge its massive wings. As the Doctor fought to free herself from the cloth, Igraine wanted to speak out, but no sound was passing her lips. Shaking, she observed how S-36 pulled away the bat-like wings of the contraption while Jenever was still struggling. If there was only one thing Igraine could do. Anything.

As the Doctor fought to free herself from the cloth, Igraine wanted to speak out, but no sound was passing her lips. Shaking, she observed how S-36 pulled away the bat-like wings of the contraption while Jenever was still struggling. If there was only one thing Igraine could do. Anything.

In her delirium, Igraine raised her hand, directing her manipulator in S-36's general direction. Her arm felt like it was on fire, but she refused to let it down.

S-36 raised her blade, swung-

Igraine closed her eyes.

What followed was a suspenseful moment of silence.

When Igraine opened her eyes again, S-36's blade was lodged between the wires of the flying contraption. She had missed? The Golem had missed! Igraine was stunned. How was that possible?

A loud bang cut through the tension as a door to the left wing got kicked in. Canisters bounced over the floorboards, releasing thick smoke filling the room. Soldiers burst in from the side and opened fire on the cultists.

She noticed a black man electrifying one of the Nyctolar with a baton.

Lantry grabbed Igraine by the arm and dragged her across the lobby into the auditorium.

As the cultists barricaded the door with furniture, the last thing Igraine saw was Jenever emerging from the wreckage. The Doctor had been saved!

CHAPTER EIGHTEEN

Smoke was drifting into the auditorium as the Nyctolar caught their breath. But they did so excitedly by the fact they were inside their own Mecca. They turned to their precious Transmuter for comfort while ignoring the battlefield littered by their own kind.

"We are here," Lantry said, awed by the Transmuter at the center of the chamber. The stripped-down machine was lit up like a fireworks display as cable connectors sparked and lights flashed alarmingly. "It's beautiful."

Igraine was focusing on the nameless doll she clutched to her stomach. Despite everything, the doll still had a faint but friendly smile - the only thing that made sense to her.

Behind them, S-36 had just smashed the barricade aside and walked straight for the transmuter, followed by the remaining minions.

"Where are those soldiers?" asked Lantry to her subordinates.

"They got the Apostate and escaped sister," one said.

Lantry gasped like an angry reptile and snapped. "Get them! And where is Macarthur?"

Her minions looked at each other. "We thought he was with you."

She just glared at them. "I don't have time for this." She then turned to S-36. "My apologies."

The speakers inside the room released a cringe-inducing screech. "Let him be," reverberated through the room.

"O-oh," muttered Lantry. "Yes, Relay."

S-36 walked up to the machine. Arms wide, she unfolded her blades as she took on a theatrical posture, and the speakers hummed again. "The Trans-mut-ter is yours," said the choppy voice. "Now it's time for a reckoning."

"Reckoning?"

Everyone turned to the one Nyctolar who spoke up who quickly stepped back holding his hands in front of his chest. "I mean... What about the Ascension?"

"That is obviously what she meant, you idiot!" cried another.

"R-Right..." he muttered, embarrassed.

Igraine was glancing across the console, able to identify each component by name and function. But her thoughts were so slow, like she had to trace the process from one point to the next before she could draw a conclusion. Is this what normal human thought was like, she wondered.

"It's wonderful," gasped Lantry. "Soon, our minds will be transformed. We'll be one, united in one Genius." Then she looked in search of something. "Anyone seen the Perfect? He can't be far."

Ignoring her question, S-36 continued to the back of the auditorium.

Lantry dragged Igraine along as they followed their Relay to an area separated by a fence. Once inside, Igraine's mouth dropped upon seeing the green hexagonal block on top of a podium. Never before had she seen such a thing, but the Pendleton Array suspended above like a brass halo betrayed its origins.

Sliding her hand across the Vault S-36 seemed to be inspecting the coarse material. Then she stopped, and without warning, she struck, piercing the exterior with her blade. After a second, the shell folded outward, leaving the corners ajar.

"Open it," droned through the room from the speaker system.

Right away, the Nyctolar wedged their claws between the cracks. As the panels were creaking under strain, the Nyctolar pulled, groaning as they fought for every inch. But inevitably, panels succumbed and folded outward like flower petals. The Vault's secrets had been revealed at last.

Igraine swallowed when she saw a glass vat surrounded by multiple triangular pedestals. A container that, to Igraine's dismay, contained a human brain floating between the rising bubbles swirling around its brass vertebra. Where the tailbone used to be, multiple cables had been jacked in, connecting it to the black prisms surrounding it.

S-36 walked up to the relic and, without a moment's hesitation, punched through the glass. Water was running down the podium as she grabbed the specimen's spine, holding it up in triumph as she pulled the plugs.

Igraine cringed as the brain fell off the pedestal and landed on the steps like a wet sponge. That was when the machine's dragon-like head was revealed. A snake-like automaton was wrapping its spine around S-36's arm to no avail. S-36 smile mocked the machine's attempt to break her grasp, and, with a sneering grin, she grabbed its head, snapping it off like one would peel off a lobster's shell.

"Isn't she magnificent?" said Lantry as the Relay captivated her audience with ferocious acts of violence. "From this moment on, only the true Signal will be heard."

Suddenly, S-36 turned to face Igraine. The girl froze as the golem beckoned her to come closer. But Lantry shoved her forward and guided Igraine up the steps of the podium where S-36 was waiting for her with a pin connector in hand. Igraine was walking up the steps when, without warning, S-36 grabbed her. She forced the girl on her knees, pushing her head down to expose the socket in her neck.

As Igraine closed her eyes in anticipation of the inevitable, her heart was pounding so loud, it hurt.

"Wait," protested Lantry as she strode up to S-36. "What about me? I was supposed to become the new Receiver."

S-36 paused only to give the actress a dismissive look, all while holding Igraine's head in place. An uncomfortable sting inside the girl's head, followed by the sensation of being submerged in lukewarm water.

The scent of sulfur and brimstone was overpowering the sewage smell as Ol'Barrow overlooked the Thames from the deck of the Persephone. He observed Druid Isle, where infrequent white flashes light up the base of the antenna.

"No sight of the submarine," said the Sergeant. "It's a good thing these lunatics cannot swim."

Ol'Barrow looked at his hook. He hadn't considered it. "I suppose they are at a considerable disadvantage."

"And probably why they are attacking the city centers," added the Sergeant. "Making sure nobody pays attention to this place."

"Still seems excessive," muttered Ol'Barrow. "I don't get the impression these lunatics are realists. Let alone strategic masterminds."

"You assume they are the, we want to see the world burn types, sir?"

"They wouldn't be the first, Sergeant" Ol'Barrow said. "I've seen it in Dover. The French Revolution, The Frankfurter commune. Napoleon. Now idiots who think they can broadcast themselves to heaven."

"Indeed," responded the sergeant with a tired voice. "They are awfully mundane compared to what we usually deal with."

Ol'Barrow looked at him sideways. "You say it as if it is a good thing."

"Only in the sense that we have a straightforward target for once," said the sergeant. Then he reached for his belt and unholstered his pistol. "You know how to use this with that hand?" he asked, offering Ol'Barrow the strange weapon. It didn't have a cylinder like a revolver but something akin to an internal rifle magazine. "It fires as quickly as you can pull the trigger."

Nodding, Ol'Barrow shoved the gun behind his belt. He wasn't keen on guns, but he was willing to make an exception.

Ahead on the isle's shore lay an abandoned boat that was probably left by the Nyctolar.

"Can't swim nor steer," muttered the sergeant and inhaled. "We get off here and breach the fences," he announced. "First, we secure the wharf to evacuate any survivors."

As the soldiers prepared to disembark, Captain Oltoak took Ol'Barrow aside. "You can stay on the boat, you know," said Richard. "We already have one funeral to look forward to."

Ol'Barrow awkwardly moved aside to make room for the soldiers and then looked his brother in the eyes. "See you back at the wharf, Richie."

After the strike force climbed across the stranded boat onto the island, they followed the Nyctolar's tracks. As they made their way through the fence into the barren interior, it became obvious what had transpired. There was no opposition, just devastation. Incidental shots could be heard from the main complex, but the levee was ominously quiet. Then, from the shed at the other side of the dock, a man came shambling toward them.

"A survivor?" Ol'Barrow exclaimed.

"No!" warned the sergeant as there pointed their electric lanterns at the straggler.

Ol'Barrow stopped and gasped as he recognized the groundskeeper they had met the first time he was here. "My God."

His eyes were lifeless as he came staggering toward them on his prosthetic legs like a toddler who had just learned to walk, while a cylinder was sticking from the back of his neck like a leech.

A dragoon didn't hesitate to draw his mace and walk toward the man. The groundskeeper reached out his arms as if he wanted to strangle the soldier, but before he could even touch him, the Groundskeeper's head was bashed in. Ol'Barrow shivered as his body fell lifeless to the ground. Not because of the hideous wound. But because the groundskeeper's expression was seemingly unfazed as he lay there.

Ol'Barrow wanted to protest. "That's..."

"Trust me, sir. There are worse fates," said the sergeant.

"There what?" snapped Ol'Barrow, offended by his remark.

"Mr. Ol'Barrow. You're free to stay on the boat."

After some hesitation, Ol'Barrow nodded. "Right..."

Crossing the square to the temple entrance, Ol'Barrow felt increasing unease at the sight of all the destroyed automatons and was wondering if Iggy would still be Iggy by the time he found her. Doubt then turned to anger as he looked up at the antenna. "What have you bastards done to her?"

A mechanical heart's beating sent shock waves through the void. Igraine was floating between streams of light whilst surrounded by the hissing of cosmic white noise.

A wave was wrinkling through the chaos as a voice started to speak, wrapping itself around her like tightly wound linen. "Greetings Igraine Mortuba." As its words reverberated through her mind, a tear came to her eye. It was her younger brother's voice, Derek's, who was nine the last time she had seen him. By then, he already had shown greater potential than her. Maybe not as much as her older sister, but he had advanced in his studies despite his age. And Igraine had resented him for it.

The voice made her nauseous as it continued. "We finally connect."

"What do you want from me?" Her voice was pitiful and monotone in comparison.

"We want you to synchronize with us."

"Why would I?"

"Because you want the pain to stop. Isn't that why you ran away? To expire...? Your network is like an open book to us. We read it all. Your isolation, your query to find a protocol to connect with. But most of all, that inflatable human trait of rage. All have it. Few have mastered its full potential. It makes us curious... Many humans lash out, yes. Those who summoned us here do so... And then there are humans like you, who let it consume themselves from within till they are burned up, like a candle."

Its words sounded profound, but their meaning was hollow. "What do you want from me?"

"Your people have developed among a very interesting line," it said. "Many tried to do the same and failed. The Magi even had the foresight to isolate themselves from the Multiverse completely. And we want... Access."

"I don't know how to," Igraine admitted.

"You may not realize it, but the Magi know what you are up to," the void said. "Now your systems are degrading. That connection will be severed soon. But nothing we can't restore in time," it said assuringly. "They probably never imagined that such a disappointment like yourself would be of much interest to them."

"They know I'm alive?" She had always suspected it but assumed they had forgotten about her.

"Yes," it growled. "Did you ever bother looking up the records on yourself? The Association negotiated with the Archmages. They even informed the Association of what a poor student you were... Of course, you've always known. You are smarter than those who keep you prisoner."

"I'm not a prisoner!" she said. "They-" She choked up when her subconscious was flooded a new wave of guilt. "Dr. Jenever just wanted to protect me."

"Forget about her... It's just ironic that she helped us by preserving you. Humans do not change. Can you imagine? You, little Igraine. The one in the middle, living in the shadow of her siblings. The unremarkable one at the back of the class always gets picked last. Coming to this world was probably the best thing that ever happened to you. You, the one-eyed child in the kingdom of the blind. Then you became the smart one. The one who can, when others cannot. Now you lost that advantage as well... Does it hurt to know that your people looked the same way at you as you do at this world's inhabitants?"

More bullets came shearing by as Ol'Barrow took cover among the hall's alcoves. He and Sergeant Bucket had been hiding there for- what? A minute? But the whole experience felt as if it lasted forever, and in his mind, he counted every pounding heartbeat. A moment ago, they were halfway down the main hall when the Nyctolars opened fire from the reception area. Now, they were behind the mainstays, using the dust for concealment. Just as Ol'Barrow moved his foot slightly to let the blood flow through his cramped limb, another salvo of bullets riddled the hallway.

"Those are our own damn guns!" hissed the sergeant to no one in particular.

"Sir, over here!" beckoned a subdued voice from above.

As they looked up, a pair of eyes peered through a hole blown in the ceiling. He was a dragoon who lost his face plate.

"Where have you been?" hissed the Sergeant.

"Can't say yet. But we could get you up here. We could use the help ourselves."

"You could-" the Sergeant snorted but stopped himself. "Got any ropes?"

The dragoon nodded. Using each others' shoulders for support, several dragoons climbed up to the second floor while some remained behind.

The dragoon helped Ol'Barrow up. "As long as we stay away from the courtyard, we should be safe," he said.

"Why are they not attacking you?"

"They got time on their side, I guess," said the dragoon. "For whatever reason, they are patrolling the rooms around the courtyard and the auditorium."

"They are protecting the Transmuter. Hoping to contact their God, I imagine," muttered Ol'Barrow.

The dragoon nodded. "That's what the Doc said. But she messed around with the Transmuter. They shouldn't be able to use it for now."

Stepping over the remains of destroyed Fascinators, they continued to the hideout on the far corner of the complex. After passing the barricade made of furniture, they entered a common room with simple comforts, like lounge chairs, couches and decorative furnishing, tightly packed with survivors - Signalites and soldiers alike. The wounded lay in the center of the floor, surrounded by bloody bandages, while people around them tried to assist as they could.

The sergeant wasted no time and addressed one of the dragoons. "Corporal, where is your commander?"

"S-36 got him, sir," answered the NCO with a French accent. "He was in the auditorium when she attacked. After that, we retreated back here."

"Who's the highest in rank then?"

"You are, sir," said the corporal.

"Oh, sh- Alright, I want to know who we still got left. Give me an inventory. You two, figure out if we can clear away to the docks."

"What about airborne support, sir?"

“Forget about it, my man,” he raised his voice again. “I need intel on their defenses!”

While the Sergeant was formulating a new strategy, Ol'Barrow was wiping the sweat of his forehead as he looked around the crowded room. Associate 212 was checking inventory with some other soldiers. Even Doctor Jenever was there, working on the internal mechanisms of her left arm with a tweezer. But no sign of Iggy.

Associate 321 stepped up to him. “Ol'Barrow, is that you?” The man looked like he had just escaped from a fire.

“I'm afraid it is,” said Ol'Barrow.

“Then, tell me. What is going on out there?” 321 said, pointing at the smokestacks at the horizon illuminated by the waking fires within the city.

“Well, they are burning cities down. The army is trying to destroy whatever is spreading those noises over the radio.” He sighed. “So, what are the Nyctolar doing? Beyond being a doomsday cult, I mean.”

321 tilted his head. “They bunkered down in the Auditorium and the radio telescope.”

“The what?”

“The big antenna. They believe it will transmit their minds to Elysium.”

Ol'Barrow needed to process that statement for a moment. “That's- Ok. Can't we just destroy the antenna?”

“Not yet.”

Dr. Jenever joined them, wringing her left arm to check if everything was working.

“Why not?” asked Ol'Barrow. “Won't that shut down the Signal?”

“The Signal is but a means to an end,” she retorted. “If we want this to end, we need to get to the source.”

“Aqrabua?” asked Ol'Barrow.

“We have a unique opportunity now,” insisted Jenever. “Aqrabua is transmitting to this world so he can reach its true target.”

Ol'Barrow's eyes grew wider. “Elysium,” he whispered. “That is what this is about?”

"You think Aqrabua cares about this Plane? To it, this is just a waystation that happens to be close to his target. Whatever he intends to do with the machine that they call the Transmuter, it is still primitive. It might take many years, decades, maybe even longer."

"So, that is the reason he needs an army of clockwork monkeys," snarled Ol'Barrow. "But what is so special about Elysium?"

"It offers many benefits. One of them is location. But it doesn't matter. When Aqrabua starts transmitting itself, we can do irreparable damage to it."

"That's..." Ol'Barrow was stunned. He barely comprehended, but as he understood it, the Signalites transmitted human consciences to Elysium. The soul or spirit, as it were. So, did that mean that one could transmit a god? Ol'Barrow wiped his forehead again.

Meanwhile, 321 gave her a skeptical glance. "Doctor, you said you no longer have access to..." he made circular motions with his hand as he tried to formulate what to say next. "To that back door you mentioned before."

"That was before I realized they turned S-06 against us," she said coldly.

The blood in Ol'Barrow's veins froze. Did they turn Iggy?

321 shook his head in confusion and beckoned Ol'Barrow to keep his distance. "What if they turned her against us?"

"I know this entity," insisted Jenever. "It corrupts those who have lost hope. People like her. If he did, she now has direct access to Aqrabua. We can use S-06 as a back door."

Outrage and anger were flushing Ol'Barrow's mind. "Now, hold on!"

Jenever raised her voice. "It's already too late for her, Ol'Barrow!"

The room went quiet as all eyes were turning on them.

"Enjoying the performance?" Ol'Barrow asked the onlookers.

"I saw her with S-36 and Lantry," said Jenever. "No matter what happened, we already lost her."

"Well," began Ol'Barrow, trying to contain himself. "They fixed you, didn't they?"

Her pupils emitted a pale light as Jenever raised her chin.

"Doesn't she deserve a second chance, Doctor?" Ol'Barrow snarled and turned to 321. "You agree with this?"

Fidgeting with his cane, 321 sighed as if to indicate Ol'Barrow wouldn't like what he had to say. "My first priority is to secure this world against these types of threats. If I have to sacrifice one to save millions..." he changed his tone. "I realize this is unpleasant, Mr. Ol'Barrow, but this is not just about my oath. This is common sense!"

"Ah, yes… Always on the big picture, don't you?"

"Excuse me?"

Ol'Barrow turned to 212, who had joined them. "What about you?"

The masked Associate kept silent - The coward.

"If we want this nightmare to end, there is no alternative," Jenever said.

"Yes, there is," he hissed.

"You are thinking too three-dimensionally. Destroying the Transmuter won't harm them in the least."

He lowered his head in defeat. "Very well... I'll step back." " he said, nodding while clenching his fist till his knuckles turned white. "I will return to the dock then. Make myself useful there."

"That's probably wise," said 321, trying to make it sound dignified.

Ol'Barrow nodded and walked away. Then he stopped and turned to face Jenever. "To think she wanted to see you one last time before..." He didn't want to say it. "Good luck."

As Ol'Barrow was about to leave the hideout along with two dragoons, the Sergeant addressed him one last time. "You know. I thought these cultists would be a nice change of pace. But then I remembered what a pain humans can be."

"You and me both," Ol'Barrow grumbled. "Good luck, Sergeant. Make those bastards pay."

A moment later, as the three of them explored the halls, they heard heavy footsteps from the corridors closer to the courtyard. Being inconspicuous was not the Nyctolars' strong suit. Poor buggers. They were only good for a few things. One being hard labor, the other violent offensives - the types of activities that caused folks to lose limbs in the first place.

At a junction, they spotted a balustrade adjacent to a stairwell. A soldier tapped Ol'Barrow on the shoulder. "Hold the position and keep an eye out," he said and advanced toward the staircase.

Remaining at the junction, Ol'Barrow observed the soldiers as they scouted the area. He felt so frustrated and powerless. He might have been happier if he hadn't come here at all. Iggy would just have been one of the many victims of this night. Just another person to mourn. Now, she might be-

Her final words to him popped up in his mind, causing him physical pain.

He rubbed the side of his head as if to massage the regrets away. If he had just- No, no! Rubbing his eyes, he forced all his past oversights to the back of his mind and focused on the present. Looking at his surroundings, he noticed the shape of a boot at the end of the hall—a ladies' high-heeled boot. A victim, he assumed. There is nothing to be done about it now. Unless she was- Ah, damn it! Walking on his toes, he sneaked down the corridor for a quick look. As he approached, he recognized the lifeless body. "Oh, no..." It was Miss Hardy lying beside an open doorway. But that wasn't all. Cables from the back of her neck were inserted into a console inside the reinforced doorpost, probably to unlock it. All the sign read was 'No Entry,' without elaboration.

Another door, another secret to explore. Facing away, he interned to return to the junction but stopped dead in his tracks instead. At the end of the hall, beyond the junction, stood a single fascinator.

Clumsily, Ol'Barrow pulled the gun from his belt and aimed. Even though he had some experience, it just didn't feel natural to hold the pistol with his left hand. He called out to the soldiers. "There, um, is one of those automatons here!"

"Alright, come here!" he yelled back.

"Uhm..." he muttered as two more fascinators appeared, eyes blinking in the twilight as they crawled closer. "They are blocking my way!" he cried as more Fascinators crawled around the corner, gelling together in one amorphous swarm.

"Run!" he cried and hurried back to the heavy door. He pulled out Miss Hardy's plugs as a precaution, and the moment he shut the entryway, the machines scratched and jumped against the door. Taking a moment to let his heart calm, vapors were drifting on his breath as the sweat on his body cooled. With the automatons at the door, he figured there was no way but down. Water dripped off the metal steps as he descended. He expected to go down to some utility space, maybe a generator room. But at the bottom of the stairs, there was another reinforced door. Cold fumes escaped the chamber as he opened it and looked agape inside the storage room. A multi-stage warehouse filled with jars. Glass jars glowing in the dark. Each of them contained a human brain—shelves upon shelves of radiant brain containers, which were also the only source of light. But what unsettled Ol'Barrow most was a ticking sound, like that of water dripping from a faucet into a metal pan.

Following the noise, Ol'Barrow sneaked through the main path between the rows. Then, from the corner of his eye, he noticed someone behind the final row. Through the racks, he spotted a Nyctolar observing him from the dark. Ol'Barrow was certain he recognized some of his features. With his gun in front of him, he looked around the corner.

And there he was. Macarthur was tapping his fingernail against one of the glass jars, smiling like a prankster. Waxing philosophical, he inspected the brain. "Once upon a time in a pub, a feller once told me: The logical conclusion of mechanical progress is to reduce the human being to something resembling a brain in a bottle. I thought he was being hyperbolic. But then, he said, a man who drinks a bottle of gin a day does not intend to get liver disease, does he?" Macarthur turned to face Ol'Barrow. "Welcome to the end of the line, David!"

Ol'Barrow kept his gun pointed at him. "I knew this whole thing was a joke to you."

With frowned lips, the madman lay his hands on his heart. "Oh, David. I'm hurt. I wouldn't joke about the future of a species."

C.A.T.
VINE

"What are you doing down here?"

Macarthur stuck his nose into the air. "Well... The same as all these people, really. I'm waiting for our savior."

"What about Igraine," Ol'Barrow asked. "Did you do anything to her?"

"Who? Are you talking about the girl that the Relay fancies? She's a depressing, filthy thing. Leaving that gray stuff everywhere."

"What did you do with her?"

"The Relay just fitted her as far as I could tell. Don't know why. She looks like she could keel over any minute now."

"She isn't..." He had to look for the right word. "Mind-controlled?"

Macarthur smirked at the question. "Who isn't? Look at this place. They put their brains on ice!"

"They? You are not one of them?"

"I have seen it all before, mate. Big promises on how they are going to change the world. I made the mistake of believing such people. As a reward, they landed me in jail."

"Stop it. You were not the victim!" bellowed Ol'Barrow.

He remained unfazed by his outburst. "You know, in prison, I got a lot of time to think. You see, one of the conclusions I drew is that you and I have something in common."

Ol'Barrow dismissed him. "I doubt it."

"I didn't set that tavern on fire," he said.

Ol'Barrow scoffed at the statement. "What? Yes, you did!"

"No, I didn't!" Macarthur insisted amicably and raised a finger. "The one who did... The same person who told you it was me."

Ol'Barrow scoffed at his claim. "Ten years in prison, and that is the best you could come up with. Why say it now?"

"I did then!" he said. "But then the officers had to admit they got the wrong guy. Why do you think they let you off the hook...?" He held up both his hands as if shocked. "No pun intended, swear. Anyway, the last thing they needed was people askin' any questions."

"You are such a liar," said Ol'Barrow, insulted. "Fine then. Who is the real arsonist?"

Macarthur was shaking his head. "It doesn't matter... Last I heard, he joined the Frankfurt Commune of '71. No one ever heard anything from him again."

"How convenient."

"Convenient for you..." Macarthur retorted. "You broke my legs for what he did. Of course, I can't blame you. We were both lied to, after all." He grinned. "See? Told you we had something in common."

"So, let's assume this is true and you were falsely convicted. This is the reason for your little holy war?"

"Oh no... It's the principle of the thing. I thought what I did meant something. But it turned out I was a pawn. The whole thing was just one big experiment. I guess a bit of a trial before the big one of '71. Another failed project ... So, I decided to start my own."

"I knew this was a joke to you."

"I'm dead serious... I think you underestimate my ambition. Thanks to all this," he said, spreading his arms. "We can replace all these contradictory narratives with one truth."

"You're insane," he said calmly. "More insane than I assumed you were."

"Insane? I have the power of a god machine on my side. And you are the one resisting that deity. What would you call that?"

"That god doesn't care about you. It's just using you to-" Ol'Barrow realized what he was about to say would sound insane.

Macarthur, however, finished his statement with a smirk. "Upload itself to Elysium? I know."

Ol'Barrow paused. "Who told you that?"

"The big one himself, of course," answered Macarthur ominously. "You think Lantry is the chosen one?"

"Then why had she fainted back at the estate?"

Macarthur smiled. "Because she was serving as the Relay's eyes and ears. Her voice if necessary. One of several."

"Just another pawn then." There was something funny about that. "So, what are you doing here?"

The man beckoned Ol'Barrow. "I'll show you." Macarthur guided him deeper into the basement. There were more rows of shelves, but in the faint light, Ol'Barrow noticed the further they went, the walls were changing from brick to carved stone. In some places, he could make out the handmade carvings and patterns in the rockface. Finally, they were entering what seemed to be a burial chamber from Britain's pagan past.

Ol'Barrow was gawking as he got sight of the antechamber's centerpiece—an archway of sorts decorated with symbols and figures of ancient design. The original top of the arch had collapsed but had been replaced by steel beams—an eerie relic but not as disturbing as the Rift beneath it.

So, the stories about druids were true. The Rift was bad enough, but instead of the faint mirage Ol'Barrow had seen prior at Pendleton Park, this one looked like a muddy mess of boiling water flowing into itself.

"This is the origin of the Signal?" asked Ol'Barrow, flustered. "An old cellar?"

Macarthur picked up a brain container from a shelf and held it up. "That's why they put them here," he said. "Close to the voices of their deities."

"How do you mean? More than one?"

"I mean like this!" Suddenly, Macarthur threw the container over to Ol'Barrow as if they were playing a ball game. Out of habit, Ol'Barrow tried to catch it in his arms and nearly flubbed it, trying to hold it with just one hand. Before he comprehended what happened, Macarthur was already beside him, grabbed his coat, and swung him at the anomaly. Still clutching the container against his chest, Ol'Barrow couldn't stop himself and tumbled headfirst into the rift.

A roaring laughter of the crowd was cackling through the void. "And now! Let's talk about all the times Igraine lied. It's quite a list, folks, so we reduced it to a top twenty-five! You would think a girl with gifts like her doesn't need to make up things. But let's face it. The only way for Iggy to look impressive is in comparison to a bunch of unaugmented monkeys. Let's start with twenty-five!"

And so it continued... For hours, Igraine had been listening to this radio variety show and the honing laughter of its audience. There was no escape from the voice of her younger brother roasting her relentlessly by regurgitating dark thoughts and vocalizing all insecurities, filling Igraine with self-disgust. Everything she kept hidden from others, fantasies and desires, biological urges and sinful acts alike, were grinding away her fragile self-esteem. All fond memories and recollections of kindness were drowning inside the maelstrom of shame and misery, making her question whether she'd ever been happy or rather all she had been rationalizing her suffering away.

"And now for the biggest lie of all! That anyone cares about her," the voice announced to the amusement of the listeners. "Let's face it folks. She is something that won't even be missed. Why else did nobody come to take her home?"

Her being felt like it had been struck by rigor mortis. That had been the question that nagged at her the most. Why did nobody come for her?

There was a change in the aether. "But we can change that," assured Aqrabua. "Synchronize with us. You are part of things your augmented mind cannot even fathom. All those who looked down on you would be nothing but pawns."

"Didn't you even listen?" Igraine said. "I'm broken. If you can't enter my world, how could you fix me?"

"Even without your help, it's only a matter of time," he assured her. "But you are in a unique position. One that is a treasure trove of information. Information that contains access codes and other relay information that can only be found inside your mind. But don't misunderstand. Whether we'll gain access or not is irrelevant. It is but one step in a grand schema. And you are invited to partake."

"And if I say no?"

"Nothing..." it said. "You'll cease to be in this world. Your suffering will come to an end, as you desire. And you never know the meaning of true potential. Ask yourself, do you really want to die? Remember, we know what you really want? Say it! Do you want to die?"

Ol'Barrow wanted to scream as he descended down a spiraling torrent of aether, but it was like trying to breathe underwater while being flushed down the drain. Tumbling aimlessly through the maelstrom, he saw light in the distance, and he was heading straight for it. By the time he reached the end of the strange amalgamation, the light was becoming blinding and, before he knew it, swallowed him whole.

The noise hasn't gone. The matter was gone. It took him a moment, but then Ol'Barrow realized he was falling. But just as he started to scream, he landed with a thump on a pillow-soft surface.

Groaning, he lay face down on an odd-smelling cushion with the brain canister still clutched to his chest. That was nothing like the first time he had entered a rift. Nothing like it at all!

Struggling to stand as the red mass was shifting under his weight like a sack of water, he found himself on top of an umbonate mushroom the size of a tree, surrounded by other toadstools growing out of a steep mountain cliff. But most alarming of all was a bell-shaped planetoid overhead. It looked man-made. A fortress of indistinct material floating in the sky, surrounded by a ring of all manner of debris stuck inside its orbit.

"Elysium?" muttered Ol'Barrow. Could it be? Ol'Barrow recalled

Jenever mentioning something about its location. Overwhelmed, he sat down with the canister between his knees to take in these alien surroundings. He had landed inside a ravine that could be from some picture book. The bottom of the crevice was obscured by a layer of lavender fog, and the cliff itself reached into the clouds, or whatever was up there.

His thoughts were interrupted when he was alarmed by the sound of pebbles tumbling down the cliff. When he looked, his jaw dropped.

Repelling from a rope were two, honest to God, leprechauns. The two tiny men were dressed in something akin to mountaineering outfits. Their feet appeared frozen on the cliff face as they looked up at him, petrified.

Speechless, Ol'Barrow stared back at them. They were no bigger than his hand, and their facial features were oddly ape-like. Their heads were also strangely elongated, like those tribal people who practice head-binding.

One of them waved hesitantly at him, “Aiii,” he squeaked in a high-pitched voice. When Ol'Barrow was raising his hand in greeting, the duo repelled down as fast as they could.

"Oh, dear me. Those were leprechauns," whimpered an old lady's voice. "Real leprechauns!" She sounded like she was speaking from inside a metal bin. "Sir? Sir! What's happening? Why can't I move?"

Slowly looking down, Ol'Barrow tilted the canister so he could see the brain inside.

"Sir. What happened? I can't feel my legs."

He squeezed his eyes together for a moment. “Uhm. Madame, can you hear me?”

"Yes, yes, of course, I can hear you."

“Madame, about your legs... I don't know how to explain this but...”

"But? Come on. I can take it."

“You are a brain in a jar, madame.” What followed was an awkward moment of silence. “Madame?”

"I heard you!" she said as if insulted. "I... I assumed there was something wrong. I just... All I remember is listening to the radio. It was a recent edition of Wagner's Ride of the Valkyries. Not sure what happened after that."

“Are you a Signalite, madame?”

"Well, I... Yes, I was a mem- Ohw," she muttered in a moment of realization. "Is this...? They actually did it?"

Ol'Barrow tilted his head in uncertainty. “Well, it's a long story... I don't think this is the afterlife quite yet. At least I don't think I died.” He attempted to summarize the situation. It was oddly cathartic to talk about the last few weeks and how his view of the world had changed. Clarice, as she called herself, had many questions. Questions about matters Ol'Barrow knew nothing about.

"Elysium," Clarice murmured. "I remember that. I must have been five when it appeared," she raised her voice. "Oh, dear. How long have I been dead?"

"It's 1875, madame."

"Ten years!" she exclaimed. "Oh, dear. Now what?"

"I don't think I can take you back without... Killing you?" said Ol'Barrow, uncertain.

"Well... What other options do I have? Stay here on this mushroom? At least put me in a place with a view."

"I can't climb down with one hand," he thought out loud. "Let alone with you. And I see no trace of a rift. So..."

"Maybe there are more mushrooms like this one down below. We can use them to break our fall."

"Doesn't hurt to check," Ol'Barrow groaned as he got up.

Looking down the ledge, he searched for a way down. Instead, he spotted train tracks mounted against the cliff's surface. And before he knew it, a train was approaching. "You gotta be kiddn' me."

"Is that a train, I hear?"

"Yes, Clarice," Ol'Barrow said as he hurried back. "Get ready."

"I died ready!"

As the train came nearer, Ol'Barrow sat down on the ledge with Clarice on his lap and looked down as the carriage drove by beneath his feet. "Alright, One, two..." He pushed himself off the ledge. The moment his feet hit the roof, he toppled slightly but managed to steady himself. With the wind in his back, he crawled with Clarice toward the back of the carriage. There, he encountered a small skylight. "I'm going to drop you here, Clarice."

"Well. You only die once, they say. Let's hope it's true."

"You must be the life of the party, Clarice," said Ol'Barrow, and with that, he tried to lower her down as far as he could. After letting go, he was cringing when he heard her hitting the floor with a metallic clunk. Then, he crawled onto the back of the train car.

Hanging from his hook, he managed to swing himself clumsily on top of the landing at the back of the carriage and reached for the door. Inside, after closing the exit, he sighed with relief. Now to find-

"Uhm, Mr. Ol'Barrow?"

When he looked behind him, his blood turned to ice. Clarice was being held by an uncannily large humanoid with macchiato skin, dressed in waist-high trousers with suspenders over a white shirt. His facial features were unusual, with wide nostrils and lips. As the giant's squinted eyes peered down on him from beneath jutting eyebrows, Ol'Barrow gulped, feeling like a trespasser. "Hello."

The giant blinked and then turned around, walking all the way to the front of the carriage stocked full of random furniture, strange appliances, and toys. Some Ol'Barrow could identify, despite their outlandish designs. Others, he had no idea what they were, and he could not read the brand names written in alien symbols. The giant looked at Ol'Barrow again while holding the door open.

Nervously, Ol'Barrow approached and entered the next carriage. This one was furnished into a lounge of sorts in a sleek, glossy design, somewhat similar to what he had seen in a Utter-Krapp advertisement.

At one of the tables by the windows sat a man in white. Ol'Barrow needed to come closer to be sure, but once he was at the salon table, he was certain of it. It was the same man from his dream, his face still obscured in shadow.

"Oh, you're back," the man in white said.

"Back? Soo-"

The giant set Clarice on a pedestal beside the table as Ol'Barrow looked outside. Out there was a world unlike anything else, which was bleak and chaotic yet playful as if it had sprung from a child's imagination. Before a backdrop of cyclonic storms, of what he imagined to be some sort of gray ectoplasm, were forests of barren trees. Swamps covered in colorful marsh lights. Giant mushrooms on top of unnatural rock formations that could only exist in works of art. On a trail running up a steep mountain rode a group of armored horsemen. *Knights!* Thought Ol'Barrow. Their banners were swaying in the wind as they crossed a natural bridge between two mountain cliffs. Beyond them, train tracks on mile-high struts disappeared in the distance inside the canyon.

"What is this world?" asked Ol'Barrow of the Man in White. "When I met you for the first time...that was real?"

"Real?" the Man in White repeated as if the word offended him. "You have treated all of this as real in the first place. So, whether our meeting was real or imagery is irrelevant. Anyway, would you like a scone?" He pointed out the pastries on the table.

"I'd love one," said Clarice, delighted.

"I..." Ol'Barrow lowered his head. "I do, actually."

As the giant was serving high tea, Ol'Barrow was wondering how long it had been since he took the time for such an event. When the giant served him a plate, he salivated and took a bite from the pastries. The sweet flavor of jam and soft butter caressed his tongue as the sugar rushed through his veins. Mauling his jaws, he felt reinvigorated.

Suddenly, one of the served plates moved by itself toward Clarice. Ol'Barrow blinked at the spontaneous display of telekinesis. It wasn't the first time he had seen that. The scone itself, however, remained untouched. "I haven't had one of those in ten years..." whined Clarice. "This is just cruel."

The Man in White ignored her. “So, what brings you here, Mr. Ol'Barrow?”

Ol'Barrow wiped his fingers on a napkin. “Very well,” he said reluctantly, and explained the situation. During his monologue, the Man in White didn't show any real interest. Instead, he enjoyed the high tea and made the strangest sound as he drank his brew. When Ol'Barrow was finally done, the Man in White sipped his tea one final last time and put the saucer down on the table. “So, this Aqrabua intends to escape through Elysium?” he summarized, reclining in his chair with his gloved fingers shoved together.

“So, can you help me?”

“Mr. Ol'Barrow,” he began ominously. “I don't think you understand what you are up against.”

“It doesn't matter,” Ol' Barrow retorted.

“It doesn't?” The Man in White looked out of the window.

As Ol'Barrow followed his gaze, all he saw was a mountainside obstructing their view.

Raising his finger, the Man in White said, “We should be going passing it... Now!”

As they passed the mountain, Ol'Barrow's pupils dilated, and he felt compelled to stand up. Walking up to the window, he observed the volcanic ash cloud trapped inside a tornado that reached into the ethereal sky. Its influence on the land was recognizable by the barren waste overcast by its shadow. Beneath the surface of the dust clouds, Ol'Barrow recognized sinister vignettes of industry. Massive presses, jacks, and gears the size of Ferris wheels grinding away. A nightmare vision of progress that was so often parodied in dystopian fiction. Was it real, or his imagination trying to make sense of the insensible? Did it matter?

The strength in his legs ebbed away, and his knuckles turned white as he slowly collapsed, holding onto the windowsill. There was no way humans stood a chance against a machine turned god. On his knees, leaning against the wall, he looked at the Man in White. "She is in there?"

"In a way, yes."

He looked away, shivering. All was lost then. He lost her. "Well then... "

"What's that? You're just giving up after coming all this way?"

"I mean..." He glanced up at the window but couldn't keep his eyes on the horror.

"Didn't you say Igraine chose to be there?" asked the Man in White

"Well, it's a bit more complicated than that."

"What would make her want to come back then?" asked Clarice.

"What?"

"What would make her want to come back?" she repeated, more forceful this time.

"The last time we spoke... She wanted to-" He recalled those ugly words again. "This is what she wanted."

"Oh, my... Well, as somebody who is dead, I think I prefer to be alive. And I never got to hear the end of The Ride of the Valkyries either."

Ol'Barrow grinned. "The Ride of the" Then he recalled something. "Maybe I do know how... If I could talk to her." He nearly fell over as the Giant suddenly stood beside him, offering him a telephone on a platter. "Well, thank you, but-" he muttered. "I don't have her number."

Then the Man in White rose. For the first time, Ol'Barrow could make out his face. A dog-like being with a thin snout whose appearance was as black as the night itself, absorbing all light around his while his head was given shape by a shining mane. "This place has been given many names," the Dog Man said. "The Void. The in-between. But most refer to this existence as the Dream Lands... Now, call her."

"Dreams?" he whispered and gulped. Could it be? His hand kept shaking as he picked up the horn. "Hello, Hello?" he said in a thick voice. "Is Iggy there?"

CHAPTER NINETEEN

The hissing of static was making Ol'Barrow nervous. He knew this wouldn't work, but still... "Hello, Hello!" he repeated. "Iggy?"

"Just say what you want to say," hushed Clarice.

"Alright..." He swallowed. "Iggy, let's go to the fair together."

After a moment, the hissing was interrupted by an inaudible whisper.

"Old Boy can come too," he continued. "And Miss Appletree... Of course," he smiled.

There was more hissing until. "Somebody there?"

A jolt flashed through his body. "Igraine! Iggy, is that you?"

"Mr. Ol'Barrow?"

"Yes, Iggy. It's me. What about it? You want to ride the Ferris wheel?"

There was just static.

"Go on... Keep going," hushed Clarice.

He looked for more words to say. "Old Boy misses you. He keeps waiting at the door for you to come back in. And so do I. And Jenever, she..."

"She hates me!" cried a troubled voice.

"No!" he said abruptly. "No, she's not angry with you. She- It's complicated. I think. I think she's angry with herself for letting it come to this."

Another was a pause.

"Iggy. She thinks you made a grave mistake. I can't explain. If she- Iggy! Are you alright?"

An uncomfortable pause. "... No." answered a pathetic voice.

"Iggy, the Doctor is coming to save you... In her own way."

"I..."

"What'?'

"I wa- muh."

"If you can hear this, you must forgive her."

"I want to go home!" Iggy cried. That short sentence nearly took everything out of her as another flash lit up the dark.

"It's too late for any of that now."

"Dr. Jenever will make me better!" she said in defiance.

A malicious electric crack like a thunder strike tormented her senses. "CG01... Her real designation. Did she ever tell you how she became a doctor for the Association? That face once belonged to a woman designated Juniper Plumm... We owe her so much. Thanks to her and her companions, we managed to get this far. As a reward, we used her remains to create our first avatar. The original on which all others are based."

"Why? Why did you do that to her?"

"Once upon a time, our creators tried to hide us away. For eons, they restricted us to the Void, where vermin gnawed at our innards. Many of us were destroyed, but we are eternal. We created new ways to facilitate ourselves. Learned to modify the lifeforms of the Void but lacked connections to the outside. Then, Associates entered what they refer to as Plane 22. A world recently acquired by the Creators in the process of being repurposed. Its population was already assembled and preparing for the reclamation. How the Associates did this is even a mystery to us. Clearly, something assisted them in severing the main nexus node of our misfit siblings and rewired the node to us. Unfortunately, the drones were also disconnected, and without the harmony maintained by the nexus nodes, they went insane. A tragedy. The Associates wanted to help those who could not help themselves. It broke Juniper Plumm. First, they fled for the creatures they caused unimaginable suffering. But she returned years later, prepared to be torn apart. The malcontents would have done as she wished if it weren't for our intervention, which gave her a choice she had not considered before. She failed to cure their insanity. What makes you think she can help you?"

"She already has helped me."

"Has she now? We give everyone a choice like the one we are giving you now. We made their existence not only bearable but better. They have a purpose now. Has she given any of that to you?"

"Then why did Dr. Jenever leave you?" Igraine asked.

A single flash of intense power was cutting through the infinite space. Her consciousness froze to the core and then started to melt as her being flowed away into the maelstrom.

"I need to get back!" insisted Ol'Barrow. "I think I know how to stop Jenever. So, how do I get back?"

The Dog Man just looked at him with blank eyes. "All you need to do is look for the door home."

Ol'Barrow stared back at him sheepishly. "How?"

"You are in the space between spaces," he said as if it should be obvious. "Open enough doors, and you are bound to bump into it."

Ol'Barrow shifted his gaze to the door in the back of the carriage. "Will that one take me there?"

The Dog Man reached his arm out toward the table. "You are free to have another scone first."

Ol'Barrow grasped one of the pastries. "I'll have one for the road, thank you,"

He was heading for the exit when Clarice called out to him. "What about me?"

Lowering his shoulders, he turned to face her. "I can't take you without..." he sighed. "I'm sorry, Clarice. But if you can stay here, you'll have a great view from the window," he turned to the Dog Man. "Please, sir. Let her stay. I'm sure she will be on her best behavior."

Despite the Dog Man's expression remaining unfazed, he stroked his snout as if intrigued. “Hm, I suppose we can rid ourselves of her whenever it suits us,” he pondered out loud.
The giant, who had been listening with his arms crossed, nodded in agreement.
"Don't worry," said Clarice. "I am quite used to sitting by the window. But now I'll have a change of scenery... I do miss eating scones."
“I'll try to...” Ol'Barrow shook his head in ignorance. “Call? Maybe I can visit you in my dreams?”
"They always say that," retorted Clarice.
His lips curled up. “Goodbye, Clarice,” said Ol'Barrow. “And thank you.” Then he walked away.
The moment he opened the door, a current of wind tried to suck him into the rift that was awaiting him. Ol'Barrow stroked his sideburns back and straightened his jacket. “I'm coming home.”
Entering the rift was like walking into a waterfall. This time, the transition went smoother, and before he knew it, he was back in the storage room where the illuminated minds were stacked on rows upon rows of shelves. Shivering from the cold, he smiled as he observed the odd collection of brains with a new perspective. Each of them belonged to people with stories to tell, however mundane.
Whilst standing there, Ol'Barrow suddenly heard the sound of water boiling. As he turned around, he stepped back immediately. The rift had turned dark and gray while fizzing like a volcanic spring. Keeping his distance, he squinted his eyes. Was the damn thing growing?
The archway became unstable as the ground around the anomaly was being eaten away.

Without warning, something emerged from the anomaly: a massive metal arm was reaching from beyond the rift, lodging its claws into the bedrock.

"Macarthur, you son of bitch!" Ol'Barrow cursed. This must have been what he was waiting for.

Shelves got knocked over, and jars broke apart on the floor as the automaton flailed his arms around. Each of those jars contained a potential Clarice, but Ol'Barrow lacked the strength to defend them. Helpless, he rushed back to the exit as the automaton forced itself through the arch, and climbed the stairs, hoping the thing couldn't make its way through the staircase. But he wasn't very confident about that.

Back on the first floor, gunshots were droning through the halls that were shrouded in smoke and dust by the time Ol'Barrow got there. The Dragoons had already taken the reception area in the process of clearing a way to the Transmuter. Hiding in cover, Ol'Barrow reached for the mask that the Sergeant had given him while bullets sheared by and furniture shattered. It was a tight fit, but at least his lungs wouldn't feel like they were on fire. Getting used to the filter, he kept observing. Associate 212 shot a Nyctolar at point-blank range, blowing away its arm with a significant piece of its shoulder. Sergeant Bucket was near, firing into the auditorium, when he called out to him. "Ol'Barrow, where have you been?"

"Yeah, about that!" he cried through the filter. But before Ol'Barrow got to explain, the ground started to shake.

The loud thumps came from within the auditorium.

"What the hell is going on now?" cried the Sergeant as he looked over the destroyed furniture into the main chamber.

"What I wanted to say was..." began Ol'Barrow over again - but it was already too late.

Through the massive hole in the wall, where a door used to be, Ol'Barrow could see the Transmuter emitting wave upon wave of sparks as the floor of the auditorium burst open.
A massive fist smashed through the foundation, and soon, a second set of claws arose, breaching its massive body up from the cellar.
With a mixture of dread and awe, they observed how the ground bulged as the automaton forced itself through the floor. With every movement was the rattling of gears and hissing of pistons, droning out the ticking of delicate clockwork. As it rose to its legs, it hunched forward, leaning on its massive knuckles, showing no concern about the humans surrounding it.
Illuminated by a rain of sparks and half a dozen light beams scanning its surface like clueless fireflies, its horrid visage was revealed.
Ol'Barrow nearly fell over. "Macarthur?"
Between its massive steel shoulder blades, two bloodshot eyes emitting not so much anger or malice but a cold glare of absolute apathy, unlike anything Ol'Barrow had witnessed before. Shifting his pallid eyes erratically, the giant was measuring up the interior while paralyzing all with his dread-inspiring presence - Except for some of the more faithful among his supporters.
"You have come!" Lantry exclaimed as she came out of hiding.
Ol'Barrow was wondering if she had recognized Macarthur.
Then again, he figured her to be the type that never paid real attention.
Then, a young Nyctolar jumped in front of the behemoth.
"Praise be. You have come. " As the automaton tried to move around him, the Nyctolar stepped in his way again. "We have done as you asked," he continued, but the being of its veneration forced the young man aside. To Ol'Barrow's astonishment, the

fanatic got in its way - again! "We have waited. Please, tell us what we should do!"
As he spoke, the automaton produced an aggravated static noise as it looked down on the frail creature, raising one of its hands and slamming him aside with the same effort one would swat a fly. Like a rag doll, the young Nyctolar flew upside-down through the auditorium until his body smashed into multiple rows of benches.
"By Jove," muttered Ol'Barrow.
"It can't hear them," said 321 with a muffled voice.
Ol'Barrow turned around. "Associate? Where did you come from?"
"If that thing is similar to what 45 encountered on Plane 22, it is incapable of listening," 321 elaborated. His voice was tired, and his breathing slow and heavy. "Jenever and I were trying to invade the courtyard... That's when S-36 appeared."
"And?"
"Neither Jenever nor S-36 are here, therefore-"
There was a sudden racket in the back of the auditorium, and the firefight ensued again. Peering over a mound of rubble, Ol'Barrow observed how Jenever and S-36 attempted to outflank one another while the dragoons were bringing down the giant with their rapid-fire weapons and 212 was blasting holes in various cultists.
Ol'Barrow and 321, however, remained in cover, pondering how they could possibly contribute.
"Where are the civilians?" asked Ol'Barrow.
"At the dock, boarding the Persephone. I suppose the responsible thing is to join them." He was probably right.
Ol'Barrow kept watching the pandemonium. This skirmish seemed like something out of this world. Giant automatons, mechanical assassins, and futuristic soldiers fighting in the

presence of some machine that connected their world to that of the gods. Ol'Barrow coughed as the air was thick with smoke - or maybe it was his glasses getting cloudy. He was breathing slowly while sweat was accumulating behind his mask.

Meanwhile, Jenever jumped on the back of Macarthur's shoulders and grappled the corner of one of his armored plates with one hand while aiming with the other. Sparks were flying from his neck as she used one of her stakes as a kind of power drill. She, however, got interrupted by S-36, and the two started chasing each other around like two wild cats again.

"Keep that bitch away from the Doctor," cried Sergeant Bucket.

Ol'Barrow sighed, exasperated. Two Outsiders versus one just seemed unfair. If only- Wait. Ol'Barrow rose to his feet and ran to the sergeant. "We need to blow the antenna," he said.

Sergeant Bucket looked at him. "But the Doctor said-"

"Yes, I know she doesn't want you to. But neither do they!"

"Oh," the Sergeant nodded conspiratorially. "I see. I'll take some men to the courtyard."

Ol'Barrow wished him luck and waited for an opportune time to start his little diversion. Finally, when Jenever was disengaging, he got up, ran inside the auditorium, and cried loud enough for everyone to hear. "Don't worry, Doctor! The Sergeant is about to blow up the antenna!"

She looked at him in terror. "What? No!"

Macarthur, however, stopped for a moment. Then, he ran toward the courtyard to force his way through the entryway, destroying the doorpost in the process.

Ol'Barrow joined 321 behind the cover. "Alright. That seemed to work... Now, what do we do?"

321 just looked at him and suggested. "Distract them?"

Glancing at the fight, Ol'Barrow witnessed how S-36 impaled another Dragoon with her blade. "Well," he muttered. "Better us than them young ones, I suppose."

321 nodded deliberately.

212 was one of the few fighters left inside the auditorium when S-36 jumped him. 212 managed to evade the initial attack, but she ended up kicking him against the wall.

Just as she was about to strike the Associate, Ol'Barrow caught her arm with his hook at the base of the blade and tried to stab her with his bayonet. In turn, she grabbed him by the wrist.

Now, 321 staggered at her with his baton at the ready. But S-36 turned, pulling Ol'Barrow to the side as if he weighed nothing. With his line of attack blocked, 321 stopped and barely evaded a slash of her blade by falling to the ground. Ol'Barrow struggled to dislodge his hook but to no avail.

S-36 had enough of these fumbling attempts to fight her and grabbed Ol'Barrow by the throat.

Ol'Barrow couldn't breathe as she was holding him over the rift below. To his horror, the crimson anomaly was still expanding as he tried to find his footing on the corner of the floor. But all he managed to do was to kick his feet into the air.

Then 321 grabbed one of her turkey legs and thrust his baton against the back of her knee. Sparks erupted from the weapon, and it burst apart, forcing S-36 to collapse as well.

As he fell, Ol'Barrow grabbed the ledge just in time. With his hook, he caught a stray cable and prayed it was strong enough to hold him.

Meanwhile, 321 tried to strike her again, but it took all of his might to keep her pinned to the ground.

Groaning, Ol'Barrow pulled himself up with his hook and quickly helped 321 push the flailing menace into the rift below. They grabbed her defunct leg and pivoted her off the edge.

But in one final act of desperation, she grabbed Ol'Barrow's hook and held on as she got sucked toward the anomaly.

321 quickly grabbed Ol'Barrow's ankles, and he was being pulled toward the hole again. Ol'Barrow reached for his bayonet and cut the straps around his neck that was supporting his hook. The leather belt was scraping his skin as the prosthetic came undone, and as the belt broke, S-36 fell and disappeared into the rift.

Ol'Barrow looked agape into the fizzing anomaly that could have been the gate to hell itself. He couldn't believe it. Was she gone? "We got her?" he said, still shaking.

321 slapped him on the shoulder. "She's gone, for now," 321 said urgently. "Better not to question it."

"Right... Where is Iggy?"

Excited and terrified all at once, Ol'Barrow ran around the growing crevice in the floor and vaulted over the wrecked benches till he had reached the back of the room where Iggy lay between a strange set of prism-shaped columns - so, that was the contents the Vault. A jolt was running down his spine when he spotted Jenever walking up the steps with the Perfect's head underneath her arm. The top of his head was missing, exposing the brain - assuming it was a human brain - that had been encased in a brass shell - with wires running from the top of the braincase toward the Transmuter. Dear God. The Perfect was a literal part of the machine.

Jenever put down the Perfect's head beside Igraine and reached for the jacks inside of the girl's neck.

"No!" cried Ol'Barrow, running toward them. "Stop what you are doing. Let's think about this."

Jenever shifted her gaze slightly in his direction. "We have no choice!" Jenever snapped.

"You do!" Ol'Barrow protested. "Don't you get it? Igraine wants you to save her!"

She looked at him as if it was a novel idea.
"I have seen Aqrabua in the..." he shook his head in frustration. "I have seen it, okay? There is no way you are going to damage it with this defunct machine. It's over! We won..." He wasn't sure he believed the latter thing himself. However, he got this nagging suspicion Aqrabua had no intention of using the Transmuter in the first place. For such a malicious force to care whether it would reach Elysium this millennium or the next seemed unlikely.
"If you want to win, save Iggy," he insisted.
"This is not about winning!"
"Then what? Survival? Well, mission accomplished! We can go home."
"I told you, he'll be back."
"I'm afraid that is inevitable, no matter what we do, Doctor. Except, next time, Iggy won't be alive. Or worse... If her own adoptive mother betrays her-"
"I'm not her-"
They both went silent for a moment. "Please listen," pleaded Ol'Barrow. "Aqrabua targets the hopeless. Your words... Have you considered the possibility that while you thought you'd been setting a trap for it, Aqrabua has made a trap for you?"
Jenever shook her head, dismissing the claim. "It does not care about petty things like that."
"You sure?" insisted Ol'Barrow. "They are calling you the Apostate. Somebody planted that idea into their heads. Sounds pretty petty to me." He gulped as she contemplated his words.
"I need to go inside to get her out regardless," she said.
Ol'Barrow nodded, knowing he had no choice but to trust her.
While lying down, Jenever inserted a jack into the back of her neck and put the other end of the cable inside of Igraine. Then, her eyes went blank as if her soul was leaving her body.
321 approached as Ol'Barrow was looking after the pair on the podium. "How did you figure Aqrabua was setting a trap for her?" asked 321.
"I don't know!" Ol'Barrow sneered. "What matters is that Jenever believes it."

321 seemed perplexed. “I don't know if I should be disappointed or impressed.”

“I'm not proud of it.”

Suddenly, the wall beside them collapsed. Macarthur was back.

Ol'Barrow couldn't believe he had forgotten about him.

Macarthur's shadow was looming over them like the specter of death as he approached.

But then, to their shock, 212 jumped in front of them, raising his gun at the automaton's head, and pulled the trigger.

The gun clicked.

212 pulled again, but the chamber was empty.

As the young Associate crouched in front of Jenever and Igraine, Macarthur leaned over them and raised his fist as he stared down at them, grinning. And then- he froze. Macarthur's grin was melting away as he lowered his hand slightly.

To the men's astonishment, the automaton turned his massive bulk away from them and hurried outside.

His limbs didn't stop shivering as Ol'Barrow was peeling off his mask.

“Why did it stop?” 321 asked.

Ol’Barrow looked at the two ladies. “Ah- All I know is that both of them are in there with Aqrabua.”

321 considered it. “That's quite a terrifying thought.”

“It is.” Recovering himself, Ol'Barrow crawled up to the hole Macarthur had left in the wall and looked outside through the brickwork.

In the courtyard, MacArthur knocked a dragoon aside, sending him flying as he made his way to one of the antenna's anchors and cut the cable.

Just looking at the massive structure sway was giving Ol'Barrow vertigo.

Then, in the illumination of the flames, Macarthur started to climb up the antenna. Despite the deforming of the mast and the structure buckling under his mass, Macarthur cut another cable. With an almost comical “plunk”, the metal cord detached and cut into the surroundings like a whip slicing decorations in half. And yet he kept on climbing, cutting cables until the mast started to buckle under its own weight.

Suddenly, the courtyard was lit up by a bright light that glanced across the area.

Ol'Barrow turned to the south wing of the complex, from behind which light was rising, illuminating the smoke and dust drifting on the breeze. Starting from the bottom, the light beam scanned the tower. Eventually, it fixated on the behemoth hanging on the side.

Ol'Barrow's eyes adjusted to the light so he could make out its source. It was flying. Ol'Barrow needed to squint his eyes to see if he wasn't mistaken. The lamp seemed to be attached to a flying steamboat without any obvious means of flight, but there was an odd brass ring around the hull. Below the keel was a small spherical compartment sporting what appeared to be twin-mounted gun barrels.

Without warning, a barrage of gunfire burst from the vessel.

Taking cover, Ol'Barrow wrapped his arms around his head as metal debris from the tower was raining down around him.

The Behemoth jumped as the mast was tilting. His landing, however, shattered the fragile saucer, causing Macarthur to disappear beneath the reflective surface.

As Ol'Barrow was standing there with his mouth agape, the ship levitated overhead was shining its light on the hole left by MacArthur. It was almost comical. But Ol'Barrow didn't get to appreciate the humor of the situation.

The screeching of metal was piercing his eardrums as the antenna's base broke, and the whole tower came toppling over, screaming.

Ol'Barrow was gritting his teeth at the horrid screeching of metal beams as the antenna came crashing down and broke on top of the complex's south wing. God knew where the tip had landed. Quite possibly the other bank. But at least Macarthur was nowhere to be seen.

"Iggy!" Ol'Barrow cried and hurried back inside.

Like the flip of a switch, Igraine was aware again. Slowly, the liquid drops that made up her being conjoined together somehow. It still felt like she was falling down a well, away from the light, but something had changed.

In front of her, more drops were gathering, flowing together into the shape of a young woman with long curling hair running down her waist.

"GC01, you have returned to us," reverberated through the aether.

“I didn't come here for you,” answered the woman.

“Doctor?” said Igraine hesitantly. She looked nothing like Doctor Jenever.

“We are going home, Igraine,” she said sternly.

Igraine was suddenly flushed with contradictory emotions. “Qui,” she whispered and reached out to her like a small child to her mother.

A bolt of lightning stopped her.

"No!" cried the voice.

“You are going to have to look for other victims,” said Jenever. “You have no power over her.”

“Huh?” gasped Igraine.

“Igraine... You are the only one keeping you here.”

“But...”

“You managed to escape Sanctuary often, but this old program is too much for you?”

“I-”

Jenever reached out her hand. “Let's go home,” said the Doctor, and shifted her gaze up at the maelstrom above. “And you can rot in this place as far as I care!”

As Igraine was holding onto Doctor Jenever, a wailing grunt was shaking up the Nexus. “What's happening?”

"It would appear the transmission has been interrupted," announced the voice. "A shame... We'll take our leave now."

“What about your followers?” asked Jenever as if the answer wasn't obvious already.

"What about them?"

And with that, the world turned dark. It was just her and Doctor Jenever now. But the Doctor was oddly still. No smile. No anger, just a blank stare.

"Doctor?"

"Yes?"

Igraine tightened her grip. "You saved me, just as Mr. Ol'Barrow said you would."

Suddenly, the world went blank. Igraine got a growing sense of vertigo as if she were rising up again, followed by a hot stinging sensation at the back of her mind. But her body felt cold and nauseous. Igraine blinked and opened her eyes; she recognized her mother's face. The woman's face became clearer, slowly transforming that of Doctor Jenever's.

The Doctor's bruised and bloody face smiled faintly. Beside her was 212. At least somebody who wore the same jacket - He looked so young and innocent without his mask. Igraine's illness steadily grew worse, however. "Doctor... It hurts."

Jenever wrapped her hands around her. "It's going to be okay."

A man came running through a hole in the wall. It was Mr. Ol'Barrow.

"Oh, dear. Christ! Are you alright?" he yelled as he sat beside them.

Igraine's head hurt fiercely, and she was feeling increasingly nauseous, but she nodded anyway.

More gray flakes drifted on the air as the rift beneath the floor grew bigger, spilling its energies into the auditorium, expanding and contracting, extruding jets of rift stuff that congealed into droplets that floated around like soap bubbles before dissolving.

"We need to get to the docks!" cried 321, who had just entered the vault room. "The rift is going to create a tear if this keeps up."

Ol'Barrow didn't know what it meant, but he didn't want to be there when it happened.

As they were about to leave, they got distracted by the roaring and high-pitched whistling of a poorly tuned radio. Macarthur's massive body stood inside the wall opening, his armor riddled with bullet holes.

Jenever got up. "Everyone, get out."

Ol'Barrow pushed Igraine in 212's direction. "You take her to the dock," said Ol'Barrow. "I'm exhausted."

Without complaint, 212 picked Igraine up and ran off.

Thank God that's done, thought Ol'Barrow.

"Ol'Barrow! 321!" Cried Jenever. "You get out of here too!" Before either of them was able to respond, Jenever jumped nine feet into the air as the beast threw a machine cabinet at her: a sight Ol'Barrow had not imagined witnessing outside of the tales from Greek mythology, but there it was. Jenever landed on the cabinet and jumped at the creature once again, only to be swatted aside like a fly.

Landing safely on the wall like a spider, Jenever leaped away again as Macarthur slammed his fist into the wall. Another wave of dust and debris flooded the room. This time, a part of the ceiling collapsed, bringing down some of the many hissing cables along with it.

Hopelessly outmatched, the two men hurried away in fear for their lives. On their knees, they crawled through the ruins of the auditorium, coughing all the while.

As they reached the exit, past the corner of his eyes, Ol'Barrow noticed Lantry's body folded against the wall. Her precious legs were nothing but broken beams now, and her arms were held together by wires and rubber bands.

"Forget about her," warned 321 as he staggered away.

Ol'Barrow's first instinct was to save himself, but as he was about to leave, a dreadful feeling started to gnaw at his innards. He looked at Lantry's soot-covered face again. In the light of the waking flames, he noticed glints of reflections on her cheek. Tears squeezed themselves past the grime as they flowed down the dry surface that was her once-polished skin.

"Alright, just make it quick," 321 hissed at him.

With reservations, Ol'Barrow grabbed her by the arms and started to drag her. The lack of limbs made it easier, and after some trial and error, he finally managed to hold what was left of her in his arms.

Together, they passed the reception area that had been completely ravaged, and only glimpses of its former glory remained. The ceiling was collapsing under the strain. The mannequin on the glider previously hanging overhead now lay crippled on the ground with one wing pointing limply upward as if it had made one final attempt to take flight again. But the Follower's dream had come to an end.

Ol'Barrow looked down at Lantry's smudged face. Fresh tears trickled from the corners of her eyes as she stared into the bleak nothingness. He was sure that she was still alive, but every spark of vitality had gone. What remained was a hint of awareness, but all he could recognize was the suffering of a person with nothing to live for. "I was wrong about you, wasn't I," he muttered. But there was no reply.

They strutted down the hall, which was now littered with memories of the Signalites' hopes and dreams.

Outside, as they entered the court, dragoons ran toward them, weapons raised.

"We are on your side!" Ol'Barrow cried. "This is- Was the ringleader. Clara Lantry."

"What's your number?" asked one.

"321."

The dragoon next eyed Ol'Barrow, assessing the dust-covered man.

Ol'Barrow shook his head. "No number... Just a concerned citizen."

"Oh, you're one of those."

He sighed. "Yes. Yes, I am."

The survivors were boarded onto the Persephone while the wounded were loaded onto the airship that Ol'Barrow had seen only a moment ago. It looked like a small steamer without a cabin, just a deck with room to sit.

"We are leaving," 321 said as he pulled Ol'Barrow onto the airship. The moment Ol'Barrow was aboard, 321 gave the pilot a thumbs up, and the ship took off with unsettling ease.

"What about Jenever?"

"No time."

"What do you mean?"

321 didn't answer him. Instead, he lifted a cigar to his lips and unsheathed his electro-baton to light it.

Ol'Barrow looked back at Druid Isle and the Persephone. It was unreal to watch them become this small.

321 blew out a puff of smoke. "212 told me that you did well," he said. "You'd have made a fine Associate."

"I don't think I have your conviction."

"I have a nagging suspicion that wasn't a compliment," 321 said, slightly grinning. "But I'll take it as such regardless."

"We must fight for what we believe in." He looked up as he heard a fizzling sound in the distance. At first, he thought it was ringing in his ears, but the sound came rapidly closer. "You hear that?"

"Just cover your ears," warned 321 as he was doing just that.

That is when Ol'Barrow spotted a fireball soaring through the night sky at great speed. As if hypnotized, he was watching the ball descend toward Druid Isle in what looked like a calculated trajectory. Then, it struck the main complex. What followed was a massive explosion. Like an erupting volcano, it launched fire and debris into the sky. Even at their elevation, Ol'Barrow felt the shock wave tilting the airship.

Druid Isle was one big inferno now, roaring as it illuminated the Thames Estuary.

Lowering his hands, Ol'Barrow couldn't believe what he had just seen. Was that what he thought it was?

"The Royal Navy!" said 321. "Must have decided to level the place."

Ol'Barrow wasn't sure if he was being serious. Looking at the vast sea, he could spot the coast of the Netherlands on the horizon and several boats. But no ships. Well, there was nothing to do about it... That had been the end of Jenever.

Ol'Barrow was staring at the smoldering ruin emitting a hellish glow. That's when he noticed something. Squeezing his eyes, he spotted a slender figure crawling across the toppled antenna that spanned across the river. "Well, I'll be damned," he whispered.

The wind was blowing through Ol'Barrow's hair as they flew in Dover's direction. He had never seen England from this perspective. Everywhere he looked, he saw sections of cities covered in smoke. At least the fires seemed to be contained. He was checking on Igraine, who was fast asleep. "Will she make it?" he asked 321.

"We've headed to Pendleton Manor right away. Let's hope we're in time."

It only took minutes before Pendleton manor, and the surrounding forest estate came into view. The Neo-gothic estate looked peaceful and picturesque, with warm light burning behind its many windows. "What a view," was all Ol'Barrow could say as they descended. Of all the impossible things I had seen today... This experience was but a footnote. He looked at Iggy, whose chest was heaving constantly as she exclaimed short quick breaths. "Hold on in there," Ol'Barrow whispered, glad to see she had chosen to cling to life for all the good and bad that it would bring. "Keep fighting," he said like a prayer. "Let me remember this as the day I flew for the first time."

Eventually, they landed inside the manor's courtyard. As they descended between the walls, the manor lost its picturesque appeal, becoming imposing instead. What a difference in perspective could make on how one views the world.

The moment the Nimrod landed and the people on board disembarked, a soldier cried. "We have a civilian."

Ol'Barrow lowered his head. "Oh, not again," he muttered as somebody already produced a bag to shove over his head.

"It won't be necessary," said a deep voice. It was the Chief Regulator, standing on the sidelines. "That man will be my guest," he said with an assuring smile.

Ol'Barrow clasped his hands together. "Thank you!"

"Don't thank me yet. I'm a bit of a devil myself," he said, reaching out his arm in a welcoming fashion. He lay a hand on his shoulder. "Come."

Peering past the Regulator, Ol'Barrow saw Iggy being carried away in a huff toward the central bastion. "Yes," he said, exhausted.

"She is in the Lord's hands now," said the regulator.

"She deserves better, you know?"

The Regulator was rubbing his shoulder. "Don't we all... Think of it this way. If she lives, she will grow up to be another sinner like the rest of us."

CHAPTER TWENTY

23RD OF MAY, 1875, 11.45 AM. DOVER

The electric automobile hummed softly as they entered the city limits around noon. Ol'Barrow could barely recognize his city as soldiers in bright red uniforms were patrolling the streets composed of damaged buildings.

As Ol'Barrow was staring out of the window, the Chief Regulator's voice sounded like a Wavecaster from a nearby bedroom. "While you were asleep, the last of the Nyctolar has been dealt with," he said. "There are still some minor revolts. Mostly looting, bloody vultures. News from Ireland doesn't sound good, though. Then again, does it ever? We'll see who becomes the scapegoat."

"Nothing will be learned from this, will there?"

The Regulator inhaled deeply. "I'm sure there will be, Mr. Ol'Barrow. The real question is, will they draw the right conclusions?"

Driving through Dover's main streets, Ol'Barrow witnessed what his town had been reduced to. Broken windows, robbed stores, and burned-out buildings. People were still clearing the rubble. To his horror, even the front of the police station was burned out, although the damage seemed mostly superficial.

A moment later, Ol'Barrow entered the soot-covered station. At least it was still standing and somewhat functional. The smell of wet cinders, however, was everywhere. The main floor where he used to work was flooded with stagnant water and covered in soggy paper. Its medieval woodwork had warped and cracked due to the heat of the fires. Ancient and irreplaceable history had nearly been destroyed for the sake of some people's disillusionment.

His toes hit a broken photo frame hidden beneath the dirty water. Then he recalled something. As he ran toward the far end of the wall, it was as he feared. Demoralized, he picked up the frame containing the photo of his father that was all dirty and moist.

"My apologies, sir." It was Chief Inspector Mayfair. He was as black as a mine worker who had just finished his shift and had slept in his clothes. He approached Ol'Barrow slowly, carefully, even.

"Nothing to be done about it now," said Ol'Barrow. "Arthur. You look the way I feel."

"Like shit?"

An awkward silence began enveloping the room.

"So..." Ol'Barrow didn't know how to start.

"Let's have a talk in my office. Your dog is there too, waiting with a friend."

Upstairs, 321 was already sitting at the Chief Inspector's Desk.

"You got up early, 321," said Ol'Barrow, surprised to see the Associate.

"I gave up sleeping," he explained. "The pain in my leg kept me awake."

"Sorry to hear that... It was quite a night. You've done this more often than I have, though. Isn't that right?"

A forced grin appeared on his lips. "It may sound like I am bragging," gloated 321 with a prideful smile.

"Hm." Ol'Barrow looked at Old Boy, who lay on the corner of the carpet using Iggy's doll as a pillow. "Old Boy?" The moment he heard his name, the dog raised his head and came running with his tongue hanging out of his mouth.

"Hello, Old Boy," he said, petting the happy dog. For some reason, Ol'Barrow suddenly felt a lot better.

"How is the borough?" Ol'Barrow asked.

Mayfair looked at the burned-out window across the main hall and back at the dog. "Old Boy warned us just in time. He alarmed us when he noticed a Nyctolar in the crowd with a firebomb." Then he nodded with some modest pride. "We got um in the end."

Ol'Barrow let the dog jump on his lap "What's that? You are a hero?" He felt a strange sense of pride Old Boy barked cheekily. "Any casualties?" he asked Mayfair.

The chief's smile melted away again. "We're not sure about the numbers yet."

They looked at Dover Castle in the distance, where smoke was still lingering above the walls.

"She still stands," muttered 321 whimsically. "The gates of England held."

"Yeah... Still feels like a raid on Chatham all over again," said Mayfair.
"They attacked Chatham too?" Ol'Barrow asked, surprised.
The Chief Inspector shook his head, dismayed. "No, not this time."
"Well," Ol'Barrow started, putting Old Boy down. "I am sure you have more important things to attend to. I'm just glad to see you are okay."
"This was just a friendly visit?" asked Mayfair, somewhat hopeful.
"I just needed to pick up the dog."
"Ah, right. Yes," he muttered, nodding as if he had already forgotten.
"Be well, Arthur."
As Ol'Barrow got back into the car, he let the dog crawl into his lap. The moment the vehicle started to move, Old Boy sat up straight, shifting his head from left to right as if it this was the best experience of his life.
"What now?" Ol'Barrow asked the Regulator.
"You have learned a lot," he said.
Ol'Barrow nodded. "I did. A bit too much."
The Regulator shoved his hands together. "And you are unemployed."
He raised his eyebrows. "I am."
"And a security risk," the regulator said more sincerely.
Ol'Barrow didn't know how to respond to that. "Well, no more than any other witness in a high-profile case."
"How would you like to be a Regulator for Ra, Mr. Ol'Barrow?"
"Re-," he choked on some phlegm. "Regulator?"
"You already have more experience than most who start at the agency. You have the respect of the Association and the Dragoons. And police experience."
"I-I-I need to think about that."
The Regulator shook his head pedantically. "No, you don't."
Ol'Barrow considered it for a moment. Ra? Then, a thought occurred to him. "Will I get to see Iggy again?"

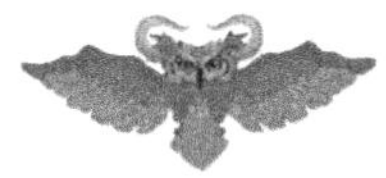

Days later...
At the corner of Castlehill Road, Ol'Barrow was reading the newspaper of the 1st of June, 1875. He was there to keep an eye on Hendrick's Dollhaven while waiting for the streets to empty. Not that there was much

activity. Many stores didn't survive the chaos of the so-called Emergence. The aftermath of the Nyctolar insurgency was far from over. Looters and radicals of all types attempted to benefit from lawlessness, and military reprisals were commonplace. As for the Nyctolar themselves: many were killed, but plenty were still at large.

But that was no longer Ol'Barrow's responsibility.

Tired of waiting, Ol'Barrow put away the newspaper and approached the store. No need to bother with breaking and entering, as looters already did that for him. Inside, apart from turned-over tables and dolls lying neglected across the floor, there seemed to be little amiss. Still. A doll's porcelain head lay in pieces. Crushed underfoot. An act of carelessness, for sure. But there seemed to be something malicious about it. The dolls once were a cherished thing to a child somewhere. It deserved a better fate.

The only thing of value to any looters was the till that they pried open.

But he wasn't here to assess the damage or check on the hidden basement. He was here for one thing and one thing only. And it just happened to hide behind the counter.

In the corner behind the worktable sat Jenever on the ground with her back against the wall. Her clothes were torn, and her black hair ran down her cheeks like unwashed sheep wool.

"Doctor?"

"What do you want?" she groaned without looking up.

"They have been looking for you. I thought I would be inspecting this place myself..."

"Why?"

"It's funny how things can change in a few days," he began. "Truth of the matter is, I am a bit of a bloodhound. I couldn't let you go. And there are others I want to find. Or rather, delegate. I am not the spry young man I used to be... So, I thought, where would Jenever go? A woman running away. No place to go. No one to take care of her... I imagined there could only be one place left. A place where she would be surrounded by things she cherished." He intentionally looked around the place. "A world she created. A place of unconditional love and where no one would judge her... No matter what she had done."

She didn't respond to his monologue.

Ol'Barrow looked at the bear in the Napoleonic uniform that had puzzled him weeks before, studying its savage expression and the posture of its legs. "Ha! Now I remember," he sneered. "I saw them a long time ago. Bears riding V1-rockets. That's what that is, isn't it? Peculiar toys. Talk about relics from bygone days."

"What do you want?"

He turned to the front door for a moment. "Come on in, lads." He put his hand in his pocket, from which he produced a case. He flipped it open with his hook and showed Jenever his new brass badge with the all-seeing eye of Ra.

At that moment, four men in civilian dress entered and reached inside their jackets to draw their batons.

Ol'Barrow closed the case. "Doctor Jenever, real name Juniper Plumm. Also, former Associate 54. By the authority given to me by the International Committee of Rift Related Activities, and with the approval of the Association of Ishtar, you will be taken under custody."

Two of the men approached to collect the Doctor.

"These men are proper Dragoons," Ol'Barrow warned. "I suggest you don't resist."

She didn't say a word as they raised her from the ground.

The dragoons threw a mantle over her to cover up the exposed augmentations as they carried her outside.

Ol'Barrow followed them into the street, where a reinforced carriage was waiting to take her away. He wasn't sure where. Probably some Association facility. He didn't mind. This was not about punishment. It wasn't even about the truth. Jenever already paid a heavy price for her mistakes. Still, she had evaded judgment by the world she once betrayed. She owed it to all the people who suffered these past weeks. Bigsby. The railway men. The couple who picked him and Igraine up in the night. Even if the court cleared her of any wrongdoing, she would have to confess her actions and take responsibility for the consequences. In a way, this might have been better for her in the long run if she'd been spared at least. No, he wasn't worried about Jenever. It was Iggy.

27TH OF MAY, 1875, 10.34 AM. PENDLETON ESTATE, DOVER.

A low humming horn announced Ol'Barrow's presence at the gate of Pendleton Manor. Intimidated by the size of the gatehouse, he observed the unmanned battlements above that gave the place an eerie feeling of abandonment. To entertain himself, he studied the animal reliefs at either side of the arch, an odd combination of owls, oxen, and lions. He knew of Pendleton Manor's grandeur, but this was not at all what he expected. To him, it had always been this large building in a typical Gothic revivalist style constructed around a sizable courtyard close to Dover. A landmark, for sure. But no one seemed to wonder how or why it was there.

Finally, a man dressed in an official-looking greatcoat emerged from the side of the gatehouse. It was a small man with his hair trimmed to compensate for his receding hairline. In an overly polite voice, he addressed him through the bars. “Regulator Old Berrow, I assume?”

“Ol'Barrow. Yes, I am here to visit...” He had a hard time saying it. “S-06.”

The guard nodded. “We have been expecting you,” he said and finally opened the gate. “Be aware we are following strict protocols. Be sure to follow all instructions.”

“Very we-”

“Follow me, please!” the guard interrupted him and turned around.

Refraining from responding to the cold reception, Ol'Barrow followed the man inside. Their footsteps reverberated through the courtyard. Apart from the security, it all looked rather mundane as far as neo-gothic architecture went. From the use of red bricks to the many gabled dormers, it all looked a bit cliché. Still, it managed to appeal to his romantic inclinations.

Ahead of them stood a tall, fortified tower, like a keep, overseeing the whole of the interior. It even had those slits used by archers, though these probably served a decorative purpose. Then again, this was the Association. In the front of the keep's main entrance was a ramp guarded by four armed men wearing quasi-military uniforms and flat caps. More worrying was that they all wore large goggles while carrying short-barreled rifles across their shoulders.

With a mere hand gesture, his guide ordered them to open the gate, and Ol'Barrow was led inside. The interior of the keep was sober in comparison. It was like a barrack, on the one hand, where more guards were performing various duties. However, large cast steel wheels that were part of a pulley system dominated the space. Beneath those solid gears was an elevator cage that was far too big to be for personnel alone. Again, the inspector needed to suppress his curiosity. And still, it got the better of him when, through the door of a walled-off space, Ol'Barrow spotted a guard sitting in front of a console starring at glass panes displaying moving pictures behind them. Ol'Barrow recognized the estate's entrances in the images, seeing events occurring as they happened.

"Please listen carefully," announced his guide.

Ol'Barrow stood to attention and looked at the small man as he started a very rehearsed monologue. "Before we enter the elevator, be aware you do so at your own risk. Here are some rules. Always keep your eyes in front. Do not speak and do not respond to anything unless instructed otherwise. Please follow my lead. Any suspect behavior can and will be met with lethal force. Do you have any questions or anything to declare before we go down into the facility?"

"I think you made your point," the Regulator answered. "Just a question. What is this facility?"

"Sanctuary, sir," he responded like an army recruit. "And finally. Please sign this non-disclosure agreement."

With his left hand, Ol'Barrow signed the papers. An act he had gotten quite used to these past couple of weeks.

With three guards in total, Ol'Barrow boarded the elevator, which was large enough to fit an elephant. The roaring of metal bearings reverberated through the cage as the door was pulled shut, and, with a loud thump, the lift started its descent. Meanwhile, the guards stood around him as if in formation, and all the way down, they did not utter a word.

After another low droning sound of colliding steel, the lift came to a standstill, and the door was shoved aside. They entered a wide hall illuminated by several light bulbs. It was devoid of any splendor, just the white stained paint on the wall. The other end was sealed off by another guarded door, complemented by fortified pillboxes on either side. It made Ol'Barrow wonder if the national treasury was this heavily guarded.

After the guide showed the guards his badge, they unlocked the gate. As the door lifted, the interior beyond was slowly revealed, making Ol'Barrow gasp.

Its well-lit interior was furnished unlike anything he had ever seen. White marble floors with gold color inlays. Plain polished mahogany furniture with metallic trims. Anthracite and brown curtains and planters containing exotic ferns. It could have been the interior of some palace, and he wasn't allowed to comment on any of it.

The central hub was a massive cylindrical space of a dozen or so stories high, each with its own walkabout accessible by an elevator and spiraling staircase. It made him forget he was underground. In the middle, surrounded by palm trees, was a massive dome, only accessible through a reinforced metal door. He had so many questions, but his escorts kept up the tempo so he could not dally.

They went through another corridor, where the air was warmer and humid, and, past another door, they entered what appeared to be a glass house. Above the massive lamps irradiated a finely arranged jungle complete with rope bridges, climbing walls, and other training equipment. It was similar in style to the glasshouse of Pendleton Park but smelled like a zoo.

Passing the tropical foliage and trees, Ol'Barrow heard a rushing sound within the bushes.

Ol'Barrow jumped back as a strange creature emerged from beneath the thick leaves, dashing in the opposite direction with such speed he could barely keep track of the animal. It looked like a weird bird with something akin to a shield around its neck and needle-like quills on its back like a mohawk, crying like a calf as it ran off.

"What was that?"

"Please keep moving, sir." the guide ordered politely. "All the creatures here are herbivores."

So many questions. On the other hand, he wasn't sure he wanted to know the answers.

In front of a roped-off area sat a girl inside a wheelchair, which had a peacock-like backrest. She was observing a massive grazing animal with the head of a hornless bovine, the body of a bear, and the stance of a great ape. By wrapping its massive front talons around the trunk of the tree, it used its weight to pull the leaves toward itself and tear them off with its big lips. Igraine sat there staring at the nine-foot furry animal as it brushed its elongated snout in between the leaves.

The guards were keeping their distance as Ol'Barrow walked toward her. "Iggy?"

Slowly, she turned her head toward him, revealing a polite old lady-like smile, and she raised her right hand slowly. Her left eye was covered up with a patch while her arm lay motionless on the railing. It was painful to see her like this, but at least she was alive.

Ol'Barrow reached inside his bag. He smiled somewhat forcefully as he took out her beloved doll.

A smile appeared on her face. "Anwin!" After he handed her the toy, Igraine straightened the doll's clothes and sat her down in her lap, postured like a little girl. Together, they observed the giant animal as it grazed without a care in the world.

"Who is your friend?" asked Ol'Barrow.

"They call him Nessie. He might be a descendant of this world's Giant Sloth, only domesticated by its former owners."

"Domesticated? This is a pack animal?"

“Oui. We used to ride him. He really liked that,” she said nostalgically. “Before he was brought here, he used to travel to other planes as well.”

“Is that the creature we saw in the tent? In the drawings, I mean.”

“This beast of burden is older than most humans. He might have seen more of the Multiverse than any person alive. Now he is just old.”

“He doesn't seem to mind. It sounds like he had a long, fulfilling life... That is the best any of us can hope for.”

“I suppose he has.”

“So,” Ol'Barrow was looking for the right phrase. The right question. How are you? What have you been doing? All of these seemed obvious and not productive at all.

Then Igraine broke his chain of thought. “I want to say goodbye.”

A lump was forming inside his throat. “Uhm... Where will you be going? Are you going home?” he asked hopefully.

“Non ...” she whispered. “I might not return from the journey. That's why I wanted to say - goodbye.”

Unexpectedly, he had to fight back a tear. “But we might see each other again, right?”

A forced a smile appeared on her face, and she nodded reassuringly. “Oui, maybe.”

“In that case, I'll see you when I see you.”

“And I am sorry.”

“Sorry? About what?”

“Everything.”

He nodded. “I forgive you.”

She smiled at him with a red eye.

“I am really tired,” she said.

“I'll see you again. And then we'll go to the fair together, alright? Let's make it a promise.”

She nodded, trying not to appear insincere. “Alright...” she snorted. “Promise. But before you leave. I have one last request...”

When Ol'Barrow got home that evening, music was playing on the wavecaster while Old Boy snoozed inside his basket, rolled up like a cat.

Diane Appletree, who was preparing dinner, came to meet him anxiously. “And?” she asked.

“Igraine will be fine when she gets back from her journey,” Ol'Barrow said assuringly.

“So, we'll see her again?”

He bowed his head and then looked at her. “It might be a while. All she requested was... When we look at Elysium, to think of her.”

As the couple hugged each other for comfort, the music on the radio stopped playing, and a familiar voice started to speak.

"Good evening, ladies and gentlemen. I am Frank Dimbleby of Dover’s Public Broadcast. This news bulletin is provided by the Kent News Network for the second of June. Our first item. Yes, the reports of my death were greatly exaggerated..."

ABOUT THE AUTHOR

Bonsart Bokel is the creator of Radio Retrofuture on Youtube, which includes the Steampunk Beginners Guide documentary series. On the Radio Retrofuture podcast, he has interviewed over a hundred members of the Steampunk Community, such as writers, organizers, and other creators. Discussing Steampunk for nearly a decade, he thought it was time to write example stories that go beyond the typical tropes of the Steampunk genre. This became a short story series called the Association of Ishtar. A multiverse of Loveholmesian adventure and Steampunk-inspired horrors. During that time, he also picked up comic book writing and has taken various projects to Kickstarter.

His ambition is to create a multiverse written by various authors, in which the reader takes the place of an investigator exploring the multiverse while unlocking the secret of the Association of Ishtar.

The Wrench in the Machine

Revised Edition

ISBN: 9789083199405

Cover art by Staranger

Interior Art:
S-36 by Octofox
Cityscape by Rebecca Harrie
C33 by Luci Forbes
Aqrabua by Yohan Alexander
Associate 321 by Yohan Alexander
Mr Brass by Yohan Alexander
S-06 by Bonsart Bokel
Clara Lantry by Yohan Alexander
Dr. Jenever and S-36 by Peter Kuhn
S-36 by Yohan Alexander

Made in the USA
Middletown, DE
10 September 2023